NEVER AGAIN

Order ID: 202-1814140-5364331

Thank you for buying from Books for Amnesty Brighton on Amazon Marketplace.

Delivery address:
Paul Wren
8 HARTSWOOD ROAD
WITHINGTON
MANCHESTER
Lancashire
M20 4RL
United Kingdom

Order Date:	Mon, Mar 29, 2021
Delivery Service:	Standard
Buyer Name:	Paul
Seller Name:	Books for Amnesty Brighton

Quantity	Product Details	Unit price	Order Totals
1	**NEVER AGAIN [Paperback] [2010] Bird, Allyson; Lane, Joel; Serra, Daniele** **SKU:** BM-FRS7-2087 **ASIN:** 190633189 **Condition:** Used - Good **Order Item ID:** 08056809921155 **Condition note:** spine unbroken. slight damp damage in corner of final few pages/back cover oct 2041	£10.50	
		Item subtotal	Included VAT £10.50 £0.00
		Shipping total	£3.00 £0.00
		Item total	**£13.50 £0.00**

Grand total: £13.50

Thanks for buying on Amazon Marketplace. To provide feedback for the seller please visit www.amazon.co.uk/feedback. To contact the seller, go to Your Orders in Your Account. Click the seller's name under the appropriate product. Then, in the "Further Information" section, click "Contact the Seller."

NEVER AGAIN

edited by
Allyson Bird & Joel Lane

NEVER AGAIN

First published in 2010 by Gray Friar Press.
www.grayfriarpress.com

Cover copyright © Daniele Serra 2010

Typesetting by Gary Fry

ISBN: 978-1-906331-18-4

Contents

Acknowledgements

'Introduction: Night of Broken Glass' © 2010. Previously unpublished.

'Feet of Clay' by Nina Allan © 2010. Previously unpublished.

'Volk' by rj krijnen-kemp © 1998. Originally published in *Nasty Piece of Work #9*.

'In the Arcade' by Lisa Tuttle © 1978. Originally published in *Amazing*, Vol. 51, No. 3 (May 1978).

'A Flowering Wound' by John Howard © 2010. Previously unpublished. (Including 'After the Earthquake' copyright © Erica Mann Jong, 1977, 1991, all rights reserved. Used by permission of the poet.)

'Sense' by Tony Richards © 2010. Previously unpublished.

'In On the Tide' by Alison Littlewood © 2010. Previously unpublished.

'Decision' by R.B. Russell © 2010. Previously unpublished.

'South of Autumn' by Mat Joiner © 2010. Previously unpublished.

'Survivor's Guilt' by Rosanne Rabinowitz © 2009. Originally published in *Black Static 14*.

'Rediffusion' by Rhys Hughes © 2010. Previously unpublished.

'A Place for Feeding' by Simon Kurt Unsworth © 2010. Previously unpublished.

'Night They Missed the Horror Show' by Joe R. Lansdale © 1988. All rights reserved. Originally published in *Silver Scream* ed. David J. Schow (Dark Harvest). It later appeared in *By Bizarre Hands* (Avon Books, 1989) and *High Cotton: Selected Short Stories of Joe R. Lansdale* (Golden Gryphon Press, 2000). It won a Bram Stoker award for Best Short Story.

'Ghost Jail' by Kaaron Warren © 2008. Originally published in *2012* ed. Alisa Krasnostein and Ben Payne, Twelfth Planet Press.

The editors would like to thank: all the contributors, and those whose stories we didn't have space to include; Peter Tennant and Steve Green for their much-valued assistance; China Mieville, Jeff Vandermeer, Norm Rubenstein, Ella Lane and Alan Bird for their support; Gary Fry for his commitment and hard work; and the musicians of Rock Against Racism for their inspiration.

In memory of
Miep Gies
(1909–2010)

Introduction: Night of Broken Glass
by Joel Lane and Allyson Bird

This is an anthology of stories in the weird and speculative fiction genres about fascism and racism. You may wonder: *why?* Shouldn't a genre anthology concern itself with genre themes? Shouldn't political realities be explored through a book of realistic stories, or a book of political essays?

The answers are in the stories following this introduction.

Racism has its origins in the manipulation of fear. Societies need an external threat to justify their own inequalities, and racism is the most popular solution. If our social structures become more democratic, 'they' will invade and take over. If 'they' are already here, controlling the 'enemy within' is a non-stop emergency that takes priority over such luxuries as equality and freedom.

While modernity has brought a much greater movement of people between populations, it has also created economic instabilities whereby capitalist societies, bound by their nature to face recurrent crises, need to invoke scapegoats in order to divide the people. The most popular scapegoats include immigrants, ethnic minorities, gypsies and the 'unemployable'.

Racism is endemic in our societies because it offers a permanent division that the ruling class can rely on to blind many people to the realities of class. It's a stable reservoir of prejudice that politicians fill but are never seen to draw from. Except it isn't really stable because its basis is not real. Its perpetuation doesn't depend on 'human nature' (as racists claim) but on the denial of human nature. It does not renew itself, and so depends on reinforcement by those who profit from it.

Fascism could be described as a politicised essence of social intolerance, applied to all forms of diversity and dissent. As a political movement, fascism arose in Italy in the 1920s and spread to Germany and Spain. While the defeat of the Nazis stopped fascism from achieving its goal of global domination, the Cold War allowed a version of it to persist in Spain until the 1970s, while the USA nurtured a fascist government in Chile in 1973.

i

The formula that where communism is a threat, fascism is an acceptable solution remains good for Western capitalism.

Fascism arose as a direct consequence of a major crisis of capitalism. Where the threat of revolution was too strong for capitalist societies to contain, fascism was employed as a means to smash the trade unions and divide the working class. Its racist and anti-Semitic ideology was a convenient propaganda tool. Fascism promoted the ascendancy of the petit bourgeois, creating a new social order based on naked power rather than traditional wealth. As Trotsky said, "The historic function of fascism is to smash the working class, destroy its organisations, and stifle political liberties when the capitalists find themselves unable to govern and dominate with the help of democratic machinery."

In the aftermath of the Holocaust, social theorists struggled to explain how a democratic society could have reverted so abruptly to barbarism. Left-wing German writers such as Adorno and Fromm, who had escaped from Nazi Germany and set up home in the USA, offered influential accounts of fascism that brought together psychology, politics and recent history. Fromm analysed the "fear of freedom" that inclined people towards scapegoating and the worship of strong leaders. Adorno called fascism "a chemically pure distillate of capitalism", and offered a controversial analysis of fascist tendencies in American society.

Analysis of this kind has led to a widespread perception of fascism in broader terms than the purely political. When we say 'fascism' these days, we tend to mean *intense social intolerance backed up with violence*. Thus the term encompasses union-bashing, lynch law, homophobia and other traditions that are embedded in our society and reinforced by the major religions.

In Britain, fascism never took root as deeply as in much of Europe. Mosley's 'blackshirts' were defeated by grassroots opposition, particularly among working-class Jews in London. Some of Mosley's British Union of Fascists went on to form the National Front – an influential anti-immigration pressure group that, once again, was defeated by well-organised opposition in the deprived areas where it sought to make political gains. More recently, it has experienced a resurgence as the British National Party, which is responsible for a high-profile racist united front called the English Defence League. BNP leader Nick Griffin has called for the party's racist policies to be backed up with "well-aimed boots and fists" on the streets.

While the BNP's dreams of taking control do not appear likely to be realised, its ideology of violence means that it can do great harm at a local level. It harnesses petit-bourgeois fear of immigration, terrorism and trade unions to offer a vision of unity through intolerance: a racial, moral and political purity that spells the end of reason, liberty and democracy. The power of racist and fascist myths to distort social consciousness remains considerable. But they are not, we would argue, as powerful as the principles of equality and human rights, and what the poet Adrienne Rich has called "the dream of a common language".

In putting together a book of weird and speculative fiction stories with anti-fascist and anti-racist themes, we were not inventing something new. There were a number of stories we wanted to reprint, and writers already involved in writing about these themes. Weird fiction deals with issues of life and death, and with causes of great fear. These include social issues. The real horrors of the twentieth century have informed its weird fiction at a deep level.

Arthur Machen's 'The Terror' used the imagery of a revolt of nature to protest against the brutality of the First World War. Franz Kafka's 'Metamorphosis' used the metaphor of a human being turning into an insect to portray the dehumanisation of Jews in anti-Semitic propaganda, isolating its victims by blighting their regard for each other. Ray Bradbury's 'The Scythe' used the image of a personalised death to embody the atrocities of Hiroshima and Auschwitz: in his story, the angel of death is a bereaved man seeking indiscriminate revenge for the loss of his family.

In Charles Beaumont's 'The Howling Man', Hitler is identified as a man "of average appearance" with a capacity to provoke evil in others. Shirley Jackson's 'The Lottery' described a tradition whereby a town's collective well-being is protected by an annual ritual: the killing of a randomly selected citizen. In Fritz Leiber's 'Belsen Express', a post-war American's irrational fear of the Nazis is focused by the collective unease of the society around him into a lethal power.

Those are examples of the kind of fiction we wanted in this anthology. The stories we have included are half reprints – going back as far as the 1970s – and half newly composed. We made two requirements of any story used. Firstly, it needed to have something distinctive and worthwhile to say about its theme. Secondly, it needed to satisfy *as a story* – to be imaginatively compelling, powerfully written and disturbing. We did not demand any specific political perspective, and we allowed 'fascism' and 'racism' to be interpreted widely – as befits an anthology of weird and speculative stories, in which imagination and reality are intimately connected.

The stories collected here span the genres of supernatural horror, speculative fiction, crime and 'slipstream'. They are mostly focused on the European perspective, though we have reprinted stories by two American writers (coincidentally, both from Texas) and one Australian writer.

Some of these stories deal with the effects of racism. Alison Littlewood's 'In On the Tide' juxtaposes an incident of racial abuse with a real fear of the unknown, reminding us that people are only 'unknown' in the lesser sense of being people we don't know. Lisa Tuttle's 'In the Arcade', a grim piece of speculative fiction, places future racism in the context of a fascist society. 'Zulu's War' by David A. Sutton exposes the racist motivation of a war crime, with a ghostly aftermath that may be rooted in guilt. Joe R. Lansdale's 'Night They Missed the Horror Show' takes us through a grim transition from familiar racism to the ice-cold fascistic violence of the KKK: a journey that feels metaphysical, but in reality may be simply part of the Texan road map.

Other stories deal with different aspects of authoritarian culture. Thana Niveau's 'Death of Dreams' examines the intolerance of emotional deviation that underlies the voyeur-puritan mentality of the tabloids. Similarly, 'Methods of Confinement' by Gary McMahon portrays the boundary between 'normal' intolerance and the instrumental reasoning of fascism – the victims in this case being those classic folk-demons of the media, prisoners. Rhys Hughes' 'Rediffusion' – a story that has Stalinism as well as fascism in its sights – satirises the vicious attention to detail of bureaucratic law enforcers. Simon Kurt Unsworth's 'A Place for Feeding' portrays the 'banality of evil': a group are united by a shared intolerance that becomes steadily more meaningful and violent.

Steve Duffy's 'The Torturer' explores the disturbed inner life of its eponymous functionary in one of the many present-day societies that judge torture to be necessary for their internal security. Kaaron Warren's ambitious 'Ghost Jail' uses a complex supernatural metaphor to portray the damaged psyche of a police-controlled nation in the developing world.

A few stories offer metaphysical images of totalitarian forces. 'The Depths' by Ramsey Campbell offers a modern version of the scapegoat myth, drawing us inexorably down through the circles of a private hell shaped by public fears. In rj krijnen-kemp's surreal 'Volk', a couple are threatened by an individual who seems to represent the malign will of a hostile society. The haunting 'Decision' by R.B. Russell examines the ultimate consequences of a willingness to obey orders. Mat Joiner's 'South of Autumn' takes us into a world of forbidden dreams and untold stories, as a writer breaks his society's taboo on giving voice to the suffering of the oppressed. The astonishing 'Beyond Each Blue Horizon' by Andrew Hook shows the power of a fascist government erasing humanity in every aspect of life.

A number of stories deal with the historical experience of Nazism and the Holocaust. 'Sense' by Tony Richards projects into the near future the Nazi strategy of picking off one minority after another, silencing protest by playing on social division. The apparently whimsical premise of Robert Shearman's 'Damned If You Don't' conceals a darkly sardonic fable about the mutual dependency of leaders and followers. Stephen Volk's 'After the Ape' links the Wall Street Crash to the rise of fascism via a bold and provocative metaphor. And in Carole Johnstone's bitterly comic 'Machine', a Second World War theme park of the future delivers a lesson in the meaning of history.

'A Flowering Wound' by John Howard weaves a lyrical ghost story around the atrocities of fascism in Romania. In Nina Allan's 'Feet of Clay', a Holocaust survivor passes on an ambiguous legacy to her granddaughter in London. 'Survivor's Guilt' by Rosanne Rabinowitz enlists the uncanny in the war against the agents of fascism. In Simon Bestwick's 'Malachi', the lessons of the past light a flame of hope in a dark future.

The book starts and ends with stories that refer to the enduring legacy of the Holocaust, underlining the message that the act of memory is one of resistance.

On page 293, we list a number of anti-racist, anti-fascist and human rights organisations. The war against social prejudice and authoritarian thinking is taking place on many fronts, and there is no single 'other side' to oppose far-right ideology. We wanted this book to raise funds as well as awareness, but we didn't want to have to justify donating the profits to an organisation representing a specific political stance – or even one that polemically takes no such stance. That doesn't mean we don't have our own political ideas, just that we leave it to readers to make up their own minds who to support.

Instead, we are dividing any profits made by this anthology between three human rights charities: Amnesty International, PEN and the Sophie Lancaster Foundation. The authors, editors and publisher will receive no payment for their contributions to this book (the publisher will be reimbursed for the costs of printing and distribution only).

Amnesty International is the leading worldwide human rights organisation. It upholds the principles of the Universal Declaration of Human Rights adopted by the UN in 1948, and has played a crucial role in opposing imprisonment without trial and punishment for protesting against a government. PEN is an international organisation set up to promote literature and human rights, encouraging translation and campaigning against political censorship.

The Sophie Lancaster Foundation is a UK charity dedicated to creating respect for and understanding of subcultures in our communities. It was set up in memory of the young woman who was beaten to death in 2007 because a gang of youths took exception to her and her boyfriend's 'Goth' appearance. The murder has led to a widening of the debate on 'hate crimes'. The Foundation – which is supported by the Bloodstock heavy metal festival – is symbolic of the need to defend individuals' artistic freedom against those with so little confidence in their own ideas that they use violence to suppress alternatives.

* * *

The far right constantly refer to their 'freedom of speech' – the same right that they openly deny to others. They shelter under democratic principles which they oppose violently. This is not a book of single-minded polemic or 'political correctness': it's a book that celebrates diverse, creative and challenging alternatives to the mentality of fear and prejudice.

Equally, this is not a book that seeks to censor imaginative writing or to keep it on a narrow track. These stories celebrate the vitality and strength of resistance to all kinds of authoritarian thinking. They speak of courage, energy, solidarity, friendship and justified anger, not of 'liberal guilt' or a fear of 'human nature'.

The weird and speculative fiction genres are powerful enough to illuminate the darkest aspects of our reality. The ghosts, shadows, night terrors and broken mornings of these stories enable us to see more clearly, and more fully, the flawed beauty and grace of the human spirit.

Feet of Clay
by Nina Allan

Allis was getting ready to leave when Noel rang. He sounded guilty about something. Allis thought he was about to tell her he couldn't come to her grandmother's funeral, but it turned out he was calling to break up with her. He told her he had met someone else and they were getting engaged.

"Her name's Nelly," he said. "I honestly never meant for it to happen."

"I don't believe this," Allis said. "I have to be at the service in half an hour."

"Here we go again," said Noel. He had reverted to the self-righteous tone she had come to hate, slipping into it as easily as a toad into a mud-puddle. "It always has to be about you."

They said some other things, things Allis did her best to forget, and then Noel put down the phone. Allis arrived at the synagogue with just minutes to spare. The place was packed. Hanne had been widely respected. She had lived through the Holocaust. Her death at the age of ninety was the end of an era.

Allis crept in at the back. Her father Jonas was already seated at the front of the hall. She had to push her way through the crowd to get to his side. Afterwards at the cemetery they stood together at Hanne's graveside to receive the mourners. Jonas Ganesh looked grey and drawn, a paler, more attenuated version of herself. She noticed her Aunt Rose was weeping openly, even though she and Hanne had never really got on. Rose Steenberg was her mother's sister. Hanne had always called her 'the stupid one.' Allis's mother Miriam shared Rose's outgoing temperament and sensitive nature but she had redeemed herself in Hanne's eyes by being academic, graduating from Imperial College with a First in applied mathematics. Rose had left school at sixteen to become a nurse. Allis drew her gently aside and took her arm.

"Are you all right, Auntie Rosie?"

Rose stared at her with red-rimmed eyes and started crying again. Her Uncle Amos, Rose's husband, shook his head.

"It's not the funeral," he said. "There was an attack on the centre this morning. Some hooligan chucked a petrol bomb through the kitchen window. We've just been to give our statements to the police. We almost didn't get here at all."

"How terrible," said Allis. "Was anyone hurt?" Rose had retired from her hospital job some years before but both she and Amos were deeply involved in the voluntary work they did for a local refuge for foreign asylum seekers. Rose especially spent a lot of her time there. She had never been able to have children, and Allis suspected that the children at the centre were very important to her.

"Farrook was badly burned on both arms," Rose said quietly. "She was right beside the window when it happened. Luckily some of the others were able to put out the fire before it did too much damage but the children were very frightened."

"Farrook is from Afghanistan," Amos added. "She was training to be a doctor, but the Taliban put a stop to all that. She came here because she thought she would be safe."

"Are you sure you're both OK?" Allis said. "Would you like me to stay at your place tonight?"

"Don't be silly. We're fine. You need to be with your father."

Amos kissed her forehead, the way he used to when she was a child. They rejoined Jonas and went back to the house, where Allis and one of the cousins had laid on a funeral buffet. People stood around in the downstairs rooms, eating and swapping stories about Hanne. There was a substantial crowd, and the atmosphere became quite cheerful. Only Jonas seemed distant and sad. Allis knew he found funerals difficult because of her mother. It was ten years now since her death but her father had never shown any signs of wanting to remarry. So far as Allis knew there had been no one else.

"Hey," Allis said to him. "You ought to eat something." She briefly touched his shoulder.

"I'll eat later," he said. "I can't concentrate with all this noise."

At around five o'clock the doorbell rang. Allis went to answer the door, expecting some late-running guest. Instead there was a man in a fluorescent jacket holding a parcel.

"Allis Ganesh?" he said. He was Pakistani and very good looking. "Sign here."

She signed the form on his clipboard and he went away. The parcel was the size of a shoebox and addressed to her. The return

2

address was Hanne's. Allis felt her heart miss a beat. It was typical of Hanne somehow, to gatecrash her own funeral. Allis closed the door and took the parcel upstairs. The first floor of the house was entirely hers. It had been her father's idea to have the place converted into two flats. Allis had been uncertain at first, but with London prices the way they were she had agreed, and in practice the arrangement worked well. She had worried what Noel might think about her living cheek by jowl with her father, but the subject never came up.

Not that it mattered now. She left the parcel in her bedroom and went back downstairs.

"Who was that?" said Jonas.

"The DHL man. It's just some papers for work."

Both Allis and Jonas were geological surveyors. Allis's mother used to call them the rock twins. Jonas had been in the same job for twenty years, working for the national survey. Allis was employed by a major petrochemicals company and was already earning more than her father. She knew some men would have minded this dreadfully, but Jonas only ever seemed pleased for her.

Jonas reached out and touched the back of her hand. "Thanks for being here," he said. "I don't know what I'd do without you."

"You don't have to," Allis said. "They'll be gone soon, don't worry."

Once all the food was eaten people began to leave and by eight o'clock they were on their own again. Allis began clearing the plates. All at once she felt close to tears. Now that the funeral was over there was nothing to distract her attention from thoughts of Noel. She couldn't tell her father, he had enough to deal with already. He sat at the table, slowly shredding a napkin into tiny pieces. She wondered how he was feeling, what he was thinking. Suddenly he raised his head, as if sensing her eyes on him.

"Leave all that," he said. "We can do it tomorrow. Let's have some coffee and watch the news."

This sense of a shared activity brought a resurgence of normality. Allis made the drinks and brought them through on a tray. The nine o'clock news had just started, and they were showing the latest footage of the war in Afghanistan. A bomb had gone off, wrecking the children's ward of a hospital and causing multiple casualties. Allis thought how different the house felt now

3

that Hanne was dead. She had never actually lived with them, but since Allis's mother had died the sense of Hanne's presence, her likes, her dislikes, her desires, had become all-pervasive. Her absence was like the lifting of a cloud.

"I'm glad she's gone," said Jonas suddenly. It was as if he had read the thought straight out of her head. Allis kept quiet, not knowing what to say in reply. Family wisdom said Hanne and Jonas were close. It wasn't the kind of thing you questioned out loud.

"She should have married and had more children," Jonas insisted. "I reminded her of things she would have been better forgetting."

"Dad," Allis said. "That's ridiculous."

"She never did tell me who my father was. I suppose I'll never know now."

Allis fell silent again. Rose Steenberg had told her the story years ago, how Hanne had come to London soon after the war. She was already pregnant, but she never told anyone who fathered her child, and nobody dared to ask because Hanne had been in Auschwitz. Everyone knew she had never been married, and there was talk that she might have been raped by one of the guards. No doubt Jonas had heard the same stories and then some. It was one of the many things they never discussed.

"It doesn't matter where you came from, Dad," she said. "All that matters is that you're here. Whoever he was, he's not important. Let him go."

She knew her words were facile but she wanted to get off the subject as quickly as possible. Talking about marriage and children would only make her think about Noel. Her father kept his eyes on the screen. It was impossible to tell what he was thinking. The local news carried a brief report of the attack on the asylum centre. There was film of the ambulance arriving, some of the volunteers sweeping up the broken glass. Allis couldn't help thinking it could have been Rose in the ambulance instead of the Afghan woman. The glass sparkled on the ground like splinters of ice.

Allis stifled a yawn. "I think I'll go to bed," she said to Jonas. "Will you be all right down here by yourself?"

"I'll be fine. You go up. You look tired."

4

Allis kissed him quickly and said goodnight. It was only when she got upstairs that she remembered Hanne's parcel. She thought again how like Hanne it was to make her presence felt, even now when she had no presence as such. She was nothing but the agglomeration of other people's memories and the few possessions she had left behind. Allis wondered what could be in the parcel. She hoped it might contain a piece of Hanne's jewellery, the agate pendant perhaps, or the garnet bracelet. She tore off the brown paper wrapping. There was an official-looking envelope containing a letter from Hanne's solicitor. The letter said Hanne had left instructions for the parcel to be despatched to Allis immediately upon Hanne's death. With the letter was a wooden box of the kind made to hold loose tea leaves, and suddenly Allis knew what was inside. She lifted the paper aside and slid back the lid. There was a rolled square of red knitted fabric, like a miniature blanket. Inside the roll of fabric was Jonny Clay.

Jonny Clay was Hanne's golem. Allis had been about seven when she had first seen him. He was a rough little pottery man about six inches high, his arms fused to his sides and his legs joined together down the middle. Allis thought he looked a little like a baby in a papoose carrier. Hanne said this was to stop him breaking apart when he was fired. He was hollow all the way through, and if you blew in through the slit of his lips he made a faint whistling sound. Hanne kept him in a wooden box at the back of the wardrobe.

"Do you know what a golem is, Allis?" Hanne had asked her. Allis shook her head, saying nothing. She didn't know whether to like Jonny Clay or be afraid of him. "A golem is a monster," Hanne said. "There are scholars who claim that the golem is just a legend, a collective delusion, the will of the Jewish people rising up to throw off their oppressors. But most of us know the truth is much stranger than that. The golem is real, all right. The golem is the strength you call on when you've no strength left."

Hanne said that golems stayed quiet most of the time, hidden in desk drawers or kitchen cupboards or in tin boxes under the bed, but if you knew the right words and signs you could bring them to life. Hanne said she had made Jonny Clay to protect her when she was in Auschwitz.

"I scooped up some mud from the yard," she said. "The mud would not have been just mud though. It was also blood and filth

5

and ash, the ashes of human flesh from the crematorium. I spread the mud on the stones behind the latrines to dry it a little and after about a day it had turned to clay. I knew how to work clay, because I had done it in school before the war started. All my friends were dead by then and I had no one to talk to. Jonny Clay looked after me. He kept me going."

Allis understood only a little of what Hanne was talking about. She heard the word blood, and the idea that Jonny Clay might have real blood inside him terrified her. Later, when she learned about the concentration camps at school, she became convinced that Hanne had baked Jonny Clay in the crematorium. She thought of her bribing a guard, or climbing inside after dark to rake through the ashes. She began to have nightmares. When finally she plucked up the courage to ask Hanne about it her grandmother simply laughed and said of course not, she had fired Jonny Clay in one of the cooking stoves in the prisoners' huts.

"Not that there was much to cook," she said. "Potato peelings if we were lucky. We used to mix them with muddy water and call it soup."

Jonny Clay had a gentle expression. It was difficult to think of him as a monster. Sometimes Hanne let Allis hold him. His outside was rough, with bits of sand and gravel baked into it, like the currants in a gingerbread man. Sometimes, if both Jonas and Miriam were going to be out, Allis would go round to Hanne's straight from school. Once Jonas arrived earlier than usual to take her home and found her in Hanne's bedroom with Jonny Clay.

"Stay and have some coffee," Hanne said. "I'll go and put the kettle on, shall I?"

"We can't today," Jonas said. "Miriam will have her tea on. I'll wait in the car."

He left the room abruptly, closing the door with a bang. He didn't speak a word for the entire journey home. Allis wondered if she had done something wrong but her father seemed upset rather than angry. After that, Hanne told Allis that their games with Jonny Clay would be best kept secret.

Allis rolled Jonny Clay in his blanket and put him back in his box. Even after all these years the pottery figure still unnerved her, and she found she had a superstitious fear of breaking it. She pushed the box to the back of her wardrobe and tried to forget about it. Now she was alone in her room she could think about

Noel. She supposed he was with Nelly somewhere, in bed most likely. They would shag each other senseless, and afterwards Noel would go over it all again, how terrible it had been for him, Allis's screaming and crying and making a scene. Nelly would pat his head and tell him it was over now, all done with, that at last they could get on with their lives.

Noel and Nelly, she thought. *They sound like a children's cartoon.* Allis choked back the tears that were starting; if she cried now there would be no end to it. She snapped on the radio to drown out the sound of her thoughts. There was an update on the news story about the asylum centre: apparently the Afghan woman had been released from hospital.

She went to the bathroom to use the toilet and wash her face. The next morning her father said he had taken the rest of the week off work and was thinking of driving north to the Peak District.

"I wondered if you'd like to come with me?" he said. "We could go and see the Blue John cavern."

Almost before she realised she was going to, Allis said yes. The thought of driving away from Noel along the motorway was so liberating it burned in her like anger.

They booked into a small hotel on the outskirts of Bakewell. There were few modern conveniences and the place had a shabby air to it, but the bed linen smelled wonderfully fresh and the high windows looked directly out on the encircling hills. Allis rested in her room for an hour, then went down to meet her father in the hall.

"Is everything all right for you?" he said.

"It's great, dad. It's perfect." She took his hand briefly and squeezed it. He seemed happy and at ease, as relaxed as she had ever known him. His eyes behind the round glasses gleamed like moss agates.

They found a pub that served home-made food, steak and ale pie and Bakewell tart. Allis ordered a glass of wine for herself but Jonas had a fruit juice and afterwards stuck to water. Allis knew he rarely touched alcohol, though she had never heard him express any prejudice against it. They talked mainly about their work, a subject they both enjoyed and that could keep them happily occupied for hours. Neither of them mentioned Hanne or the attack on the asylum centre. At one point Allis thought briefly of

7

Noel, probing the subject gingerly with her mind as she might probe a cut or graze to see how it was healing. Pain rounded on her like an angry cat, as if irritated by her attention. She let it alone, wondering if she would ever escape her father now that Hanne was dead. Jonas was the least possessive, least worldly of men, yet there was an inevitability in them ending up alone together, growing old and brittle and grey like two sticks in a ditch.

So what if we do? she thought. *Would that be so terrible?* She listened contentedly as Jonas told her about the last time he had been in the north. She loved his quiet, slightly hiccoughing laugh, the way he recounted inconsequential details just for the simple pleasure of telling a story. He was rarely so forthcoming at home.

They stayed in the pub until closing time, then made their way back through the darkened streets to their hotel. The little town felt watchful and alive, steeped in the rich, lithe blackness of the surrounding moor. Allis fell asleep almost at once. When she woke it was past eight o'clock. She felt rested and renewed, as if the more difficult parts of her past had been erased overnight. She had not slept so well in several weeks.

The sky was blue as lapis. They drove out across the moor towards Castleton and Edale, where the Blue John caves were and where they planned to walk a short stretch of the Pennine Way. Allis was surprised at how confidently her father handled the car. In London he rarely drove, and when he did he often appeared nervous and despondent. The narrow moorland roads seemed to excite him, releasing from within him the hawkish, need-fuelled expectancy of a gold prospector. He hurried the Renault along, hauling it without ceremony over the potholed tarmac and steep passes, his elbow resting casually on the rim of the open window.

Allis saw that her father loved this country and knew it intimately. She wondered why they had never been here as a family when she was a child, apart from one short week in Scarborough when she was ten.

They went on the Blue John tour, propelled in a wooden skiff through a low-ceilinged, water-filled passageway into the main cave, its walls shimmering with massed deposits of fluorspar and barite. Allis could not help remembering a piece of music Noel had liked, that he had sometimes put on in the evenings when they were alone together, Debussy's *Submerged Cathedral*. She had never much liked being underground, and was glad when they were out again; though her father seemed perfectly at ease, happy even, asking questions of the guide and reaching out to touch the gleaming bands of crystals in the surrounding granite.

They had lunch in a café in Castleton and then headed up into the hills. There was a sweet breeze, reminding Allis of the fresh chlorophyll smell of the bedsheets in the Bakewell hotel. Every now and then the wind dropped and the sun beat down full strength, its heat vast and mauling as a copper furnace.

Eventually they stopped the car and got out. Allis rolled on her back in the springy grass, shading her eyes from the pouring sunlight with the back of her hand. The earth beneath her was powdery and dry, with a sharp, acrid aroma she found quietly intoxicating. Jonas stood on a granite boulder, looking out over the moors. Against the scintillating blue of the sky he looked gaunt and grey as a dolmen or a blasted tree. Aunt Rose and especially Hanne had made much of his thinness, his small capacity for food, yet he was seldom ill, and it had been her mother in the end who had died.

Surveying the land, Jonas was in his element.

"There's yellow fluorite over there," he said, pointing. They hiked towards a narrow ravine, clambering in and down among the jagged rocks. From the leg pocket of his jeans Jonas produced one of his extensive collection of geologist's hammers. He bent to the ground, retrieving some shards of fallen granite, and with practised taps of his hammer began splitting them along their fault lines. As he had predicted, the rocks were full of quartz, the clumps of yellowish crystals that were the more common variety of the Blue John fluorspar that was mined from the hillside below. Watching the careful, expert way he worked, Allis felt a sudden flare of anger at Hanne, who had chided her father for his lack of ambition and who, or so it now seemed to her, had done her best to keep them divided.

It was Hanne who had paid for Allis to go on school field trips, who had bought Allis her first laptop computer. She often said her most heartfelt desire was for Allis to make the most of herself. Her words made Allis feel both honoured and subtly pressurised. They carried within them the sense of Hanne's belief that her father had *not* made the most of himself, that he had failed

9

Hanne in some way. Allis disliked this unfair criticism of her father as much as she felt determined to show her grandmother that she would not fail, that she, unlike Jonas, could do what was required of her.

I must have been crazy, she thought. *I let that mean old woman cast her spell on me, when I could have been out here every summer with my dad.*

"Dad," she said suddenly. "You know the package that came the day of Gran's funeral? It wasn't from work. It was from Gran."

Jonas laid his hammer aside on a rock and brushed his hands briskly downwards over his jeans. Twin streaks of dust pointed raggedly towards his knees.

"What was in it?" he said. Allis was struck by how little surprised he seemed by what she was telling him. It was as if he had known or guessed all along.

"That pottery figure she used to keep in her wardrobe. You know, Jonny Clay." She hesitated. "I got such a fright when I opened the box. I was scared of Jonny Clay when I was a kid."

Jonas sighed. He sat down on one of the boulders and took off his glasses. He looked naked without them, and much younger. He also looked very like Allis. For a moment Allis felt as if she were standing in front of a mirror.

"Me too," Jonas said. "I was terrified of that little clay goblin, and she knew it. She used to make me hold it and play with it. But the worst thing was the stories she used to tell me about it and where it had come from. The one she told most often was how Jonny Clay saved her life one night, during the forced march across Poland. I was six when I first heard that story, but she must have repeated it to me a dozen times afterwards, a hundred. The details varied but the main story was always the same, how the SS knew they were losing the war and so they decided to hide the evidence of what they'd done in the concentration camps. The dead were incinerated, or buried in mass graves. The sick and the dying were simply abandoned where they lay. Those prisoners still fit enough to walk were taken out of the camps and made to set off on foot back towards Germany. It was winter, and even for the Germans food was in short supply. The prisoners had no proper outdoor clothing and they were all on the edge of starvation. Hundreds of them died every day. Hanne was

10

ill and exhausted and the day came when she knew she had no more strength left, but Jonny Clay told her to hang on until evening. She was so cold she could no longer feel her feet. She knew that all she had to do was stop walking, and one of the SS guards would shoot her dead on the spot. She said the idea began to take her over. It became as comforting and necessary to her as the idea of walking in through the lit doorway of one of the cottages they glimpsed from time to time through the trees. But Jonny Clay told her to wait, and so long as she kept her fingers wrapped around him she was somehow able to find the will to keep on moving.

"In the end they were allowed to rest in a forest clearing. She knew from the night before, and all the nights before that, that the respite would only last a couple of hours; but on that night she didn't care, because she knew she would be dead by morning. But soon after she went to sleep she was woken by a terrible outburst of screaming and gunfire. When she opened her eyes she saw that the camp fire the guards had made for themselves had grown to an enormous pyre. In the light of the roaring flames she could see the figures of the guards, darting about in panic as they tried to escape the monstrous thing that was attacking them. As Hanne watched, one of the guards was flung forward into the fire. He fell backwards, writhing on the ground, his raised arms already swarming with flames. He was squealing like a pig, she said; then something huge and black descended, crushing his blazing form into the ground the same way you might crush a moth that had set itself alight in a candle flame.

"The black thing was the vast, ash-booted foot of Jonny Clay, Jonny Clay grown so huge he blocked out the moon.

"Hanne closed her eyes after that, but she could still hear the sounds, the thrashing and shrieking as Jonny Clay tore the guards apart and roasted them on the fire. In the end the screaming stopped. Hanne heard the leaves crackling as something enormous and heavy came out of the clearing towards her. Then she was lifted up and carried away. She was carried for what seemed like hours. Finally she was laid down gently on a pile of straw and dead leaves. She dreamed that Jonny Clay was lying beside her, keeping her warm. When she woke up the next morning she found she was in a cow barn at the edge of a village. Someone had covered her with old grain sacks, and it was this that had stopped

11

her from freezing to death during the night. Jonny Clay was in her pocket, just like always. There were black marks on his head and body, as if he had been rolled in the cooling embers of a camp fire."

He was silent for a moment, looking out across the wild expanse of the surrounding moor. "The thing that scared me most was not what happened to the guards but the idea that I had been named after Jonny Clay, that somehow Jonny Clay was my real father. I worried about that for years. I never said anything to Hanne. I knew she would either laugh at me or else tell me that the thing I most dreaded was true. As I grew older the whole idea began to seem ridiculous, but I did wonder about my mother. I wondered if she had been driven insane by the things she'd seen."

Allis was silent. She remembered how Hanne had laughed when she'd asked if Jonny Clay had been fired in the crematorium. She could not imagine what it had been like for Jonas, growing up in the shadow of Hanne's terrible past. *He had no one to talk to*, she thought. *Whereas I have always had him.*

"What was the name of the village where Hanne was found?" she said at last.

"Przdyno. It's in the middle of nowhere. No one could ever explain how she came to be there. The prisoners she was with ended up miles away. Many of them died from the cold but those that survived hid out in the countryside until the Russians arrived. Years ago, before I met your mother, I flew to Paris to talk to one of them. When I asked how they escaped from the guards, the man told me they hadn't needed to escape, because they woke up to find the guards dead. It looked like they had turned on each other."

He fiddled with his glasses, opening and closing the frames and then polishing the lenses on the front of his T-shirt. "How are you doing, Ally?" he said suddenly. "Has something happened with Noel?"

Allis glanced at him sharply, trying to gauge from his expression how much he might know, but his eyes were still fixed on his glasses. "We broke up," she said. "He left me. He's going to marry someone called Nelly. Apparently I'm selfish and self-obsessed."

"The man's a fool, Ally. You're too good for him."

"I know you're right." Something seemed to give way inside her then, and suddenly she was crying, the tears coursing down her face like liquid quartz. Then her father came to sit beside her. He took her hand, kissing the tensed, wet knuckles. She buried her face in his shoulder, weeping as she had not done since she was small. At last her grief wore itself out. She raised her head, blinking in the afternoon sun.

"I'm sorry, Dad, you must think I'm an idiot."

"He's the idiot. You're better off without him. And it's me that should be saying sorry. I'm sorry about Hanne. I should never have let her fill your head with all that rubbish. I should never have left you alone with her."

"Don't be crazy, Dad. She was just an old lady. She liked telling stories, that's all."

She smiled at him through the last of her tears. She felt an overwhelming joy that no matter what happened in their lives they would always belong to one another. *We're made of the same stuff*, she thought. *The rock twins, just like mum said.*

They went and found the car and drove back to Bakewell. That night she dreamed of Noel. He was kneeling above her, his hands grasping her hips, raising her body towards him, preparing to fuck her. But as he entered her she realised it was not Noel's face looking down at her but the reddish, pockmarked mask of Jonny Clay. His expression was oddly tender, his full terracotta lips parted to reveal the shadowed emptiness of his hollow abdomen. She came as she woke, pressing both hands into her crotch, the tears starting again from her eyes. Her nipples felt sore, as if the starched sheets had been chafing her skin.

She lay awake for a couple of minutes and then fell back to sleep, glad it was Jonny Clay that she had been with and not Noel.

She knew Jonny Clay had a past, that the golem was once a powerful symbol in Jewish mythology, and once she was back in London Allis decided she would like to find out more. There were a surprising number of books on the subject of golems. In the stacks of the university library Allis found everything from arcane philosophies to pulp novels of the nineteen-forties. Many were just hearsay and folklore, overripe fantasies by would-be disciples of Gustav Meyrink and Elmer Shapiro. The books Allis found most interesting were those few that took a scientific approach. Especially fascinating was a pamphlet by a Lithuanian named Mical Velius, *The Golem of Prague and his Thousand Sons*. It

13

went into some detail on the matter of clay, and in particular which kind of clay had the highest success rate when it came to activation. Velius maintained that the ordinary red clay golem was almost entirely without consciousness, a blunt instrument, and that for a golem with intelligence as well as strength it was necessary to utilise more refined materials. He recommended the feldspar clays of Lvov, or the highly plastic blue clay that could be dug only from the banks of a minor tributary of the Upper Volga. He added that the power of the golem could be further enhanced by mixing additional elements, such as iron and gold, with the basic clay.

In a chapter entitled 'Golems and War,' Velius stated that a woman who had lost her husband would sometimes call upon the golem in the service of providing her with a son.

Allis returned the books to the shelves and signed out of the stacks, wondering what she thought she was doing there in the first place. The books reminded her of Hanne, of her solitary obsessions and unhealthy beliefs. She wanted nothing more to do with them.

The Steenbergs had asked her to tea. As she hurried to the tube station Allis wondered if this was their way of checking up on Jonas, of finding out how he was coping after Hanne's death. She did not mind this subtle intrusion into their privacy. She knew her aunt and uncle meant well. In any case, there were some questions she wanted to ask Rose.

The Steenbergs' house was full of banners and placards.

"We're having an open day at the centre," Rose said. "We want to get people on our side, let them know about the work we're doing. We've got speakers coming from all over the country. I'm helping to organise the publicity."

"Do you think that's a good idea? What if that BNP lot turn up again?"

"They're the reason it's important that we do something, show them we're not afraid. Muslims, Christians, Jews, we've all got to stand together against these people. We already know what happens when we don't. You only have to remember what happened to your own grandmother."

"That's not going to happen here, Auntie Rosie. Things are different now."

"It happened to Farrook, just two weeks ago. Things are never different, anywhere." Her voice had risen in pitch, and Allis saw her hands were bunched into fists. "Please say you'll come and support us."

"I will if I can. I don't want you to get hurt, that's all."

Rose laughed and some of the tension went out of her voice. "I'm a big girl now," she said. She patted her substantial bosom. "I can look after myself. But you're a dear child, Allis, and such a clever one. Your grandmother was so proud of you."

Allis hugged her and kissed her cheek. In the brief moments of physical contact she caught the fleeting, fugitive scent of her mother Miriam. She thought how strange it was that Rose should speak of Hanne whom she had not liked instead of her sister Miriam whom she had adored. No one in the family ever talked about Miriam. It was as if the loss was too new, too raw. It was easier to speak of Hanne, who everyone had admired but no one had loved.

"Did Gran have friends?" she said suddenly. "Friends she knew before the war, I mean?"

Rose's expression became guarded. "I don't know about that. Your grandmother was a very private person. I do know she had two sisters, and there was a girl they adopted too, a child whose parents died or something. She had the same birthday as your gran, I remember that now, though of course they weren't proper sisters, they weren't related. And there must have been a man too, I suppose, your father's father." She frowned. "She never really talked about the past. Coming to London for Hanne was like crossing the Rubicon. Everything she knew got left behind."

Except Jonny Clay, Allis thought. *Jonny Clay was all she had left*. She thought of Farrook, the Afghan woman, who had escaped to England and what she thought was a new life, only to have a petrol bomb thrown at her by pathetic little tin-pot fascists.

Suddenly she felt angry and ashamed.

"I'll come to the open day," she said to Rose. "Of course I will."

Later when she arrived home she found a package had been delivered for her. The package was from Noel, and contained the few odds and ends she had left behind at his flat: an amethyst ring, a book on fossils, a Bob Dylan CD. There was no note. It was the lack of a note that made her feel like killing him.

15

It also made her feel curiously free, as if she too had made a lucky escape.

In the end Allis missed the open day, because it clashed with a seminar she had to attend at Strathclyde University. She stayed up in Glasgow overnight and caught the train back to London soon after breakfast. It would have been quicker by air of course, but she was nervous of flying, and in any case the slow journey south was always a chance to become reacquainted with old friends: the rugged wind-chafed features of the border country, the hunched black back of North Cumbria, the grey-eyed vistas of Lakeland. All were a familiar source of joy.

She pressed her face to the glass, watching as the landscape narrowed, flattened towards the Midlands, became more populous. She realised once more how good it felt to be anywhere that was far away from Noel. It was the first time she had thought of him in twenty-four hours. When her mobile went off suddenly she jumped, convinced for a moment that it would be Noel, that her careless thoughts had summoned him like a demon. In fact it was her father. She picked up at once, surprised. Jonas hardly ever called her on her mobile.

His voice sounded tinny and distant.

"I'm sorry," Allis said. "I can hardly hear you. The signal's weak."

He was telling her he wouldn't be there when she got home. "I'm at the hospital," he said. "Amos has had a heart attack."

Allis drew in her breath. She had thought for a moment it was her father who was hurt or ill. She felt a flash of guilty relief that it was only her uncle.

"My God," she said to Jonas. "What happened?"

"Some of those BNP thugs turned up at the centre yesterday. You know, at the open day? One of them got into an argument with Rose and knocked her down. I don't think he meant to exactly. As soon as he saw what he'd done he ran away. Amos went haring after him, and you know Amos, he's not exactly built for speed these days." The line went blank, and for a moment Allis thought they had been cut off. When Jonas spoke again he sounded further away than ever. "He's still critical, so they've got him sedated. I've told Rose she should get some rest but she won't leave him. I've been here with her most of the night. I stepped

16

outside for a minute so I could phone you but I ought to go and make sure she's OK."

"You go," Allis said. "I'll be there as soon as I can."

She broke the connection, feeling numb. What she wanted most of all was to get out of the train at the next station and travel north again. She did not want to see Amos, lying unconscious and maybe dying in a hospital bed. She did not want to see Rose, her eyes reddened from crying and insisting it was all her fault. It was too much like déjà vu. She had told her father she would take a taxi from Euston but at the last minute she changed her mind and made for the tube. She reasoned it would make more sense to go home first, to dump her stuff and change her clothes.

The house was blessedly quiet. She went upstairs, stripped naked and stepped into the shower. The sound of the falling water was like the Pennine rain. In her bedroom the possessions Noel had returned to her still lay in a heap on the dressing table. Seeing them there was somehow awful, and she wished she had put them away before leaving for Glasgow. As she dressed herself again in clean clothes she imagined she could hear Hanne's voice, speaking to her from inside the wardrobe.

These men are criminals, all of them, she said. *Are you really going to let this happen again?*

She remembered waking up in Bakewell, Jonny Clay's harsh embraces still hot on her skin. The old books said the proper way to activate a golem was with cabbalistic markings. These should be painted onto the clay with manganese oxide, which when dry was a reddish brown, and symbolic of blood.

Allis wondered if real blood might not be stronger, then remembered that Jonny Clay had real blood baked into him already.

In her mind she could see Jonny Clay, making one great bonfire of the whole of the city of London.

That should smoke them out, she thought. *The cowards*. She wondered how they would report it on the news.

Volk
by rj krijnen-kemp

Hermann Oade stared at the dead thing which lay before him. Approaching, he had attributed the lack of any shadow cast on the floorboards to the dim light of the landing; but now he saw that the thing was flat, virtually two-dimensional. It appeared to have had its life cruelly and systematically squeezed out, as if by some inexorable mechanical process. Its very flatness made it appear larger than it had in life. The tail was now as broad as a strip of toilet roll, the body, big and round as a rug, the eyes as wide as pfennigs. The fur was now merely erratically sketched lines that heightened the illusion of largeness. The thing was a stiff, cardboard caricature of what it had once been.

It had once been a cat.

Oade exhaled through his teeth as he squatted down to examine the dead thing more closely, the buttons of his waistcoat precariously taking the resultant strain. He shifted his parcel (white sausage and black bread) from one arm to the other. The grey, tiger-striped markings were familiar, recalling an animal he had cause to know well. The object had once been Ziggy, one of Elise's beloved "children".

What to do? After an anxious day at the factory, he had anticipated with relish a good meal, some music, a relaxed evening, but now his proposed itinerary had been disrupted by this distasteful dilemma of a dead cat. To leave it would be an atrocity; to dispose of it would entail the descent of many flights of stairs. At any rate, the very thought of touching the thing was nauseating. It looked stiff, but he imagined it flopping in his hands like a soggy towel. The prospect of moist white sausage lost its appeal. The lifeless eyes accused him, staring from a face as flat and thin as a slice of black bread.

Oade's appetite vanished completely.

The click of a lock disrupted his indecision. He stood and turned. The door across the landing, bordered by fantastical maps of cracked plaster, stared back at him. The old gossip had been spying again. It would have been no surprise had she been responsible for the thing on the doorstep; she was always whining about the pets, and the music.

Sighing, Oade delved into his pocket and withdrew his key. He would let the cat lie for the moment. He moved his hand towards the door, finding it unexpectedly open. It swung back into darkness, decanting cold air laden with the ammoniac scent of cat's piss and sweet rot of alcohol. Wrinkling his nose, he entered the room and fumbled along the wall for the switch.

The light snapped on. Oade dropped his package and stepped backwards, crunching his heel into the macabre feline doormat.

Propped against the damp, mould-smudged wall sat Elise Oade, her abandoned violin and an empty schnapps bottle at her side, a small kitten cradled in her lap. Her head had fallen forward and she was breathing deeply in oblivious sleep. Around her were the remaining eleven cats. Some were already deflated of life and lay beneath the others like furry blankets, others in various stages of disintegration. Those that still resembled themselves were splayed upon their dead and dying fellows, shivering and mewling piteously, while the ones in whom the process was clearly more developed were formless, damp bags of jelly. Some of these latter still moved.

Oade hurried across the room. He lifted one of the cats out of the way, then hurled it at the wall in a spasm of disgust when its skin peeled beneath his fingers, revealing bones as soft and sticky as over-boiled pasta. It slithered back to the floor, turning a quivering head, hissing as it sank and spread into a quaking pool of fur. He lifted Elise with gentle care and took her to the only other room in the apartment, the bedroom, where he set her down. Then, with equal care, he picked up the violin, caressing it and whispering endearments as he returned it to its case. The small kitten, seemingly unaffected by the dreadful affliction, he placed on the bed beside his wife. Then he rummaged through a drawer, extracting an old sack and, as an afterthought, a pair of gloves.

Elise Oade awoke, with dry mouth and pounding head, finding herself alone in darkness. She could hear movement in the next room, furtive and sneaking. Easing herself delicately from the bed, she crept to the door. Opening it, she winced at the light. The room wavered, a sheet of blinding white, forcing her to close her eyes and grip the doorframe for support.

She heard a tattoo of heavy footsteps.

"You look like Death." It was Hermann's voice, low with warmth and concern.

Elise allowed her husband to guide her back to the bed. She sat on its edge as her eyes became accustomed to the light seeping past the open door.

"What has happened here?" he asked, sitting beside her, placing his arm about her shoulders to ease her quiet sobs.

"Where are my children?" Her voice strained through tears.

"Disposed of." The reply was curt, though not unkind, attesting to the repugnance of the deed. The memory of that still-squirming sack, the long trek to the ground floor, deserted streets, the squealing when at last he let fall his burden into the inky waters of the river, was a nightmare best forgotten.

"Ziggy. I couldn't find Ziggy. I called and called…"

"What has happened here?" he repeated.

Anger mastered her grief. "It was that bitch, Frau Winkler," hissed through her teeth.

Oade remembered the door that had snapped shut behind him when he had been crouched over Ziggy, recalled his suspicion. Had the old gossip stooped to poison?

"She knocked just before dawn, a few moments after you had left for the factory. She complained about my children, again. She called them dirty and flea-ridden and noisy, and said that she wouldn't have to put up with them for much longer. She said she had gained an ally."

"Who?"

"She said that Volk, the new man upstairs, had told her that he would be speaking to the authorities."

"Herr Volk is in league with the authorities!" Oade's whisper held terror and awe in equal measure.

They were both whispering now.

"I was frightened and furious, Hermann. I went straight upstairs and banged on Volk's door. He didn't answer. I listened. He *was* there. I could hear him shuffling about, wheezing like a steam train. I was mad. I put my mouth to the keyhole and shouted that I didn't give two damns about his authorities…"

"Elise!"

"…and if he hurt my babies, then I'd hurt him."

20

"Elise, my treasure," Oade reproached, "to speak so, and to a gentleman who has, or may have, the ear of the authorities. What were you thinking?"

She ignored the question, continued her narrative. "It started with Melinda. She just *collapsed,* sunk in, as if her life were being sucked out by some blood-drinking ghost. Then it happened to the others. Oh, Hermann! I didn't know what to do…"

Not a religious man, but a cautious one, Oade crossed himself.

Her pretty eyes flooding with tears, her voice threatening a wail of hysteria, she stumbled on. "I drank all of your schnapps. I'm sorry, but I couldn't bear watching them die. I tried to play to them, but the music went wrong. I called for Ziggy. They were all dying, except… So horrible!" Her final words were a scream, choked back into sobs.

Oade hugged her close. "Shush, my pet." He looked up at the high ceiling, felt the fragility of their privacy. "He may hear you."

"What do I care whether he hears or not?" Elise, also turning her face towards the ceiling, shouted, "Murderer! *Vampyr!*"

Oade, hushing her, became conciliatory, rational. "Darling, my pet, such allegations, and without a shred of proof. We must be careful what we say, ever vigilant of our words, lest they betray us. Try to put it behind you. Play some music for me, and we shall attempt to pass the evening together as pleasantly as is possible." He was worried that Elise, always sensitive, could be pushed to a point where her mind would no longer run the stave of sanity, so much had she suffered of late. He hugged her again, crooned soothing nothings to her.

"Proof?" She was wide-eyed. "My belief is surely proof enough. I know that he murdered my children." And what real proof is there of anything, her eyes challenged, save that someone believe that thing to be true?

Oade reflected. In such a splintery mood, his wife would only respond to humouring. She had worked herself to the tension of the slenderest string of her violin, was at a pitch higher than its highest note, and only sympathy would re-tune her to base reality.

A discontented miaow startled them both.

With a cry of delight, Elise fished the kitten from where it had crawled beneath the blanket. She held it up. It hung between her hands, blinking and purring at its mistress.

"Jarmilla, you little dear!" She pulled the kitten to her, caressing its warm head with her cheek.

Oade reached a decision. He stood and walked out of the bedroom.

Elise followed, still cuddling and stroking little Jarmilla. The animal appeared to be in high health and spirits, exhibiting none of the symptoms that had claimed its elders.

"Hermann, what are you going to do?"

He was stood in front of the fireplace, looking into the old, chipped mirror and adjusting his tie. His reflection gazed uncertainly back: a pale, balding man lost in milky fog, struggling with something snaked tightly about his throat.

"I shall go up and talk to Herr Volk," he said. "I desire that this whole matter be cleared up, and I hope to return with an assurance that your fears are totally without foundation." It was the benevolently paternal tone that he used with boys in the factory.

"Very well, Hermann." Knelt on the floor, she was pouring a saucer of milk, stroking the grey cat and cooing affection.

Oade paused at the door. He looked tenderly upon his young wife, playing prettily with her remaining pet. Despite her traumatic swings of mood, her delusions of persecution, her occasional drinking bouts and unpredictable strangeness, she remained the most beautiful person that he had ever known. Since they had had to sell his piano, her violin playing had sustained him, become the only link with an otherwise lost world of bliss. Regarding her now, he felt determination flood him like hot blood.

Closing the door behind him, he strode across the landing and knocked.

Forewarned, he mused, is forearmed.

A few seconds later he knocked again, harder. Waiting on the chill, damp, dimly-lit landing was not pleasant.

A few more seconds and the door, ever so slightly, opened.

"Yes?"

Perhaps the glint of an eye could just be detected in the dark sliver between door and doorframe.

"Frau Winkler, I…"

"Oade. Go away. I am not well." Her voice was birdlike, rasping and high-pitched, with a tarry gurgle beneath each word, as if she were screaming from beneath fathoms of dark water.

22

"Frau Winkler, neighbour, I wondered whether we might have a word about Herr Volk?"

He was answered with silence. He remembered the moment when the mewling had suddenly ceased as the sack slipped beneath the surface of the river. He waited, expected the chain to slide back and the door to open.

"I mayn't speak to you. Go away!"

The door slammed shut with finality. He heard bolts grate into place; then, receding, the sound of shuffling, slippered feet, accompanied by a low, discontented clucking, "Volk...Volk ...Volk..."

Buttoning his jacket against the pervasive cold, Oade turned towards the stairwell. Dark shadows latticed the steps, a blackly alternative staircase seemed to overlay the real, ascending in skewed angles to the infinite void beyond the stars. As he climbed to the highest floor, he could not escape the feeling that he was pacing up those other, odd, sidereal stairs.

Elise gloried in playfulness, barely aware of her husband's departure. When the saucer of milk was finished, she found the white sausage and fed it to the kitten in small, wet gobbets. It purred, then ran off to sport alone, leaving her to muse on the freedom of cats. Cats are the ideal anarchists, attached to no one but those whom they choose, obeying no law but instinct. Yet even such near-perfect liberty does not make them safe from injustice, torture and death. Gracefully, she crawled across the floor towards her pet, softly miaowing her half of a mysterious conversation.

"Then, you shall have music!"

She fetched her violin from the bedroom.

As she brought the instrument to her chin, the animal curled at her feet, staring up with round eyes. She fingered the first few notes of a sonata, shutting her mind to the depletion of her audience.

"Stop that noise!"

She lowered the violin with a start. Oade was stood in the doorway, one hand clutched to his forehead.

"I have a headache." He entered the room, closing the door behind him with precise delicacy. He brushed what looked like a cobweb from his grey jacket. "I would prefer that you refrain from playing this evening."

As she returned the instrument to its case, she asked, "Did you speak with him?"

"God, it stinks of cats in here." He made for the bedroom door.

Feeling stung, she asked again, "Did you? Did you talk to Volk?"

His back to her, Oade bowed his head, ran fingers through his thinning hair. "Yes, I spoke with him. *Herr* Volk is a fine, upstanding gentleman, a man of the people. He understands things. He was most sympathetic, and said that it must be as I suspected, some nasty animal illness. He was going to speak with the authorities to see whether we could be transferred to a dwelling where so many cats might be more suitably accommodated, perhaps with a garden. But we have lost our chance of that, of course." His tone was cold, his words snapped and clipped like scissors.

Elise was cut. Tears threatened, but she held them back. "Then he is with Them," she observed.

"He is a... fine man, and you must cease your insane slanders. Goodnight." The bedroom door slammed shut like an inarticulate rebuke.

Weeping silently, Elise strolled over to the window, Jarmilla following at her ankles, whipping its tail back and forth in sympathy with her new mood. She wondered what it would have been like had she been permitted to keep the child, her real, human baby. Unstable, they had said, not a suitable mother. Pulling aside the curtains of yellowed lace, she looked down into the street.

Outside, it had begun to snow.

"Insane," she whispered. "Insane slanders." Then she turned and followed her husband to bed, still accompanied by the kitten.

Dreams of dread and death plagued the conjugal night.

When Elise awoke, she thought that Oade must already have left for the factory, as his customary weight was gone from the mattress. She reached for the bedside lamp.

The light showed him still there, beside her, beneath the blanket that was bizarrely tented by his so thin limbs. Shallow-breathing and skeletal, Oade's flesh had fled from him as he slept.

His eyes were open, pleading. She placed her ear to his mouth, straining to hear the words that stilted the rhythm of his breath.

"From beyond," he hissed. "He is from where the music fails."

Music. It seemed all that was left.

She recovered the violin and sat on the bed. Bow poised between slender fingers, she began to improvise a melody, nearly a melody, atonal and melancholy. Beneath her sad notes, she came to imagine she could hear another sound. She increased the volume, pressing hard on the catgut; but there it remained, that sound, also growing louder, a measured scrape, a slithering, as if in the room above, Volk's room, some bloated, satiated thing was dragging itself across the floorboards. She bowed frantically and the music rose to a continuous, mad arpeggio, a requiem of feline wailing, a Paganinian frenzy that climaxed as Oade melted into oblivion. As his life drained into air, her music ceased. Everything ended on that final, high, sustained, fading note; life, love, music, all were gone from her world, only silence remaining.

Elise sat, bent over her now voiceless violin, on the edge of the bed. Of Oade, there was nothing left but a voided sack of skin, as empty as his wide, sightless eyes.

Jarmilla, forgotten, had hidden within a shadowed corner of the room.

Motes of dust laded the grey morning light.

In some high place, a door opened and closed. The thud of heavy footsteps echoed in the stairwell.

Elise broke the surface of her asphyxiating sorrow. She leaped, with a scream of which she was entirely unconscious, towards the doorway. The startled kitten mimicked her screech and dived beneath the bed. Flung by fear across the sitting room, Elise fetched up against the window, fumbled briefly with the handle, threw the panes wide and leaned out. Far below, cobbles glistened frostily, like scales on the back of some great serpent. A few people, wrapped in heavy coats and with the brims of their hats pulled low, paraded wearily along the street.

Another step sounded loudly upon the stairs.

Elise leaned further out of the window. "Help me!" she cried. "Help!"

The stream of people was swelling, all flowed in the same direction.

25

"Please, help me!" she cried again.

From the midst of that anonymous sea of jostling clones, a face was raised towards her. Across the vertical distance, Elise stared down into dark, dead eyes that peered from grey skin drawn taut to the skull. The vacuum in that glare sucked at her soul, hungered for her blood, her music.

Footsteps reverberated upon the stairs like the collective heartbeat of the crowd.

Elise understood. As an unseen hand fumbled roughly with the door handle, she jumped. For a moment, she soared angelically, the slight cotton of her nightdress billowing like wings, then she plunged down to fall among the innumerable dead where they queued before the gates of Inferno.

In the Arcade
by Lisa Tuttle

Eula Mae woke. She peeled the sheet away from her perspiring body and sat up. Man, she was hot. The moon shone directly into the room through the uncurtained window, falling in a pool on the bed and giving the white sheets an almost phosphorescent glow against her dark skin.

She swung her legs over the side of the bed. It was strange to be awake so late at night. Everything was so still. Her husband slept silently in his half of the old, spring-shot bed. Eula Mae wondered what, in all this silence, could have awakened her.

It was odd, to be awake when everyone slept. She didn't think it had ever happened to her before. To go back to sleep seemed the only reasonable thing to do now, but she wasn't the least bit sleepy. She got up and walked to the window. That moon certainly was big and bright and low in the sky.

She put her palms flat on the rough, paint-peeling windowsill, ducked her head beneath the sash, and leaned out into the night. No lights gleamed from any of the crumbling tenements that lined the street, and only two street lamps shone – the rest stood darkly useless, bulbs shattered by children or angry drunks. Nothing moved. There was no sound. Eula Mae frowned slightly, and listened. The quiet wasn't natural – there should have been *some* sound, if only the far-away monster of traffic making itself heard. Did everyone and everything sleep without dreams? It was not natural: it was the stillness of a machine at rest, not the restless sleep of a city. She strained to hear the sounds she knew she should hear.

There! Was that...? But now Eula Mae could not be certain. Had she heard that faint humming noise, or had she only felt the blood and breath traversing the highways of her own body?

Eula Mae sighed deeply and wondered how close to morning it was. She would not sleep again this night. She shifted her weight from one foot to the other and raised her eyes to the moon.

The sight of it shocked her, and shook the centre of things. The known world, her world, ceased to be. The moon had always been there; she'd looked at it almost every night of her life. And now she looked up and saw not the familiar moon at all, but a simulacrum, a falsehood, a stage moon: a light. Nor was that the night sky it shone in – attached to an invisible ceiling, the light shone down through swaths of deep blue drapery. The familiar horizon became limited and strange. If that was not her moon, this could not be her city. Where was she?

"Howard," she said unhappily, turning back into the room. A cry for help. "Oh, Howard, wake up."

The still form did not stir. Eula Mae sat on the edge of the bed, which sagged still more under her weight, and put her hand on her husband's bare shoulder. His skin was smooth and cool.

Her lips formed his name again, but she did not speak it. She had suddenly comprehended just what was so unnatural about his stillness. He was not breathing.

She moaned and began to shake him, trying to shake him back into life, to get him started again, knowing it was hopeless.

Oh, Howard. Howard. Howard.

He lay there like a doll, like a bolster on the bed, still and sleek and cool. He was somewhere very far away from the close heat of the room.

Eula Mae sat with her hands resting on her husband's body. Tears ran down her cheeks. She did not move. Perhaps, if she were still enough, she would go where Howard was. But the sobs forced themselves up from her gut, wrenched her body, made her shake.

Then the fear prevailed. The fear made her get up off the bed (slowly, trying not to jar the body), the fear made her stop crying. She had to go somewhere, she had to be with someone. She fumbled about in the big metal wardrobe, seeking her clean housedress, but it took too long, and the sagging, hanging door on the locker kept swinging inward, bumping her, and the fear overruled all. She had to get out. She thought of her children, sleeping in the next room. She would take them and go to her sister's place.

The front room was dominated by the big bed where the children slept. Eula Mae noticed the wrongness as soon as she stepped through the door. There was no sound. Taddie's usual adenoidal snore didn't ripple the air – none of them, in fact, were breathing. She forced herself to go close to the bed, but she couldn't make herself touch them. If she touched them, felt them lifeless beneath her fingers, they would be turned into strangers for sure.

The facts were almost too stark to question. She wondered only why she, out of them all, had been permitted to awaken. Her mind searched restlessly, almost without her volition, for a prayer that would mean something.

Friends lived downstairs. She could go to them. The latch on the front door was stubborn, as always, but tonight it seemed a sinister stubbornness, locking her deliberately in a room where everything once familiar had been changed to evil. The door finally opened to her, groaning querulously, and she ran down stairs that tore with splintery mouths at her bare feet.

"Annie! George!" She pounded at their door. Her voice bounced from wall to wall in the ill-lit corridor and came back to her ears, thin and strange, frightening her so that she shut her mouth and used only her fists to call for help.

Nothing. Eula Mae was afraid to go out into the unnatural night, lit by the make-believe moon – this building was, at least, a known shelter – but she could not stay here among the dead. Her sister Rose Marie lived just up the street, in an identical tenement house, in a nearly identical two-room apartment. Her sister Rose Marie would take her in.

Eula Mae heard a scuttling sound. Roaches. Oddly, the sound was reassuring. It was familiar; it meant life here in this deathly still place.

She went into the street, not looking up. Her head was beginning to ache. She put her hand to her forehead, where the pain seemed to be centred, and felt the familiar imprint of the six-pointed star. She pulled her fingers away hastily, for their touch seemed to acerbate her headache. She remembered a radio programme she'd heard once, about a woman who had fallen and bumped her head and then forgotten everything – who she was and where she lived. Could something like that have happened to her? But what could she possibly have forgotten that would make sense of all these changes in her world?

The door of Rose Marie's building always hung open, and Eula Mae entered the narrow little hallway nervously. The mailboxes on the right wall had been smashed into useless metal, and she was afraid every time she came here that someday whoever had smashed those boxes would be waiting to smash *her*.

As always, reprieved once more from a smashing, Eula Mae scurried up the creaking stairs as rapidly as she could without stumbling.

No one answered her calls or her poundings. No one in her sister's apartment, and no one up and down the hallway, although the sound must have been heard throughout the thin-walled building. Were they all gone? Frightened? Deaf? Could everyone be dead?

Finally, Eula Mae broke in the door to her sister's apartment. It was not difficult: Eula Mae was a powerfully-built woman, although she did not think of herself as physically strong.

The front room was littered with children. One narrow cot held two, and the rest were on pallets on the floor. Eula Mae picked her way among them. She could hear no breathing, but did not want to investigate more closely.

A curtain separated the front room from Rose Marie and Jimmy's bedroom. Eula Mae pushed through the curtain and heard the welcome sound of soft snoring.

Her heart leaped with gratitude. "Rose Marie? Jimmy? Wake up!"

The slight, sibilant snores continued undisturbed. Eula Mae approached the bed. "Hey, get up!" she said loudly, and bent over her sister.

But no breath came from Rose Marie's nostrils, and no heartbeat disturbed the pink nylon ruffles of her negligée. Jimmy was snoring: he slept beside his dead wife. Eula Mae was outraged by this, and she leaned across the body of her sister and shook Jimmy's arm vigorously.

"You! Wake up! Quit that snoring and listen to me! Hear me? Wake up!"

Not even the rhythm of his snores altered. He slept on, as unreachable as Rose Marie.

Eula Mae straightened up and let her arms fall to her sides, realising that she was quite alone. She was accustomed to making decisions, to running both her own life and the lives of other people, but she'd never been alone, and in a situation she flatly did not know how to handle.

She went back down the hall that reeked of long-forgotten meals, and down the treacherous stairs, and back into the deserted street. She would try to find someone, anyone, any friend or

30

stranger to assure her that she was not the last person left alive; then they would decide what to do.

As she walked silent streets she remembered something her youngest brother had said. It might have been just another of the stories he loved to make up – just another of his innumerable horror stories about the omnipresent Whitey – or it might have been true.

"They've got a gas," he said. "They pipe it into rooms and kill everyone there. They tell us something like 'this way to the showers' or 'wait in this room till the doctor gets here' and then," his eyes glittered, "then they slip a tube under the door, or pump gas in through pipes in the vents and…. a few little coughs, a choke or two you hardly notice and…. zap…. everybody's wiped out. Snuffed."

Eula Mae had been a little bit afraid of him when he'd told her that: he'd enjoyed the telling so much; he had looked gloating and sly, not much at all like her beloved little brother.

"That's the way the Man solves the nigger problem," he'd said cheerfully. "He just puts 'em all to sleep, like dogs with rabies."

When she came out of her reverie, Eula Mae saw that she had walked much farther than she would have thought possible. She had walked straight out of the city and into the countryside. She stepped from concrete onto a dirt road, and looked around in wonder. The sudden transition was mysterious; Eula Mae *knew* she could not have come so far in such a short time – true, she had been preoccupied, but she doubted she had walked even a mile yet. By all that was logical, she should still be in the heart of the city. Yet she looked around and her eyes gave her evidence of a cotton field, a watermelon patch just across the road, and some tumbledown wooden shanties a bit further away.

She walked on towards the shanties, and went right up to one. But then she hesitated before mounting the steps to the dilapidated porch. A dog slept there, nose between his paws. Or did he sleep? The dog did not stir, nor give any sign that it knew she was there, staring at it. Had it indeed been a gas? Some mysterious gas, sprayed over all the areas where blacks lived? But if that were true, why had she lived on?

She walked past the shanty, continuing down the road, although her head hurt more with every step and she wanted to lie down somewhere, to rest, to be free of the pain that was knocking about inside her skull, burning a hole in her forehead. But she feared that if she rested she would never rise again.

So she walked on, she walked on – she walked quite suddenly into an invisible wall.

She backed off, staring stupidly at the horizon, at the moonlit dusty road which stretched before her. Then she tentatively stretched out a hand, and the hand went right through everything – the sky, the grass, the road, the distant shacks – and touched a hard, flat, smooth, invisible wall.

Eula Mae began to walk slowly alongside the wall, one hand outstretched and touching it to assure herself of its presence. She walked that way, following it, for some distance. It was eerie, seeing her hand pass through the landscape and touch something solid she could not see. But she did not have strength to spare for wondering. Her headache was almost overwhelming, and she had to fix all her attention upon moving, just moving. Reasons and answers would have to come later, if they ever came, just as rest would come later. For now she would have to move, because she was afraid to stop or turn back.

Once, Eula Mae looked to her right, away from the wall, and was startled to see that she was walking along a street only four blocks from where she lived. Why had she never tried to walk through the wall, towards the buildings that seemed to be there? Or had she? She could not remember. Perhaps it was not important to know if her universe had always been circumscribed by this wall, or if this was a recent change.

Abruptly the wall ended, projection merging with reality in a solid building. It was just another broken, dying tenement, like so many others in the neighbourhood. This one was scarred with 'Condemned' signs, and a door gaped blackly open.

Eula Mae hesitated a moment, the pain in her head holding her back like a brutal fist. She gasped slightly, and pushed herself through the doorway.

The hall it opened on was short and dark with a door closed at the opposite end. Eula Mae fumbled with the knob, and the door opened onto a blaze of light.

When she opened her eyes – slowly, against the pain of the headache and the glaring brightness – Eula Mae saw that she had opened a door leading into a wide, white-walled corridor lit by fluorescent ceiling panels. It was nothing from her world.

She looked up and down the hall. White walls, punctuated by doors, stretched in either direction. She saw no one, heard no one, and hesitantly entered the hall. She looked back at her door and saw, in stark black letters at the top of the doorframe, one word: NIGGERTOWN.

The pain in her head, which had become so persistent that she could almost ignore it, suddenly seared and stabbed with a new intensity. Eula Mae gnawed her lip to keep from whimpering. It was foolish to go on; foolish not to go home where she could lie down... but she thought of lying next to her dead husband, and knew she could not go back with nothing accomplished. If she was a fool, well then, she was a fool. She would go on.

She walked away from Niggertown. She came to a door labelled 'Little Israel' and hesitated... and then walked on. Eula Mae saw that the corridor had a turning just ahead and her pace quickened.

At the turn, the hall opened into a large, circular gallery. It was empty of people. All around the walls projected booths or stalls, similar to those found at fairs and amusement parks of all sizes – the sort where tickets are sold and goods dispensed. And as at a fair (and seeming to Eula Mae to be very much out of place in this clean, large, empty, well-lit hall), each booth was decorated with garish signs and posters, each proclaiming the particular attraction to be purchased at that booth.

'Niggertown' – the word garish in red and black – caught her eye, and she let herself be drawn to that booth.

Clowns in black-face. It was a depiction Eula Mae was accustomed to. Thick-lipped, pop-eyed, fuzzy-headed darkies. Mammies with their babies, little pickaninnies, young bucks in overalls strumming banjos.

SEE, shouted the caption above one picture. *Customs held since tribal days in darkest Africa!* Above a cartoon of soulful darkies looking heavenward was the suggestion: *Join the happy darkies in heart-warming 'spirituals' and sing your blues away!*

Centred amid all the garish drawings was a box set in a bold typeface. Eula Mae read it, her lips moving slightly as she grappled with each word.

Guaranteed Satisfaction! Observe first-hand a vanished way of life. See them tremble before you, the hated 'honky' – OR, for the thrill of a lifetime, never to be forgotten, SEE LIFE THROUGH BLACK EYES! Yes! Our surrogate people are so real, so lifelike, that only a trained expert can tell the difference. Plug right in and instantly you see, hear, smell, taste, and feel, just as you can in your own body. Walk among them undetected in an android nigger body – they'll accept you as one of the 'tribe', never suspecting, while you –

Voices. They cut through her confusion and the pain in her head. Eula Mae was frozen like a rabbit before headlights. Which way to run? People – she had been looking for people, but what if –

Caution won. She stumbled behind the poster-bedecked booth, crouched, and waited.

Clicking footsteps: boot heels. Eula Mae peered around the side of the booth, and terror flowed over her as she saw who was there.

Two white men, fine, blond, strong, Aryan types. The pride of the world. One wore coveralls and carried a tool-kit; the other was a guard of some kind, in a grey and black uniform, swastikas shining discretely from his shoulders.

The worker was complaining; the guard listening with a slight smile curling his lips.

"It's just that it's so damn unnecessary. It's an unnecessary expense to maintain real people – the public wouldn't know the difference if we replaced 'em all with androids. It'll have to be done eventually, when they die out, so why not replace 'em all right now? The surrogates wouldn't give us this kind of trouble."

"You're probably right," said the guard. "The public wouldn't know – the public is very gullible. But the Old Man himself sometimes comes around here. He'd know.... he likes..."

"*He* comes *here?*" asked the other in awe.

The guard frowned at being interrupted. He had stopped walking in order to speak his piece, and he expected the other to be properly respectful of his words.

"Yes. This is one of the last places you can see such things... most other arcades are composed entirely of surrogates. Some of them very fine, true, but not the real thing. And to some, like the Old Man, having the real thing is very important. It makes him

34

very proud, to be able to come here, to see a way of life he's wiped from the earth..." The guard began to walk again, and the other fell into step beside him.

As they turned the corner out of sight, Eula Mae could still hear the guard's fine, resonant tones going on: "But, of course, even the Old Man will not last forever... when he finally goes then you can have all your replacements, and you'll only have to maintain your surrogate people."

Voice and footsteps faded out. Eula Mae got to her feet, slowly and painfully. Her head hurt too much to think, almost too much to move. She could only wish she'd never awoken, never noticed that there was something wrong with the moon... It took her minutes to gain the strength and the will to take a few steps forward, and she was so engrossed in this simple action that she did not hear the returning footsteps until it was much too late.

She heard one voice say quietly, "Ah, there it is."

And then the pain in her head blazed up, she went blank, and she crumpled in a heap in the centre of the big arcade.

A Flowering Wound
by John Howard

I open to you like a flowering wound,
or a trough in the sea filled with dreaming fish,
or a steaming chasm of earth
split by a major quake.

You changed the topography.
Where valleys were,
there are now mountains.
Where deserts were,
there now are seas.

Erica Jong, 'After the Earthquake'

It's when I uncover his head. The man must have almost made it out as the building collapsed: there is hardly any rubble on top of him, but his legs are pinned under a concrete lintel and his head is covered by part of a shattered door. That is how I find the man, clawing away at bricks and concrete with my bare hands as the others all around are doing. Then I recognise his hand from the wristwatch. I pull the wood away from his head. I am surrounded by sobs and cries, the shouts of commands and curses. Floodlights and torches shine over the debris: searching eyes hovering over it. The man's eyes are closed, his face and hair covered in dust. There is a trickle of blood, already dried. But his head moves slightly and he is breathing. I resist the impulse to try to brush flakes of concrete and brick dust off his face and cradle the man in my arms. In any case his feet are still buried by concrete blocks and chunks of wood. I turn away, shout for help.

For a moment I'm dazzled by a torch. It flickers into my eyes and then plays on his face.

"You've found someone?" Radu says. He points the torch again and kneels down beside me, bending in close.

"He's still alive," I manage to say.

"He's a fucking yid," Radu says. "Can't you tell? Half the apartments in this place were yid apartments. We hadn't got them all out yet. Now it's too late anyway, eh?"

I lean in, trying to put myself between the man and Radu. In case he speaks; his mouth is trying to move, to open and form words.

"It'll be all right," I whisper.

"Leave that," Radu shouts. "No, wait."

Radu pushes me out of the way and smashes the torch against the man's forehead. The light goes out, but not before I see that his mouth stops trying to open.

"Sorted," Radu says. "The carcass can be dealt with later. There's still plenty of Romanians to save yet."

The man – the man's name is (was; no, it must be is) Sebastian. His apartment high in the Charlton Building is white and clean; the Boulevard seems so far below that a different air and sunlight applies. He puts a book back on the white shelves.

"So is it because I am Sebastian Vidranu, that yid who has a flat in the exclusive Charlton Building in Brătianu Boulevard, and I'm sleeping with you, and we both enjoy it? So that means I'm assimilated, I'm really as Romanian as you and your friends are, after all? Please, Mihai!" He sits down opposite me. "You're better than that! Aren't you? Do you think that you make up for some sort of defect I have, fill in a cavity, make me one hundred percent human? Is that it? Yes Mihai, you've rubbed off on me all right, you know that don't you? You have. Is that what this is about? Have you decided you're sorry?"

I stand up and make as if I'm leaving. The man turns his head to look at the wall of books ranked row upon row.

"Yes!" I shout. "To all of that. But I don't mind. I know I'm a Romanian. The Legion is right. We need a national cleansing and renewal. Anyone, anything, who is not one of us, who is against the nation –"

"So what am I then, Mihai?" he shouts back. "Can you answer that? You're here, aren't you? What am I then? Is something wrong or am I ill? Or is it maybe you needing to be cured of what you are?"

The earthquake strikes in the early hours of a November morning. It lasts nearly five minutes. Houses, offices, shops, churches cave in and fold up all over Bucharest. When the earth is quiet again the most prominent casualty is the Charlton Building, the tallest apartment block in the city and a stunning example of the modernist style in architecture. Dominating the Boulevard, the complex includes offices and a cinema. The brightly-lit future is brought to us in a ruled majestic line of sleek white structures cutting sharply through the irregular streets and gardens of the old city.

The rescue attempt is a dismal failure. Immediately the tremors finish fading away, German military engineers stationed in the city offer to help. But with pockets of air becoming exhausted and water mains flooding the basement under the enormous pile of wreckage that is all that is left of the tower block, our Legionary leaders insist on us doing the work ourselves, and mainly with our bare hands. Some have shovels to begin with if they're lucky. We waste our time.

The gendarme doesn't even bother to try and shoot at me as we run. He eventually gives up the chase and falls behind. Winded, panting for breath and covered in sweat, I find myself on the Boulevard, sprinting along it and keeping close to the buildings lining its clean empty length. It seems safer than any of the streets leading into it. Then I hear shouts and more firing and I dodge into a deeply recessed doorway. The man is standing on the other side of the thick engraved glass doors, solidly set into their ornate brass and bronze frame. We make eye contact for a moment: that is all. The door is as unmoving as a wall, as the pillars supporting the concrete tower soaring above. I almost bounce out onto the pavement again, but I look back over my shoulder and see the door opening slowly. He beckons me inside.

Later Sebastian says that he has not left his apartment for several days. He is prepared: the place is well-stocked with food and drink. His servant is back in Cluj until things calm down again. He offers to sew up the tears in my jacket himself; he says his father once taught him the basics of the trade. I empty the pockets and a Legionary medallion falls out and clatters across the polished inlaid table.

"I wonder why that didn't fall out earlier," Sebastian says. I pick it up and look again at the profile of the Captain on the face and the outline of the country shaped on the reverse. The light glances off its bright clean surface.

"He is a great man," I say reverently. "I met him once. His time will come."

Sebastian starts to work. Then he says, "I think there's something I need to make clear to you." He bites off a length of thread and puts the needle away.

Radu knocks back another plum brandy and says, "What happened to you?"

I start to explain, but he grins and hands me a full glass. "Drink that," he laughs. "Maybe you haven't heard, then. We've got Carol scared. He's holed up in the palace. He might think he doesn't need us, but we certainly don't need him. We'll soon sweep him away, with his Jewish clique and the rest of them."

Someone makes a joke about Magda Lupescu, King Carol's mistress. Loud laughter echoes around the tiny overheated room, and I join in. But some of us are missing. Soon we will hold the roll-call, when we will hail the martyrs' names, crying out the responses, making them proudly.

I drink, fingering the medallion in my pocket. I can't tell which of the raised textured surfaces I feel between my finger and thumb are which: the Captain or the country. It doesn't matter. They are one, the dead and the living, and I am with them and them in me.

When King Carol abdicates in September and the National Legionary State is declared, Legionaries are taken into the Government and we go on to the streets in celebration. We have endured months of national humiliation, losing territory to the Bolsheviks, to Hungary, to Bulgaria. Carol and his camarilla escape from the nation they leave betrayed and mutilated. But we perform our own recompenses.

Sebastian says he has to find 75000 lei or leave his apartment. I turn away from the balcony. "I'm afraid I can't –"

He jumps up from the Bauhaus sofa, comes over to where I'm standing. Behind me he rests his hands on my shoulders. "I know. I'm not asking you," he says. I can feel the man's warm breath on the back of my neck; I smell his cologne and stray traces of the expensive imported bourbon we are both drinking. "The money is no problem. I can raise it. You know why it's getting more and more difficult to remain here. István isn't ever coming back from Cluj – I told him it's too dangerous for him here. You know why that is." Sebastian kisses the back of my neck. "But I don't want to leave, do I? There's someone who makes me want to stay. Anyway, I was born in Bucharest. I have a lovely home here. I have a right –"

"You have no rights," I say to myself, moving my lips but not making a sound. "No, I don't want you to leave here," I say. "But that's when I'm here, up in the air." Sebastian begins to laugh gently. Then his broad shoulders start heaving as he laughs harder and louder. The man says he doesn't want to tell me why he's laughing so much; why he finds it so funny.

I start to say that it's not only when I'm with him in the apartment, but all I do is to stop his laughter with my mouth.

I ask Radu what happened to the bodies found in the rubble after the earthquake.

"They were disposed of correctly," he says. "You've seen we know how to look after our own, and to do it well. Other Romanians were buried with only the rites of Holy Orthodox Church. Other Christians by their rites, I suppose. And as for anyone else –" Radu stops suddenly and puts his glass down, still half full of spirit. He looks me straight in the eye; through me, I feel. "You're thinking about the Charlton Building, aren't you? About when you were doing your bit with the rescue work."

Radu still stares at me. For a moment his face assumes a distracted, almost vacant gaze, as if the mind behind it, looking out of the eyes, is turning its attention away; then it comes back almost at once. "Mihai, I know what this is about. It's that yid you found, isn't it? Was that the first corpse you'd ever seen? I think I envy you!" He calls for more brandy, and slops some into my glass. "Do you really want to know what happened to those corpses? I don't think it was nice. I could ask around. But why are you so interested, Mihai? Anyone would think that you knew the man or something. Hey, you didn't, did you?" Radu bellows with laughter at the absurdity of it.

I forget how many times I deny it.

I stand on the pavement, staring at the ruins of the Charlton Building. The mountain of rubble has been cleared away; only the walls of the cinema and a few shattered concrete pillars are still standing. Scavengers pick through the scoured earth and surround a bonfire. The Boulevard is busy with people and traffic. Workmen scurry around; the exposed wall of the apartment block next to the site is being propped up with massive wooden supports, and cracks are being examined minutely. Furniture and suitcases are piled up on the pavement: the tenants are being moved out as a precaution.

I continue walking north along the Boulevard, towards Piața Romană. The white canyon of modern buildings is becoming grey and dusty; smooth white walls are cracked and pitted, exposing concrete frames and brick fillings. I wander the streets around the Boulevard and Calea Victoriei, and all the way back down to the river. I try to lose myself in the city, but it isn't possible. I know the bars and cafés, parks and street corners all too well. At ground level the future is stalled, mired in mud and cobbles. It is as much my city as Sebastian's; I tell myself I am part of building it up, making it worthy of the renewed society we strive for. I cross the Boulevard again and again, backwards and forwards, ignoring the traffic and the way people look at me. A tram narrowly misses me; I step back on the rail but the tram is gone, leaving behind gasps, and cries of derision and fright. For hours I wear tracks into the pavements, slowly and deliberately rubbing the tangled printed plan off the map. I am hiding Bucharest as I penetrate it further. I rub it out, I dream of pulling it down as the hours slide into twilight. I can no longer bear to go home or to the Legion House. I am back at the ruins of the Charlton Building again when a voice makes me stand still.

"Mihai."

I stare at the man.

"Mihai, are you all right?" he says. "What's wrong? Don't you know who I am? It's me." He takes hold of my arm and starts to pull me slowly along the pavement. "Come on, let's go home to the House and have a drink," he says. "You'll be among your friends again."

I say the man's name, and immediately don't remember which one comes out. My legs blossom with pain, cracking as they

41

give way under crushing weight. I cough and choke. The skin and bone of my left temple splits in an agonising budding of blood. As the darkness sweeps in, my mouth opens and I bloom in a flower of concrete fragments and brick dust, voicelessly spreading, spreading.

Sense
by Tony Richards

November, 2012

This area had changed so much. Pulling down the shutters on his tiny jewellery store late that afternoon, Frank Aaron was forced to admit it. When he'd been growing up here, this street would have been bustling, everyone preparing for the coming Sabbath. Whereas these days, it was practically deserted.

He clamped the heavy-duty padlock in place, straightened, and made his way home.

A good few of the neighbouring shops had closed down, their empty windows covered up with flyers for rock concerts. Except that many of those were out of date. And had been covered, in their turn, by posters from the NBP, the Sword of St. George standing out prominently in the growing dimness.

"Nazis," his friend Stewart called them. Frank wasn't so sure. The economy was in the toilet. The current party in office wasn't doing any more about it than the last one had. Maybe a fresh approach…?

He loved *erev Shabbat*, the evening of the Sabbath. The familiarity of it, the closeness. All the family gathered around the dining table as one bonded unit. The prayers said and the candles lit. It had been that way since he had been a little child.

At which point, Frank had an insight. He genuinely thought, the way most people in the country seemed to these days, that things needed to change. But at home, and in his personal life, he didn't like that word.

A yell brought his gaze up. On the opposite pavement, a group of half a dozen tall black boys – he thought they might be Somalis – were tussling with each other. He was worried at first that it might be a gang fight. But they were only playing.

Frank watched them suspiciously. He knew that they were only teenagers, and he had been high-spirited at that age. But there was something deeply alien about them. And it wasn't the colour of their skin… he was friendly, after all, with the Olawis, two doors across from his house. Those were decent, lovely people.

43

These were... what? Not at all like his little community. They cared nothing for family; doubtless their fathers were long gone. They cared nothing for education either; they could be seen out on the street during the hours when they should have been in school. And they talked constantly about 'respect,' but seemed to have not much of that, for the district, the people around them, or even themselves.

They'll integrate eventually, the way our people did, he tried to tell himself. But they seemed to have no will to do so.

He reached the corner leading to his street and turned down it, dead leaves blowing around his shoes. And was halfway along when he heard footsteps running up behind him. When he glanced across his shoulder, the same six boys were hurrying towards him. One of them had produced a crowbar, seemingly from thin air.

He realised what they were going to do and turned away, trying to escape.

But however hard he pumped his legs, he couldn't manage to run fast enough.

A couple of days later

"Of course they're British," Ray Kingdom was saying, on the TV screen above the hospital bed.

Frank had a fractured skull.

"But why should this country be forced to import criminality? We've enough bad boys of our own, after all. We're a wicked lot, us Brits."

Most of the audience laughed.

"What the New Britain Party is proposing is this. Immigrants, and their children–"

"Second generation?" the interviewer broke in.

"Yes. If they're prepared to abide by the laws of this country, they're welcome to stay. But if they're not, maybe they'd be happier somewhere else. So we'd withdraw their citizenship and require them to leave."

There was a round of applause. And Frank would have nodded, but it hurt too much to move his head.

One disgruntled soul in the audience shouted, "You going to start gassing people next?"

"You're not listening to me. Anyone law-abiding is welcome to stay. Wouldn't that make for a better country?"

It certainly sounded like it made sense. The local elections were coming up. And he usually voted for some small, moderate party. Maybe he'd consider something different this time?

August, 2013
The Citizenship Act had been amended just last week to include third and fourth generation immigrants who committed crime. Frank had to admit, the area felt a whole lot safer. What had happened to him last year... it wasn't common any more. He felt glad of that. He still had partial memory loss, and suffered from awful migraines sometimes.

But things in general were looking up, he told himself as he walked home from the shop. Business was improving. Both his daughters had got into university. The world seemed more cheerful, and less cluttered.

A yell brought his gaze up. On the opposite pavement, a group of half a dozen white boys – each of them wearing a Sword of St. George armband – were following a woman in a burka down the street. They were keeping their distance, but were yelling at her angrily.

"What you dressed like that for, then?"

"You hiding something?"

"Maybe you'd be happier somewhere else?"

Frank couldn't be sure, under the long black robes that she was wearing. But the woman seemed to be teetering on the verge of trying to break into a run. The same kind of burst of speed that he'd been forced to attempt last year. Dressed the way she was, though, she could never manage it.

He felt a twinge of sympathy for her, having been in a similar position once. But then he told himself, *What does she expect, dressed up like a crow like that? She's brought it on herself.*

And actually, he didn't completely trust Moslems, or like some aspects of their religion very much.

"We're talking fundamental differences," Ray Kingdom said on the TV that evening.

The General Election was coming up in a few months.

"Of course they're British, legally. But there is a direct opposition between Islamic attitudes and democratic ones. What we're proposing is this. They sign an affidavit stating that they put this country and its values first, and their religion second. Otherwise, they're not allowed to vote."

Which seemed reasonable to Frank, who'd been born here and had always considered himself a patriot.

Someone set fire to the local mosque that night. Which saddened him, not least because he could still remember when it had been a synagogue.

January, 2014
Everything had settled down at last. There had been weeks of riots when the election results were made known – a hung Parliament, with the NBP holding the balance of power. Millions of pounds worth of property had been destroyed, and three people had died.

"What's wrong with these idiots?" he'd complained to his friends. "They have to accept how the public voted."

Except his friends were getting fewer these days. A good number of the people he'd grown up with had moved away to Canada, America, or Israel. He thought they were overreacting. Ray Kingdom had never said a single word about their kind.

The local mosque had not been rebuilt as such and was now a Kwik-Fit. After the election, the NBP's researchers had matched the electoral roll to those people with Moslem names who had not signed the affidavit, and had used the expanded Citizenship Act to have them deported.

The area was still changing. Several eateries and stores had closed down, becoming bookmakers or off-licences instead. It left the main street with a good deal less character, he had to admit. But was a little blandness so great a price to pay for better safety?

Mr. Olawi appeared from a parked car and stopped in front of him, looking grave and shaken.

"Luther, are you all right?"

Frank tried to put a hand on his shoulder, but the big Nigerian shook him off. His eyes were bulging and seemed glassy.

"Toby was attacked last night." His eldest son. "A knife barely missed his heart. It was the same kind of thugs you people voted for."

Us people? He meant white?

"How do you know?"

"They were wearing armbands."

46

Which proved nothing, Frank thought. But he was still mortified. He'd known little Toby almost since his birth – a fine, polite, intelligent boy.

"Which hospital is he in?"

It turned out to be the same one he'd wound up at after he'd been mugged. He visited, but Toby was sullen and uncommunicative for the first time ever. And as soon as he'd recovered, they all went back to Nigeria.

The family who moved into their house were not what he'd expected. There were five of them, a father and four teenaged sons. No mother in evidence. The father seemed to own no shirts, and went about constantly in his undervest. The sons were all crop-headed and wore armbands. They seemed to drink from cans constantly, crushing them up and tossing them in the gutter. They were always out on their front porch, and continually making noise.

He went across rather nervously to ask them to tone it down a little when they disturbed the prayers on *erev Shabbat*.

The eldest boy started to get up, his eyes ice cold, his mouth puckering. His fists clenching. When suddenly, the father appeared in the doorway. Laid a hand on his son's shoulder. The boy settled back down unhappily.

"Sorry about that, mate," the man grunted. "You naff off and say your prayers, and put one in for me."

"Course he's British," one of the boys muttered when Frank turned away.

The whole group of them snorted with suppressed laughter.

June, 2015

Several coalitions had collapsed. The economy had grown inexplicably worse again. There was another election, which got no clear result. So it was held a second time the following month. People were exhausted with the whole damned thing.

"...cannot be trusted," Ray Kingdom was shouting.

It was *Prime Minister's Question Time*. Just yesterday afternoon, a Moslem teenager had tried to set off a bomb on a bus, and had burned himself to death instead. Several other passengers had been taken to hospital with minor injuries, mostly caused by the panic that had ensued.

"I accept that it's not fair to some. I understand that some of them are fully integrated and accept our values. But the safety of the British public must come first."

Several MPs booed. He shouted back, "Do you want the blood of innocent Britons on your hands?"

The Citizenship Act was expanded hugely, requiring all Moslems to leave. There were more riots. And a lot more rioters killed this time, the police on huge pay rises and heavily armed. Several MPs resigned. There were by-elections, and the NBP got a three-seat majority.

"Can you tell the difference – on a street, on a Tube train – between a Hindu and a Moslem?" Ray Kingdom yelled from the front bench. "Can you tell the difference – on the street, on a Tube train – between a Namibian Christian and a Somali fundamentalist?"

"Look at their identity cards!" someone shouted. They had recently been introduced.

"People can fake names! We can't fully trust *any* of them!"

And Frank could see that most of that made a kind of sense. Nobody was being picked upon without good reason. Nobody was being hurt. And none of what had been said applied to him or his – admittedly dwindling – community. He felt like he was on the right side of this argument.

Before they were forced to do so, most people with darker skins were leaving. Even people with olive skins, in fact. There had been an Italian restaurant on the high street Frank had eaten at since he'd been a little boy. The original owner's son – Marco – had continued the business. It was gone, and so were that whole family – grandparents, toddlers, all. The windows were now bare. Posters with the Sword of St. George began to obscure them.

Later that same month, a mob of some eight hundred youths in armbands ran amok in Chinatown. The TV news broadcasts kept showing it until an emergency decree under the Security of Information Act shut them down.

Frank had never really thought about the Chinese before. They seemed to exist on the edges of your consciousness. Kept completely to themselves. But they were hardworking, he knew that. And had never caused any trouble. So why pick on them?

Later on, there was footage of Ray Kingdom condemning the attacks. But for the first time, there was something rather insincere about the way the words came out, which made Frank uneasy. He started feeling very glad that he looked just as British as any other man.

The trouble was over and done with in one night, though, and he finally decided it was not significant.

February, 2016

A lot of the abandoned shops and eateries on the high street had not reopened. There were posters everywhere. One convenience store had turned into a games arcade, from which a constant racket of electronic pings and gunshot sounds emerged. There were boys with armbands on every corner, apparently with nothing much to occupy them. They sneered at Frank when he went quickly by.

A man about his age, but more scruffily dressed, was handing out copies of *The Briton* up ahead of him. PLENTY MORE TO ACHIEVE, SAYS KINGDOM, read the headline.

Frank reached out for the one being proffered, but the man jerked it away.

"I thought they were free?" he asked.

The man stared at him wordlessly.

It was disturbing. But there always had been, always would be, ignorant people who took a blinkered view of life. Frank walked off sadly, trying to push the incident to the back of his mind.

This area had changed *so much*. There was practically nothing that he recognised. He had hardly any friends at all left around here any more. And he realised, perhaps for the first time, how broad and general a term 'friendship' was. The man at the corner shop where he bought his morning paper, who'd always smiled at him and exchanged a few friendly words. The young couple from the dry cleaners, who'd come outside and helped him one time when he'd slipped over on a patch of ice – they'd waved when they'd seen him through their window after that. The little Kurdish girls who used to play hopscotch on this very stretch of pavement, and wished him a good morning when he passed.

All gone. He was surrounded by unfamiliar faces, uniformly pale and grim and drawn.

And then he realised he was wrong. There *was* someone he definitely knew. Walking towards him was the unmistakable portly figure of Ivan Bremman, one of the regulars from his synagogue. They'd often sat together, chatting in hushed tones during the service.

Frank started raising a hand to signal to him.

Then thought better of it.

Parked against the kerb was a large, unmarked black van. Three men stepped from the shelter of it – they were plainly clothed and wore no armbands. But they confronted Ivan in the street and appeared to ask him a couple of questions, then looked at his identity card.

Frank could see the man's head shaking. What exactly was the problem? It didn't make any sense.

And then something incredible happened.

All three men were young and tall. And two of them suddenly hooked their arms around his friend's and hustled him in the direction of the van. The third pulled the back doors open. Ivan was pushed inside.

Were these police? They didn't look like it. An awful feeling of suspicion began to creep over Frank. His brow became clammy, his palms damp.

He'd been going to open up his shop, just like on any other normal day. But now he turned around and started heading back the way he'd come. *Get back home, where you'll be safe.*

There was a shout behind him. When he glanced over his shoulder, the back doors of the van were firmly shut. One of the men was pointing at him. They began to move in his direction.

Frank reached the corner leading to his street. Went around it, just as his pursuers' pace began speeding up.

He started to run.

But however hard he pumped his legs, he couldn't manage to run fast enough.

In on the Tide
by Alison J. Littlewood

Dan made his way down the path to the beach. The salt smell was always with him but he took a deep breath, enjoying the briny sharpness. He passed Fergal's shed on the way down, saw the man sitting outside. Dan grinned and waved, but didn't stop to talk. He could already see Alfie and Janice standing on the shoreline, skimming stones into the foam. Their mouths opened and closed but all he could hear was the waves, over and over, comforting in their constancy.

Dan waved a hand in greeting and they sat on the rocks, shifting until they found bits that didn't spike them through their jeans. They stared out across the sea as far as the Hebrides.

Alfie had a cigarette. He pulled it from his pocket, trying to be nonchalant. Dan knew he should be nonchalant too but couldn't help staring as Alfie lit up and raised it to his lips, just for an instant, and blew out an insubstantial wraith. Dan's old man smoked and he knew it didn't look like that, not quite, but he didn't say anything.

"Chuffing hell," said Janice, "would you look at that." She pointed.

A figure walked along the beach. Even though his back was to the sun, Dan knew who it was. He frowned.

"He's in your class, is he no?" asked Janice. Dan nodded.

"Chuffing hell."

The figure grew closer. He was wearing normal clothes, at least. A brown sweater, blue jeans. Only his black, wiry hair bore the signs of somewhere else. And his face, of course. It was Sukhjeev Singh. He had joined Dan's class at the start of term.

Sukhjeev kept walking, drew close enough to hear them. Dan saw he carried a fishing net over his shoulder, a ridiculous thing, red mesh on a stick. The lad was too old for such a thing. He should know better.

Alfie didn't comment on the net, however. He waved his cigarette in the air. "Hey, chocolate," he called out. "Watch out: ye'll melt if the waves get ye."

Sukhjeev stopped. He didn't quite look at them, just looked down the beach the way he was headed.

Janice sniggered. "Yeah, chocolate."

"Curry," said Alfie.

Janice turned to Dan. "Can you smell curry?"

"My dad says he's a Paki," said Alfie. He threw his cigarette down, stamped it under his heel. "Go back to Pakiland, Paki."

Sukhjeev spoke in a low voice. "I'm from Arbroath."

"Are ye fishing for curry fish? You won't find any curry fish here."

"Yeah, he's fishing for curry fish."

Sukhjeev edged away, holding his net closer to his body.

"That's it. Back to Pakiland."

"Maybe he'll find a curry fish there."

"Saves stinking us out."

Laughter rose as Sukhjeev turned and picked his way back towards the path. They watched him go. Sukhjeev didn't walk right, Dan noticed. He walked like he knew they were watching him walking. Dan swallowed and turned away. Noticed a shape caught in the waves. It lifted and lowered, lifted and lowered, just offshore where the rocks fell away and the sea grew dark. He caught his breath.

"Bloody Paki." That was Alfie. Dan knew it was Alfie and that he should turn round and laugh with the others, but he could not.

The shape lifted and fell. Something floated from it, pointed towards the shore. It looked like a pale, bloated hand. Tendrils spread on the surface of the water, like hair. Dan's gorge rose. It was as though his throat was blocked; he couldn't breathe.

"What's biting you, Danny boy?"

Dan didn't answer, just raised a hand and pointed towards the water. Whatever it was, it was wrapped in bladderwrack, a shining, slime-smelling sheet. Dan's hand shook.

"What's wi' you?" Alfie slapped him on the head.

"There," breathed Dan. "A body. Do ye not see it?"

Alfie stepped forward, leaned towards the water. "What the chuff you on about?"

"There. Right –" Dan pointed again, but this time he didn't see it. He didn't see it at all. The waves were clear, breaking against the shore as they always did. Dan let his hand fall to his side. "I thought –"

"Ye slack twat." This time, though, when Alfie clipped his ear he did it softly.

Dan shook his head, shrugged. Turned to see them staring at him.

Janice spun on her heel then, and shrieked with laughter. Dan jumped.

"Did he say Arbroath?" Janice said, her voice shrill. "Arbroath – Arbroath smokie!"

After a moment, they dissolved in helpless laughter.

Dan saw Fergal outside his shed, spreading a fishing net around him, testing it for tears. The net looked massy and heavy: a real fishing net. Dan waved and jogged down the path towards him, then saw Fergal wasn't alone. Sukhjeev Singh leaned against the shed. Fergal must have said something to him because Sukhjeev's shoulders shook with laughter. Then he caught sight of Dan and stopped shaking. In another moment he'd said his goodbyes and walked off down the path.

Fergal looked up and saw Dan. He waved. "Pull up a chair, young man," he called out, and they grinned. It was a joke, their joke. Fergal only had one chair, and that was Fergal's. Dan sat on the path and wrapped his arms around his legs, watching Fergal's callused fingers on the net.

"Where you off today, sailor?" asked Fergal.

Dan grinned. "China, maybe. Or Japan." He thought of a film he'd seen, Jackie Chan wiping out an army of bad guys using only his feet.

"Japan, aye? I've been to Japan."

Dan knew he had. Fergal had been everywhere. Now Dan was supposed to ask about Japan, teasing it out of Fergal. He pressed his lips together.

"Something wrong?"

Dan frowned. "I just wondered."

"Oh, aye?"

"Has there been a body washed up around here?"

Fergal started. "A body? What's that, now?"

"I just thought –"

"Thought what?" Fergal raised his eyebrows.

"I might have seen something. I thought it was a body, but –
it can't have been. Only I wondered."

Fergal grinned. "There's no body in these parts, lad. Not
exactly the place for swimming, is it? There's no been a body
washed up on this coast for years."

Now he had Dan's attention. "For years?"

Fergal sighed and put down the net. "Ye no miss anything, do
ye?"

Dan shook his head. Grinned. Now Fergal had to tell.

"There was an Italian washed up on this beach. A prisoner o'
war. He was taken away with the rest, and put on a big ship, see.
An' as it sailed the Germans torpedoed it, and in came the body.
Tha's the only one I ever heard of."

Dan frowned. "Was he a soldier?" When Dan used to play at
soldiers they hadn't shot Italians, only Germans.

"He owned a chip shop, so I heard."

"Eh? What're you on about, Fergal?"

Fergal threw back his head and laughed. "'S true as I'm
sitting here. He ran a chip shop in Fife. A Fife man born; it was his
father came from Italy, before the war, before this chap ever
thought of frying a fish."

"What?"

"It was in the war," Fergal said, as though that explained
everything. "The Italians joined the other side. An' so Winston
Churchill, he decided we shouldn't have no Italians in Scotland.
They were all rounded up, the men anyway."

"Are ye sunstruck?" Dan squinted at Fergal. Last birthday his
dad had taken him to an Italian restaurant in Oban, and they ate
pizza and spaghetti and laughed with the waiters. One of them had
bright red hair and freckles and was no more Italian than Dan was
a Chinaman, but he'd put on the voice anyway. Seemed to like
doing it. Dan had done it too; he had fun doing the voice. No one
hated the Italians.

"There was this big boat, see. The Arandora Star. She was
built as a cruise ship, and a fine one. Big chandeliers, state rooms,
quoits: all that."

Dan didn't know what quoits was, but he remained silent.

"They stripped out all the luxuries and put in barbed wire.
Then they took the Italians from their beds – didn't tell no one
where they were going – and locked them on the ship."

54

"So where were they taking them?"

"Prisoner of war camp, most likely. Only they got torpedoed first. The Germans thought she was a warship, didn't they. Most of the bodies were never found. Guards and Eye-ties and crew - the fish must've eaten 'em all alike, I reckon. No one told 'em they were any different."

"That's ridiculous," Dan said. "Winston Churchill ne'er did ought like that. He was a hero."

"He did, that. Course, the ship was off Ireland, by then, but the sea carried them home. One of the bodies washed up right here." Fergal pointed. Below them, down on the shoreline, Sukhjeev Singh peered into a rock pool while waves broke at his feet.

"You know, ye shouldn't let tha' lot pick your friends for ye," said Fergal.

Dan whipped his head around and looked at him. Fergal picked up a blue-green strand of net, ran his fingers over it.

"I've got to go." Dan jumped to his feet. "I'll see you later." He took a step towards the beach, hesitated, then turned back the way he had come. He felt Fergal's eyes on him, but didn't turn around.

In school, they were doing careers. They went around the class and asked everyone what they wanted to do. Then the teacher nodded, as though they'd made a good choice. Dan thought about Janice. Her class had already done careers and Janice had said, "A ballet dancer, miss," and the teacher nodded and everyone laughed.

He turned around. Sukhjeev sat on his own. The desks were in pairs, but nobody sat with Sukhjeev Singh. Dan wondered, if there was another Asian kid in the class, whether they would hang about together even if they didn't like each other. He thought they probably would.

It was Sukhjeev's turn. "I want to be a banker," he said. The teacher pursed up her lips before she nodded, as though he'd made a very good choice. The other kids didn't say anything, though there was a wave of movement: legs shuffled, pens rearranged.

"Daniel."

Dan looked at the teacher. He didn't know what he wanted to do; then he did. "I want to go on the boats, miss. I want to be a

55

fisherman." He could go as far as China or Japan if he wanted, just like Fergal.

The teacher nodded. Another good choice.

Dan turned to the window and thought about that shape, rising and falling in the waves. Outside the sky was blue and clear, a rare, beautiful day.

The Italians had been on a boat. Even with the barbed wire and guns, that would have been something. A big boat, Fergal had said. Dan thought of the torpedo hitting, everything breaking apart and letting the sea rush in; open-mouthed fish, waiting to eat them all, and he shivered.

"They're taking our jobs," said Alfie, flicking ash from his cigarette. "Everyone knows it."

Sukhjeev was there again, picking his way around the rocks in the distance, looking down at his feet. Occasionally he bent and dipped his net into the water.

"Arbroath smokie," said Janice.

At first Dan didn't know what she meant, then he remembered and his lip twitched. He didn't know why Singh kept on coming down here. This was their place, everyone knew it. He remembered the lad standing by Fergal's shed, and scowled. "He wants to be a banker."

"That'd be right. Taking our money, too." Alfie breathed out in a long hiss. "We should teach him his place."

Dan looked up to see Alfie flick his stub into a rock pool. It floated there.

"Come on, then," said Janice. She jumped to her feet.

Alfie stood too, leading the way. "Hey, smokie," he called. "Wait up, smokie. We only want to talk to you."

Sukhjeev retrieved his net from the pool. It dripped, trailing a line of thread or seaweed, Dan wasn't sure which. Sukhjeev waited for them, not speaking.

"Smokie, smokie," chanted Janice.

Sukhjeev raised his eyebrows. Glanced briefly at Dan, then looked away.

"Look at him. He doesn't speak the language," said Alfie. "Ar-broath smok-ie, right? You smokie. Me whitey. Looky-looky."

Janice snorted.

56

"My name is Sukhjeev."

"Suk-what? Fuckwit, more like." Alfie turned to Janice, receiving her laughter.

"We should hang him out like a smokie." Janice jabbed a finger towards Sukhjeev's trousers. Sukhjeev shifted his feet, took a step back.

"Damn right," said Alfie. "You ever seen a Paki's cock, Jan?"

She giggled. Dan looked from one to the other. He glanced towards the sea, the dark swell of the waves.

"Come on then, curry, drop your trews. Show the lady."

Sukhjeev looked over his shoulder. Back at Alfie. His eyes were bright.

"Drop your trews, I said."

Sukhjeev stepped back, slipped on the rocks. One foot dipped towards the pool and he pulled it back. Alfie was at his side in a moment. "You do it, or I'll do it mesel."

Behind Dan, a wave broke. The sound of it was loud in his ears. He looked towards the path. He hadn't seen Fergal at his shed, but that didn't mean he wasn't watching.

Sukhjeev threw down his net and put his hand to his zip.

"Take 'em off," said Alfie. "Take 'em right off."

Sukhjeev paused. Undid his button and slipped his trousers down. His legs were stick-thin.

"And the rest."

Sukhjeev took his eyes from Alfie's face, looked down at the ground. Then he slipped his underwear down to his knees.

Janice shrieked with laughter, pointing. "Paki cock," she said. "Paki cock."

Dan looked. Sukhjeev's cock was pale and curling against his dark hair. Dan's throat was dry. He could hear the waves breaking at his back, and it wasn't like a constant thing, any longer: each time, it was new. Could bring something new. The presence woke behind him. It bored into the back of his skull; Dan could feel its eyes. Something the sea brought, like a gift. Its clothes drenched, flesh drenched, swollen with the sea and the slimy creatures that made their homes within it. He could smell a rank, sour odour.

Nibbled eyeballs. Holes in cheeks. Water streaming from smooth, limp hair. Bloated fingers, reaching for his shoulder.

Dan whirled around and saw the sea breaking on the shore. Rock pools stretched into the distance, right across the bay.

57

When he turned back Alfie had Sukhjeev's trousers in his hand and was waving them over the rock pool. The cuffs were wet. Sukhjeev had pulled up his underwear, was watching his trousers dangle.

Dan reached out and caught them in his fist. "That's enough," he said. His voice shook. He couldn't meet Alfie's eye but the trousers went limp in his hands and he knew the older boy had let go. Dan threw them to Sukhjeev and Sukhjeev caught them, started to pull them on.

"Shit," said Alfie, disgusted. "Come on, let's leave them to it. Loverboys."

He and Janice retreated, their shadows rippling and spiking on the rocks.

Dan looked up to see Sukhjeev fastening his zip. Sukhjeev met his eye. It took him a moment to speak. "I don't need your favours," he said.

Dan saw that Sukhjeev's eyes were wet.

The boy strode away, heading back towards the town, pumping his stick-thin legs. Dan opened his mouth to call after him. He had seen Sukhjeev's fishing net, still lying on the rocks, trailing its sad red nylon. He closed his mouth again.

When Dan turned to look for Alfie and Janice, they had already gone. There was only the sea, quieted once more, beating out its ever-present rhythm.

Fergal twined new thread into the net, joined it beneath one of the floats. He stuck his tongue out between his teeth. Then started the game again. "So, Japan," he said. "Mount Fuji. There's a garden there with seven stones, but wherever you stand, you can only see six of them. It's supposed to mean something."

"What?"

"I don't know. Something about life."

Dan shrugged. "Maybe I'll go to China." He tried not to glance at Sukhjeev's fishing net, where it leaned against the side of Fergal's shed. Fergal hadn't said anything about it, and neither did Dan.

"I was in the navy," said Fergal, "before I took to fishing. Did you know that?"

Dan shook his head.

"You don't get to see all those places on the fishing boats. Plenty of squalls, though. Plenty of rain."

Dan sighed.

"You don't want to go fishing, Danny, not really. You should get a real job – then you can go on fancy holidays."

Dan shook his head, looked down at the sea. There was a breeze coming in and it was cold on his face. It struck him he had never asked Fergal to show him how it was done, to learn the way of it: to gain red calluses on his palms, sun-raw skin on his face. He wanted to go on the boats, sure, but never really thought about fishing. He only liked to roll the unfamiliar words around in his mouth. Kuala Lumpur. Jakarta. Malaysia. Those words.

He shook his head. "Tell me about China." He half-closed his eyes, leaned back.

"There are men there as big as houses. The goats have razor-sharp teeth."

"Fergal."

"It's true. They eat noodles longer than the Great Wall. And you can't go on the Great Wall unless you've got great shoes. They check."

"Stop it." Dan laughed.

"Who's this?"

Dan heard it too. Footsteps came down the path, then a figure rounded the corner. It was Sukhjeev. Fergal grinned at the boy, gestured to the path in front of him. Sukhjeev looked at Dan but sat down anyway, wrapped his arms around his legs.

"How about India?" Fergal said to Dan. "Why don't you go there? You've been, haven't you, Sukhjeev."

Sukhjeev nodded. "I visited once," he said. "We went all over Kerala. We saw the spice plantations and the lagoons. It was beautiful."

"I've been to India," Fergal said. "An amazing place. We landed at Mumbai and I went to Chor Bazaar. It sold everything you could imagine."

"Ah. I have never been there. Did you visit Kerala? My family came from there, originally. My father –" Sukhjeev broke off. Looked up at Dan, who had scrambled to his feet.

Fergal looked at him too.

Dan pointed to the path. Alfie and Janice had paused on their way down, were staring at them.

"I have to go," said Dan.

"No, you don't. Come on, sit a while." Fergal paused. "Invite your pals if you want to."

Dan shook his head. "It's OK. I'd better go." He looked pointedly at Fergal. "See you later." Then he ran towards his friends.

When he reached them he caught Alfie's eye. At first Alfie didn't say anything. Then he nodded, jerked his head towards the sea. Dan suddenly didn't want to look. He could hear the waves though: a thick, oily sound. The tide would be coming in and he wondered what it brought. Whether it lifted a black, sodden shape in its swell.

Dan pushed the thought away. They started walking down the path and he turned to Alfie. "You brought smokes?" he asked.

Alfie grinned. "Wouldn't you like to know."

They went down to the sea together, and when Dan looked into the waves there was nothing there. The sea broke against the shore as usual, just the same as it ever was. Dan imagined setting out on it, heading away, past the horizon to somewhere new.

At night, when Dan lay in bed, he often thought about the Arandora Star. He imagined it a big, fine ship, sailing a dark sea lit only by brilliant stars, headed who knew where. Away from here. He tried not to think about the torpedo, about what came after.

Alfie rummaged in his pocket and brought out a cigarette. It was crooked and he straightened it between his fingers. "You first," he said, handing it to Dan.

Dan lit up, leaning back against the rocks. He inhaled, making sure Alfie could see. Breathed in deep. Felt it choking his lungs, fought the urge to cough. He breathed out a thick plume of smoke.

Dan opened his eyes, looking straight up at the clouds, listening to the sound of the sea. The thing the waves had brought wasn't out there any more: it was inside him. He could feel it in his belly. The weight of it was rising and falling, rising and falling, dark waves that rolled greasily. He thought of the Italian who ran a chip shop, trying to breathe salt water. Sukhjeev Singh, letting his trousers fall to his ankles.

Dan made a sound back in his throat. Felt the cigarette being snatched from his grip. He let it go. He knew that he didn't want to be a fisherman, didn't want to stay here; didn't want to be

60

Alfie's friend. He only wanted to go somewhere far away, somewhere different, where no one even knew who he was.

Decision
by R.B. Russell

Frank Wilson feels unwell the moment he wakes up on Friday morning. He has to roll over to quieten the incessant ringing of the clock. It's still dark; it feels like the middle of the night. He has set the alarm to come on a little earlier than usual to make sure that he can run through the presentation one last time before taking the train into the office. It depresses him that the proposals had been his last thought before going to sleep the night before, and are in his mind again immediately he wakes up. He consoles himself, however, that the words are still in place, the rehearsed arguments come automatically, and in just a few hours time it will all be over and done with. He reasons that when the Turk's Head opens at midday he'll be there with his colleagues either celebrating the award of the contract or commiserating with them because they've lost it. Whatever happens, he's so sick and tired of the project he'll be pleased just to be able to move on to something new.

It's the first day of December, and for a few moments after he pulls back the bedroom curtains there doesn't seem to be anything at all out there beyond the black glass. His head is throbbing and he feels a little faint and dizzy at the apparently dark, illimitable expanse of space that greets him. It disorientates him, but then he sees a light come on at a window in the house opposite. The world shifts vaguely and inevitably into place.

He washes and dresses before going downstairs, where he tries to turn on the kitchen light. He immediately trips the electricity. The bulb has blown, and in the darkness of the hall he fumbles for the door to the cupboard under the stairs. Once he has got it open he feels inside for the fuse-box and the one switch that he will need to reset everything.

Unfortunately, to his frustration, he doesn't seem to be able to turn the electricity back on. Each time he tries, the main switch flicks back off. He gropes around for his toolbox and finds the torch. Now he discovers that he can only reset the electricity for all the other circuits in the house when the one for the lights remains off. This doesn't seem to make any sense to him but he's not feeling well enough to worry about it. He really does have more pressing matters to concern him, and his head is so painful he is unable to think about more than one thing at a time. He packs his briefcase by torchlight and, locking the front door after him, goes out into the freezing cold early morning.

As he walks toward the station he rehearses his introduction to the presentation, hoping that the twenty-minute walk will clear his head. When it fails to do so he buys painkillers from the small shop that is already open on the corner by the roundabout. He hopes the pills will have kicked in by the time the train delivers him into the city centre.

But the headache refuses to leave him all day. In fact, it gets worse. Wilson knows it's the stress, but he hasn't realised before now just how much he has been feeling the pressure. It's behind his eyes and in his temples. To make it worse the presentation is delayed until after lunch and drags on through the late afternoon. By the time they're finished he's almost unable to stand upright. It isn't just behind his eyes; his eyeballs actually hurt. It doesn't help that the clients decide they will not make their decision that day after all. It's not unreasonable, of course, but they had previously promised their judgement would be immediate; they'd implied that they'd already made up their mind.

Tidying up the conference room afterwards, Wilson knows that his presentation has been crucial; has he done such a bad job that they are reconsidering awarding his firm the contract? It seems entirely possible: he had lost the thread of his argument a number of times, and he knows that he hadn't always given the most coherent answers to their questions. He would have insisted that somebody else present the scheme to the clients, but he had been the only one with enough expertise.

He gets off the train that evening and walks back home, just wanting to take some more painkillers and go straight to bed. The pain is still in his eyes, behind them, and around his temples and over his scalp. It's the weekend and he's grateful that he can probably just stay in bed until he's recovered. It'll take at least a whole day and a night in a darkened room, he's certain. But then, as he passes the Crossroads public house on the corner of Albert Road the sudden and unexpected idea of a large glass of whisky causes him to stop. He reasons that it might just help. He rarely drinks spirits, and he certainly has no desire for his usual drink of bitter. No, he is certain that whisky is what he needs, and so he goes inside and orders. He reasons that it'll relax him, and he can tell that being so tense for so long has caused his condition.

Apart from the barman the bar is empty and Wilson is served straight away. He doesn't feel revitalised immediately, in fact he feels a little nauseous. He knows it's probably psychological, but the spirit seems to make the headache ever so slightly easier to bear. Without hesitation he orders another. He knows he'll have to leave after the second glass if he is to get an early night and a good sleep. But he is also wondering whether he ought to find something to eat first.

"You are very unwell," says a woman who appears alongside him.

"Do I look that bad?" he asks.

"Not in yourself," she says. "But your aura is all wrong."

"My what?"

"Your aura. Everyone has an aura, but only a few of us can see them."

"I'm sorry but I don't believe in auras. I've got a stinker of a headache and I'm sure I'm giving off enough signals to show how ill I feel. There's no need to fall back on hippy shit like auras."

She looks upset, which is the result he's hoping for. He decides she's probably a little older than he is, and a do-gooder as well as a hippy.

"It's all over the place," she continues.

"My aura? What, is it the wrong colour?"

"No, colours are often different. Yours is a kind of greeny-yellow, but it's a complete mess."

"Thanks for your concern, but another quick drink and I'm going home to bed. That should sort it out."

"I don't think it will, but I'm sure I can help, if you'd like me to."

"How?"

"Sit on this stool."

He doesn't know why he does as she says. He's hostile towards her not only for spouting rubbish about auras that he doesn't understand, but because all he wants to do is drink the second whisky and leave. He doesn't want to think about anything else; he knows that a primal sense of survival will allow him this last drink and the short walk before he collapses, and he's not sure that he's up to anything else.

Sitting on the barstool he is still taller than the woman as she stands before him. She has to lift up her arms to put her fingertips on his temples and their faces are very close. She smells of patchouli and wears far too much make-up. This close to her, he can see how she has plastered eyeliner around her eyes and her lashes are lumpy with mascara. Her face is caked with foundation in an attempt to mask her imperfect skin. No, he decides, she's quite a bit older than he first thought; at least ten years older than he is.

He would have continued to find fault with her but suddenly he realises that the pain in his head has slightly diminished. He is relaxing and slowly he feels a surge of positive feelings for this woman who seems to be not just restoring him to health, but adding something else. As her fingers massage his temples an intense feeling of peace and well-being is replacing the tension and the pain. He smiles at her and she smiles back, and he realises that all the faults he had detected in her were entirely the result of him feeling so unwell. By the time she removes her fingers his head feels clear. He can tell that his whole body has previously been incredibly tense, and now that the tension has been removed he simply feels tired. Tired, but also very relaxed.

"Thank you so much," he says, quietly and sincerely.

"You're welcome," she smiles. "And now I suppose I'd better be on my way home."

"Can I buy you a drink, to say thank you?"

"No, I don't drink. I don't normally come into bars at all, but I saw you walking in here and I had to come and help."

"My name's Frank Wilson," he says, and puts out his hand rather formally. He's pleased when she takes it.

"I'm Lottie Rainbow."

"And how do I find you again if I'm ever in need of your healing?"

She laughs, opens her purse and draws out a card. He takes it and gives her one of his own.

"Rather than a drink, how about something to eat?" he suggests. "There's a little restaurant back up by the roundabout and their food is pretty good. They start serving about seven, which is in only a half an hour...."

65

She considers the proposition, studying the card he has given her.

"I really would like to thank you," he continues. "And I'd be fascinated to know what it is you did to me just then."

"Oh, it's all hippy shit, really," she says distracted, still staring at his card. "Rubbish about energies and kundalini."

"I really am a little more open-minded than I was five minutes ago."

"Do you really work for these people?" she asks, pointing at his card.

"Yes. Why?"

"I've got to go home first. But if you really want to buy me dinner I can come back and tell you why you shouldn't."

As she leaves he has a presentiment of trouble and starts to regret organising the date. However, he feels so much better and though there is still some residual pain and underlying tension, he's sure that if he continues to relax it will all melt away. He takes a small sip of his whisky and decides that he no longer needs it. He can't quite waste it, though, and decides that he'll reconsider once he has visited the toilets. He tells the barman he's returning for it and goes through to the back of the pub.

He is thinking of the woman, Lottie Rainbow, as he stands at the urinal and starts to relieve himself. She's not particularly attractive, and certainly not what he thinks of as his type. As she is a self-confessed hippy, he knows he's in for a lecture if they meet and he wonders if he can find some way of cancelling it. He's pleased to have his life back after thinking of nothing but work for weeks, and the woman suddenly feels like an awkward obligation.

Wilson is not particularly aware of his surroundings and pays no attention to the fact that somebody else has come into the toilets after him. He's still thinking about the woman.

And then he's suddenly pushed up against the wall with a violence that would make him cry out if he'd been able to take a breath. A heavy body is pressed up against him and he can't move. His hands are down in front of him so he can't fight back. The side of his head is forced up against the white tiles but he can't see his assailant because a large hand is over his face. But he can see the big ugly black gun. His attacker forces the barrel into Wilson's mouth and he gags.

"Shut the fuck up," the man says in a rough, accented, but controlled voice. "Or I'll blow your fucking head right off."

Wilson is so scared that he feels limp; without this man's weight pressing him to the wall he knows he would collapse onto the floor. He can smell the man's aftershave or cologne even over the rancid tang of urine and chemical cleaner. Wilson feels cold with the fear, and he's aware of his own urine running warmly down his leg.

"I've got a little job for you," the man hisses into Wilson's ear. "An easy little job. Are you going to do it for me without any kind of argument?"

Wilson makes a whimpering sort of sound that's meant to be affirmative.

"Good, well. All you have to do is exactly what I say. Then you won't get hurt. Now face the wall and don't try and look back at me."

And with that the man steps back and loosens his grip. Wilson has to hold onto the urinal so that he doesn't fall over. He looks determinedly at the white tiles in front of him, resolved to do everything the man demands.

"Now, you're going to deliver a little package for me. Okay?"

Wilson nods vigorously, still staring forward. He senses the man move forward and then feels him slip something heavy into Wilson's jacket pocket.

"Take that to the Hare and Hounds. You know where it is? Go in there and look out for a man with a tattoo on the back of his neck. Give him the package, discreetly, and then get out of there."

"Okay," Wilson says weakly, barely able to get the word out.

"If he's not there, then wait till he turns up. I'll be following you, watching, and if you don't do exactly as I've told you I'll make sure you get a bullet in the back of your head."

"Okay."

"And I know where you live," he says, and despite Wilson's fear he wonders if this is a bluff. "I know where to find you if you do anything you shouldn't. If you tell anyone, or ask for help; if you go to the police... Now, you can count to twenty, slowly, before turning around. You'll go back into the bar, calmly, and finish your drink. Then you're to go straight to the Hare and Hounds. I'll be just behind you so don't look back."

Wilson nods, and he can hear the man walk to the door, open it, and leave. The door slams shut and Wilson wants to relax but can't; he knows the man is out there, waiting for him. His whole body prickles painfully with sweat and he wants to cry, but he makes himself count to twenty, slowly, as he was told to do. When it is reached he makes himself wash his hands and walk out of the toilet. He's unable to control his shaking. The place is empty apart from the man behind the bar, who frowns at Wilson as he goes back to his drink and takes it up in a trembling hand.

He swallows the whisky in a gulp and thanks the barman. His shaking is uncontrollable as he goes out into the cold night and walks back towards the railway station. It has been raining in the short time that he's been inside and every surface is slick with water. The cars pass him, their headlights shining off every surface, and Wilson's senses are spinning. All he knows is that he has to deliver the package, the dead weight in his jacket pocket, and the nightmare can be at an end. He doesn't dare turn around to check whether the man is following. He is sure that he can hear footsteps: hard-soled shoes clicking on the pavement behind him.

The restaurant where Wilson is meant to be meeting the Rainbow woman is all lit up, and as he approaches it he can see the staff inside preparing for opening. He doesn't look in as he passes for fear that the man behind thinks he's turning his head towards him. Wilson crosses the road and goes under the railway bridge. Another hundred yards further on he can see the Hare and Hounds. It's not a pub he's ever been inside before; it has a reputation for fights at weekends and serves a younger clientele. When he goes through the door, though, he does feel some slight degree of comfort from seeing a couple of groups of men and women already inside.

"Discreet" is what the man had said he should be, so Wilson asks the barmaid for a pint without looking too closely at anyone. When his drink is ready he automatically takes a large sip, but feels his stomach trying to reject it. He wipes his mouth on his sleeve, then looks around him.

To one side of the door are two couples. The women sit under the window on a meanly-upholstered bench looking back into the room. Their partners both have their backs to Wilson; they have short hair and are wearing T-shirts, so he can immediately see that they are of no interest to him. At the back of the room are five young men around a pool table, laughing, not taking the game too seriously. He has to be careful not to be seen staring at them, but as they wander around the table Wilson can tell that none of them is the man he wants.

The package is weighing heavier in his pocket. When the landlord appears he comes straight up to his customer and asks if it has started to rain. Wilson wonders if this is the discreet rendezvous that is intended, and he very nervously says that it has.

"You alright, mate?" the man asks, and Wilson tells him that he's had a bad day.

The landlord talks inanely about the weather, and then politics, and Wilson is desperate to hand him the package if only he'll turn around so that he can see his neck. He has to make sure he has the right person. And then one of the men at the pool table calls out a question to the landlord. He turns to answer and Wilson can see that he is not the man he wants.

Looking around the pub there is nobody else inside. There is no other bar as far as Wilson can see; the only other door leads through to the toilets and he can't find the courage to go and check there, not after his recent experience.

He forces himself to finish his pint, finding it easier after the first few mouthfuls. He orders another, taking it over to a seat close to the door so that he can examine anyone who comes inside.

A mirrored clock behind the bar shows that it is a quarter past seven. Wilson does not think at all about Lottie Rainbow waiting in the restaurant for him. He is unable to think about anything other than handing over the package that is still in his pocket. He has to stop sipping nervously at his pint because it is now going down too quickly, while time itself seems to be slowing down. Time is somehow stretching, obtaining the painful maximum out of every minute that passes. Wilson eventually has to order another drink and explains as nonchalantly as he can to the landlord that he's waiting for a friend who might or might not be arriving. He's not sure how convincing he sounds; he's feeling sick, his head hurts once more and his bladder needs emptying again. He hardly dare leave the pub for fear of missing his rendezvous, but he's also scared of going into the toilets. As he debates what to do he can smell his own urine and he feels totally wretched. The tension has returned and he's feeling as ill as he did earlier that evening, before he met Lottie Rainbow. The memory of the gun in his mouth makes him retch and the landlord and the young men look over at him.

Before he knows what he is doing he is up on his feet and walking through the group of men playing pool, heading towards the toilet door. He goes through to a very dim and smelly Gents that he is not necessarily comforted to find empty. Locking himself in a cubicle he retches repeatedly into the toilet bowl. His stomach muscles ache when he stands back up, and he wants to get back out into the main bar quickly, among people. He manages to make himself stay long enough to relieve the pressure of his bladder once more, and then goes back out.

He's feeling slightly better, a little more in control of the situation. For the first time he wonders if he is being set up; if it isn't just some horrible practical joke. He's almost tempted to take the package out of his pocket and examine it.

Returning to the bar he notes the old couple walk in, and when he is standing back by his table he looks around at them. He can't see the back of the man's neck because his hair comes down over his collar and in a moment, without thinking about what he is doing, Wilson decides to leave the remains of his pint untouched and walk straight out of the pub.

It is as though he's temporarily forgotten his errand and his fear of the man who had forced him to undertake it. In the distance, under the railway bridge, Wilson can see the lights of the roundabout, and he thinks about the restaurant where the woman would have been waiting for him. He stands on the pavement and then remembers the man with the gun.

But he is walking away now, not going back into the pub. He turns into an alleyway that he guesses will come out on a footpath that will take him under the railway. Once he is on the path he sprints down towards the junction. He turns there through ninety degrees, and he's under the bridge and back out on the main road with the roundabout off to his left. There is another road opposite, though, and he runs down it less desperately, but with a regular stride that covers the ground just as quickly. Each step on the hard pavement jolts his aching head. At the end of the street he turns left into another and out towards the road he would normally take to get home. He's almost sure that he will have shaken off any pursuer.

Now he walks, so as not to draw attention to himself. He looks behind him nervously, but there is nobody around. When he reaches his house he looks around again, and once through his front door he locks it behind him. He remembers that the lights don't work and he actually laughs, thinking he wouldn't turn them on anyway.

A little light on the telephone is blinking on and off and he walks over to it automatically. He knows that he ought to phone the police, but he's scared to do so after the warning he was given. He presses the button on the telephone and the first message plays:

"Hi, it's Lottie Rainbow. I'm really sorry, but I'm going to be late for the restaurant. I hope you get this and aren't sitting there for hours waiting for me, thinking I've stood you up."

The second message plays after the first:

"I'm really sorry. You've not replied to my earlier message so you're probably thinking I'm just a silly hippy after all. If you're not too mad with me and still want to talk, you've got my number."

He picks up the receiver of the phone automatically, but he doesn't know if he's about to call the police or the woman. If only his head didn't hurt so much he might be able to make the right decision. And then he remembers her ability to help him earlier that evening, and decides that she should be able to advise him what to do. Her card is in his pocket, the same one that now holds something sinister.

He removes the package very warily, and puts it carefully down by the telephone. It is surprisingly heavy for its size. Even in the dark he can tell that it's something metal wrapped in light-coloured paper, but he doesn't have the courage to open it.

He then takes out her card, but has to get the torch to make the call.

"Hello?" she answers after a couple of rings.

"Hi, it's me, Frank Wilson."

"Oh, I'm so sorry I stood you up. I did go to the restaurant later, but you must've left. I feel so awful."

"No, don't worry at all. Something happened, something horrible. And I don't know what to do."

"Can I help?"

"I don't know. I think I should probably call the police. But I must admit that I'm worried."

"Do you want me to come around?"

At that moment Wilson hears what sounds like somebody trying to open his front door.

"No," he says to her quietly, fighting back the fear, "that might put you in danger too."

"Danger? Oh my goodness. Well, why don't you come around here? I'm at 32 Richardson Street."

"I'll come over immediately."

Wilson leaves the house as quietly and as quickly as he can by the back door. He's able to vault the fence to his neighbour's house and goes around by their path to the road. Keeping to the shadows, he walks away as stealthily as he can. He tells himself that he can't be certain there was anybody at the door, but he's pleased to have somewhere else to go. He knows how to find Richardson Street, and he even has the presence of mind to hide in a doorway for five minutes to make sure that he is not followed. The streets seem deserted, with cars only passing at the distant junction of whichever road he is on. He also takes an intentionally convoluted route to Richardson Street.

With a feeling of imminent relief he walks up the path to number 32 and the lights are on behind the curtains. He has decided he will probably call the police from her house. He knocks cautiously at the door, but his heart rate suddenly increases when he sees it is already open. Fear thrills through his body; he knows instinctively that the woman has not left it open for him. Something is wrong.

Wilson is afraid for her, but he pushes the door inwards very carefully and quietly, ready to run away if he has to. After listening and hearing nothing, he takes a cautious step inside the dark hall, and then he hears her muffled cry from the room to his left. There is light seeping insidiously around the edges of the door. He can't leave now, he tells himself. Shaking almost uncontrollably, he opens the door but does not go into the room.

The woman is tightly bound to a chair and gagged, while the man is standing behind her with his ugly gun in his hand. She looks petrified; she's white, and the heavy mascara has run down her cheeks where she's been crying. It seems wrong that the room is so warm and smells of incense and there is soothing music playing in the background.

72

"It's time to make a decision," says the man.

Wilson feels unwell the moment he wakes up, and has to roll over to quieten the incessant ringing of the clock. It's still dark; it feels like the middle of the night. He remembers that he had set the alarm to come on a little earlier than usual, but then that he had already been to work and made his presentation. It has to be Saturday. His head still hurts abominably; the pain is not only in his eyes and temples but around the back of his head and neck.

It is some seconds after he has woken up that he remembers the events of the previous evening. At least he can remember them up until the time he walked into the woman's house on Richardson Street.

He gets out of bed suddenly, in horror, desperate to recall what happened next, but he can hardly think of anything because of the pain. It feels like there is a vice clamped around his head. He is unsteady on his feet, dizzy and feeling sick. Everything seems to be conspiring to stop him remembering what happened, but that seems in many ways a merciful thing. He tries the lights but they won't work, and when he stumbles into the bathroom he's unable to see where the painkillers are in the cabinet. He needs the toilet, he stinks of urine and beer, but his priority is to fight the pain he's in. He'll have to go and find the torch before he can look for the pills properly. He feels so bad that he even considers calling for a doctor, but he remembers he was meant to be calling the police.

Wilson feels his way down the stairs carefully, one hand on the banister, the other massaging his temples. He runs his hand up over his head, massaging it with his thumb and forefinger, but when he gets to the back of his neck it suddenly stings like hell.

Down in the hall he finds the torch where he had left it by the telephone. He turns it on and sweeps the beam around, and nothing seems immediately out of place. In the living room everything is as it was, but his heart sinks when he sees the package. Again he thinks of the man, the bound woman, and what might have happened. He forgets that he was intending to go back up to the bathroom to find the painkillers. Instead, he picks up the small, heavy parcel that is somehow the cause of his trouble.

Frank Wilson puts the torch under his arm and rips open the paper to reveal a black metal box with a hinged cover. When he opens it there is nothing inside; it is empty.

And then the lights come on. He jumps; he is petrified. He can see through the door into the hall that the cupboard under the stairs is open and there is nobody there.

He can instinctively tell that he is alone in the house, but what worries him is that the curtains are open and now anyone outside can see straight into the house. The glass is black, as though there is nothing there beyond the windows. He stands unmoving, uncertain whether or not to pull the curtains closed or switch off the lights. And then the pain grips his skull in a spasm and he clamps his hands over his head, massaging it but to no avail. When he touches the back of his neck again he feels it sting once more, and looks into the mirror above the fireplace. He hopes to see what he has done to himself, but can't turn his head properly; it hurts too much, and his eyes cause him too much pain when he tries to focus on anything. He has to get the small mirror from off the wall by the front door and bring it in.

With two mirrors he is able to see, in the reflection of the reflection, the raw new tattoo. It's a scabby mess; he can nevertheless make out the crooked legs of the ugly symbol.

South of Autumn
by Mat Joiner

He was back at the Wall again.

It stretched up and up into night, and every brick was a dead human face, mortared with old blood. Faces beyond count, bruise-marbled green, plum, blue, battered into shapes they should never have worn, shot and split. Their grey lips were kept shut with crude stitches. In most cases he had to guess their age or sex; he could have used their injuries to tell them apart, to name them, but it would have made him no better than a butcher.

He wore brittle grey overalls, his prison uniform. A spotlight pinned him like an insect. *No*, he thought and looked away, but the Wall was before him wherever he turned. He began to follow its length, keeping a few yards between them. If he couldn't unsee the Wall, he was damned if he would touch it.

The quest always started this way, looking for a door, window or end, but there were only ever faces. The one mercy was that their eyes stayed shut; if the Wall was to gaze on him... Perhaps they slept, buried in their own deep nightmares.

The voice of a gaoler said, *You will always be a prisoner.* Another, that sounded like his own, added: *You belong to the Wall,* and now he was looking for his own face, unsure he would recognise himself; but he always woke before he found it.

Tadeusz's mouth was dry, the rest of him glazed with sweat. It was almost midnight. He switched on the light and scrubbed himself with cheap soap. His body was raw and unwelcome to him, a library of scars. Welts latticed his back; cigarette burns formed constellations on his belly and thighs. He could hide them under clothes but always felt them.

His coat draped a pile of books on the studio floor. Putting it on caused a small avalanche. Among the rubble were reprints of his own work. *South of Autumn. The Wrong Moon. Hearth Tales and Fireflies.* After his trial he had learned the original editions had been burned; he still felt a dull rage about it. *The dreams of a dissident fouling young minds* was the verdict of the True Wheel censor. Or children's books, to anybody sane. At one point having

75

a Tadeusz Volmic on your shelf could mean your kids were taken in for re-education.

His typewriter and drawing board gathered dust; his only new work lay under the new plaster on the walls, where he'd attempted to paint the nightmare out of him. The result was a horror, easy to paint over. "I never worked well with colour," he'd told Yelena.

She was sleeping in the upstairs flat. He could wake her and talk it through: it would only be the thousandth time. Twenty-odd years as lovers, two as friends – he could not ask her to be a confessor again. "You have to go outside sometime," she had said; and true, this window offered a poor view of the city. *No curfew,* he thought. He picked up his cane and went out.

He lived in the Old Town and his house was typical of the area, tall and narrow with deep balconies and dagger-sharp gables. On a clear night he could hear the river and its grey swans, a few streets away; now just the wind playing banshee, making his bad knee ache.

Tadeusz already wanted to go back in. That figure in the lighted window could be an informer. Those shadows could hold a punishment squad. He thought of the neighbour who'd sold him out. The cosh. The boot. Then: *Stupid. Stupid. The True Wheel's gone. You've put your imagination to better use than this.*

He limped on through backstreets and passed the Church of Sofia the Intercessor, a snail-shell in copper and blue glass. Hard to believe it had once been firebombed. They were holding mass; the building thrummed with song. Tadeusz wasn't a believer. His mother had been devout, Nana an old pagan. From her tales he had distilled his books of the UnKin: his own name for her First Folk. ("They were here before we came to the world," she'd said once. "Through the earth, on the wind, between the trees. They're still here. They see the forest under our cities. But they're hard for us to spot, boy; they wear several kinds of skin. Likely you'll unsee them, or think it's shadows, tinkers or beasts.") The books were selling again now, and people wanted more. But the only stories he could tell now were the horrors everybody knew.

The Unfurled Wing advertised their policies on street kites strung from lamp-posts and balconies. Tadeusz could see these streets as they were a decade back – the posters of the Wheel, statues with tape-recorded slogans. For every midnight mass and wine parlour now, he remembered curfew patrols and bullet-pocked walls. He was hard put to know which year he was in. Every time someone passed him, he tensed, expecting a militia man to call "Hey citizen where you going? Get over here." A quick glance at your papers. Another name to be crossed out. A vanishing, a statistic. The Wheel had rolled over so many, and Tadeusz saw their faces most nights.

Two years free, and you're still waiting to be executed.

He was in the flea market, with its smells of bruised fruit and hand-me-down clothes. Under a wrought-iron clock one stall was open. A stocky man looked up from his paper. He could offer a bag of sweet chestnuts, chicory coffee from a samovar. Tadeusz took both. While he was waiting for his drink, he gazed back over the city. The moon came and went in a churning sky, giving Iruganecz the look of a zoetrope town. It was only this, and his insomnia, that made the skyline wriggle and fold its many roofs into a new shape, a grim poem of a building, part fortress, part fairy-tale castle. His prison.

Tadeusz gaped, and when the coffee seller shook him the skyline was only that, a city at night. He mumbled, "The Edifice. I've just seen it..."

"It's gone, mate. Knocked down, like everything those bastards built."

But they built other things too, in our minds. That's how they live on, Tadeusz tried to explain. All that came out was a shapeless babble. He listened to himself in horror. The coffee-seller thrust a paper cup at him, and said with gruff kindness, "Look, that's free, don't worry." He didn't add: *Leave me alone,* but Tadeusz did anyway. At last he knew where he was going.

The Edifice, or its site, was on the west side of town, two stations on the Kremow Line. Only the mad and the homeless take trains after midnight; there was nobody else on the platform or in his carriage. Something had stopped him buying a return ticket.

He knew it had been demolished. The Unfurled Wing had seen to that. Cranes, wreckers' balls, even Sofian priests to bless the bruised earth. (Tadeusz often thought about that rubble: what houses had been built from it, what echoes might they hold? Black marketeers, it was said, were selling bits of the Edifice to Wheel sympathisers for enormous sums. He imagined prison bricks waiting to be bloodied again in the fists of backstreet gangs.) The prison site was made a Memorial Garden. Tadeusz was asked to lay a plaque at its opening, but refused: too much like erecting his own gravestone.

A figure stood at the Garden gate, its shape uncertain under a paper lantern. Was this it, then? Closer, he saw a tall woman wrapped in shawls. Under a bright headscarf, her face was pointed and fine-boned. She reminded him of someone he couldn't name. Her eyes were large, and full of light.

She put a gloved hand on his chest and pushed him back, just a little. "No further. This is a private place."

"It was once," Tadeusz said. "Then the people stormed it, and broke it down. Now anyone can walk here."

"Not tonight. Any other time, this land is yours. I can't let you pass."

Sofia knew what she took him for: some Wheelist vandal, perhaps, rather than some grizzled idiot with sunken eyes and chestnut crumbs in his beard. "I have to go in," he insisted. "This is the last place I'd want to come, but... What this place was, it's still strong." He wiped his eyes, disgusted with himself. "It's a call, you see. I have to face it."

She cupped his face, very gently, and stared deep into him, sniffed him. "What are you? A pilgrim?"

He almost laughed. He only said, "I... lived here once. Seven years."

"Ah," said the gatekeeper. She sniffed him again. It was such a relief to find another lunatic in the night that Tadeusz hugged her, very briefly. She herself smelled like deep woods and animals in shadow. She stepped back to let him pass, out of the range of the light. All that remained of her were green-flashing eyes, a voice that said, "Walk on then, storyteller."

He knew that face now, though it belonged to a man long dead: he said, "Bartolemu? Did you know him? Did you call me?" but the woman had passed into night.

The Garden was laid out in a spiral: willows for remembrance, evergreens for the Sofia. Wind coaxed creaks and whispers from them. There were flower-beds laid out in knotwork, pale stone monuments, benches here and there (he would not sit.) What had he come here to face? Shadows flitted past him; he turned as quick as he could. There was no bogeyman with a cog tie-pin and an automatic pistol. He searched the ground for traces of the Edifice. Nothing. Ah, well. He carried the prison with him. He let his memories build it over again. Tier on tier, jag and spire. All the voices. The clang of old iron. A mumbled prayer, a hollow laugh, wardens cursing. The copper tang of shed blood, the reek of the slop bucket. The bite of a hypodermic. The flickering nightmares of the re-education films. Steering by these echoes he might find his cell. Most of his seven years Tadeusz was solitary. A few men had shared his cell, but it was only Bartolemu he remembered. A wiry young man with black hair and eyes the colour of old moss, and pretty: he drew the rape gangs, suffered worse than anything Tadeusz had experienced. After the attacks, Tadeusz had held him – nothing more, though he would have drawn Tolem given the materials – through the night, and told him stories.

Bartolemu never cried. Sometimes his eyes burned. Other days he was jaunty, the smiles looked real. They played chequers with pebbles and scratches on the floor. Tadeusz never knew his crime. He was a fixer, a fence, producing tobacco or loved ones' letters like conjurers' tricks. "What can I get you?" he'd asked Tadeusz, who answered grimly: "A magic door."

He had a north country accent, a deepwood youth turned city spiv. One night, the wardens had crashed into their sleep and dragged Tolem out. He never came back. Tadeusz's cell was the other end from the execution yard, but it was easy to imagine the shots, then and now, and what might have been done to Tolem in his last moments.

"I'm sorry," he said to Bartolemu and the dead he hadn't known, in the Wall and unmarked pits. "I'm sorry." Perhaps he was one of them, and hadn't remembered the firing squad. He didn't know. He didn't know. The thought so horrified Tadeusz that he dropped his cane and hid his face. He heard wind chimes, and took them for warden's keys. He was ready to step in the cell one last time. But there were sparks moving among the willows, and in the grass at his feet: they had no place in his prison. One landed in his palm. A firefly, this early in the year? He cupped the insect, careful not to crush it, and moved to the Garden's heart, where he saw the pilgrims.

There was a temple of sorts here, a domed place held up with fluted columns. They were singing dirges in a tongue he didn't know, full of trills and crooning, and laying wreaths: leaves that

79

flashed metallic colours, roses like petalled moons. They were no less strange than their tribute. Tall shadows wearing porcelain masks. Brindled foxes with long-fingered hands. Sharp-eared men and women with twitching tails, fronds or feathers growing at the temples.

He knew them well. They weren't as he had drawn or written them, but they were his UnKin, Nana's First Folk; or as good as. One among them was incongruously dressed in pea coat and corduroys. The moon found strange colours in his black fringe, like a magpie's wing. The angles of his face had changed, but Tadeusz recognised him.

So the Wheel came for you as well. Tadeusz watched Bartolemu and his people make their valedictions. Even in mourning, they were beautiful. He felt like a voyeur, and he might have left them to their ritual. But the wind changed direction, bringing his scent to the UnKin. Silence fell; they turned to look at him. Their eyes were unreadable; they might be poised to fly or fight. Very slowly he reached out to pluck from the bushes around him a fistful of ivy, a few unopened roses; limped into the temple and laid his small shabby tribute on the ground. He bowed his head. He would not look up, even when their strange hands found him. Fingers of fur or shadow or air brushed his face and passed on. They were singing coronachs again. From the edge of his eye he saw them dancing. Someone remained with him, helped him up.

"Storyteller." The name Tolem had given him back in prison. "We didn't expect guests…" Bartolemu's eyes were huge, hair tousled and full of leaves. He grinned crookedly; Tadeusz supposed it was a welcome of sorts.

"I met your sister… your daughter?… at the gate." They walked among the monuments; shadows kept pace with them, watching Tadeusz. He tried returning the favour, but his eyes slid off them.

"She smelled me on you. It was the only way you got in." There was pride in Tolem's voice; it might have been fatherly. "What you did back there was –"

"– a gesture. We should have known what had happened to you; we could have *helped* each other."

"Perception's a strange thing, don't you think?" said Tolem. "How many years had you stopped seeing us, except as folk tales, or in your books? Which I've never read, by the way. We were charming enough, a bit twee, a bit strange, but no threat to your new reality. Seen and unseen. It suited us too; we had peace. Even when your Wheel rose, we thought we were immune. We'd forgotten the mad could see us, and the Wheel were the maddest of all."

Tadeusz remembered something Nana had said: "Those who have the eyes don't always have the heart."

Tolem nodded. "Tadeusz, how many of your people overlooked what was being done to them, just to survive? Would they have really noticed us?"

"You looked..." Tadeusz hesitated. "Normal, no, *human* enough when I knew you."

"I had to. Some of us wouldn't run. Disguise or death, which would you choose? These," he fingered the points of his ears, "these took the longest time to grow back. But I wouldn't give up my tail, until some Wheelist fucker with an axe took it. Well, that's pride for you. Leaves you with a stump. I was just about passing for human when they arrested me. I could have shown you what I was, but they would have killed us both. The way it went was bad enough."

"I imagined the worst. Seeing you now, I thought you'd escaped."

Tolem chuckled. "You'd have written it so I'd become a shade, and passed between the bricks. No, they shot me. Silver and iron, they could kill me. Lead, no. But it hurt like *fuck*, and when I woke, I clawed my way up through corpses and earth. There are pits like that all over the land, still waiting to be found. I know where they are; I can see through the soil to the bodies. But they burned my people, and they're lost to us." He shuddered, and the fear made him something Tadeusz could recognise. He did not flinch when Tadeusz touched his arm. "And that's why we're leaving. We can't bear this land, your kind, any more. There's been too much damage done. We'll find places where we can heal and forget you. All that was left was to make farewells to our dead, and then you came blundering in. I still don't know how you found me."

"I thought I was called here; I didn't know what I'd find. An end to it, I suppose."

Bartolemu whispered in his ear, "You summoned yourself. Storyteller, how many more trials can you go through? Sit down." He guided Tadeusz to a bench and brought out a crumpled cigarette packet. "I found a taste for these. One more thing to lose when I go." He offered Tadeusz one, then winced. "No, you wouldn't now. I'm sorry."

Tadeusz took a cigarette. It had been years; he coughed and coughed, but he only smelled tobacco burning. "Don't call me that. 'Storyteller.' It's bullshit. I stopped writing a while back."

"I'm not asking you to write, *Tadeusz*. It's been, what, five years since we met? Tell me how it's been with you. Pretend we're old friends who met on the street."

It wasn't easy. Tadeusz kept halting, asking for a smoke, telling things out of sequence. The Wall, the ghost prison rising over the city. How his relationship with Yelena had failed. His life had no plot, he found. He wrapped up his dog-ends in a handkerchief to dispose of later. "That's it. What there is to tell. Where will you go?"

Tolem shrugged. "South of autumn, and left of the sun." It was an old saying. "We won't meet again."

"Stay. We could learn so much from you."

"You'll have to teach yourselves."

"Then take me with you. Except you can't, I know that."

"You and me, alone, that might work. We could live in peace. The others wouldn't allow it. We had hopes for your kind once, many moons ago. Your minds could change shape, even if your flesh was fixed. You were our little cousins. But all that's happened shows your minds are stuck too."

Tadeusz bridled at this; but then, what shape was his own mind in?

"You're not dead yet, Tad. Go back, live with Yelena, yourself, best as you can. Write. Help root out whatever's left of the Wheel."

"I'll start with myself then." He couldn't feel the Edifice around him anymore; it had gone back to its hiding place. It might take a lifetime to break it down.

"I could do one last thing for you. I told you back then I was a fixer, but you never asked for anything. Call it a parting gift. I can't take away the scars. The memories, yes, but it wouldn't be right." Tolem's fingers were long and clever; they spidered over

Tadeusz's skull, and went inside. There was no pain, a tickle behind his eyes perhaps, the strangeness of another's hand sifting through his thoughts. Soon Tolem pulled away. He kissed Tadeusz on the forehead. "Take back your dreams," he said, then something in his own language, a blessing or goodbye. He turned and loped off into the trees. Others followed, leaving strange tracks in the dew.

Tadeusz sat there till dawn greyed the Garden. The wreaths of the UnKin – he wondered what they called themselves – were fading in the new light. Then he went to find a train.

The Wall was before him again. Tadeusz looked down at himself. He was wearing ordinary clothes, a pullover and an old suit, and in his buttonhole was a strange flower, an opal rose that sang.

He stepped forward and touched the Wall. It was nowhere near as bad as he had thought; just cold flesh, webbed here and there with frost. He kept his hands on it till the faces thawed enough to open their dim eyes. *Wake now,* he said. *Wake. I'm here for you.* A little more of his heat, and the lips parted, breaking their stitches. *Tell me your stories, your names.* He stepped back, and waited for them to speak.

Survivor's Guilt
by Rosanne Rabinowitz

As I enter the meeting hall near the Thames I breathe in the scent of tobacco and wet clothing, perfume mingled with fried fish, the malt and yeast of beer flowing freely. Strains of Spanish guitar are already wafting from the auditorium.

Two fresh-faced students are taking tickets. But there are also Yiddish-speaking East Enders hawking *Frei Arbeter Stimme*, as well as a few of the more moneyed Marxists copiously donating into the collection bucket. There's a bunch of literary folk whispering over well-thumbed books. I hear people speaking many languages: Polish and Spanish, Russian and German, as well as several varieties of English.

I feel at home, though my original language is so obscure and ancient there's no chance of hearing it even in this glorious babel.

I peer through the crowd, though I'm not sure who I'm looking for. Even under the best of circumstances, Gunther won't be here in person.

I used to believe that he had died in Munich, shot by the Freikorps. Now I'm not so sure, and tonight I hope to discover the truth.

"Hi Mara," someone greets me. I nod at people I've worked with in the Freedom group and the Anti-fascist Welfare Committee, a few from the Independent Labour Party. But I keep to myself, too anxious to socialise. I have my notebook and pen with me, ready in case I want to pass on a message. I haven't written anything yet. Gunther was the writer, not me.

On stage are two guitarists, a trombonist and a stocky woman who looks like she could also throw a few good punches as she belts out the tunes. "...*La luchamos contra los moros, mercenarios y fascistas. Aye, Manuela,*" she proclaims in ringing contralto while the guys "*rumbala rumbala*" behind her.

People clap and stomp. "*Vive le quince brigada! rumbala rumbala*"

The music rattles at the doors of my mind and I let them swing open, just a little. In come the images, snatches of thought. For a moment I'm with the people making the music.

I'm where those songs come from. I see:

The narrow streets of Barcelona hung with banners: *No Pasaran.*

Wind, smoke, explosions among olive groves.

Women wrenching up cobblestones from the streets for barricades.

And there is the fresh sting of defeat, filling my mouth with dirt.

But that only makes me want to raise a clenched fist and storm the nearest barricade, though there are none on the streets of London tonight. This song summons the music of my early childhood, the music of bloodsuckers, godless mountain-demons and monsters. We have our own songs of persecution, our songs of battle. No matter that the songs of my dwindling tribe are about defending some far-flung pile of rocks none of us would want to live on now. And even though they're sung in a language unknown to humans, I hear those songs in the chords of many struggles, far beyond Spain.

"Want a programme?" A child tugs at my dress. "Take one and make a donation. It'll help the refugees." Other children are underfoot or helping out. A while ago you wouldn't see so many. People were wary of attacks from fascists, but since we routed Mosley's crew at Cable Street a few years ago there haven't been many physical attacks.

I hand the boy some coins and take a programme from him. The bill includes music hall performers, a jazz group, a classical violinist and a Basque dance troupe. And sandwiched in the beginning is a reading of new work by the elusive writer, Arto Westman – by his agent.

Can this agent be trusted if I want to pass on a message? I worry that I might write something that could give either of us away.

The singer is asking for requests.

"A las Barricadas!" Shouts for a Spanish anarchist anthem don't go down well with some Communist Party members, who grumble and mutter.

But one of the guitarists grins and strums the opening chords.

"Negras tormentas agitan los aires..."

"Would you like to buy a copy of *Cloudforests*? Special edition with the Left Book Club, authorised by Arto Westman to aid the fight against fascism!"

This time the vendor is a woman in her twenties.

"No thanks, I have my own copy." I take the book out of my pocket and show her an earlier German edition. "I have all of Westman's books. But this is my favourite."

Cloudforests evokes the lives of workers on a coffee plantation in the mountains of Chiapas, southern Mexico. The author uses a mixture of Spanish, English and a smattering of native languages, but makes every word understandable by context. It is a book about resistance and dreams. It is full of colour and light and what it feels like to walk among the clouds.

Yet there is a cadence in some phrases that connects this distant place to more familiar city streets, as if that part of Mexico isn't so far away from Munich after all.

Westman's collection of stories about a general strike in Seattle also made me think of Gunther. Though the stories take place in the wet and windy Northwest of America, I find lines of dialogue we both could have uttered after some turbulent beer-soaked meeting where workers also set about transforming a city.

I'm not the only one who sees this connection. There are rumours that Arto Westman is a German who fled the repression of the Bavarian workers' councils in 1919. Like many refugees deemed too dangerous to stay in England or the US, he lives in Mexico. He avoids any personal attention. There are rumours he is a man I believed to be dead. *Gunther.*

I remember teaching English and Spanish to Gunther, how quickly he learned and his love for language. He said he wished he could be fluent in every language in the world, a true internationalist. I wondered if I could ever risk teaching him mine.

Meanwhile, he taught me how to run a printing press and forge documents. Perhaps he also showed me how you can keep changing your name, yet stay true to yourself.

After an amnesty in the twenties, many spoke freely about the Bavarian uprising, but others stayed in the shadows. Erich Mühsam had written: *You are no longer a fugitive, Gunther. Let us know if you're still alive. Now we can let the truth be known.* But Erich was later tortured and murdered in the Oranienburg concentration camp.

86

Let me know if you're still alive, Gunther. Have you wondered the same about me?

Or were you sure it was the end when you heard those shots on the road behind you?

"Black storms shake the sky, dark clouds blind us..."

There were many dark clouds in the skies twenty years ago. There are dark clouds gathering now that will do more than shake the sky. They will drench the earth with blood that will never sustain life.

But in 1919 there were also moments of hope, and we drew together in the middle of one.

"Alza la bandera revolucionaria que llevará al pueblo a la emancipación..."

I'm humming the tune as I make my way to a seat closer to the front. I have my notebook ready. All I have to do is write a short note to his agent to pass on. I'll let Gunther know I'm alive and give my address. Then he can write back. If he wants to.

A stout man who looks uncomfortable in his suit gets on the stage, introducing himself as Jack from the dockers' union. "We'll have more music after a reading on behalf of Arto Westman, a popular author known for keeping a low profile. But he's standing up to be counted in his own way. His agent and close friend will read some new work."

I let loose a gasp when I see who is getting on the stage. Then I come close to laughing out loud.

It is Gunther himself, now a robust man in his forties. His skin is tanned and weathered. The grooves down his cheeks and along his mouth are deep, put there by a life lived outdoors. Now his hair is grey instead of blond, but the contrast of his dark eyes is just as startling.

Does he really think he can get away with posing as his own agent? It's ridiculous, but I can't stop grinning. He always was a cheeky guy! Then, many of the people likely to recognise him after twenty years are already dead.

I look down quickly. Exchanging letters over thousands of miles is one thing, letting him see me is another. I have my own reasons to stay in the shadows.

In those days I cut my hair short and wore modern straight-cut dresses without a corset, as radical women did. We were denounced as 'mannish', but I doubt I earned that particular epithetic with my plump figure.

Now my hair is long and curly again. I wear a full dress cinched at the waist in the current style. But those changes are only superficial. If I had prepared for this I could have applied cosmetics to appear older. Worn glasses to obscure distinctively green and tilted eyes. Gunther said they had attracted him when we first met, though we argued constantly.

I make do with letting my hair fall in a veil in front of my face, as I did when I was a child shielding myself from the nuns meant to be caring for me. Those strands of hair had to hide the hunger that surely showed there. Then I would sneak out a window at night and run through the woods and finally feed myself. For a while I was free from black-garbed figures and the muttering of prayers, free from those who would burn me if they knew.

I never thought I'd repeat that gesture here. I raise my programme and peer over it through my hair. It must look odd, but I wouldn't be the only eccentric in this audience.

"I'm sorry that Artie can't be here," Gunther says. "He really doesn't travel. He's much more at home in the mountains and the forest, or at home learning to play piano with his beloved Lucia, and of course typing away at his next book. And by his own admission he's *lousy* at speaking to an audience anyway, so he won't inflict such an ordeal on you."

Gunther, you don't fool me with that American accent! I still hear hints of German, traces from other places too.

The groove along the side of his face deepens for a moment, like a wink. "Artie hasn't been on this side of the Atlantic for a very long time. OK, maybe in the early days he'd been tempted to return to his native Finland for the sake of a good sauna. But then he discovered the traditional Mayan sweat bath, which he recommends highly. Mexico is now his home and he doesn't like to leave it. So he sent me instead to read something he wrote very recently, together with an introduction and message of solidarity."

Native Finland! Not only am I trying not to be seen, I have to work harder not to giggle again. Already the man in the next seat is looking at me with the expression of one of those nuns about to *shush* me in church.

88

Of course, I've come up with far-fetched stories in my own time.

I wish we could sit together and laugh at all our disguises over a glass of schnapps.

Now I can't resist. I touch his mind, in a way I've only done once or twice before.

Even then there was so much static on its surface, so many layers and contradictory thoughts. There were words, already in several languages, words assembled for newspapers, leaflets and proclamations. Most of this was submerged by a dense layer of fear as heavy steps thundered above our heads, or when our guards cursed and the lorry rattled as it brought us to our execution. That was just before I kicked open the door...

Now his mind is layered with another twenty years. It is dense with subterfuge, meanings hidden in other meanings, more jokes that make me smile. And I find a feeling that I don't recognise at all. It is calm but purposeful. Warm, with an edge that can turn white-hot.

Gunther clears his throat: "Artie writes: 'This is new and very rough. Maybe I won't ever put it in print. But I want it to be read. I've denied much of the past out of necessity, but it's now necessary that this past doesn't get buried. As our comrades rose up in Spain, we had an uprising in Germany twenty years ago. The Nazis – and all those in power – try to bury that history, and we have to bring it into the light. This is dedicated to a comrade I knew and loved in those days.'"

A woman sits in the front row, watching with pride. Lucia. She stands out from the crowd with her green open-work shawl and dangling earrings. Her hair is long and dark, with flashes of white at the temples. She gives him a brief nod of encouragement.

Arto – Gunther – begins to read.

"You went by many names. So did I. Though we were lovers you didn't tell me everything. When we had to hide. I thought you whispered 'be still' in my ear though your lips didn't move."

No! I expected stories about coffee-bean pickers, strikers in Seattle, rebellious oil field workers and adventures riding the rails across America. Not this, even after his introduction.

He doesn't mention the name I used. But then he knows enough not to do that, being an old player of the name-game himself.

Now that he's slipping out of his role as agent for 'Artie', he leads me back to Munich.

He writes about the cold, the comfort and camaraderie. Twenty inches of snow fell at the beginning of April that year. As I listen to him I can be in the room we shared in the noble's villa we helped occupy. Homeless families had moved into the many rooms upstairs, and we converted the front room into an office that housed Gunther's printing presses. Travelling comrades came to stay, sharing news of unrest in Augsberg, Vienna, Berlin and Budapest.

We slept next to the office. It was a comfortable room, its great windows framed in gilt. But with the shortage of fuel it was very cold, and snow seeped through cracks in the ornate frames. I wasn't really affected by the cold, but I often felt him shivering next to me. Then I'd move closer, and we'd make love.

"Our secrets were never shared but they bound us together," Gunther reads.

Yes, there were things we never found out about each other. It didn't matter. Gunther was already used to fleeing, changing identities. It was only right that I kept my secrets too.

Like him I was absorbed in revolution and art, though I worked in a hat shop at the time and didn't do anything overtly artistic. But art was not just for artists, it was for everyone.

On the day the Räterepublik was proclaimed, crowds of jubilant workers decked out in their best clothes promenaded and conspired in the most fashionable avenues. Soldiers had turned against the war and ran through the streets, tearing epaulettes from their officers' shoulders. The red flag streamed over the Wittelsbach Palace, where typists leaned out from the silk-curtained windows of the former Queen's bedroom to cheer the crowds below. We walked hand-in-hand into the palace where vast rooms filled with the tread of workers, farmers and revolutionary soldiers. We also heard some heavy snoring as exhausted comrades recovered from days of turmoil on the plush palace sofas.

But we ran up the stairs in a burst of exhilaration. While curious citizens and countless new committees and councils were occupying most of the palace, it was quiet up there. We found an empty room and sat on a divan. I started to think about storming another mansion over a century earlier, near Manchester. Blood from a mill owner, the pent-in motion of his struggle making its flavour sharp. The fruity fumes of fine wine looted from the pantry, a boy devouring handfuls of red preserves. Flames moving through each shattered window and licking out the hole that had been the front door, great hollow groans as the central beams collapsed.

"The first time I did this..." I started to say.

"Did what? Take over a palace?" Gunther stretched out on the divan, his head on my lap. His voice was muffled, sleepy. His eyes were only half open, barely visible behind his lashes. Perhaps he needed rest too.

The intoxication of revolt was loosening my tongue. It also made me hungry.

I stroked his hair, and leaned over to kiss his neck. "Do you want to know more? I'm older than you think..."

He cut me off with an affectionate laugh. "I didn't think you were vain about your age! None of that matters. The past doesn't matter when everything is about to change. There's too much to take in. Don't you see more at times like this? Look out the window. It's just a grey day in November, but even that grey is beautiful."

"Yes, it is," I agree. The clouds were slate grey, edged with pearl where the sun struggled through. So what do old names and places matter while we're looking at this?

"Art is bread," someone once said. Does that mean poems can be potatoes, and ballads can be blood? While we grappled with ending a potato shortage, we also pondered poetry.

Europe must be rebuilt from the ruins of the Great War, its foundations laid anew. How could we create architecture, painting and drama to imagine and remake this world? Writers, artists and actors even formed their own councils to do this.

As I listen to Gunther read, I remember another meeting. It was in the open air, with thousands thronging the streets. I see his friend Ernst Toller proclaiming a poem in memory of Kurt Eisner,

91

a leader of the Räterepublik. Eisner's assassin had explained: "He is a Jew, he is not a German. He betrays the Fatherland."

Ernst Toller was still in his twenties, dark and intense and persuasive. People responded to his eulogy with tears, others called for arms. Then we moved off to the ordnance depot to get them, along with soldiers and sailors with red flags. The workers and poets of Munich rose again.

Who says words can't change things?

Later, our comrade Gustav Landauer drew up plans for a people's theatre and a free school system that encouraged children to truly experiment and learn.

Landauer came to a bad end with all of his fine plans, beaten to death by the Freikorps paramilitaries. This could have happened to me. But being who I am, I escaped.

And for the very first time, it's clear that Gunther did too.

I look at him, a healthy man who had escaped and survived, and remember the one time I tasted his blood.

We were hiding in the narrow space under the floorboards of a house just outside Munich. We'd been speaking to members of the farmers' union about distributing food. Then the Freikorps unleashed its attack through the region.

Gunther reads more, and I remember...

Splinters brushed my face. Feet pounded above us, sending tremors through the wood.

Words from every language I knew merged in my mind. Were those men searching for witches? Or Reds?

I knew how to hide. I was hiding in a cave when the local dignitaries shackled and burned my family in 1703, on the side of a mountain facing the Bay of Tivat in Montenegro.

"They're worse than Turks. They are witches, vampires, unnatural women."

We can live forever, my mother had told me. But she didn't. She died in agony. We don't die very often, but when we do it takes much longer.

"You must live and bring down the people who do this to us," I heard her whispering in my mind. I've tried, I wanted to tell her. I'm trying now, and I will try again.

When I was young I heard of those who rebel against the nobles and the churches, against all exploiters. It didn't matter that these people were not like me, or that others of my kind urged me to stay out of human troubles.

Later I took to the streets of different cities, in different times. I thrived on that as much as blood. I fed on freedom as their control unravelled, turning to strands of orange, bright against the darkness that is my ally.

But I'm still not prepared when it comes to *this*.

The floor vibrated against the side of my face. Things were falling, breaking. I imagine a mirror, a picture of a woman I glimpsed before we closed the floor over us. Drawers pulled out, a rip of fabric.

Do the men making the floor shake above us wear black robes or uniforms? Do they carry pikes and bayonets, or machine guns? Of course, they speak in German. They're the Freikorps, sent by the social democratic government to crush the workers' councils of Bavaria as they did in Berlin. They couldn't get regular soldiers to do this.

Gunther's human scent is sweatier and saltier than mine. Warmth spreads from the points where our bodies touch. I move my thigh closer so we connect there too. He laces his fingers between mine. Our fingers slip and slide, clasp and unclasp against each other. His smothered gasps make me hunger more.

Once I believed I couldn't be close to a lover without the blood. I always had to get under my lover's skin. I wanted the red stuff that kept them alive to sustain me too. For a long time I didn't need that with Gunther. I didn't even touch his mind.

But I have to do it now. His blood will give me strength to fight if it comes to it. And he needs something from me.

What can I offer to help him live through this? Give him calm, give him dreams. He keeps his secrets close. But I might have to reveal some of mine.

Do you hear me? We can't talk, but I'm speaking to you. We have to be calm. We have to slow down. There isn't much air.

I turn my head so my lips are at his throat, watch his eyes close.

I came so close to doing this as we watched the sky from a window in the palace. Now everything has changed again.

His blood tastes of adrenaline, with a whiff of earth. It carries fear and anger. The anger tastes good. Bubbles of it explode and tickle my tongue. It gives me power and clarity, but I can only take a little.

What do I give him? I surround him with treasured memories. *Smell the sea and the great rosemary bush near the cottage. And look...* The mountains in front are blue with patches of brown and green. Those between them are solid blue, and beyond them the mountains turn to smudges of pale grey and silver.

I used to dream about what lay behind the mountains I couldn't see. To think of another world waiting to be discovered there always made me happy.

I also show him a woman gathering stones; then potatoes, bread and cheese as market stalls are overturned. I show the crash of machinery and breaking chains – and then I'm barging into a forbidden room full of light and mirrors.

Afterwards, I saw the question in his eyes. I felt it grow in his mind. But Gunther was always discreet, and ready to find a rational answer: *I was faint, I was crazed and half-conscious.*

We never had a chance to talk about it. Though we survived that search, the Freikorps picked us up in Munich shortly afterwards.

There's a gust of laughter from the bar next door, but everyone in this room is very quiet. Maybe it's the quiet that brings me back to the meeting hall.

Gunther has paused, then he starts again. "You showed me scenes from some other life, a world that takes on colour after luminous colour, colours veiled by shadows that hint of far away. Seeing them was like listening to music full of defiance, made all the more powerful by notes of loss and melancholy. I still hear the echo of those notes.

"Now that I write to you after keeping silent so long, I wish you were here to tell me where those colours came from. And after you saved my life, I still wonder if I could have saved yours."

No, no, Gunther! I had to kick you out of that lorry. I *made* you leave me behind, while I tried to help the other prisoners. That was the only way.

He seems to be a happy man, but perhaps a worm gnaws at the core of that happiness. Being in Europe again has unsettled him. Being here in London, where we first met at a conference to stop the coming war, has prodded that slumbering worm of guilt.

Gunther is reading an intimate letter, a direct and clumsy appeal to someone he believes is no longer able to answer. But I can, I can!

I don't have to look far into his mind to see that he wrote this in his hotel room last night. He was pacing and scribbling, Lucia first urged him to get in bed. Then he read to her, and she urged him to finish it. Her generosity shines from her as she listens. *You are here with me now because of her.*

"After so many years I miss you as if the loss is new." The paper shakes in his hands. "I want to show you all I've seen since, the colours of cloudforests and of desert. Perhaps visions and dreams won't stop the onslaught to come, but they may be all we have left."

Is it wrong to let him go on like this?

He pauses and looks over the audience. And I look downwards, hold my programme higher and think about what I should do.

"Sometimes I think you were fortunate," Gunther reads. "You didn't live to see how the men of the Freikorps made Germany what it is today. You didn't see the defeat in Spain and the rise of Hitler. You never lived with the despair that took our comrade Ernst Toller."

A month ago Ernst was found strung up by the waist cord of his bathrobe in his hotel room in New York, three days after Franco held his victory parade in Madrid. He was 48. Ernst had donated the last of his money to help Spanish refugees. Before he killed himself, he'd heard that his family in Germany had been sent to a camp.

Had he been suffering from the guilt of a survivor? A well-known playwright, Ernst had spent five years in prison for his part in the uprising while others had been beaten to death or executed.

But if you live while others die, you can only go on writing and fighting and doing your best. Perhaps he gave up even on that when he heard about his family.

Perhaps I should have emerged from my own 'death' to talk to Ernst about living with survivor's guilt – over 200 years of it.

"You stayed pure in your defiance."

Now you're talking nonsense, Gunther. Pure is the last thing I am.

"You spoke to me in my thoughts, though it could have been a delirious dream. I don't believe in God. I don't believe in angels. But you didn't seem to belong on this earth."

I'm not human, but that doesn't mean I don't belong here. That doesn't mean I'm pure.

Tell them how we clashed when we first met at that conference.

You can even talk about our housekeeping arguments in Munich. Or when you tried to stop me from going out at night by myself. Your current lover has shown herself to be much less possessive than you.

Tell them how arrogant you could be.

And why don't you tell them how arrogant I can be. It would only be fair.

Lucia leads the clapping. Bravo!

She had encouraged this hurried eulogy. But what if the dead woman suddenly proved to be alive? I understand she's Gunther's editor and friend as well as lover. She runs a crafts shop in San Cristobal de las Casas and also illustrates books. She works hard and enjoys what she does, she believes in Gunther and herself.

Now I know what was strange about recent thoughts I grasped in his mind, a flavour I would taste in his blood now if I tried it.

They expressed a contentment that doesn't lead to complacency. It doesn't diminish the will to fight, but gives you the strength to do it. In over 200 years of life, I don't think I've ever felt that.

Will I destroy their happiness if I come forward? Will it disrupt Gunther's view of reality – even his grip on it?

He steps down from the stage. He's not far from me. I can reach out and touch him. Or I can sit here and leave him in the closest thing there can be to peace. Lucia should be able to talk him out of survivor's guilt: *You did what you could.* Perhaps working on this new story will lift the burden.

Jack, master of ceremonies, returns. "We have more music..."

A sharp *crack* against one of the high windows along the auditorium interrupts him. Jack hesitates. When there's no further sound he begins again. "We'll have some performers who made their name in the music halls..."

Another *crack*. It could be nothing, but someone goes to investigate. The musicians start to set up.

Now there's a rumbling from outside, there are voices. Something else hits the window, spreading a spider web of breakage. A boy cries out.

A broad-shouldered muscle-bound bloke runs in from outside and takes the microphone. He doesn't look like he's about to sing 'Doing the Lambeth Walk'.

"Attention! There are fascists outside trying to disrupt this event, but there are more than enough of us to see them off! All those who want to fight go to the door and grab some ammo! And those who can't fight, remember there's no shame in that. Stay here and enjoy the music. Let's show them we won't be intimidated, and let the show go on! *No pasaran!*"

People start shepherding children towards the stage, furthest from the door and away from the windows. Others draw up close as a singer in braces and a fake handlebar moustache bounds onto the stage along with three women in spangled swimsuits. *"When trade is very rocky and you has to take the nocky,"* he sings. *"It's best to face the music like a brick."*

The pianist begins playing. Then he pauses and listens, as if wondering whether to join the fight. But Lucia signals from the audience that she'll take his place, and he leaves. She positions herself on the piano stool with the poise of a dancer, and launches into a jazz-inflected accompaniment.

While the moustached man urges those near the stage to clap along, everyone else scrambles towards the door. Veterans of Cable Street and Aragon, wily ghetto guerrillas escaped from the Continent, East End dockers and liberal doctors ready for first aiding, progressive students, the burly contralto and her bandmates...

And then there's me.

I'm spurred as echoes of slogans reach the auditorium. *"No Jews and Reds... No immigration!"*

The cracked glass gives way. As I come closer I hear the impact of punches, hits and kicks from outside. The performers continue with a frantic gaiety, as if it's their duty to keep the captive part of the audience entertained. Moustache man bellows: *"If your creditors come down on you for everything you owe, you must bash them on the crumpet with a stick!"*

I pick up a chair and snap its leg off. I know from experience it will prove an effective and flexible weapon, especially with my extra strength. The chair itself will do as a shield.

Just as the wood crunches and I pull the leg free, I find myself looking straight into Gunther's eyes as he joins the surge to the door. He jolts with the connection as if it's a physical shock, scattering thoughts of guilt and longing through the air. *Have I conjured a ghost with my reading?*

Before he says anything, I break another leg off the chair and hand it to him.

Rediffusion
by Rhys Hughes

They came for me just after midnight, those devious inspectors, opening my door with a special key and rushing into my living room before I had a chance to even get out of my chair. I had always imagined I would have plenty of time to hide the television in a cupboard before they entered, but the reality was quite different. I was helpless and they were merciless and they took my machine as evidence.

True, I had ignored no fewer than three warning letters, but I hadn't felt guilty in the slightest about not buying a licence. Still don't, in fact. At no point in my longish life had I ever entertained the notion of obtaining one. The expense was simply absurd. The best part of a full week's wages just for the minor privilege of viewing one outmoded and rather staid channel among thousands. It didn't seem right.

I was surprised the inspectors had the power to handcuff me, kick me with fake leather boots and bundle me into the back of a van. Clearly the law had recently been changed in this regard without my knowledge. Was it even a criminal offence to watch television without a licence? The thug sitting in the back of the van assured me it was, then he slapped me in my insolent mouth, breaking a tooth.

The van swayed around bends, accelerated over a bumpy road, slowly climbed a steep hill somewhere. I had the impression we were leaving the city, but when it finally stopped and I was let out, I found myself blinking up at the renowned corporation tower, a building not more than few miles from my house. Later I learned that the driver had taken a lengthy detour so he might claim higher expenses.

I was pushed up the stone steps and through the gaping portal into the impressive lobby, but my guards didn't let me loiter in this cool spot for more than a few seconds before yanking me down a narrow passage that twisted and coiled like an intestine and ended in a blank wall. A narrow metal ladder speared into the ceiling at this point and I was told to climb it on my own. I did so unsteadily.

A dozen rungs later, I emerged into a wood-panelled chamber. A hatch beneath my feet closed silently, cutting off my retreat. I was standing in the dock of an improvised courtroom, facing a judge who was nothing more than a gigantic image on a vast plasma screen. Two smaller screens displayed the prosecution and defence lawyers, but the stations were badly tuned and the pictures fragmented.

It seemed I was late for my own trial and that the process was already over, for the judge was midway through his condemnation. "Unspeakably guilty of living as a broadcast parasite," he intoned, "and therefore wisely sentenced to more years in prison than shall be deemed unseemly." It was an odd sentence, both verbally and judicially, and I was too bewildered to utter an objection. I merely wept.

I had expected a warning, possibly a fine, certainly not imprisonment, and a wave of revulsion engulfed me. I staggered out of the dock, tried to locate the exit, sought to elude my fate, to flee. Instantly three new guards jumped out from behind furniture to apprehend me. One drew a futuristic gun out of a silver holster. He aimed it at my head and pulled the trigger, and a hidden spring released its energy.

From the barrel of the gun emerged a cardboard bolt of lightning that jabbed me in the centre of my forehead, then bounced harmlessly off. At the same instant, one of the other guards pushed me to the floor while the third placed his mouth next to my ear and cried, "Bzzzzzt!" I realised this was a typical stratagem of the corporation, a cheap prop rather than a real weapon, a low-budget special effect.

"You've been stunned by the ray," said the marksman.

"If you say so," I replied.

"Don't move at all, you're paralysed," he added.

"For how long?" I asked.

"Until we get you into your cell. Don't forget. Sensation will return to your hands, then your legs, then your mind. We'll be watching to make sure you do it in the right order."

I said nothing, figuring that the paralysis was also supposed to extend to my tongue. They carried my stiff body out of the courtroom and down a wide corridor to a door that opened onto a large courtyard. At the centre of the courtyard stood a brick prison. I was amazed to see such a building hidden within the corporation

100

tower. Tiny barred windows perforated the dizzy heights of irregular turrets.

The perspectives didn't seem right, but then I recalled how an ordinary television set can manage to fit imposing mountain ranges and undulating deserts into the width of a screen, and my surprise decayed as rapidly as a neglected cosine wave or bowl of forgotten cherries. The sentry posted at the prison gate shook his head fiercely, as if he sought to restore reception to a misfiring cathode ray tube.

"An awkward customer, resisted arrest, I see."

My bearers nodded and lowered me slowly into his extended muscular arms. "He's rather a crafty one."

"Soon reduce him in size," came the reply.

Then he turned and ran into the prison at a speed I deemed absurd and dangerous down a succession of dim curving corridors, narrowly missing other sentries and prisoners, clearly anxious to demonstrate his unnatural strength and stamina. His heavy feet slapped the flagstones like tsunamis of molten basalt. Despite my official paralysis, I made appreciative noises to humour him. I even sniggered.

Skidding to a halt before an open cell, he brusquely cast me inside and slammed the grey door, then raced back the way he had come. I landed on a low bed and my subsequent injuries were minor or imaginary, so I stood and flexed life back into my limbs, obeying the recommended sequence to satisfy any secret cameras that might be observing. Then I realised the key to my door was on the inside.

This oversight seemed too bizarre to be plausible, but I took advantage of the opportunity to slip out of my cell and tiptoe along the corridors. At first I was anxious and excited, then it dawned on me that the prison was actually a complex labyrinth and that I was profoundly lost. The laxity of the security measures was merely an illusion. The outer exit must always elude my desperate wanderings.

Two guards with buckets and brushes turned a corner and yelled at me to halt. I panicked and ran, nursing my aching jaw and whimpering. Then I tripped and sprawled. I heard the slurp of paint and felt the rough caress of bristles. They were painting vertical lines on my clothes, the traditional convict stripes. After they finished, they casually sauntered away and left me alone, but now I was branded.

I remained on my hands and knees and crawled down a side passage to an open door. The space beyond was an ugly forest of legs, a recreation area of some sort, a communal room. I scuttled like a crippled crab to the nearest vacant chair, hauled myself onto it. Now I was part of an audience facing a television screen. The other members of this audience were also prisoners and we watched in silence.

Cheap soap operas were followed by light news bulletins and domestic shows concerned with cooking, gardening, finance. Cartoons were also in evidence. After an hour, the situation became unbearable and I whispered this fact to my neighbour. "I have been incarcerated for neglecting to pay my television licence and yet I'm clearly allowed to enjoy free television in prison. How ironic is that?"

He rubbed his bleary eyes and replied, "Not very, considering we're all inside for the same crime. Only licence dodgers are permitted to rot in the private dungeons of the corporation. But it seems you are labouring under the delusion that television is provided to prisoners as a privilege or act of compassion. Even here a license is mandatory. Don't you have one? Theft of corporation images is serious."

"You are joking, surely?" I spluttered.

He shook his head. "The inspectors are vigilant and unforgiving. They always punish cheating eyes."

"This news is terrible. What should I do?"

"Buy a licence, of course."

"But I have no money or means of making any!"

"That is not a valid excuse."

"In that case, I won't enter this room again. I'll forsake the pleasures of televised broadcasts and remain in my cell. But as this is my first day, I'm not sure how to get back there."

"All dungeons are identical. Take your pick."

"I thank you for your advice. Please don't reveal the fact I sat here and absorbed one full illegal hour of broadcasting. In future I'll ask my guards for books or magazines instead."

He plucked my sleeve and pulled me back. "Even if you don't watch it, you still need a licence for any working television set on the premises. It's futile for you to attempt to hide."

102

I shook him free and fled the recreation area, my heart pounding. Then I soothed myself with the thought that I was merely the victim of a subtle jest, an experiment with practical paradox. An imprisoned licence avoider being forced to obtain a licence for a television set provided by the prison authorities. Utterly ridiculous! Yes, it was a jest. There could be no other sensible explanation, none at all.

I soon located an unoccupied cell, possibly even my own, and fell into a troubled sleep on the uncomfortable mattress. When I awoke I saw that an envelope addressed to me had been slid under my door. It contained a warning letter from the corporation. Apparently, the inspectors had been alerted to the fact I didn't have a valid licence. I sat trembling on the edge of the bed, awaiting developments.

They came a few days later, dragged me away, pushed me up a ladder into another courtroom. Again I was found guilty by a flatscreen judge in a digital wig, then prodded, pinched and buffeted down endless corridors and through a door into a courtyard in the centre of which stood a smaller prison. I laughed unhappily. Prisons within prisons. A new sentry clasped me in his arms, hurried me inside.

This prison was full of broadcast parasites who had defaulted not once but twice, and we were made to feel doubly accursed. I had the impression that the process of relocating me here had somehow reduced my physical size as well as diminishing my self-esteem. Body and soul shrunk to fit an implacable credo, the unbending and illogical will of the corporation, the nightmare of rigorous absurdity.

The corridors of my new home were thin and confusing. I stumbled on the communal television room on my second day and stood silently at the entrance, swallowing hard. When I returned to my cell, the expected letter had already been delivered. It accused me of attempting to exist without a licence despite having access to a television. Inspectors would shortly be dispatched to deal with the anomaly...

They came with their usual sarcasm and fists. This prison contained its own virtual courtroom and judge, its own courtyard that was the location of a third prison, to the entrance of which they dragged me. Then another strong sentry and bare cell, another automatic violation of the television licensing laws, another

103

threatening letter. An appalling process had been set in motion. An inward spiral.

The prisons grew progressively smaller, but so did I, so did my guards, and everything shrunk in perfect proportion, like a cannibal who boils his own head in the same pot as the skulls of his victims. One morning I had a visitor who was not an inspector. He identified himself as a corporation lawyer working for the best interests of the convicts. He entered my cell wearing a silk suit and oily smile.

"There is another way," he declared simply.

"Kindly elucidate."

"Experiments are taking place on living specimens. Any prisoner who volunteers will be spared the indignity of constant arrest, trial, relocation. Your sentences are adding up into something resembling a paragraph, a page, or even a book, of despair. This can be stopped easily enough. You merely need to sign this form."

Without looking, I asked, "And if I do?"

"A series of controls will be fitted into your nervous system. Knobs or buttons that can adjust your colour balance, your contrast, audibility, even the particular channel of your thoughts, whenever we desire. Your spinal fluid will be drained and replaced with a metallic solution that will enable you to receive corporation signals."

"And if I decline this generous offer?"

"You will continue to occupy smaller and smaller prisons until you are trapped inside an institution no larger than a single pixel on a screen. That will be the point of no return, the dot of ultimate doom, the final spark of closedown, the singularity of sorrow!"

I chewed my lip. "May I think it over tonight?"

He nodded sourly. "I suppose so, but you must give an answer before the inspectors come for you at noon tomorrow. In the meantime be aware that the governor of the corporation, Bogie Laird, is visiting this prison in disguise. Nobody knows what form he has chosen, so it's imperative to be humble to every individual you meet."

I blurted impulsively, "Are *you* Bogie Laird?"

He snarled and raised his clenched fists, his silk suit splitting its seams as his muscles expanded. "How dare you be so perspicacious? I predict a traumatic final episode for you…"

Then he lurched out of my cell, howling, his suit rapidly disintegrating as he went, leaving me in an acute state of agitation. But I recovered soon enough and emulated his example, vacating my cubicle and going for one of my usual random strolls. Down one passage I heard a bland vibration, a refreshing change from the ceaseless babble of televised entertainment, and I felt compelled to investigate.

In a tiny room that stank of stale tobacco smoke and was slippery with spilled tea, a brace of off-duty guards sat around a prisoner who had recently been modified. Standing rigidly to attention, eyes popping with static, lips humming a monotone, the volunteer grimaced while one of the jaded guards slapped and shook him, restoring coherent reflections to his pupils for just a few moments at a time.

I wanted to jump forward, make my indignant presence felt, sweep an admonishing finger across every bored face. I wanted to express my fury in a mighty shout. "So this is how you spend your free time? Surfing dead channels within the hopeless eyes of a prisoner! But do any of you have a valid licence to watch him? The corporation will be informed if you don't and inspectors will be activated!"

But before I could make the leap, it occurred to me that the prisoner in question might be none other than Bogie Laird in a new disguise, and the more I pondered this possibility the more convincing it became, so I lost my nerve and slipped away before I was noticed. My one chance to mock the system had been lost, my final opportunity to use irony as a retaliatory weapon had faded and dissolved.

Naturally enough, after this incident, I was reluctant to submit myself for treatment and so the hideous cycle of arrest, trial and incarceration in diminishing prisons continued. After many years I reached the smallest of them all, a mere dot. I was trapped inside a single pixel on the screen of a television I presumed was unlicensed, a machine whose owner must soon be visited by the inevitable inspectors.

Instead of eschewing the recreational facilities of my enforced abode, I wasted half my free time sitting in front of the communal television. Still without a licence, I was also without fear. Arrest entailed no motion at all, for there was nowhere even smaller to send me. It was therefore possible to safely ignore all warning letters. On some level, the lowest imaginable, I had finally cheated the authorities.

But the entertainment on offer left much to be desired. Every channel displayed the same unchanging image, a room full of people who sat with their backs to me. They were dressed in grey clothes and their bald heads glistened in the glare of an unspecified light source as they watched with grim reverence something beyond the screen. I studied them intently and thought about them during my walks.

Recursion can be a terrible thing, and one day I found a service ladder to the roof and climbed onto the tiles, my hands rouged with rust from the corroded rungs. There was no safe descent to the courtyard below. On all sides reared the walls of the next smallest prison, and above those loomed the higher walls of the third smallest prison, and over those leered the still taller walls of the fourth smallest...

And so on, all the way back to the almost forgotten beginning. Prisons within courtyards, courtyards within prisons, prisons within the courtyard of the corporation tower. The concave surface of *that* impossible building appeared unimaginably remote now, as unattainable as the inner shell of the universe, and the lights of its windows burned like artificial quasars at the perimeter of a synthetic reality.

The spectacle was unbearable, so I looked directly upwards instead. At the furthest limit of a cylinder so immense and imposing it contained all the misery I could ever conceive for myself, I beheld a glass screen with blurred faces on the other side that were mostly fixed to the fronts of bald heads. Then I knew this truth. If I am part of a fictional drama and not a factual documentary, I might not go mad.

A Place For Feeding
by Simon Kurt Unsworth

"Ah, ah, aaah," said the woman with the beige coat and the too-red lipstick, waving an admonishing finger in the air in front of her, and Angela didn't realise at first that the woman was directing it at her, so she carried on.

Shaun had been good that afternoon, better than usual, but he had been getting squally these last few minutes. Knowing that he wouldn't stop, would only get louder and more demanding, Angela had stopped shopping and found a café, got herself a drink and prepared to feed him. She undid another button on her blouse and then reached in and pulled down the cup of her bra. Then it was simply a matter of lifting Shaun to her breast and readying the large square of muslin in her other hand so that she could drape it over her shoulder to give both her and Shaun some privacy. It was as she moved Shaun's lip to her nipple so that he could latch on that the woman made the "Ah, ah, aaah" sound again, wagging her finger more forcefully, and then said, "You! Miss! Not in front of my children, you don't!"

Even then, Angela wondered what the woman was talking to her about, though that she was talking to her had become clear: she was looking directly at Angela as she spoke, and the wagging finger (topped, Angela saw, by a long nail painted the same too-red shade as the woman's lips) was stabbing now, poking emphatically at her. It didn't make sense, not at first; Angela wasn't doing anything, was she? Just sitting, having a cup of tea while Shaun fed from her.

So what, then? Angela wasn't doing anything to cause offence, nothing to generate such a strong reaction. The woman's face was actually *wrinkling*, her lips pulling back from her teeth and twisting her face into an expression of disgust, as though she'd smelled or seen something foul. Angela glanced down at herself, wondering if she'd spilled something or walked something in on her shoes, but no, there was nothing. Nothing except her long skirt and flat shoes, her coat over her knee and her plain blouse above them, and Shaun nestled at her left breast, partially covered by the muslin. He was content now that he was feeding, his cheeks expanding and contracting in sweet little ballooning motions as he sucked and swallowed. Just Shaun, and then Angela paused. Shaun? Was it Shaun, Angela wondered before realising that it was, it was *Shaun*, it was Shaun *feeding* that the woman had a problem with.

She was so surprised that she didn't respond, didn't move, and the woman said angrily, "Don't you ignore me, missy! It's disgusting, doing it like that, in front of people, in front of my *children!*" and she actually hissed the last word. Her finger stabbed forward, now no longer up vertical but a savage horizontal, jerking forwards and back as she spoke. The red nail flashed as the café's overhead light caught in it, streaks like the glint of fishes' scales darting across its surface. Angela looked around the café, hoping she would see a friendly face, but everyone seemed to be looking at her disapprovingly. One young girl was even nodding as the woman spoke, and that really hurt Angela's feelings; the girl had a small child in a buggy by her side, and Angela had hoped she, at least, might be on her side. The café windows were slick with condensation, misting the world beyond to pastel smears through which the shapes of people passing were little more than insubstantial blurs.

"I'm sorry," Angela started, meaning to tell the woman that she was sorry, she didn't understand what the problem was, but the woman interrupted before she could get any further.

"You ought to be sorry, exposing yourself to my sons like that!"

"Exposing myself? How? I don't understand," Angela stammered, but knew that she did. Behind the woman, two small boys glared at her; one looked to be about six, the other a little older, perhaps eight or nine. The elder of the two was peering intently at Shaun, at her almost-exposed breast.

"That!" the woman said furiously, jabbing her finger forward again, this time extending her arm so that it was at nearly full stretch. "We don't want to see you do that while we eat. It's *disgusting.*"

"It's not disgusting," said Angela, not liking the way her voice wavered as she spoke. She wished that Steve was here, he'd have already told the woman what she could do with her fingernail and her "Ah, ah, aah" sounds and her ridiculous, upsetting attitude to Shaun feeding. Trying to gather herself, she went on.

108

"He's just having a feed, it's perfectly natural,"

"So's going to the toilet," the woman retorted, still hissing, "and we have a place for that and it's not in the middle of a café where everyone can see and where decent people are trying to take their sons out for a meal."

"Can see what?" said Angela, still trying to remain calm, to not cry, hating how this woman was making her feel, small and angry and strengthless. She had never been good at conflict, never liked standing up for herself, always wanted to try to walk away to avoid the fight if she could. "I've covered him, he's just having a feed. He's hungry."

"He might well be hungry. We're all hungry, you know, but I don't want to see him have his drink. You should do it somewhere else. It's disgusting," the woman repeated. "In public. And don't think that little cloth helps, either; we saw you before you put it there, and we know what's happening behind it now. I can *hear* him."

Angela couldn't speak; her cheeks burned in helpless, impotent fury. Shaun was four months old, was the sweetest, brightest thing there was, and being able to feed him herself was the thing she was most proud of in her whole miserable life. All the struggles of her life before, all the terrors and pains of his birth and of her and Steve's hopes and wishes for him, they all fell away when he fed from her. She wasn't successful, she wasn't popular, she had neither a good job nor good prospects, she was just Angela who had got pregnant at nineteen and had somehow managed to have a perfect little baby and stay in a relationship with his father. Shaun needed them, needed *her*, and finally she had found something she was good at; she had taken to feeding Shaun easily, as he had taken to feeding from her. And yet, here was this woman, this *cow*, undermining her, attacking her, making her feel bad.

"It's the healthiest thing for him, it's so much better than formula," Angela tried again, hoping to somehow persuade the woman, make her see things from Angela's point of view.

"So you think you're better than those of us who chose to feed our children using the bottle do you, better than those of us who chose to respect other people's sensibilities?"

"What? No, I never said that," said Angela, feeling the tears start. She hated people like this, people who could twist what she

109

said, who were quicker with words and who always had an answer, no matter what she said. "I just meant that –" but the woman interrupted her again.

"You just meant that you're better than me, that I should just ignore you because he wants it. Well, let me tell you, missy, if you let him have everything he wants as he wants it, he'll grow up spoiled. Perhaps I should let my boys do what they want. How about that, Oscar? Would you like to just do what you want, when you want it?"

"No, mum," said the older of the boys, still peering intently at Angela's chest. She could almost see the hope in his eyes, the hope that her blouse would flap, that he might catch a glimpse of something. Angela reddened more, if that were possible, feeling the burn spread from her cheek to her forehead and down her neck, knowing that a dark flush was appearing down her throat and spreading across the bony hollows of her collarbones.

"There!" said the woman, triumphant. " 'No, mum'! He knows that he won't be able to live his life getting what he wants, he's not selfish. Both my sons had the bottle, had *formula*, not when they wanted it but when I wanted them to, and they've turned out fine. Better than fine, perfect! So don't give me your nonsense about 'better for him'!"

"But it is, it's the best thing for him, it's from me, how can it not be, the companies lie about how good formula is because it isn't, but my milk is, it's perfect for him," and Angela was crying now, tears of shame and anger rolling down her cheeks, fat and hot and corrosive. Out of the corner of her eye, she saw the manager of the café come out from behind the counter and start to thread his way between the tables towards her. *Oh thank God*, she thought, *he's coming to tell her to leave me alone*. She looked up at him gratefully as he arrived by her side.

"Miss," he said quietly. He was only small, she saw, short and slight and wearing a thin white shirt and a tie with a pattern of green and blue and red triangles.

"Miss," he repeated, and he looked down as he spoke, refusing to meet Angela's eyes. "You'll have to stop, I'm afraid. It's upsetting the other customers. Please. There's a room you can use, where you and he can have some privacy."

Angela felt like she'd been punched, and couldn't speak. Any sound she might want to make seemed suddenly trapped in her throat, swelling and painful. She tried to swallow and found she was unable, that her tongue was clumsy and dry in her mouth. Shaun suckled on, oblivious.

"Miss," said the man a third time and reached out for her, his hand stopping nervously between them and hovering before falling back to his side. "I'm really very sorry but you really can't do that here. It's offending people. We have a place you can go, please come with me. Please."

Angela wanted to say, *What about me? I'm offended, for me and for my son, he just wants to have a drink and so do I, my feet hurt and I'm tired and I want to sit here and wait for the food I've ordered and for my son to be allowed to finish his feed, please,* but she didn't. Instead, she inserted a finger into Shaun's mouth and gently prised him off her breast, slipping the cup of her bra back up with a practiced motion at the same time. Shaun grouched, but only a little; he would be content for a few minutes, but he hadn't finished feeding yet and would become demanding again soon. She lifted him to her shoulder, cradling him against her, using her other hand to hold her blouse together rather than rebutton it. She kept her head down so that the woman and the manager wouldn't see her tears, wouldn't see the expression on her face. The manager reached out to help her with her coat but she knocked his hand away, saying stiffly, "I'm fine."

As she followed the manager, Angela saw that the woman was sitting with her arms folded, a broad smile on her face. *It makes her look like a frog,* Angela thought bitterly, *a big horrible frog with a big ugly tongue. I'll bet kissing her must be horrible, I bet she tastes horrible, like old ponds and slimy plants,* and the thought made her smile. "Look at her," said the woman, "no shame. She thinks this is all a big joke." Angela hurried on, carrying Shaun and uncomfortably aware that she was leaving her bags of shopping and his pram by the table, and she wanted to be somewhere else, anywhere but in the café. She wished the ground would somehow magically open and spirit the two of them away, but beneath her feet the tired linoleum remained stubbornly whole. Ahead, the manager's skinny buttocks and curved back guided her on.

The room was a storeroom between the two toilets. It was half full of boxes and it smelled of cleaning fluid and musty air and old, pale urine. The bulb dangling from the ceiling was low-

111

wattage and waxen, the light it cast a seeping yellow that showed the room in the colours of old photographs. The floor was plain concrete, gritty, and Angela heard it crack and pop under the soles of her shoes. It was cold, and there was no furniture that she could see.

The manager fumbled behind one of the piles of boxes and finally pulled out a folding chair, opening it and setting it against one wall. He had to shift one or two smaller boxes out of the way as he did so and he grunted as he pushed them, a little animal sound like the noise Shaun sometimes made as he filled his nappy. After the boxes were moved, he turned to Angela, his face a mask of misery. "I'm sorry," he said, "but there's nothing I can do. I'll make sure no one takes your table and that your things are left alone, and your food will be ready when you've... when he's finished. Can I get you anything else?"

"No," said Angela, not trusting her voice to say more. "Please just leave us alone."

Once the door had swung shut the room was gloomy, the darkness seeming to magnify the odours into a rich landscape that hung around her and Shaun as she sat down. The chair wobbled, Shaun griping as she clenched him tight. He could tell she was unsettled, and it disturbed him. She cuddled him for a minute and then tried to get comfortable in the chair, which wobbled again as she shifted. Finally, he calmed enough for her to try to let him feed; she let her blouse fall open and lowered her bra cup again, moving Shaun so that he could take her in his mouth. At first, he didn't latch on properly so that the initial sucks he took of her were painful. Wincing, she repositioned him, trying to concentrate on him and not on the woman, not on the other people in the café or the manager, not on this horrible room or the smell, just on Shaun and feeding him and being what he needed.

The sound of a door closing came from behind Angela, making her jump. She twisted slightly, careful not to disturb Shaun who was latched and feeding better now. The wall was only plasterboard, she saw, more a divider than a wall. It looked damp and soft, and the sound from the room beyond travelled through it easily. It was the men's toilet, she thought, as she listened to heavy footsteps and then another door closed and there was a click she thought was probably a lock. "No," she whispered out loud as another noise erupted, a horrible bodily sound, flatulent and full.

Someone groaned and then broke wind again and Shaun wriggled in her arms and she realised that she was holding him tight, her arms trembling. There was a third sound from beyond the partition, another groan, and then the noise of water splashing and Angela was on her feet and speaking out loud again.

"No," this time not whispering but saying it clearly as though she were talking to the person beyond the wall. "I will not feed my son listening to the sound of someone going to the toilet, I will *not*." She gently broke Shaun's latch, ignoring his emerging wail of protest, and lifted him back to her shoulder. Then, as calmly as she could, she buttoned her blouse back to the top and picked up her coat. It had wetness on it from the floor, dark patches standing out against the beige material. Steve had bought her the coat for her birthday and she was suddenly angry – no, not angry, *furious*. Not enough that they made her feed Shaun like this, like some animal, they had made her coat messy. It was hers, not theirs, and they had messed it up. Well, that was it. She was going to take Shaun back and go and sit at the table and she was going to show the manager her wet coat and explain to him politely about the sound of the man on the toilet and how she wasn't going to make Shaun have his food listening to it, and then she was going to eat her food and let Shaun feed and if the woman or her children didn't like it, they could go and eat in the cupboard. They could *all* eat in the cupboard if they wanted, and if they tried to stop her feeding Shaun, well, they'd have a fight on their hands. She had had enough.

As she got to the doorway, Angela heard the sound of the door further down the corridor opening again and footsteps coming towards her. She waited until the person, the man, had passed and she had heard the sound of a more distant door open and close, so that she knew he was back in the dining area, and only then did she come out of the cupboard. She went quickly, carrying Shaun against her front like her badge and shield and armour. Her heart fluttered in her chest, birdlike, and she wished she were stronger, braver, because she knew that she wasn't going to say anything to the manager, she was just going to sit and eat as fast as possible and hope Shaun didn't start to cry, and if he did she was going to get up and gather him to her, get her things and leave. She hadn't the words or the strength to fight, but maybe if she sat quiet they'd leave her alone. Taking a deep breath, she went back into the main body of the café.

Shaun's pram and her bags remained where they had been, untouched, but now there was a bottle on her table, a baby's bottle full of thick white liquid. Angela looked at it and then up, around the people in the café. The woman had her head down, was shovelling a forkful of food from her plate to her mouth. Oscar was looking at Angela with undisguised interest, his round face creasing into a frown of disappointment when he saw that her blouse was fully buttoned. The other child was also eating, his actions mimicking his mother's. There was an old man sitting at the table beyond the woman and children, his face red. *Was he the one in the toilet?* she thought, *the noisy one?* Glancing away, she saw other tables, other people. A younger man wearing overalls and a paint-spattered fleece, an older couple who were both reading, another old man who was peering at her, the light reflecting across the lenses of his spectacles. Other people had entered in the short time that she had been in that horrible room with Shaun: a group of young girls in fat anoraks covered in gold and silver logos, and a couple dressed in smart clothes like they'd just come out of an office. By the door, the young girl, the one with the child in the buggy, was looking at her. Angela caught her eye long enough for the young girl to look deliberately down and then back up; Angela repeated the action and saw the bottle again. She put Shaun back in his pram, where he gurgled happily to himself and played with the dangling fish of his mobile, and then looked at the girl again, who smiled at Angela. Picking the bottle up, Angela walked across to her and said, "Is this yours? I think you might have left it on my table by accident."

"No, it's for you. Well, for your baby," said the girl.

"No, thank you," said Angela politely, a feeling of unreality washing over her, "he's breast-fed, he doesn't need a bottle."

"Oh, I'd disagree," said the woman suddenly from behind Angela. From *right* behind her. "You can't fill boys, not with just the breast," she continued, her voice almost conversational. "They need something extra. Besides, it'll help him sleep through."

"No," said Angela again, trying to turn but finding her way blocked by the woman, who was really very close now. "Formula isn't what he needs; it's not as good as my milk. I don't want him to have a bottle. I'm the only food he needs."

114

"Nonsense," said the woman, reaching over Angela's shoulder and taking the bottle from her hand before Angela could stop her. "This young woman's been very kind to let you have this, you should be grateful. After all, it won't hurt him."

"No, please, stop," said Angela, trying again. She managed to twist part of the way around this time, but then the woman stepped further forward and bumped into her, knocking Angela back against the nearest chair and causing her to stumble. Her knees caught against the seat of the chair and she sat heavily, the upright of the chair catching her painfully.

"He'll like it," said the young girl. Her voice was breathy and excited.

"He will," said the neatly-dressed woman, and the man with her nodded. The girls at the other table giggled.

"No, wait, please," said Angela again and tried to rise, but then the manager was in front of the woman and was pushing Angela back into the chair. For such a small man, he was surprisingly forceful, and she had time to think that he was the only man besides Steve to touch her in over two years, and then she couldn't see the woman any more. She reappeared in Angela's view, was now by Shaun's pram and appeared to be leaning over and peering inside it. Angela saw that Oscar had beaten her to it, however, and had already taken Shaun out. Taken him out, was holding him, was holding her baby.

"Put him back," Angela shouted. Oscar ignored her; everyone ignored her except the manager, who said "It's for the best, really. We all talked about it, and we all agree."

"No, formula can give them poorly tummies, he doesn't need it, leave him alone, let me go," said Angela. Her voice cracked as she spoke, rising to a shout, and then she was struggling, pushing against the manager, trying again to rise. He forced her back down, calling out, and the younger man came over and sat in the chair next to her, leaning over to grip her arms tightly.

"Everything'll be fine," said the manager, but he wouldn't look at Angela as he spoke; his eyes were tightly shut and his shoulders were hunched up as though he were trying to cover his ears. She opened her mouth to scream and the younger man squeezed her arms painfully tight and said in a quiet voice, "Don't. You'll only make it worse. Besides, you'll thank us in the end."

115

"Please," she repeated. "He's my baby, I don't want him to have a bottle, I want to feed him myself, let me go and we'll just leave and we won't come back."

"It's okay, love," said one of the old men as Angela started to sob. "You don't want to listen to any of the rubbish they tell you. He'll be fine, he'll enjoy it, and it's better for everyone, isn't it? You can go anywhere with him if he's on the bottle, can't you?"

"Of course you can," said the woman, taking Shaun from Oscar. "You're only young, you think you know everything but you don't. I've had two, and this way is so much easier for everyone."

Angela gasped as the people in the café crowded around her, pressing her back into the chair. The smell of hot bodies filled her nostrils as she screamed, once, before a hand that was heavy and tasted of soap and grease clamped across her mouth. She couldn't see who the hand belonged too in the melée, only that it was connected to an arm that snaked away around the side of her head. Another arm wrapped around her stomach and pulled her hard against the chair. The manager let go of her shoulders and backed away, and just before the gap he left was filled with more bodies, Angela had the briefest glimpse of Shaun. He was in the arms of the woman, her face bent down towards his, and she was smiling widely and holding the bottle to his lips.

Night They Missed The Horror Show
by Joe R. Lansdale

For Lew Shiner,
a story that doesn't flinch

If they'd gone to the drive-in like they'd planned, none of this would have happened. But Leonard didn't like drive-ins when he didn't have a date, and he'd heard about *Night of the Living Dead*, and he knew a nigger starred in it. He didn't want to see no movie with a nigger star. Niggers chopped cotton, fixed flats, and pimped nigger girls, but he'd never heard of one that killed zombies. And he'd heard too that there was a white girl in the movie that let the nigger touch her, and that peeved him. Any white gal that would let a nigger touch her must be the lowest trash in the world. Probably from Hollywood, New York, or Waco, some god-forsaken place like that.

Now Steve McQueen would have been all right for zombie killing and girl handling. He would have been the ticket. But a nigger? No sir.

Boy, that Steve McQueen was one cool head. Way he said stuff in them pictures was so good you couldn't help but think someone had written it down for him. He could sure think fast on his feet to come up with the things he said, and he had that real cool, mean look.

Leonard wished he could be Steve McQueen, or Paul Newman even. Someone like that always knew what to say, and he figured they got plenty of bush too. Certainly they didn't get as bored as he did. He was so bored he felt as if he were going to die from it before the night was out. Bored, bored, bored. Just wasn't nothing exciting about being in the Dairy Queen parking lot leaning on the front of his '64 Impala looking out at the highway. He figured maybe old crazy Harry who janitored at the high school might be right about them flying saucers. Harry was always seeing something. Bigfoot, six-legged weasels, all manner of things. But maybe he was right about the saucers. He'd said he'd seen one a couple nights back hovering over Mud Creek and it was shooting down these rays that looked like wet peppermint sticks. Leonard

117

figured if Harry really had seen the saucers and the rays, then those rays were boredom rays. It would be a way for space critters to get at earth folks, boring them to death. Getting melted down by heat rays would have been better. That was at least quick, but being bored to death was sort of like being nibbled to death by ducks.

Leonard continued looking at the highway, trying to imagine flying saucers and boredom rays, but he couldn't keep his mind on it. He finally focused on something in the highway. A dead dog.

Not just a dead dog. But a DEAD DOG. The mutt had been hit by a semi at least, maybe several. It looked as if it had rained dog. There were pieces of that pooch all over the concrete and one leg was lying on the curbing on the opposite side, stuck up in such a way that it seemed to be waving hello. Doctor Frankenstein with a grant from Johns Hopkins and assistance from NASA couldn't have put that sucker together again.

Leonard leaned over to his faithful, drunk companion, Billy – known among the gang as Farto, because he was fart-lighting champion of Mud Creek – and said, "See that dog there?"

Farto looked where Leonard was pointing. He hadn't noticed the dog before, and he wasn't nearly as casual about it as Leonard. The puzzle-piece hound brought back memories. It reminded him of a dog he'd had when he was thirteen. A big, fine German Shepherd that loved him better than his Mama.

Sonofabitch dog tangled its chain through and over a barbed wire fence somehow and hung itself. When Farto found the dog its tongue looked like a stuffed, black sock and he could see where its claws had just been able to scrape the ground, but not quite enough to get a toe hold.

It looked as if the dog had been scratching out some sort of a coded message in the dirt. When Farto told his old man about it later, crying as he did, his old man laughed and said, "Probably a goddamn suicide note."

Now, as he looked out at the highway, and his whiskey-laced Coke collected warmly in his gut, he felt a tear form in his eyes. Last time he'd felt that sappy was when he'd won the fart-lighting championship with a four-inch burner that singed the hairs of his ass and the gang awarded him with a pair of colored boxing shorts. Brown and yellow ones so he could wear them without having to change them too often.

So there they were, Leonard and Farto, parked outside the DQ, leaning on the hood of Leonard's Impala, sipping Coke and whiskey, feeling bored and blue and horny, looking at a dead dog and having nothing to do but go to a show with a nigger starring in it. Which, to be up front, wouldn't have been so bad if they'd had dates. Dates could make up for a lot of sins, or help make a few good ones, depending on one's outlook.

But the night was criminal. Dates they didn't have. Worse yet, wasn't a girl in the entire high school would date them. Not even Marylou Flowers, and she had some kind of disease.

All this nagged Leonard something awful. He could see what the problem was with Farto. He was ugly. Had the kind of face that attracted flies. And though being fart-lighting champion of Mud Creek had a certain prestige among the gang, it lacked a certain something when it came to charming the gals.

But for the life of him, Leonard couldn't figure his own problem. He was handsome, had some good clothes, and his car ran good when he didn't buy that old cheap gas. He even had a few bucks in his jeans from breaking into washaterias. Yet his right arm had damn near grown to the size of his thigh from all the whacking off he did. Last time he'd been out with a girl had been a month ago, and as he'd been out with her along with nine other guys, he wasn't rightly sure he could call that a date. He wondered about it so much, he'd asked Farto if he thought it qualified as a date. Farto, who had been fifth in line, said he didn't think so, but if Leonard wanted to call it one, wasn't no skin off his back.

But Leonard didn't want to call it a date. It just didn't have the feel of one, lacked that something special. There was no romance to it.

True, Big Red had called him Honey when he put the mule in the barn, but she called everyone Honey – except Stoney. Stoney was Possum Sweets, and he was the one who talked her into wearing the grocery bag with the mouth and eyeholes. Stoney was like that. He could sweet talk the camel out from under a sand nigger. When he got through chatting Big Red down, she was plumb proud to wear that bag.

When finally it came his turn to do Big Red, Leonard had let her take the bag off as a gesture of goodwill. That was a mistake. He just hadn't known a good thing when he had it. Stoney had had the right idea. The bag coming off spoiled everything. With it on, it was sort of like balling the Lone Hippo or some such thing, but

119

with the bag off, you were absolutely certain what you were getting, and it wasn't pretty.

Even closing his eyes hadn't helped. He found that the ugliness of that face had branded itself on the back of his eyeballs. He couldn't even imagine the sack back over her head. All he could think about was that puffy, too-painted face with the sort of bad complexion that began at the bone.

He'd gotten so disappointed, he'd had to fake an orgasm and get off before his hooter shriveled up and his Trojan fell off and was lost in the vacuum.

Thinking back on it, Leonard sighed. It would certainly be nice for a change to go with a girl that didn't pull the train or have a hole between her legs that looked like a manhole cover ought to be on it. Sometimes he wished he could be like Farto, who was as happy as if he had good sense. Anything thrilled him. Give him a can of Wolf Brand Chili, a big moon pie, Coke and whiskey and he could spend the rest of his life fucking Big Red and lighting the gas out of his asshole.

God, but this was no way to live. No women and no fun. Bored, bored, bored. Leonard found himself looking overhead for spaceships and peppermint-colored boredom rays, but he saw only a few moths fluttering drunkenly through the beams of the DQ's lights.

Lowering his eyes back to the highway and the dog, Leonard had a sudden flash. "Why don't we get the chain out of the back and hook it up to Rex there? Take him for a ride?"

"You mean drag his dead ass around?" Farto asked.

Leonard nodded.

"Beats stepping on a tack," Farto said.

They drove the Impala into the middle of the highway at a safe moment and got out for a look. Up close the mutt was a lot worse. Its innards had been mashed out of its mouth and asshole and it stunk something awful. The dog was wearing a thick, metal-studded collar and they fastened one end of their fifteen-foot chain to that and the other to the rear bumper.

Bob, the Dairy Queen manager, noticed them through the window, came outside and yelled, "What are you fucking morons doing?"

"Taking this doggie to the vet," Leonard said. "We think this sumbitch looks a might peeked. He may have been hit by a car."

120

"That's so fucking funny I'm about to piss myself," Bob said.

"Old folks have that problem," Leonard said.

Leonard got behind the wheel and Farto climbed in on the passenger side. They maneuvered the car and dog around and out of the path of a tractor-trailer truck just in time. As they drove off, Bob screamed after them, "I hope you two no-dicks wrap that Chevy piece of shit around a goddamn pole."

As they roared along, parts of the dog, like crumbs from a flaky loaf of bread, came off. A tooth here. Some hair there. A string of guts. A dew claw. And some unidentifiable pink stuff. The metal-studded collar and chain threw up sparks now and then like fiery crickets. Finally they hit seventy-five and the dog was swinging wider and wider on the chain, like it was looking for an opportunity to pass.

Farto poured him and Leonard up Cokes and whiskey as they drove along. He handed Leonard his paper cup and Leonard knocked it back, a lot happier now than he had been a moment ago. Maybe this night wasn't going to turn out so bad after all.

They drove by a crowd at the side of the road, a tan station wagon and a wreck of a Ford up on a jack. At a glance they could see that there was a nigger in the middle of the crowd and he wasn't witnessing to the white boys. He was hopping around like a pig with a hotshot up his ass, trying to find a break in the white boys so he could make a run for it. But there wasn't any break to be found and there were too many to fight. Nine white boys were knocking him around like he was a pinball and they were a malicious machine.

"Ain't that one of our niggers?" Farto asked. "And ain't that some of the White Tree football players that's trying to kill him?"

"Scott," Leonard said, and the name was dogshit in his mouth. It had been Scott who had outdone him for the position of quarterback on the team. That damn jig could put together a play more tangled than a can of fishing worms, but it damn near always worked. And he could run like a spotted-ass ape.

As they passed, Farto said, "We'll read about him tomorrow in the papers."

But Leonard drove only a short way before slamming on the brakes and whipping the Impala around. Rex swung way out and clipped off some tall, dried sunflowers at the edge of the road like a scythe.

121

"We gonna go back and watch?" Farto asked. "I don't think them White Tree boys would bother us none if that's all we was gonna do, watch."

"He may be a nigger," Leonard said not liking himself, "but he's our nigger and we can't let them do that. They kill him, they'll beat us in football."

Farto saw the truth of this immediately. "Damn right. They can't do that to our nigger."

Leonard crossed the road again and went straight for the White Tree boys, hit down hard on the horn. The White Tree boys abandoned beating their prey and jumped in all directions. Bullfrogs couldn't have done any better.

Scott stood startled and weak where he was, his knees bent in and touching one another, his eyes as big as pizza pans. He had never noticed how big grillwork was. It looked like teeth there in the night and the headlights looked like eyes. He felt like a stupid fish about to be eaten by a shark.

Leonard braked hard, but off the highway in the dirt it wasn't enough to keep from bumping Scott, sending him flying over the hood and against the glass where his face mashed to it then rolled away, his shirt snagging one of the windshield wipers and pulling it off.

Leonard opened the car door and called to Scott who lay on the ground, "It's now or never."

A White Tree boy made for the car, and Leonard pulled the taped hammer handle out from beneath the seat and stepped out of the car and hit him with it. The White Tree boy went down to his knees and said something that sounded like French but wasn't. Leonard grabbed Scott by the back of the shirt and pulled him up and guided him around and threw him into the open door. Scott scrambled over the front seat and into the back. Leonard threw the hammer handle at one of the White Tree boys and stepped back, whirled into the car behind the wheel. He put the car in gear again and stepped on the gas. The Impala lurched forward, and with one hand on the door Leonard flipped it wider and clipped a White Tree boy with it as if he were flexing a wing. The car bumped back on the highway and the chain swung out and Rex cut the feet out from under two White Tree boys as neatly as he had taken down the dried sunflowers.

Leonard looked in his rear-view mirror and saw two White

122

Tree boys carrying the one he had clubbed with the hammer handle to the station wagon. The others he and the dog had knocked down were getting up. One had kicked the jack out from under Scott's car and was using it to smash the headlights and windshield.

"Hope you got insurance on that thing," Leonard said.

"I borrowed it," Scott said, peeling the windshield wiper out of his T-shirt. "Here, you might want this." He dropped the wiper over the seat and between Leonard and Farto.

"That's a borrowed car?" Farto said. "That's worse."

"Nah," Scott said. "Owner don't know I borrowed it. I'd have had that flat changed if that sucker had had him a spare tire, but I got back there and wasn't nothing but the rim, man. Say, thanks for not letting me get killed, else we couldn't have run that ole pig together no more. Course, you almost run over me. My chest hurts."

Leonard checked the rear-view again. The White Tree boys were coming fast. "You complaining?" Leonard said.

"Nah," Scott said, and turned to look through the back glass. He could see the dog swinging in short arcs and pieces of it going wide and far. "Hope you didn't go off and forget your dog tied to the bumper."

"Goddamn," said Farto, "and him registered too."

"This ain't so funny," Leonard said. "Them White Tree boys are gaining."

"Well speed it up," Scott said.

Leonard gnashed his teeth. "I could always get rid of some excess baggage, you know."

"Throwing that windshield wiper out ain't gonna help," Scott said.

Leonard looked in his mirror and saw the grinning nigger in the back seat. Nothing worse than a comic coon. He didn't even look grateful. Leonard had a sudden horrid vision of being overtaken by the White Tree boys. What if he were killed with the nigger? Getting killed was bad enough, but what if tomorrow they found him in a ditch with Farto and the nigger? Or maybe them White Tree boys would make him do something awful with the nigger before they killed them. Like making him suck the nigger's dick or some such thing. Leonard held his foot all the way to the floor; as they passed the Dairy Queen he took a hard left and the car just made it and Rex swung out and slammed a light pole then popped back in line behind them.

The White Tree boys couldn't make the corner in the station wagon and they didn't even try. They screeched into a car lot down a piece, turned around and came back. By that time the tail lights of the Impala were moving away from them rapidly, looking like two inflamed hemorrhoids in a dark asshole.

"Take the next right coming up," Scott said, "then you'll see a little road off to the left. Kill your lights and take that."

Leonard hated taking orders from Scott on the field, but this was worse. Insulting. Still, Scott called good plays on the field, and the habit of following instructions from the quarterback died hard. Leonard made the right and Rex made it with them after taking a dip in a water-filled bar ditch.

Leonard saw the little road and killed his lights and took it. It carried them down between several rows of large tin storage buildings, and Leonard pulled between two of them and drove down a little alley lined with more. He stopped the car and they waited and listened. After about five minutes, Farto said, "I think we skunked those father rapers."

"Ain't we a team?" Scott said.

In spite of himself, Leonard felt good. It was like when the nigger called a play that worked and they were all patting each other on the ass and not minding what color the other was because they were just creatures in football suits.

"Let's have a drink," Leonard said.

Farto got a paper cup off the floorboard for Scott and poured him up some warm Coke and whiskey. Last time they had gone to Longview, he had peed in that paper cup so they wouldn't have to stop, but that had long since been poured out, and besides, it was for a nigger. He poured Leonard and himself drinks in their same cups.

Scott took a sip and said, "Shit, man, that tastes kind of rank."

"Like piss," Farto said.

Leonard held up his cup. "To the Mud Creek Wildcats and fuck them White Tree boys."

"You fuck 'em," Scott said. They touched their cups, and at that moment the car filled with light.

Cups upraised, the Three Musketeers turned blinking toward it. The light was coming from an open storage-building door and there was a fat man standing in the center of the glow like a bloated fly on a lemon wedge. Behind him was a big screen made of a sheet and there was some kind of movie playing on it. And though the light was bright and fading out the movie, Leonard, who was in the best position to see, got a look at it. What he could make out looked like a gal down on her knees sucking this fat guy's dick (the man was visible only from the belly down) and the guy had a short, black revolver pressed to her forehead. She pulled her mouth off of him for an instant and the man came in her face then fired the revolver. The woman's head snapped out of frame and the sheet seemed to drip blood, like dark condensation on a windowpane. Then Leonard couldn't see anymore because another man had appeared in the doorway, and like the first he was fat. Both looked like huge bowling balls that had been set on top of shoes. More men appeared behind these two, but one of the fat men turned and held up his hand and the others moved out of sight. The two fat guys stepped outside and one pulled the door almost shut, except for a thin band of light that fell across the front seat of the Impala.

Fat Man Number One went over to the car and opened Farto's door and said, "You fucks and the nigger get out." It was the voice of doom. They had only thought the White Tree boys were dangerous. They realized now they had been kidding themselves. This was the real article. This guy would have eaten the hammer handle and shit a two-by-four.

They got out of the car and the fat man waved them around and lined them up on Farto's side and looked at them. The boys still had their drinks in their hands, and sparing that, they looked like cons in a lineup.

Fat Man Number Two came over and looked at the trio and smiled. It was obvious the fatties were twins. They had the same bad features in the same fat faces. They wore Hawaiian shirts that varied only in profiles and color of parrots and had on white socks and too-short black slacks and black, shiny, Italian shoes with toes sharp enough to thread needles.

Fat Man Number One took the cup away from Scott and sniffed it. "A nigger with liquor," he said. "That's like a cunt with brains. It don't go together. Guess you was getting tanked up so you could put the old black snake to some chocolate pudding after a while. Or maybe you was wantin' some vanilla and these boys were gonna set it up."

"I'm not wanting anything but to go home," Scott said. Fat

125

Man Number Two looked at Fat Man Number One and said, "So he can fuck his mother."

The fatties looked at Scott to see what he'd say but he didn't say anything. They could say he screwed dogs and that was all right with him. Hell, bring one on and he'd fuck it now if they'd let him go afterwards.

Fat Man Number One said, "You boys running around with a jungle bunny makes me sick."

"He's just a nigger from school," Farto said. "We don't like him none. We just picked him up because some White Tree boys were beating on him and we didn't want him to get wrecked on account of he's our quarterback."

"Ah," Fat Man Number One said, "I see. Personally, me and Vinnie don't cotton to niggers in sports. They start taking showers with white boys the next thing they want is to take white girls to bed. It's just one step from one to the other."

"We don't have nothing to do with him playing," Leonard said. "We didn't integrate the schools."

"No," Fat Man Number One said, "that was ole Big Ears Johnson, but you're running around with him and drinking with him."

"His cup's been peed in," Farto said. "That was kind of a joke on him, you see. He ain't our friend, I swear it. He's just a nigger that plays football."

"Peed in his cup, huh?" said the one called Vinnie. "I like that, Pork, don't you? Peed in his fucking cup."

Pork dropped Scott's cup on the ground and smiled at him. "Come here, nigger. I got something to tell you."

Scott looked at Farto and Leonard. No help there. They had suddenly become interested in the toes of their shoes; they examined them as if they were true marvels of the world.

Scott moved toward Pork, and Pork, still smiling, put his arm around Scott's shoulders and walked him toward the big storage building. Scott said, "What are we doing?"

Pork turned Scott around so they were facing Leonard and Farto who still stood holding their drinks and contemplating their shoes. "I didn't want to get it on the new gravel drive," Pork said and pulled Scott's head in close to his own and with his free hand reached back and under his Hawaiian shirt and brought out a short, black revolver and put it to Scott's temple and pulled the trigger.

126

There was a snap like a bad knee going out and Scott's feet lifted in unison and went to the side and something dark squirted from his head and his feet swung back toward Pork and his shoes shuffled, snapped, and twisted on the concrete in front of the building.

"Ain't that somethin'," Pork said as Scott went limp and dangled from the thick crook of his arm. "The rhythm is the last thing to go."

Leonard couldn't make a sound. His guts were in his throat. He wanted to melt and run under the car. Scott was dead and the brains that had made plays twisted as fishing worms and commanded his feet on down the football field were scrambled like breakfast eggs.

Farto said, "Holy shit."

Pork let go of Scott and Scott's legs split and he sat down and his head went forward and clapped on the cement between his knees. A dark pool formed under his face.

"He's better off, boys," Vinnie said. "Nigger was begat by Cain and the ape and he ain't quite monkey and he ain't quite man. He's got no place in this world 'cept as a beast of burden. You start trying to train them to do things like drive cars and run with footballs it ain't nothing but grief to them and the whites too. Get any on your shirt, Pork?"

"Nary a drop."

Vinnie went inside the building and said something to the men there that could be heard but not understood, then he came back with some crumpled newspapers. He went over to Scott and wrapped them around the bloody head and let it drop back on the cement. "You try hosing down that shit when it's dried, Pork, and you wouldn't worry none about that gravel. The gravel ain't nothing."

Then Vinnie said to Farto, "Open the back door of that car." Farto nearly twisted an ankle doing it. Vinnie picked Scott up by the back of the neck and the seat of his pants and threw him onto the floorboard of the Impala.

Pork used the short barrel of his revolver to scratch his nuts, then put the gun behind him, under his Hawaiian shirt. "You boys are gonna go to the river bottoms with us and help us get shed of this nigger."

"Yes, sir," Farto said. "We'll toss his ass in the Sabine for you."

"How about you?" Pork asked Leonard. "You trying to go weak sister?"

"No," Leonard croaked, "I'm with you."

"That's good," Pork said. "Vinnie, you take the truck and lead the way."

Vinnie took a key from his pocket and unlocked the building door next to the one with the light, went inside, and backed out a sharp-looking gold Dodge pickup. He backed it in front of the Impala and sat there with the motor running.

"You boys keep your place," Pork said. He went inside the lighted building for a moment. They heard him say to the men inside, "Go on and watch the movies. And save some of them beers for us. We'll be back." Then the light went out and Pork came out, shutting the door. He looked at Leonard and Farto and said, "Drink up, boys."

Leonard and Farto tossed off their warm Coke and whiskey and dropped the cups on the ground.

"Now," Pork said, "you get in the back with the nigger, I'll ride with the driver."

Farto got in the back and put his feet on Scott's knees. He tried not to look at the head wrapped in newspaper, but he couldn't help it. When Pork opened the front door and the overhead light came on Farto saw there was a split in the paper and Scott's eye was visible behind it. Across the forehead the wrapping had turned dark. Down by the mouth and chin was an ad for a fish sale.

Leonard got behind the wheel and started the car. Pork reached over and honked the horn. Vinnie rolled the pickup forward and Leonard followed him to the river bottoms. No one spoke. Leonard found himself wishing with all his heart that he had gone to the outdoor picture show to see the movie with the nigger starring in it.

The river bottoms were steamy and hot from the closeness of the trees and the under and overgrowth. As Leonard wound the Impala down the narrow, red clay roads amidst the dense foliage, he felt as if his car were a crab crawling about in a pubic thatch. He could feel from the way the steering wheel handled that the dog and the chain were catching brush and limbs here and there. He had forgotten all about the dog and now being reminded of it worried him. What if the dog got tangled and he had to stop? He didn't think Pork would take kindly to stopping, not with the dead burrhead on the floorboards and him wanting to get rid of the body.

128

Finally they came to where the woods cleared out a spell and they drove along the edge of the Sabine River. Leonard hated water and always had. In the moonlight the river looked like poisoned coffee flowing there. Leonard knew there were alligators and gars big as little alligators and water moccasins by the thousands swimming underneath the water, and just the thought of all those slick, darting bodies made him queasy.

They came to what was known as Broken Bridge. It was an old worn-out bridge that had fallen apart in the middle and it was connected to the land on this side only. People sometimes fished off of it. There was no one fishing tonight.

Vinnie stopped the pickup and Leonard pulled up beside it, the nose of the Chevy pointing at the mouth of the bridge. They all got out and Pork made Farto pull Scott out by the feet. Some of the newspapers came loose from Scott's head exposing an ear and part of the face. Farto patted the newspaper back into place.

"Fuck that," Vinnie said. "It don't hurt if he stains the fucking ground. You two idgits find some stuff to weight this coon down so we can sink him."

Farto and Leonard started scurrying about like squirrels, looking for rocks or big, heavy logs. Suddenly they heard Vinnie cry out. "Godamighty, fucking A. Pork. Come look at this."

Leonard looked over and saw that Vinnie had discovered Rex. He was standing looking down with his hands on his hips. Pork went over to stand by him, then Pork turned around and looked at them. "Hey, you fucks, come here."

Leonard and Farto joined them in looking at the dog. There was mostly just a head now, with a little bit of meat and fur hanging off a spine and some broken ribs.

"That's the sickest fucking thing I've ever fucking seen," Pork said.

"Godamighty," Vinnie said.

"Doing a dog like that. Shit, don't you got no heart? A dog. Man's best fucking goddamn friend and you two killed him like this."

"We didn't kill him," Farto said.

"You trying to fucking tell me he done this to himself? Had a bad fucking day and done this."

"Godamighty," Vinnie said.

"No, sir," Leonard said. "We chained him on there after he

129

was dead."

"I believe that," Vinnie said. "That's some rich shit. You guys murdered this dog. Godamighty."

"Just thinking about him trying to keep up and you fucks driving faster and faster makes me mad as a wasp," Pork said.

"No," Farto said. "It wasn't like that. He was dead and we were drunk and we didn't have anything to do, so we —"

"Shut the fuck up," Pork said, sticking a finger hard against Farto's forehead. "You just shut the fuck up. We can see what the fuck you fucks did. You drug this here dog around until all his goddamn hide came off... What kind of mothers you boys got anyhow that they didn't tell you better about animals?"

"Godamighty," Vinnie said.

Everyone grew silent, stood looking at the dog. Finally Farto said, "You want us to go back to getting some stuff to hold the nigger down?"

Pork looked at Farto as if he had just grown up whole from the ground. "You fucks are worse than niggers, doing a dog like that. Get on back over to the car."

Leonard and Farto went over to the Impala and stood looking down at Scott's body in much the same way they had stared at the dog. There, in the dim moonlight shadowed by trees, the paper wrapped around Scott's head made him look like a giant papier-mâché doll. Pork came up and kicked Scott in the face with a swift motion that sent newspapers flying and sent a thonking sound across the water that made frogs jump.

"Forget the nigger," Pork said. "Give me your car keys, ball sweat." Leonard took out his keys and gave them to Pork and Pork went around to the trunk and opened it. "Drag the nigger over here."

Leonard took one of Scott's arms and Farto took the other and they pulled him over to the back of the car.

"Put him in the trunk," Pork said.

"What for?" Leonard asked.

"'Cause I fucking said so," Pork said.

Leonard and Farto heaved Scott into the trunk. He looked pathetic lying there next to the spare tire, his face partially covered with newspaper. Leonard thought, if only the nigger had stolen a car with a spare he might not be here tonight. He could have gotten that flat changed and driven on before the White Tree boys even

130

came along.

"All right, you get in there with him," Pork said, gesturing to Farto.

"Me?" Farto said.

"Nah, not fucking you, the fucking elephant on your fucking shoulder. Yeah, you, get in the trunk. I ain't got all night."

"Jesus, we didn't do anything to that dog, mister. We told you that. I swear. Me and Leonard hooked him up after he was dead... It was Leonard's idea."

Pork didn't say a word. He just stood there with one hand on the trunk lid looking at Farto. Farto looked at Pork, then the trunk, then back to Pork. Lastly he looked at Leonard, then climbed into the trunk, his back to Scott.

"Like spoons," Pork said, and closed the lid. "Now you, whatsit, Leonard? You come over here." But Pork didn't wait for Leonard to move. He scooped the back of Leonard's neck with a chubby hand and pushed him over to where Rex lay at the end of the chain with Vinnie still looking down at him.

"What you think, Vinnie?" Pork asked. "You got what I got in mind?"

Vinnie nodded. He bent down and took the collar off the dog. He fastened it on Leonard. Leonard could smell the odor of the dead dog in his nostrils. He bent his head and puked.

"There goes my shoeshine," Vinnie said, and he hit Leonard a short one in the stomach. Leonard went to his knees and puked some more of the hot Coke and whiskey.

"You fucks are the lowest pieces of shit on this earth, doing a dog like that," Vinnie said. "A nigger ain't no lower."

Vinnie got some strong fishing line out of the back of the truck and they tied Leonard's hands behind his back. Leonard began to cry.

"Oh shut up," Pork said. "It ain't that bad. Ain't nothing that bad."

But Leonard couldn't shut up. He was caterwauling now and it was echoing through the trees. He closed his eyes and tried to pretend he had gone to the show with the nigger starring in it and had fallen asleep in his car and was having a bad dream, but he couldn't imagine that. He thought about Harry the janitor's flying saucers with the peppermint rays, and he knew if there were any saucers shooting rays down, they weren't boredom rays after all.

131

He wasn't a bit bored.

Pork pulled off Leonard's shoes and pushed him back flat on the ground and pulled off the socks and stuck them in Leonard's mouth so tight he couldn't spit them out. It wasn't that Pork thought anyone was going to hear Leonard, he just didn't like the noise. It hurt his ears.

Leonard lay on the ground in the vomit next to the dog and cried silently. Pork and Vinnie went over to the Impala and opened the doors and stood so they could get a grip on the car to push. Vinnie reached in and moved the gear from park to neutral and he and Pork began to shove the car forward. It moved slowly at first, but as it made the slight incline that led down to the old bridge, it picked up speed. From inside the trunk, Farto hammered lightly at the lid as if he didn't really mean it. The chain took up slack and Leonard felt it jerk and pop his neck. He began to slide along the ground like a snake.

Vinnie and Pork jumped out of the way and watched the car make the bridge and go over the edge and disappear into the water with amazing quietness. Leonard, pulled by the weight of the car, rustled past them. When he hit the bridge, splinters tugged at his clothes so hard they ripped his pants and underwear down almost to his knees.

The chain swung out once toward the edge of the bridge and the rotten railing, and Leonard tried to hook a leg around an upright board there, but that proved wasted. The weight of the car just pulled his knee out of joint and jerked the board out of place with a screech of nails and lumber.

Leonard picked up speed and the chain rattled over the edge of the bridge, into the water and out of sight, pulling its connection after it like a pull toy. The last sight of Leonard was the soles of his bare feet, white as the bellies of fish.

"It's deep there," Vinnie said. "I caught an old channel cat there once, remember? Big sucker. I bet it's over fifty-feet deep down there."

They got in the truck and Vinnie cranked it.

"I think we did them boys a favor," Pork said. "Them running around with niggers and what they did to that dog and all. They weren't worth a thing."

"I know it," Vinnie said. "We should have filmed this, Pork, it would have been good. Where the car and that nigger lover went off in the water was choice."

"Nah, there wasn't any women."

"Point," Vinnie said, and he backed around and drove onto the trail that wound its way out of the bottoms.

Ghost Jail
by Kaaron Warren

Rashmilla arrived early at the cemetery, knowing she would need to battle with the other beggars for a good place, not too close to the grave of the much-loved leader, not too far away. Cars stretched for a kilometre, spewing exhaust as they idled, waiting to park.

Rashmilla's face was dirty because the water didn't run every day. She waved a laminated letter at the people, a piece of paper which proved her house burned down and her five children, too. Many carried such a letter. They shared it. Once, a house did burn down with five children, but it was not Rashmilla's house. Not her children. There was a fire, when Rasmilla was seven, her mother's house, her twin sister burned to death. Her childhood ghost, now, always seven, always with her.

Rashmilla had a sack full of dried peas to sell. Most people refused the peas with a wave of a hand. "Please, for my children," she said, holding out her hand. Her childhood ghost wreathed around her neck like a cobra.

People gave generously; they always did at funerals. It was the fear of punishment in the afterlife, punishment for greed or cruelty. Rashmilla waved peas at the outer mourners and was about to push her way further in when she noticed a young child trapped in a closed circle of gravestones. Whimpering. His family ignored him; they did not like to think about how he could be saved.

Rashmilla stepped in, ignoring the whirl of angry spirits, letting her twin sister snarl at them. She told the child, "It's okay, I can help you," then stepped out again. He kept whimpering and Rashmilla hissed, "Sshhhshhh, they don't like voices. Voices make them envious and wild."

She walked slowly around the circle, reading the dead names in a stilted, cautious way. Then she worked at each gravestone with her fingers, finding the one which was the loosest. This, she pried up and tipped over.

The circle broken, the boy stepped out, silent now. He glared at his family, as if to say, "A strange woman had to save me." Rashmilla put her hand out to the mother. "Please," she said. The woman ignored her. Rashmilla stepped forward; she would be paid for helping the boy.

"You need to say thank you." It was the Police Chief, come himself for the important funeral. He stood beside Rashmilla, twice as broad across, two heads taller than her.

The boy nodded, his mouth open. He glanced sideways, looking for his mother to help him out of trouble.

"Saying thank you would be a good idea," the Police Chief said, his voice gentle. "Give her money."

The boy ran; Rashmilla shook her head. "It doesn't matter," she said. "I didn't do it to be thanked."

"Why then?" The Police Chief leaned closer, intent.

"Simply that those ghosts need to be told."

"What about this man's ghost? Whose death we mourn?" Police Chief Edwards said. He led her to the graveside, pushing through as if the other mourners didn't exist. Her childhood ghost muttered in her ear.

"Did he die in peace?" Rashmilla whispered. Her childhood ghost nodded, much braver.

Police Chief Edwards didn't smile or respond. Rashmilla thought he would beat her. She said, "His peaceful death will give him quiet," and the police chief smiled.

A small man, dressed neatly, threw himself into the mud. "Murder! Murder!" he wailed, and he threw both arms up, reaching for the Police Chief, as if beseeching him to take the act back.

Out of nowhere, men appeared, police sticks in hand.

"Such bitterness," Police Chief Edwards said to Rashmilla. "Such anger. It was an unfortunate death."

"Who killed this great man?" the small, neat man shouted. "Who silenced his great voice, who stilled his tongue and stopped his hand? Ask the question, ask it! Murder! And the guilty dare to stand here!" He squealed as the policemen dragged him away.

Rashmilla shut her eyes, not wanting to see, but the men were close, so close she could smell hair oil. She stepped back from the conflict and tripped over a stone, too fast for her childhood ghost, who leaned forward, wanting a better look.

"I want to talk to you. Don't be frightened." Chief Edwards looked at her ghost, not at her. "In the van. We'll sit in the van and I will buy all your peas. Your day will be done." He held out his elbow to her. "Come on," he said. "I have tea in the van. I will read your letter."

He was being very kind to her. Nobody read her letter; no one cared about her house fire. He held her arm with gentle firmness.

In the van he poured her a tin cup of tea. It was black and strong and she felt the energy of it filling her as she sipped it.

He watched her, a smile on his face she didn't like. He said, "There was a man buried here today. I will not lie and say that he was a good man; for all I know he beat his wife and spent his children's school fees on beer. But he still deserves to rest easy. Lies will send him to a restless grave. That mourner should not tell lies about how he died."

The van had thick walls, Rashmilla thought. She could not hear the prisoner in the back. She nodded. "I heard what he said. He said this man was murdered."

"He wishes to discredit the very people who save this country."

She closed her eyes, but her childhood ghost watched, sitting on her lap.

"I saw what you did for that young boy."

"I don't need a thank you."

"What you both did for that young boy."

She blinked at him.

"I can see her. Your ghost."

"Most can't."

"It's a talent which can be learned. It can be useful."

"Not useful. A nuisance. Always the one to tell those bad ghosts what to do."

"Yes, I saw that. You have a way with them."

"I know them."

Chief Edwards considered her. "You come to the barracks in three days and ask for me. I think I have a job for you."

"A job? At the barracks?" She imagined herself with a bucket, a mop, hot, bloody water.

"The job is not at the barracks, no. At the Cewa Flats. We are helping people to relocate. You must have heard. You come in three days, and I will tell you what I need you to do."

* * *

"Selena in the Morning here, DJ to the disaffected. Up and at 'em, people, we can't change the world from bed." Her voice was sexy, deep. She liked to talk in that way, like silk between the fingers. "I hear they've cleared the Cewa Flats because beneath them are the remnants of early settlers. Treasures, power. Police Chief Edwards wants it cleared because he wants that shit for himself. He's willing to risk the cancer, I bet."

She played a message from him: *"Because the breath is all that remains when we die. All that remains of us. The body can be burned, can be buried. The breath exhaled is the very essence of us. If that is tainted, cancerous, then no passage from earth will be gained."* His voice sounded so reasonable. *"It's for your own good to leave this place. This is no place for families. Children don't belong here."*

* * *

Lisa Turner, already at the computer, getting an hour in before leaving for the newspaper office, listened and smiled. She liked to start the day with Selena.

Lisa wondered how she managed to stay sharp, out of their reach, when she spoke the truth. They didn't like the truth.

Selena whispered in her heartfelt voice, "He's gonna rip up that yard for something buried. His Great Malevolence is gonna dig the crap out of it and we all know what he's gonna find. A few old stones the museum would be interested in, nothing else. The man is a fool."

Selena launched into her soap opera, names changed to protect the innocent, but she went too far with it, and the next morning Lisa tuned in like she did every day, only to hear the dull voice of a company man, playing sweet tunes and letting the words rest. "We don't need words," he announced. "Now is the time for music."

Lisa's editor Keith led the protest to bring Selena back to the airwaves. He used the newspaper and printed sheets, on the street, in letter-boxes, no names on there, no trouble. He used his contacts, his power. "Freedom of Speech the Victim," the campaign ran. Enough letters in, brave people willing to risk arrest

137

to have their say, and it was "Thank you, all of you," from Selena. A week after her removal she was back on the air. "I laughed so hard I split my pants when they banged on my door. No one wants to see my split pants. I have to be serious for just a moment. Thank you for wanting me back. I'll try to make it worth your while. I've got this for you: I've heard there's only one place in the city where electromagnetic interference means no bugging devices can be used. Cewa Flats. So if you're making a plot or think someone's watching you, this is the place for you. Sorry. I said I'd be serious and I lasted about a minute. Carry on without me for three minutes forty-five seconds," and she played a local song of hibiscus flowers and the river running clean.

Lisa and Keith arrived at the Cewa Flats to cover the evacuation of the families. She'd driven past the flats many times. At first she'd felt guilty, in her good car with her warm clothes on, seeing the children in torn singlets, bare legs. Rubbish piles. She'd felt all the guilt of privilege. But that faded; she got busy, distracted by bigger stories. She drove past without even noticing now. The flats were so small you could see through the front window and out the back. Four storeys high, ten rooms on each storey, six buildings. All the corners broken off, and a great crack running down the middle of building C, so broad she could see sky through it. Graffiti, written and written again, illegible and meaningless. The bricks, once pale yellow, were dark red. Lisa knew it was a chemical reaction within the pigment, but it looked blood-stained.

The children ran barefoot, in shorts too small, shirts too big.

Plastic bags full of belongings, the people waited for buses to transport them to their new homes. Lisa helped one woman with five children, each carrying two bags.

"We have nothing more," the mother said. Lisa had some canvas shopping bags in the car, and she gave them to the woman, helping her transfer the things. Grey, beige, some washed-out colours. Wrapped in a torn shawl was a hard box; the woman nodded at it. "All we have. My grandmother's coin of release."

Lisa knew a lot of these people came from kidnapped slaves.

The mother spoke with her hand over her mouth. Others did too, and some wore masks covering half their faces.

The children were mostly covered with headscarves.

"I can't breathe," one skinny little girl complained. "And this doesn't smell like air."

"You don't want to breathe until we leave. You don't want to catch Cancer of the Breath," the mother said to her.

Lisa shook her head. "You know there is no such thing. You can't get cancer of the breath."

"Oh? Then what is in my mouth to make this?" The woman dropped her bags, reached up and grabbed Lisa's ears, pulling her close.

The breath was awful, so bad Lisa gagged.

"You see? Even your white girl politeness can't stop you."

"That's not cancer of the breath. It's your teeth and gums."

"If you had children you would understand. You would not risk your child's breath to stay here."

"You should wear a scarf," the skinny little girl said to Lisa. "Your face is ugly and pink and shiny too much."

Lisa cared little for taunts about her burn scars. She was proud of them, proud of where they came from, though she never spoke of what she had achieved in getting them.

Other children rolled an old tyre to each other, a complex game with many a side.

A policeman gestured to the family. "The bus. Come on."

The mother gathered her children and they squeezed into the bus on laps, arms out the window.

"I'd like to come, see where you're being settled," Lisa said. The woman waved her away with a flap of the hand.

Keith had been helping another family. He said, "I'm imagining where they're going has to be better than this." He patted her shoulder. "I'm looking into the land reports. You chase this story up."

Lisa followed the buses to the new settlement, forty-five minutes away. The air was cleaner out there, and the shacks lined up neatly, each facing away from the door of the next. There was the sense of a village about it.

Lisa watched the children run around and explore. The parents calling to each other, laughing.

"It seems okay," she reported back to Keith.

"What did you expect? A work camp?"

"You never know. I haven't figured out his justification for getting rid of them."

Three days later, Keith's house was seized under the 'Uncontrolled Verbiage' ruling. He had written his editorial without restraint. He'd lived life too easy; he didn't know how it could get. He wrote: *No one with any critical assessment thinks the transfer of families from Cewa Flats is solely to benefit the children, although anyone can see that the people are far better off. Their new place is much finer; it is the motivation I call into question.*

He rang Lisa, told her he was going to stay at Cewa Flats before they came to arrest him. "Last place they'll expect me to be. And I can do some good there, you know. Prove this breath cancer bullshit isn't true."

"And if you're there, others are there; they won't be able to go ahead with the redevelopment. It's not like they can pull the place down around you. People will be watching. I'll be watching."

"You be careful, Lisa. You write only the truth. Give the rumours to Selena."

They both laughed.

"Truth in print. Gossip on the radio. As it should be."

Lisa understood about covering up; many days she buried small pieces of information, anything which might connect her to the long-past fire. She did not regret her actions, but she was terrified of the results.

* * *

Selena in the Morning said, "I've got it here. The land assessment report of the Cewa Flats, and I'm not going to tell you who gave it me. It's real, though. You know I said there were treasures buried? It's a little more than that. According to the report, the land itself is worth something, and the dirt, it's full of some sort of shit we need. Why should The Government get it, just like that?" The radio went quiet for a moment. Then music.

Selena was silent for three days, then Lisa pushed her way in for an interview with Police Chief Edwards. She lied; said it was a piece about mothers' cooking, how good it is, favourite recipes.

He was a big man, charming, with a dazzling smile. If she'd met him at a bar, any pick-up line would have worked.

He was furious when he realised where she stood. "How dare you? I am not a monster. I want families to be safe from people like you and your cancerous words." He threw her out, hissing, "Write nothing. Say nothing."

That night, Lisa heard a crash of glass downstairs and reached for the phone. Voices, and she knew for sure there was someone in the house.

She dialled Keith but his mobile didn't work; all she heard was a high-pitched squeal. Then she dialled her neighbours, hoping one would at least look out the window, shout at the invaders. No answer. Finally, in desperation, she called the police. She flipped open her computer and logged on at the same time.

The phone rang a dozen times. She heard the men downstairs, moving around as if they were looking for something. She quietly shut her bedroom door, then moved to look out the window. It was barred; she had no chance of getting out that way.

"Hold, please," the operator said.

Music, some old pop song, played on bells. "Help," she whispered. She hid in the cupboard. She didn't care what the men took; they could have it all. She didn't want to disturb them. They carried machetes, these home invaders, and guns. They would not always try to kill, but she knew that many arrived already out of it on booze or drugs.

"Hello?" she whispered into the phone. Footsteps on the stairs.

"Can I help you?" The cold, hard voice of the operator.

"My home is being invaded," she whispered. She gave her address. "Hold, please." The operator was remarkably calm; unaffected.

"Lisa Turner?" This came through the door. They knew her name.

"Lisa Turner, we have a warrant for the repossession of your home due to uncontrolled verbiage activity."

Lisa felt deep relief. Every day she spent in fear that her moment of activism would catch up with her, the grieving relatives perhaps would track her down and ask her why people had to die for her cause. Lisa did not regret the fire. The building had been on sacred ground and the activities inside destroyed the souls of the true residents of the country. She was sorry that people had to die, but it had been necessary. She had lost contact

141

deliberately with those who had instigated the attack; they had considered the deaths a victory, whereas she felt great pain, great guilt, and knew that she would have to atone for it one day.

The police operator hung up on her. As the men entered her room, Lisa hit *send*, and her notes went out to a dozen journalists and activists around the world.

She expected to be interviewed, locked up, but they gave her thirty minutes to pack her bag and leave her home.

They recommended a hotel for her to stay in, which made her laugh. They would watch her every move, listen to her every word.

Before he ran, Keith had told her, "We can't put friends or family at risk. If you need to, come join me. Don't go anywhere else. If they take your house, go there. It's the first stop. We'll get the bastards."

They confiscated Lisa's car too, so she hailed a taxi to take her to the Cewa Flats. They passed through a roadblock at the end of the street; Lisa wondered who it was they were keeping out. All the way the driver cleared his throat, spitting out the window. When they arrived, he turned and smiled at her. His teeth were red. "I'll be out of this country soon. I keep my mouth shut. I'm just waiting for my visa to come through."

"You know it won't, don't you? You know they're not letting anyone out. They've cancelled all visas, all passports."

He shook his head. "University Girl. You don't know how this country goes. You shouldn't tell lies to us."

Lisa climbed out, paying him a generous tip. "Good luck with it," she said. He gave her such a look of hatred she shut the door poorly and had to do it again.

The flats were dirty and huge up close. She stepped forward, over a grey, cracked path. The front dirt area was empty of people, a rare thing. Even after the families left, the young men remained, and they would hang together in clumps, moving as one large mass, always something in their hands to be tossed up and down, up and down.

None of the young men were here. In their rooms? Lisa looked up at the many dark doorways. Doorless.

An old woman took her hand and squeezed it. "I am Rashmilla. I will guide you through the spirits." She had an odd

142

shape, lumpy around the chest, as if she had a child hidden in there.

"Up there," she pointed. "You find a room up there. You scream if they bother you and I'll send my sister to talk to them."

Lisa saw the lump in Rashmilla's chest wriggle.

"You can see her?" Rashmilla whispered. She began to unbutton her dress; Lisa backed away, wanting to escape.

"If who bothers me?" Lisa said. "I have friends here, you know. They don't bother people. They speak the truth."

"I'm not talking about your friends, dear," Rashmilla said. "You will know when you meet one."

It was hard to tell a vacated room from an inhabited one. Families had left in a hurry, leaving rubbish, belongings behind. Small clay pots, some with grey ash to the rim, sat in many corners. Mouldy cushions, piles of mice-infested newspaper, remnants of clothes.

Lisa poked her head through a door on the top floor, saw a man sprawled on a mat and pulled back.

"Who's there? Who is it?" he called. "I'm at home."

Lisa backed away. He hadn't seen her and she didn't know him. He sounded desperate; too eager.

She changed her tactic after that; walked slowly past each door and tried to have a sideways peek through the shuttered window. The walls had posters, dismal and ancient attempts to bring colour and life to the small, dank rooms. They seemed embedded, welded to the walls.

She carried a small suitcase. She'd left the rest of her things behind in her house; she imagined the police would have been through everything by now and taken what they wanted. She found a room with a mat and a pile of empty, rusted tins, each with a dry residue at the bottom. She put down her suitcase and tried to find comfort. The rooms were three metres square, space for a mat and a sink which also did as a toilet, she could tell.

Looking from her window, all she could see were buildings: dark, rank, decrepit.

It was late – past eleven – and quiet. She curled onto her mat. It was hard and thin with smooth stains at either end. She pulled out a shirt and used that as a shield for her face.

In the morning, people started to emerge. A sense of community filled her. Of possibility. She could hear people talking quietly, and footsteps, people moving around, making breakfast and, she hoped, coffee. She recognised faces: people she knew. From the inside out the room didn't look so bad. She had a view, when she stood on her toes and squinted, of a small shrove of trees which would bear fruit during the wet season. With a small breeze she fancied she could smell the fruit. It was intoxicating, like the first sniff of a good wine.

She liked wine. Felt an emptiness for it. That first sip around the dinner table, already knowing that the conversation would become freer the more people drank. That soon they would be shouting, making plans, talking of outrages, human rights and moving the country forward.

She saw Rashmilla one floor down in the building to her left. She called out but her voice seemed muffled. She tried again but then... She opened her mouth to call out again and from her feet, from through the floor, rose a tall thin ghost, a man with red lesions along his cheekbones. He raised his fist and she flinched, unprepared.

He thrust the fist into her mouth and out, so fast all she felt was a mouthful, then nothing but the taste of anchovies left behind.

She reached to grab him but he leapt over the balcony, over so fast he blurred in her eyes.

She heard nothing.

She looked over and there was nothing, only Rashmilla looking up, her face serene.

Lisa ran; got to the stairwell, turned around and the ghost was right beside her, fist raised. With his other hand he shushed her, finger to lips.

She hated to be shushed. "I won't..." she started, but the fist again, in and out of her mouth again, how the hell? She couldn't even get her own fist in there.

She watched him this time over the side and down to the ground where he seemed to... disintegrate.

Lisa dragged herself down the stairs. There were people in many of the rooms, most with their hands over their ears. Others moved up and down the stairs, purposeless. She knew some of them, had sat and talked all night with them, but none of them acknowledged her or seemed willing to even meet her eyes.

Rashmilla slid up to her as she reached the bottom step. "I don't want peas," Lisa said, waving her away.

"Have you understood?"

Lisa's eyes adapted; she could see a young girl, the ghost of a young girl, resting herself on Rashmilla's chest. Lisa could see her face, her teeth, she could see the dirty scarf she wore around her neck.

"I understand I won't stay here." Lisa stepped away. Rashmilla grabbed her arm, reached out and touched Lisa's scarred cheek.

"You were burned badly in a fire. I look at you and think of loss. Of all the things gone in the fire."

Rashmilla had the skin of a child. Soft, pale brown, unblemished; it was wrong for her.

Lisa pushed past; Rashmilla hissed, "You behave ugly, you get the cancer of the breath."

"I don't believe you."

"It doesn't matter if you believe or not. This is not about belief." There were deep holes here, dug by bored children.

Lisa reached the stone path and trod carefully this time, lifting her foot over it.

Something grabbed her ankle, both ankles, and pulled her back. No time to prepare, she landed with a crack on her chin and lay there, pain blurring her thoughts of all else.

"You can't step over the gravestones," Rashmilla said, shaking her head. She dabbed at Lisa's chin with a filthy rag. "They moved them so carefully, laying them down one by one. It doesn't matter, though. The ghosts don't care about how gentle they were."

Lisa crawled from stone to stone and saw that Rashmilla was telling the truth: the names, the dates of the long-dead, the recently-dead, their stones laid close together.

Lisa pushed herself up and ran to her room, ignoring the whisper of the ghosts around her.

She turned on her laptop to send some emails, get some action. The outrage at such desecration; surely that would get a response. Her first message was to Selena. There was a woman of power, with a voice. Selena needed to know the place wasn't safe, that it wasn't a good place to meet. There were ghosts.

145

The battery was dead though, and she felt a sense of great disconnection.

Rashmilla knocked at their doors one by one. "You will listen to the speech," she told everyone, "You will listen when he speaks."

"Listen," her childhood ghost echoed, "Listen to the man in the van."

Police Chief Edwards, broadcasting through the speakers of his large white van, said, "Language is a violence. You lepers bring cancer of the breath to the people; it is best you are kept away from the deserving, the good people of this land who support what we are doing and accept it."

Lisa saw Keith, waved at him, wanting his help. *Look at me, look at me.* He scratched under his arms and went back inside.

She circled around Rashmilla, then went up the stairs to Keith's room. The smell of human waste was terrible. Did they all use the sinks? With barren ground surrounding the buildings, she couldn't see why people would use sinks for their toilet.

Keith lay on his mat. She had never seen him inactive; it looked odd. Even when he rested he would read, take notes, do something. He lay there, almost motionless.

"Keith," she said. "It's me. I'm here."

There was a stirring around her, like bats she couldn't see.

"They don't like you to talk loud," he said. He got up. "I'd ask you in but there's not really any room."

"There isn't. This place is awful, Keith. It's haunted."

"It's safe," he said, but his eyes were closed as he spoke.

"It's not safe. There are ghosts here who don't want us to speak."

"They don't like noise. They don't mind quiet talking."

"What about talking about our situation?" she said. Keith curled up away from her, blocking his ears with his shoulders, his hand over his mouth. At her ankles she felt a tugging, and she looked down to see the ghost of a legless man, his fist drawn, his face livid.

"Quiet," Keith whispered.

"I'm not staying here, Keith. This is not a haven. Haven't you realised that?"

The look he gave her made her feel shallow and empty.

146

Keith turned his back to her, curled up on his mat and hummed softly.

"We'll get out of here," Lisa said. "I'll find a way and we'll get out."

Keith gave a low moan, blocking his ears. Lisa felt a cool breeze behind her and turned to see a gelid old ghost of a woman, shaking with fury. The woman lifted her arms and flew at Lisa, clutching her fingers at Lisa's throat.

Lisa choked, trying to suck in air. It smelt like old potatoes.

The old woman thrust her thumbs into Lisa's mouth and pinched. The pain brought tears to her eyes. Her terror was so complete she felt as if no other word would ever come from her.

The old woman vanished in a faster-than-light flash. Lisa turned to see Keith sitting up, hugging his knees.

"Shhh," he said.

She left him and went to lie on her own mat, to think. Surely she was able to think.

The moment she closed her eyes her head was filled with voices, a mess of noise she couldn't make sense of. The voices were flat, dull; it sounded like thirty people reading the newspaper aloud in a language unfamiliar to them.

She lay with her eyes open, letting her body rest. She felt a deep exhaustion. She had not felt such sustained fear since the fire. That, at least, had been a tangible threat with an obvious course of action; if she was caught, she would confess and never give any names away.

Here... but there was something she could do. She scrabbled for her phone and found it. The battery was fully charged, but she could get no signal except a high- pitched squeal which made her want to jump out of the window.

Lisa tried again, and again, and once more to step over the stone path, but she couldn't. The ghosts screamed in her ears; she felt a pop, as if her eardrums had burst, and a sharp pain which felt like a knitting needle in one ear and out the other.

"Can you call someone to visit? I have a friend I want to contact."

Rashmilla shook her head. Her childhood ghost laughed, spun around.

"You can't leave."

"Will you call her for me? I'll pay you."

Rashmilla shook her head. "You don't want me to leave the ghosts alone. They are nice when I'm here."

"Nice?" Lisa looked at her to see if she was making a cruel joke.

"They behave for me."

"Why can you step out?"

"They don't know if I'm a ghost or a woman."

"If we lift the stones will the circle be broken?" Lisa felt nausea and pain when trying to talk. The ghosts of two young boys with yellow eyes pulled her backwards.

"They are set in concrete. Cannot be lifted. You could read the names but they don't want to be released."

"Her name's Selena. She's on the radio."

Rashmilla nodded. "I know that lady. The Police Chief calls her Sell. He says, *Sell, what do you think,* but he doesn't listen to her answer. I see through every window. Sell lies naked with the Police Chief."

"Selena?" Lisa had never felt so stupid, so naïve, so ill-informed and betrayed. Her career was a joke; she could not research, write or investigate to save her life.

"How do we stop the ghosts?" she asked, looking over her shoulder. The ghosts rose up, snarling, teeth bared in fury.

"There is no way," Rashmilla said. "They don't like noise, they don't like talk, they are caught by the endless circle of stones."

A taxi pulled up, and a young man stepped out. Lisa knew him, the editor of a local 'radical' magazine. She'd met him a few times at drinks, and they'd spoken of change, of effecting change. She'd e-mailed him at the moment her house was taken. She didn't know if he'd responded or not.

"Don't step in," she tried to shout, but the ghosts of the young boys kicked her shins, knocked her to the ground and hovered their filthy faces in hers. There were bleeding cuts on their cheekbones.

Rashmilla stepped out to greet him, then helped him into the circle. Her childhood ghost ruffled his hair, looked into his ears.

"Dale," Lisa said. One of the ghost boys grabbed her tongue, spat in her mouth. "Dale, lift the stones," she said, but he didn't hear her, didn't recognise her in the dirt. He caught his toe on a

148

jagged corner and tripped. He broke his fall with the heel of one hand, and a sharp edge sliced into the soft mound and blood oozed out.

He walked his arrogant, hip-thrusting walk, past her to the stairs. Rashmilla helped him, but Lisa could see the ghosts hovering behind her, waiting for her to release him.

A scream came, harsh and odd in the silence.

She still had the energy to step forward and look, see what had caused the noise. Other people did too, men and women dragging themselves out of their small, stinking rooms to see Keith, fallen or pushed, splattered on the ground.

There was a sigh, a collective sigh, not of sorrow but of pure envy. "Lucky lucky lucky lucky lucky," Lisa heard, the people whispered, "Lucky lucky lucky" but none of them leapt over, none of them had the strength or the power to die.

Lisa opened her mouth to let the noise out, but around her the ghosts waved their fists and she swallowed it down.

Lisa thought of all the silenced voices and how many more there would be. Soon this place would be empty again, starved husks removed or left to rot or to be buried by anyone who had the strength.

She felt a great sense of impetus, of gravity.

Lisa said, "Do you have any matches?"

Rashmilla said, "Give me money." Lisa gave her all, gave her everything she had.

She thought clothing would burn well, so she went upstairs and put everything from her suitcase on. The T-shirt with 'Bali – Party Town' on it that she wore to bed. The scarf her mother knitted her. The jeans she bought in Hong Kong and wished she'd bought ten pairs, because they were perfect.

She put all that on. She collected a can of fuel from under the stairs and stood there, out of sight. She struck a match.

The ghosts were furious, ripping out her hair, tearing it out in chunks, tripping her. The ghosts came at her and she felt her energy leaving. She had to finish it.

Lisa struck another match. She heard whining behind her. Rashmilla said, "What are you doing? You have made them angry." Her childhood ghost clung to her, hiding her eyes in the torn material of her dress.

Lisa set fire to her scarf, to the long sleeves of her shirt, to the cuffs of her jeans. She fell to her knees as she burnt, screaming with pain, so full of it she no longer noticed the ghosts. From the great heat to cold. She had been under anaesthetic three times before and this felt like it: the cold starting at the entry point, in the arm, and pumping with the blood till her heart was chilled to stillness.

She grabbed a gravestone and she felt something shifting, moving inside her. Her ghost lifting. The body slumped; her ghost flew up.

"You won't last. You are not meant for here," Rashmilla said. "You can't escape. We have tried." Her childhood ghost shook her head.

"Shhh," Lisa said, and thrust her fist into Rashmilla's mouth.

Keith joined her, fresh ghost, lacking bitterness, unconfined. They moved together, waiting for Police Chief Edwards, for Selena and others like them. Ready to fill their mouths with fists and hair, ready to stop their words and change the world.

The Torturer
by Steve Duffy

Usually, he's home in time for supper. His most recent promotion means he rarely has to work evenings, not like the early years of their marriage when he was used to pulling long shifts at unsociable hours. Undoubtedly, status has its compensations. On the other hand, it's a longer drive home to their new house in the suburbs. You win some, you lose some, he tells himself.

He steers his convertible off the broad tree-lined street and parks up in the driveway, a meticulously laid sweep of herringboned brick of which he's excusably proud. A well-built man in the peak of physical condition, he stretches his limbs till the tendons creak, till the cramp of rush-hour driving is eased. He lopes over to the knot of children – his own, the neighbours' – playing soccer on the lawn, and traps their ball. Teasingly he rolls it back to them, calls for the return pass. The neighbour-children are shy, and he tries unsuccessfully to include them in the fun with an impromptu game of pass-and-run. In the end he's playing by himself, more or less: juggling the ball on his instep, keepy-uppy, ten times, a dozen, twenty. Losing control, he boots it high over the trees out into the street, bellowing with laughter as the children scatter.

Inside the house, there's a peck on the cheek for his wife on his way through to the back yard, where he romps for a while with the dogs, two tubby German shepherds getting on in years, retired guard dogs from the old facility. He drags them playfully back and forth by their coarse ruglike neck fur, forces them over onto their backs, into the attitude of submission. Their heavy outdoor smell accompanies him back inside the house.

Upstairs in the bathroom, he chucks his shirt and underwear into the laundry basket, showers for ten minutes precisely and dries himself slowly in front of the mirror. Towel too vigorously, and you'll only sweat again. What's the use of that? Of course he showered at work, at the end of his shift; but this is different. This is the start of the evening, *his* time. Quality time. The home shower is part of his routine, and has little to do with strict hygienic necessity. He takes pleasure in the way his mind switches off beneath the steaming hot jets; the way the water courses the length of his body, sleeking down his abundant body hair, washing away the day and all its clamours, all its niggling inconveniences.

Supper is eaten as a formal meal in the dining area. He admonishes through mouthfuls of roast the children who sit half-turned from the table, sneaking peeks at the TV through the room divider while they eat. Loudly he organises the clearing of cutlery and crocks, directing the young ones to carry their plates through for Mother to put in the dishwasher, one-two-three, smart little soldiers on kitchen duty. Afterwards, they go through to the lounge as a family and watch television, the remote control never leaving his hand. He argues with the newsreader, groans at the weatherman, then roars with bullish hilarity at the slapstick antics of the two popular comedians: the tall skinny one, the little fatty, their pratfalls, their disasters. So comic, you can't help but laugh.

Bedtime is nine-thirty sharp, which is a trifle late for the youngest, but much too early for the eldest – or so she protests. He dismisses her complaints with a look and a finger drawn across the throat. By ten, his wife is back downstairs from bathing and bedtime stories, and he sends her for another bottle of his favourite imported beer. When she returns from the kitchen his hand is already extended, waiting.

An hour or so later, his wife is yawning horribly, hands covering her thin nervous face. He sends her off upstairs with a kiss and a promise from the depths of his recliner. Early-to-bed has never been his way; it reminds him too much of the old days, when he was obliged to submit to the rules, rather than enforce them. More and more it's his pleasure to sit in the darkened lounge, not really watching the television, his mind elsewhere, thoughts that drifted through the day now winding down to rest.

When the national anthem plays over stock patriotic footage – the flag that waves so proudly at the national shrine to the martyrs, the head of state taking the salute at the Heroes' Day parade – he comes automatically to his feet, startled from his reverie. As the last glorious notes die away and the screen resolves to static, he points his remote control at the TV and clicks it off.

The sudden dark disorientates him: he'd assumed there'd be a light on somewhere. Gradually his eyes adjust, and he begins to pick out familiar shapes in the gloom. He gropes his way through to the kitchen for more beer, squinting as the light inside the big

152

refrigerator blinks to life. He takes the rest of the tray – three bottles left of the eight – out onto the front porch.

Towards two a.m. the torturer is still sitting on his porch, smoking and drinking steadily. The street is quiet; the windows of the neighbouring houses are for the most part dark. Somewhere a steeple clock chimes the hour, *clang, clang*. He gets up, yawning horribly; the beer has gone to his head, and he takes a second to find his balance. He uncaps the last bottle on the porch rail – a slap of the palm across the angle of bottle-top and woodwork – and swigs, long and deep. Beer in hand, he strolls over to his convertible.

It's a foreign model, something he picked out from the pound around this time last year, thirsty on the juice as you'd expect but pretty much untouchable on the straight. From the back seat he lifts a vinyl sports holdall, slings it over his shoulder and walks to the open garage. There, he dumps the bag on a workbench and switches on the fluorescent strip. With a stuttering buzz the starter kicks in; one drowsy moth flutters up from its roost among the tools towards the humming tube.

He rummages in the bag, pulls out a heavy elasticated strap with metal hooks at each end, the kind of thing motorcyclists use to secure luggage on their pillions. The woven fabric covering of the strap is noticeably frayed in places: some of the elastic core is exposed and starting to unravel. Here and there on the red and yellow fabric are dark, wet-looking stains. You might think the strap had been gnawed by a large dog, perhaps, but the German shepherds have never been near it. They may urinate occasionally against the wheels of the car, sniff the whitewalls for the spoor of other dogs, leap into the passenger seat even, but they know better than to touch the holdall. The whole family knows better than that.

Experimentally, he tugs at the strap, stretching it like chest expanders to the fullest extent. The fraying is really quite bad. He shakes his head at the damage, and tosses the compromised strap away into a corner of the garage where the children leave their toys. Something catches his eye there in the corner. The junior trials bike belonging to his middle boy sits propped up on its frame. A plastic safety helmet, gloves tucked away inside, is secured to the saddle by a pair of straps exactly like the one he has just discarded.

He retrieves the frayed strap from the floor, and swaps it for

153

one of those securing the helmet. Pulling the new one taut a couple of times, he grunts in satisfaction. He zips his latest acquisition away in the holdall, glancing out through the open garage door as he does so. Tree-shadowed lamplight falls on the quiet street and empty sidewalks. Away towards the city, the distant sound of sirens, not uncommon in these days of the curfew's reimposition. Here, in the comfortable suburbs, nothing.

He shoulders the holdall, retrieves his beer bottle from the workbench and walks back out onto the porch. With one giant swallow he downs the rest of the beer, then unslings the zipped-up holdall. He hefts it for weight, swings it by its strap, then tosses it, clear across the lawn, straight into the back seat of his open-top convertible. It's a circus shot! He shoots, he scores! The laughter jerks out of him – he hadn't meant to laugh, and it takes him by surprise. He looks at the empty beer bottle in his other hand for a moment, then hurls it too, out towards the sidewalk.

It sails end over end in a high arc into the night, crashing through the foliage of the plane trees before shattering into pieces in the middle of the street. The sound of breaking glass shears through the stillness, such panic in the brittle detonation, such unease. It mingles with his laughter, more deliberate this time, louder and more evidently drunken. Up and down the street, lights click on in some of the houses. These lights are soon extinguished – all the good folk hereabouts are sensibly loath to poke their noses into other people's business – and by the time the torturer stumbles up to bed everything is calm once more.

The bedroom is dark, thick velvet curtains drawn tight. Out of consideration for his wife he does not switch on the bedside lamp, though he knocks it over noisily in the process of tugging off his pants. The room sways and lurches as he wrestles with his boxer shorts. His stomach sends up a premonitory flux of hot acid. His head, his fucking dizzy – Jesus… Convulsively, he dives on to the bed, like a swimmer breasting a wave contaminated with sewage. The pillows piled against the headboard carry – or so it seems to him – the smell, or taint, of sleep, of dreams. He beats them down with his slackening fists and lapses almost immediately into profound, overwhelming unconsciousness. Sooner or later, he will be visited by dreams… by one dream in particular, recurring most nights.

There will be a passage, a corridor he's seen a thousand

times, though never yet in the waking world. Its bare concrete floor stained with liquid waste, its unrendered breezeblock walls, remind him of the cattle market in the rural province where he grew up – the stink is the same, he recognises it immediately. He remembers the market, how the ranchers would bring the beeves in their hundreds to be sold, then slaughtered onsite. He was just a child then, waiting hours on end for his terrible, magnificent father to conclude his ponderous deals, and while the old man haggled he would go and watch the cattle being driven up the ramps.

Staring into those mournful liquid eyes with their astonishingly feminine lashes, long streaks of gluey tears gumming up the canthus, he would feel nothing but contempt for the cattle and their Christ-like submissiveness. Sometimes he and the other boys would pelt them with stones as they bucked and jostled in their stalls, and laugh at their frantic bullocking panic, their high-pitched snorts and bellows. Dogs would roam the perimeters of the pens, sniffing the excreta that flowed along the reeking gutters, yelping submissively at the slaughter-master's kick. In the darkness of the far sheds, the dim aproned men with the bolt guns and the hammers, waiting, always waiting. All events proceed toward their necessary conclusion.

This corridor, the dream-passage, is something like the antechamber of that abattoir from long ago, even down to the stink, the sweetish, slyly intimate mixture of shit and piss and muck-sweat. It winds and rambles, the corridor, it draws him on through compound twists and turns to a huge room beyond, an enormous room, bare and echoing, unfeasibly large and utterly empty. It is so massive, the room, that as he stands at one end of it the further end is lost in the shadows. Slowly, with an indecision he's schooled himself never to feel in the waking world, he steps forward into the vast open space. He has walked no more than half a dozen steps when the lights go out.

The panic that overwhelms him is unmitigated and immediate. Though she does not know where he is in that instant, though she knows nothing of the detail because he has never told her and she never dares to ask, still his wife has become familiar with this passage of his nightmare, from outside as it were. A helpless spectator of the effects, yet innocent of their unknowable cause, still she recognises the change that comes over him in his sleep: the lather of sweat that coats his body, the sheets pulled

155

clear of his threshing limbs. She knows only too well the sound he makes, the sound of a small and frightened child, so utterly incongruous it might almost be laughable. But in this bedroom, laughter has absented itself indefinitely.

Meanwhile in the dream, after a chaotic and terrible caesura, the lights come on again, and the torturer is sitting in a chair that is turned towards the wall. The unrendered breezeblocks, bare of stucco or plaster, are perhaps an arm's length away from his face. Behind him, the long room recedes into infinity. He is aware of this, perhaps through some quality of the echoes, of the movement of the air; but he cannot see it, for he cannot turn his head even a fraction of an inch. In fact, he is immobile: he does not move, nor seek to move, because he knows he cannot stir a muscle.

Are there restraints that bind him to the chair, are there clamps or belts or irons? He believes so, though when he looks there's nothing there. Still, he cannot move. He is naked, and he cannot move. There are rules in this dream-room of the dream-world. There are rules, and he does not, cannot know them. He should have memorised them beforehand, he should be able to reel them off by rote, but he cannot. He knows only that somehow he has broken them, these awful ancient rules. And now, immobilised and helpless, he awaits his certain fate.

The sounds behind him seem to come from a long way away. It is these sounds, perhaps, that first evoked the memory of the slaughterhouse: soft snorts, the clanking of chains, the scraping of a hoof on rough concrete. He is conscious of some other being that shares this space with him, of a presence in the room. In a school book once he saw a drawing of a minotaur, and the awful image will not be erased from his thoughts in this instant.

When the footsteps come, slowly and deliberately, he will be so still and so quiet, though they seem to take forever to reach him. When the footsteps stop, and the last of their echoes roll off the wall in front of him, even then he will remain quiet, as quiet as a little mouse. Even when he hears the breathing behind him, a dry, slightly ragged panting, he will be motionless as a statue. And when he feels the hands reach round, grasping, pinching, he will not make the slightest response. Those stiffly probing fingers which press and squeeze and poke, which force their way inside him and penetrate the very centre of his being: not even these will stir him to a reaction. No conscious reaction at least, although no, oh no, oh please God no... Tearless, unyielding, his eyes will stare directly ahead as he feels his shameful erection swelling despite his every effort. He will not be responsible, he will not acknowledge anything. He will see only the grey roughness of the breezeblock wall, and he will not make a sound.

When he wakes up, bedclothes twisted in his fist, pillows strewn across the floor, prick stiff as a truncheon, he will remember nothing. Not in the morning shower, where his slick oily night sweat is sluiced off in incomprehensible haste; not at the breakfast table, at which he is notoriously unapproachable even after his third cup of strong black coffee. Not in the honking, shunting gridlock of the drive into town, nor yet in the astringent camaraderie of his fellow law enforcement professionals as, some fifteen minutes late – *fucking traffic, this city, I tell you* – he enters the duty room.

Not ever, in these waking hours. Outwardly, inwardly, he is himself, inviolate, untouched and unaffected. Only an echo, perhaps, comes back to him: an apostrophe in the day's frantic diatribe, a turning aside to the secret sharer, the hidden self. A beat as he pauses, one hand on the door-knob of Interview C, the room they call the dungeon. In this instant of fugue, this *déjà vu* unfixable on any conscious level of his memory, his cheek is brushed as if by the wing of a moth in the dark; reverberations from a rough wall of breezeblock, the hum of a fluorescent strip light, the shattering of glass in the night.

A bull enraged by clustered flies, he shakes his lowered head. His hand tightens on the metal knob, and he flings opens the door. Impetuously, at a rush, he enters the windowless room, the centro-symmetrical universe of *how*, but never *why*. Why? *Because.*

Reconciled, assimilated, overfilled with darkly radiant bonhomie, he greets his colleagues gathered round the dentist's chair. His voice is loud, far too loud for such a cramped, unventilated room. With ogreish enthusiasm he begins to tell the subject, the bruised and bleeding man strapped into the chair, what will happen to him, there, in the chair, in the room. The door swings shut on them, the jovial torturer and his slumped prey. The corridor relapses into silence; a silence as oppressive as terror and despair.

Methods of Confinement
by Gary McMahon

*The degree of civilisation in a society can
be judged by entering its prisons.*
— Fyodor Dostoevsky

The return journey was often worse than actually travelling there.

Sheila boarded the old bus that would take her from the prison gates to the train station in Leicester, where she would be required to wait at least another half-hour before a train arrived to take her home to Yorkshire – via a forty-minute layover in Derby, of course. All this way just to spend a couple of hours struggling to fill the silence that yawned between her and David like a vast hole in the floor, neither of them willing to get too close to the edge. Sometimes she wondered why she even bothered to visit him at all, and if it really made any difference to his state of mind.

Just as the bus set off it shuddered to an abrupt halt. The doors rattled open and somebody below Sheila's eyeline struggled on board. "Thanks, love," said a coarse, heavily accented voice she thought she recognised. "Thought you were gonna go off without me."

Sheila took her book out of her handbag – a novel by Paul Auster, an American writer she'd recently discovered through a work colleague – and opened it at the first page. She glanced up to see who was struggling along the narrow aisle, directly behind a small, fair-haired child. Sheila's suspicions were confirmed: it was the woman she'd spoken to briefly back at the prison, in the ugly little waiting room before her visit. Small, undernourished, with bony hands and a flat chest; dyed blonde hair scraped aggressively back into a severe ponytail, sallow complexion. The woman's pale eyes darted from side to side, looking for someone to latch onto.

Sheila hid her face behind Auster's words, squeezed shut her eyes and prayed that she would not be disturbed. She was relieved when the woman took a seat a few rows down from her own, vocally encouraging the silent boy who accompanied her to take the window seat as she slipped into the space next to him.

A chapter into her book, Sheila glanced up and saw that they were already approaching the train station. Checking her belongings, she waited until everyone else had disembarked before standing and making her way down to the front of the bus. She paused for a moment, making sure the woman was nowhere in immediate sight, before finally setting foot onto the steps. "Thanks," she muttered to the driver as she descended. He just stared ahead, through his windscreen, ignoring her. *I'm not one of them*, she felt like telling him. *I'm a good person, an honest person. Not one of them.* But it would serve no use; the driver had her tagged as a loser, as if she had a symbol tattooed onto her forehead.

Stepping down onto the concrete footpath beneath a cold grey sky, she experienced a moment of disorientation. What was she doing here? She should be at home, or perhaps returning there after a day spent working at the office. Certainly she should not be here, standing in the premature twilight, preparing to get on a train. She looked up, straining to see a hint of brightness beyond the sullen clouds, but the sky was darkening fast, signalling the inevitable approach of an early November night.

Behind her, the bus doors crashed shut. The engine grumbled, but the vehicle remained where it was, parked at the kerb. When she looked back, into the cab, the driver seemed to be grinning in her direction. Sheila hurried away towards the station, feeling even more alienated.

The platform was dotted with other prison visitors whose faces she recalled from the bus, most of whom were women dressed in cheap sportswear – tracksuits and training shoes – or the occasional pair of grubby denim jeans. Sheila felt out of place in her plain knee-length skirt and sweater, the expensive jacket she'd recently bought from Debenhams with her yearly bonus draped across her shoulders like a truncated cape. She moved to the end of the platform, furthest away from everyone else, and stared into empty space.

The darkness crowded in around her, making her feel strangely oppressed. A man on the opposite side of the station, separated from her by the train tracks, staggered to the edge of the platform and stood there, swaying. As she watched, he unzipped

159

his trousers and began to urinate onto the tracks. It was a depressing sight, and Sheila was unsure which troubled her most, the fact that he was so obviously drunk this early in the evening or his casual display of vulgarity.

"Put it away, man. You don't know where it's been!" The voice sounded alarmingly close to her right ear, and when Sheila spun around to confront its owner the last thing she expected was the woman from the bus – the one she'd been trying to avoid – standing next to her, a vicious sneer carved into her heavily-made-up features. "Dirty bastard," she said, turning to Sheila. Her eyes were dull and flat, as if all colour had been bled from them, and her lips were pale and thin. The fair-haired boy stood at her side, staring at the urinating man. His face was devoid of expression.

"Oh, hi," said Sheila. "Yeah, that's pretty grim."

"I'm Caitlin. I saw you on the bus, but you looked really into your book so I didn't bother to give you a shout." The woman's rush of words sounded oddly like a challenge. Sheila did not respond; she was unsure of what to say and of the reaction she might provoke.

"Getting chilly." Sheila shrugged her arms into her jacket and fastened the buttons across her chest, then stood waiting for the woman to either say something else or move away.

The boy said nothing. He did not even stir.

"I'm Sheila." She put out a hand, but the gesture went unnoticed. Or perhaps Caitlin didn't understand what it meant.

"We didn't get much of a chance to chat in there, did we? In the prison, I mean. I looked for you outside, when I went for a fag, but you weren't there." Again that subtle note of menace: the woman's voice held a note of antagonism, as if she were deliberately attempting to elicit a defensive response.

"I don't smoke," said Sheila.

"Ah. That explains it, then. She don't smoke, Joe. Hear that, eh? Don't smoke." She stretched out the sentence as if she were speaking to someone with learning difficulties – perhaps that explained why the boy was so quiet and unresponsive.

"Do... do you know when the train's due in?" For some reason, Sheila was beginning to feel uncomfortable that the boy was so unmoving. She knew exactly what time the train was scheduled to arrive – in seven minutes' time – but it was all she could think of to break into the odd atmosphere.

"Soon," said Caitlin, and it sounded like yet another non sequitur. "It'll be here soon." The smile she wore was unnatural, more like a sly expression of mirth than a friendly gesture meant to put one at ease.

The man opposite had stumbled away to sit on a wooden bench against the ticket office wall. His head lolled to one side as he slept, and in the growing uneasy silence Sheila fancied she could hear the low, abrasive sound of his snoring. Two men in dark grey uniforms appeared at his side. Sheila suspected they had stepped out of some hidden doorway from the ticket office, but could make none out in the gloom.

"Who you visiting?"

Caitlin's question took her by surprise, so she answered without pausing for thought: "My brother, David."

"What's he in for?"

She was aware that this kind of information was usually shared freely between family and friends of the criminal fraternity, and almost worn as a badge of identification; she'd heard the other sisters and mothers and fathers and brothers discussing their loved one's crimes without hesitation back in the prison waiting room. But Sheila was not of their world, she and David came from a different place. Raised in a typically middle-class household, they'd enjoyed privileges people like Caitlin would never have known. It was wrong, she knew, to think of herself as apart from them – weren't they all simply citizens of the same societal melting pot? – but she could not help the things she'd been taught, the ideals and ideas planted in her head since childhood.

"Shy, are you?" Caitlin moved closer, her arm touching Sheila's thigh, as if sheer physical presence might loosen her tongue.

"Assault and battery," she said finally, giving away just enough to sound convincing. "He got into a fight in a pub."

Caitlin nodded sagely, as if that explained everything. "Mine, too," she said. "My ex, that is – Joe's dad. Tried to murder his new girlfriend's ex-fella. Kicked his head in and got caught for it. The bugger's in a coma, but he ain't dead yet. My ex says that should make 'em let him out sooner, but it won't happen. Gave him a longer sentence instead, and called him a danger to the public."

Sheila nodded, not knowing how else to respond. She felt the other woman was boasting – and perhaps in Caitlin's social circle, these were indeed things to be proud of, incidents upon which to build a reputation.

She wished the train would hurry up and arrive. Glancing at her wristwatch, she saw that there were still five minutes to wait.

So she thought about David instead: about what he'd done and whether or not he deserved his draconian sentence. She supposed he did – the attack had been unprovoked – but at the same time, she knew her brother was not a violent man. Something had snapped inside him; but because of his insular nature, he would not tell anyone what had occurred to spark such an act of uncharacteristic brutality. One night he'd simply walked into a local pub, ordered a pint of cider, drunk it in one swallow, and then turned to the person nearest to him at the bar and hit him in the face. Then hit him again. And again. When the man fell to the floor, David had begun to stamp on his head.

In his youth, David had been such a gentle child, a loving little boy. His sensitive, caring nature had often led to trouble. Sometimes he was bullied for being slightly fey; the rest of the time he tried to help his playmates by offering a shoulder to cry on.

That night in the pub it had taken three other men to overpower David and drag him away from his victim, and one of them had received a black eye for his trouble. According to witnesses, David never stopped smiling throughout; and he was still smiling when the police arrived to take him away.

"You listening to me?"

"Uh… sorry?" She turned to Caitlin and shrugged. "I was… miles away," she added.

"I was just telling you about Joe, here. How he's a bright lad. His dad's thick as mince, but the laddo here is sharp as a tack. Aren't you, Joe?"

As usual, or so it seemed, Joe stared straight ahead, not even part of the same world. Sheila thought perhaps this was some kind of coping mechanism, part of a decision the boy had made long ago, when he realised what he had for parents. If what Caitlin had claimed was true, and Joe was indeed a gifted child, then surely he was simply retreating from the world and trying to block out his surroundings. For all anyone knew, he might be mulling over one of Einstein's lesser-known theories in his head.

162

The man opposite must have woken. When Sheila looked over to where he'd been sitting, the bench was empty and the station guards were no longer in evidence. A discarded newspaper fluttered on the ground under the seat, but the section of platform was otherwise deserted. She glanced along her own length of platform, and was puzzled to find that it looked far less crowded than before. Seven or eight adults stood in animated clots, with children moving around them in slow circles, where before Sheila might have sworn there were fifteen or twenty. Nor had she previously noticed the bags and suitcases that were piled nearby, as if waiting to be loaded.

Caitlin continued to talk, but Sheila had long ceased listening to whatever it was the woman was trying to say. Instead, she recalled something David had told her on the phone a month ago, during one of his short, infrequent and uncomfortable calls: *We're all locked up, but some of us get to choose the prison.* It had sounded trite and self-serving at the time, but right now it seemed to hold a ring of truth.

When she'd pushed him further today, the smile had slipped and his tone had darkened, lending the rest of his monologue a sense of tension that she'd never before experienced in his presence. *At least I get three square meals in here, and some discipline, some order. Books to read. Time to reflect. Regular exercise. Don't get me wrong, it isn't pleasant; but it's better than some of the jails I've seen out there... There are others in here just like me, men who have taken a choice instead of being forced into a niche that doesn't fit them. I am not alone.*

Was that it, then? Had life simply become such a gaol to David that he'd decided to change cells? If his philosophy was sound, then Sheila realised that she, too, was stuck in her own prison, serving a sentence that consisted of marking time in a featureless office with people she barely even spoke to except to talk about work, paying off the mortgage on her tiny flat, and accruing personal debt until her eventual release – which meant, of course, the day she died.

Sheila looked along the train tracks, peering into a darkness that seemed to swell and grow at an alarming rate, and waited to catch sight of the lights on the front of a train.

"...and I said, 'Oh, you can't do that to me,' but he just lit up another fag and started laughing." Caitlin's unfocused babbling was almost soothing; if she weren't speaking, the silence might prove too great to bear.

At last she heard the train's lumbering approach, and as she leaned out over the platform and into the empty air above the tracks, she saw its black hulking shape between the two concrete platforms. The design looked out of date but not particularly old, like something from a 1960s advertising campaign. The paintwork was chipped in places, and a thick coating of grime concealed most of the bottom half of the train. For some reason the lights were off, but still she felt relieved that it was finally here. Surely those were not bars across the windows, and the man hanging out of an open doorway on the side of the train was not dressed like a prison guard. It was simply a new uniform; the rail companies were always trying to update their public image without spending too much money in the process.

The train growled and slowly halted, its nose stopping just beyond where Sheila stood at the end of the platform. The carriages were dark; there was nobody inside the train. This must be the first stop on its route. There was no reason to be afraid, and she certainly should not feel reluctant to climb aboard.

"You coming, love?" Caitlin pushed ahead and dragged open one of the heavy doors. Darkness remained in place behind it, like a solid wedge of shadow stuck in place. The small woman grabbed her son's hand, and Sheila felt the sudden urge to grab his other arm and pull him away, sheltering him... but from what? The lightless train? His skinny vulgar mother? A hopeless future? Or the dour prison cell of the rest of his life?

Sheila fought her weird compulsion and watched the two figures as they clambered up the hollow steps and into an empty carriage. A light flickered on above their heads, illuminating the sparse interior, and the illusion of bars at the windows faded. They were nothing more than streaks of dirt on the glass; greasy handprints left by former passengers. But why were there so many, and had those other people been palming the glass in panic, trying to summon someone to get them off the train?

The others waiting on the platform shuffled slowly and patiently aboard, barely enough of them now to fill a single carriage. Through the windows, the seats looked dusty and worn; cigarette burns marred the upholstery, empty drink cartons and food wrappers layered the floor.

164

Caitlin was staring through the glass, a troubled expression mottling her pallid brow, her tiny hands resting against the pane. Little Joe sat next to her, staring at the back of the next seat. Frantically, Caitlin began to wave her aboard. The boy slowly turned his head. Were those tears in his eyes, or was it simply another trick of the poor light and the dirty windows? His face, when it came into view, was bleak and loveless and flat as a warning poster pasted to the glass. Caitlin started hammering her fists against the window, her face becoming dark with agitation: she was afraid that Sheila might miss the train.

Sheila took a single step back from the edge – that was all it took to heed her brother's obliquely-worded advice, and to decide upon an uncertain future. Her only regret was that she'd been unable to save the boy.

As the train pulled away from the platform, the lights began to flicker once more, and Sheila watched sadly as the uniformed man she'd glimpsed earlier loomed over Joe and his mother and wrapped them both in an inescapable embrace.

The prison train surged into the darkness, destination unknown.

Damned If You Don't
by Robert Shearman

"I want to make a complaint."

And Martin felt a thrill of courage, and for just a moment the first sensation of actual happiness since he'd arrived in this God-forsaken place. Here he was, always rather a timid man – both in the bedroom and in the boardroom, which is why he'd never accomplished much in either, but Moira had never complained, bless her, and even if he'd never had the nous to rise to managing director like everyone else his age at least he'd never been sacked or demoted or what was the word they used now, yes, *reassigned*, no, they'd always kept him on, he was just too solid to lose. Solid, that's what Martin was, steadfast, reliable. But timid. Never one to rock the boat. And yet, here he was, all five foot three of him, squaring up aggressively to someone who must have been at least eight foot tall. And that wasn't even counting the horns.

Of course, Martin realised, in that split second when he felt so brave, he wasn't being as brave as all that. He'd chosen this demon specifically. Yes, he was eight foot tall, but that was distinctly diminutive for a demon since the rest of them were much larger and more ferocious. And there was a blond tuft around the demon's horns which made him look almost endearing.

The demon turned both of his red rheumy eyes on to Martin. He didn't encourage him to go on, but neither did he *discourage* him, which was all to the good. Martin floundered anyway. He'd been so intent on summoning up the nerve to start complaining he hadn't given much thought on how to continue.

"It's my roommate. I'm not happy with my roommate," said Martin. "I didn't even know we'd be *getting* roommates. I haven't shared a room with anyone in forty years, not counting Moira. And Moira was bad enough with her snoring, I used to have to wear ear plugs. I don't suppose I could have a room to myself? No, okay, too much to hope for. But if I'm going to be here for a long time, and I think that's the idea, I should at least get a better roommate. Not that one. It's just…" and here he ran out of words for a moment, and then found a feeble conclusion, "…not on."

166

The demon looked as if he were going to say something very cutting, then changed his mind, deciding that eternity was long enough as it was. "Martin Travers," he boomed.

"You know my name?"

"I know everyone's name. Your roommate has been especially selected for you."

"Right," said Martin. "I see. Right. And how..." and he felt a bit of the old fire coming back; he'd come this far, he might not get the courage again, "how exactly was he chosen? A lucky dip or, or, or what? I mean, I'm just saying. I don't think there was much thought to it. That's all."

"Your roommate is very clean," said the demon.

"Yes."

"Doesn't smell. A friendly personality. Snores much less than this Moira of whom you speak."

"Right. Good, I'm sure..."

"Frankly," said the demon, dropping some of the booming cadence from his voice, "you're in Hell, and you could have done a lot worse, mate."

"But he's a dog."

"He is indeed."

"I'm not trying to make a fuss," said Martin. "But I deserve a human at least. Surely. I mean, I could do better than a dog. I'm not a, for God's sake... I'm not a murderer or anything..."

The demon shrugged. "Everyone's equal here. No segregation based on gender, race, age, sex... or species." He grunted and leaned forward confidentially – Martin felt a little nauseous as he was caught in an exhalation of fetid breath. "Personally, I preferred it in the old days. Lutherans on one side, Calvinists on the other, and never the twain shall meet. What we've got now..." He waved a claw disparagingly at nothing in particular but the whole denizens of Hell, "It's just political correctness gone mad."

"The thing about dogs is they make me itch."

The demon sucked air through his teeth in what was actually intended to be a gesture of sympathy, but sounded instead like a terrifying death rattle. Martin recoiled as if he'd been struck.

"I'll see what I can do," he rumbled. "Okay? But I'm not promising anything."

"Thanks," said Martin. And unsure what else to do now, nodded, made an attempt at a friendly smile, and went back to his room.

The demon watched him go. He wished all the damned would leave him alone. All the bigger demons laughed at him about it. It was that tuft of hair over the horns that did it. Every night he'd shave it off, but by morning the bloody thing would always have grown back.

The dog was waiting for him.

"Are you all right?" he said. "You just took off without a word. I was worried."

The funny thing was, it was only if you looked at him full on you could tell he even was a dog. Try out of the corner of your eye, or stand to him sideways, he seemed to be just another faded soul bouncing around in eternal damnation.

"I'm sorry," said Martin. "I was just a bit... you know."

"I do know," said the dog. "It takes a while to get used to! Don't worry about it." And he gave a friendly little smile, then panted cheerfully with his tongue hanging out. "What's your name?"

"Martin," said Martin.

"Nice to meet you, Martin," said the dog politely, and offered his paw to shake. "My name's Woofie."

"Vuffi?"

"No, Woofie. I'm German."

"Ah."

"Yeah."

They smiled politely at each other.

"I've never been to Germany," said Martin.

"Oh, it's nice," said Woofie. "Well, bits of it."

"Yes."

"Rains sometimes, mind you. And gets a bit nippy in the winter."

"Same as anywhere, I suppose."

"Yeah, I suppose," said Woofie, and smiled. "Still, I liked it."

They smiled politely at each other again, and Woofie even affected a friendly tail wag. Martin would have done the same, had he had a tail.

168

"Anyway," said Woofie. "I don't want to get in your way. You know, but if there's anything you need..."

"Thanks."

"Make yourself at home. Well, it *is* now. Do you have a preference...?" he added, nodding at the bunk beds.

"Oh, I don't want to impose," said Martin.

"It's no problem. Whichever one you want. All these years here, I've been in both. I'm happy either way. Don't worry," Woofie said, perhaps seeing the involuntary look of disgust on Martin's face, "I don't moult. And they're clean sheets."

"Well, I suppose the top one might be more fun," said Martin. "If you're sure you don't mind."

"Hey," said Woofie generously, "I know what it's like to be the new guy. We've all been there. Anything I can do to make it easier. There's a spare wardrobe over there, it's all yours. Washbasin in the corner."

"What about the toilet...?"

"We never need to go," said Woofie. "Funny that. First couple of days I was here I was frantic looking for the litter tray, till I realised I didn't need one. And yet they give us a washbasin. I've never quite worked that one out."

Woofie politely offered Martin use of the sink before they went to bed, but Martin let him go first. He watched his new roommate wash his fur, and brush his fangs, and a part of him thought he was about to scream and the scream would never stop, *I can't be in Hell with a dachshund.* Woofie wiped the sink clear of his gobbets of toothpaste, looked up at Martin. "It's free when you want it."

As Martin washed, he looked into the mirror. He stared at this timid little dead man, standing at five foot three. And if he tilted his head all the features he recognised vanished, and he saw a soul like any other. Every day, he realised, he'd look in this mirror when he washed, and he'd never be able to forget that he was dead, that he'd only ever been meat hanging on a frame, and that the meat was now rotting and the frame could be seen underneath. That's why Hell came equipped with washbasins. Not because of the sink, but the mirror. Martin sighed heavily, and all the stale meat of his face wobbled, and the soul framework dimmed a little. He heard Woofie let out a little snore, already asleep and dead to the world. And he didn't know why, but it reassured him, just a bit.

For the next few days, Martin waited for the tortures to start.

"It doesn't quite work like that, though," said Woofie. "I'm not saying there *aren't* tortures, but I've been here for ages and no-one's started on me yet. I don't like to say anything in case it reminds them."

In the meantime there were the shopping malls to wander around. None of the shops were ever actually open, but Martin didn't have money to buy anything anyway, and it was reasonably good fun to look through the windows. There was a nice local cinema which screened films every evening, some of them even only a few months after general release. And Woofie kindly invited Martin to join his bowling team. They'd all go bowling three or four nights a week, and some of the players were really rather good. They were all dogs, and seemed a little reserved around Martin because he was a human. Martin felt a bit offended by that – if there were any qualms to be had, he should be the one having them. But none of the dogs said anything for Woofie's sake, and when Martin bowled his first strike, after a week of practice, all their congratulations seemed genuine enough.

"It's like the holiday village I once stayed at in Lanzarote," said Martin. "Hell isn't so bad."

But of course it was.

"What are you in here for?" Martin asked his roommate once, as they were getting ready for bed. He wasn't especially curious. Just making conversation.

It was the first time he'd ever seen Woofie irritated. "That's not a very polite thing to ask, Martin."

"Oh. I'm sorry."

"It's okay."

But a few days later, as they were riding the mall escalator up and down for kicks, he asked him again.

Woofie sighed. "Tell me what *you're* in for first."

Martin was more than happy to do so – in fact, he'd just been waiting for the excuse to let it all out. "It's because I don't believe in God, apparently. They told me that when I arrived."

"Uh-hum."

170

"The thing is, I thought I *did*. I went to church most weeks, you know. Always thought there was some sort of higher presence or something."

"Uh-hum."

"Turns out I only believed I believed. But actually I didn't."

"They hate it when you're wishy-washy," said the dog. "You'd have been better off not believing in God at all. They'd have respected that."

"I wouldn't have gone to Hell?"

"Oh yes. But you'd have been able to sleep in on Sundays." And then Woofie told Martin the reason why *he* was in Hell.

Martin was surprised and impressed.

"Don't be impressed," said Woofie. "It's nothing to be impressed about."

"It seems a bit unfair," suggested Martin gently.

"It *is* unfair. Most dogs go to Hell because they weren't kind to their masters. They bit them. Or wouldn't come when they called. Or wouldn't chase the sticks they'd throw. Dogs not doing what dogs are meant to do."

"Yes, I can see that."

"And I'm here because I *didn't* bite him. Frankly, I was damned right from the start. If I'd been lacking in my dogly duties, straight to Hell, no questions asked. But as a good dog, loving and patient to my master, I was serving Adolf Hitler."

"So, really," said Martin, "it's just guilt by association."

"Yeah," said Woofie. "When he told me to fetch a stick, I was just following orders."

"Did you tell them that?"

"Of course I did. They said that's what *everybody* said. Throughout history, the same feeble excuse. So," and he gestured with his paws at Hell, "this is where I finish up." As it turned out, he was gesturing at the time towards a Virgin Megastore, but the point was still made.

"I can see why you'd be bitter about that," said Martin.

"Oh, I don't know," said the dog, and he shrugged. "If I'm going to be damned anyway, it might as well be for something impressive… It *is* impressive, isn't it, really?" he asked shyly.

"It is impressive."

"I said you looked impressed."

"You did and I was."

"You know Strudel the poodle, who won the bowling last night? He belonged to Goering. I mean, just think. Bloody *Goering*. How embarrassing." Woofie allowed himself a proud smile. "If you're going to be in Hell because you were once the prized pet of a Nazi, better to be Hitler's than some jumped-up SS Kommandant with ideas above his station."

"I take your point," said Martin, and for a moment felt embarrassed that the evil which had sentenced him had been so banal in comparison.

"I can't stop looking back," said Woofie. "I feel guilty. Of course I do. I think, if only I had been a better dog, maybe I'd have been a more calming influence."

"No," said Martin.

"If I'd distracted him for just one more hour with my squeaky toys, that would have been another hour he wasn't setting up death camps..."

"You can't think like that," said Martin. "What could you have done? Nothing, you could have done nothing."

"I hope this won't make a difference between the two of us," said Woofie. And he reached out for Martin's hand with his paw.

Without thinking twice, Martin squeezed it. "Of course not," he said. "It doesn't. Really, really."

Martin didn't bring the matter up again. They bowled together as usual, watched the same movies, took turns to use the washbasin. And, if anything, Woofie seemed more relaxed around his roommate. The polite friendship was replaced by something warmer and more honest; Woofie let down his guard and beneath the affable doggy exterior there was a really sharp sense of humour. His mocking impersonations of the rest of the bowling team, all done behind their backs, used to have Martin in stitches – they were cruel, but so accurate, especially the way he imitated Rudolf's stutter or Ludwig's limp. And it all helped single Martin out as his *special* friend, the one he would never laugh at privately, the one that he truly took seriously. Martin felt quite proud of that.

"You may as well get it over with," said Woofie one night. The lights were out, but Martin couldn't sleep, and he was pleased to hear the voice of his friend rise from the bunk beneath him. "Ask me what he was like."

"Who?"

"Who do you think? Come on. Everyone always wants to ask. It's all right."

"All right. What was Hitler like?"

"He was okay," said Woofie. "Quite generous with treats. Didn't like me lying on the bed, but was usually good for the odd lap. Even as I got older and fatter, he never minded me climbing onto the lap for a cuddle. He wasn't a bad master at all. Of course," he added reflectively, "he had his bad days. When he'd got things on his mind, and he did a lot, actually, as time went on. Then sometimes he wouldn't find the time for walkies. But, you know. He did his best."

There was silence.

"And at this point everyone asks whether I knew I was being fed and petted by an evil man. Go on, ask it."

"I don't want…"

"It's all right, really."

So Martin asked the obvious.

"I was his first dog, his childhood pet. So you've got to bear in mind that when I came on the scene he hadn't done anything yet. Well, anything that was particularly *evil.* He'd done a few things that were *naughty,* but really, refusing to eat your greens, or reading under the bed covers after lights out, or graffitiing over pictures of Otto von Bismarck… I mean, you wouldn't say that was especially untoward. I know what you're going to say. That surely I could have seen *something* there. The seeds of the man to come. Say it, you might as well."

"Did you see the seeds of the man to come?"

Woofie paused. "Do you know, Martin, no-one's ever asked me that before?"

"Really?"

"I'll have to think about that." And so he did. And then, at last, the voice gentle in the darkness:

"It's not as if he ever had the chance to discuss matters of state with me. But I don't think he'd have been ashamed. I dare say he'd have explained the need to burn the Reichstag, or invade Czechoslovakia, he'd have explained the concentration camps. I'd have only had to ask. I honestly think he was just doing his best. Muddling through, like the rest of us. Trying to be a good person. I'm not saying all his decisions were *good* ones. And that he didn't get carried away. Who wouldn't, you or I in the same position,

173

who wouldn't? But people think of him as a demon. And he wasn't. Well, we know what demons look like. And he was just a man, you know. Just a man with his dog. Like you and me. Well, like you, anyway. Yes," Woofie said softly, as he thought about it, "Adolf Hitler was a lot like you."

"Thanks," said Martin, and meant it.

"Why didn't you want to ask? No-one else has left it for so long."

"I just supposed," said Martin, "that it must get a bit irritating. Always being in his shadow. People never asking you about *you*, only the famous person you hung out with."

There was silence for a while.

"But I was in his shadow," said Woofie. "I was his dog."

More silence. For a while Martin thought Woofie had fallen asleep. And then:

"Thanks, though. That's really thoughtful of you. Thanks."

"That's okay."

"You're my best friend."

"You're my best friend too, actually."

"We can cuddle if you like," said Woofie. "I don't mean anything funny," he added hastily, "just cuddling. If you like. I mean, there's nothing funny about a man and his dog sleeping together, is there? If you like."

"I'm not sure there's room," said Martin slowly.

But there was room, if Martin leant into the wall a bit. And Woofie wasn't very big, he curled into the spaces left by Martin's body as if they'd always been designed to fit together like this. If Martin laid against Woofie sideways he was rubbing against his soul, but face on he could feel his fur, and the warmth of it was more comforting than he could have believed.

"Good night, Martin," said Woofie softly.

"Night." And within minutes Martin heard the snoring that told him his new best friend was asleep. And he had only a few moments to realise how reassuring that snoring was, how much gentler than Moira's, how much more *right*, before he was fast asleep too.

"Good news," boomed the demon. "You're being transferred tomorrow morning."

174

Martin tried to work out how he should respond. "Oh," he said eventually.

"Well, don't look too bloody grateful," muttered the demon as he stomped off. He was having a rotten day already. Since he couldn't shave the tufts of fur round his horns, he'd set about plucking them out with a pair of tweezers. This only succeeded in drawing attention to them still further, and the overall effect made him look a bit camp. He rather suspected – accurately, in fact – that behind his back in the staff room the piss was being ripped out of him quite mercilessly.

Martin wondered how he should break the news to Woofie. But that was the one thing he needn't have worried about. He was waiting for him when he got back, the body unnaturally tense. Martin thought he might have been crying.

"Hello," said Martin, for want of anything better to say. Then, "I'm sorry."

"Was it something I've done?"

"No. No, that's not it."

"What is it? Just tell me what I ever did that was wrong."

"It's not you, Woofie. I'm sorry. It's *me*. It's my fault, it's me, I'm sorry."

Woofie looked so sad, with his big dog watery eyes boring into him. Martin wished he'd be angry – bark at him, nip at his ankles, *anything*. Anything other than this quiet and this hurt.

At last Woofie said, "Is it because of the whole Hitler thing?"

"No," Martin hastened to reassure him. "It's because you're a dog."

Silence.

"It's nothing personal."

Silence. For the first time since he'd met him, the dog made Martin itch.

"So it's not because of what I've done. It's because of who I am."

"Well. Yes. Sort of."

Woofie stared at him. "That's sick."

"Yes," said Martin. "It is. I'm sorry. Is there… is there anything you'd like? Anything I can do, or…"

"No," said Woofie. And then he changed his mind. "Yes," he said gently. "I'd like my bunk back. The top bunk. My favourite bunk. And all to myself. Please."

So that night Martin slept on the bottom bunk. Woofie hadn't spoken again all evening, and he stared up at the little sagging mound from the bed above him, and he wanted to touch it, *prod* it, just to get some sort of reaction, even to have an argument, just so there could be an ending to this. But he didn't dare. In the morning, Woofie seemed kinder, even to have forgiven him.

"Best of luck, Martin," he said, and offered him his paw.

"And best of luck to you too," said Martin warmly. "And thank you for everything." He made to give him a little pat on the head, but Woofie stepped backwards instinctively. He'd gone too far.

Martin's new roommate was a human called Steve. Steve was very polite and almost friendly. He didn't give Martin the top bunk, but really, why should he have? It turned out that Steve was a rapist. But, as he told Martin, it had only been the once, and it was a long time ago, and he felt very sorry about it. And besides, Martin didn't know the child in question, so he decided not to be bothered about it.

And Steve let Martin hang out with his friends. At the shopping malls, at the cinema, at the bowling alley. It had been a long time since Martin had spent time in the company of humans, but he soon adjusted. Inevitably there were occasions when he'd almost run into Woofie: the first time was a bit awkward, and he could see that Strudel would happily have jumped at his throat. But Woofie barked something in his ear, and with bad grace Strudel turned his back on the fair-weather human and got back to his ten pin bowling. And that was the worst of it. After that, whenever Woofie or Martin realised the other was near, they'd simply not make eye contact as discreetly as possible. It was never not embarrassing – but it was an embarrassment that Martin could cope with with increasing ease as the years went by.

It may have been on his third or fourth Christmas in Hell that Martin received a card. "Something addressed just to you," said Steve with a sniff, as he handed it to him. Most of the cards would say 'Steve and Martin', and one or two might be for 'Martin and Steve'. Never Martin on his own.

"Dear Martin," it said. "Long time no speak!" And the exclamation mark dot was a happy face, just trying a bit too hard.

Martin took a breather from hanging the tinsel – Christmas decorations are always very popular in Hell – sat on the bunk, and read the card properly.

Dear Martin,
    Long time no speak! How are you? It's been ages.
    This is just to wish you a merry Christmas, and let you know an old friend is thinking of you. Because we are old friends, aren't we? I know we've lost touch, but I didn't want you to think there were any hard feelings. There really aren't. I only want the best for you. I only ever did.
    I catch sight of you every once in a while, and I keep meaning to say hi. But either you look very busy, or I'm very busy, so it never happens. Which is so silly! We must catch up one day. That'd be lovely.
    All the old gang are well, and send you their best.
    Lots of love, Woofie.

And the 'love' had been written with a hesitancy that made it all the more emphatic. And then, in a different pen, there was a P.S.

    P.S. Look, if you're up for it, and I'm sure you have other plans anyway – but still, no harm in asking. We're thinking of having a party at New Year's. Nothing very fancy. If you've nothing better to do, and I dare say you have, do come along!

And then, same pen, but written later:

    I miss you.

Martin reread it. He wondered if he should send a card back, but really, Steve took care of all that.

"Shall I hang it with the others?" said Steve, reaching out for it.

"Sure," said Martin. "Why not?"

And then, some time in January, the announcement came.

Hell was getting too full. There simply wasn't the space for many more damned souls. So someone had decided they had

177

better send an emissary to God, and find out what should be done about it. And when he came back, the emissary said that he'd looked long and hard, and it turned out there *wasn't* a God after all. He wasn't sure there had never been one, but if there had, he certainly wasn't around any longer. And this had caused a bit of consternation – who was going to solve the overcrowding problem now? – until it was realised that his non-existence solved the problem in itself. After all, it seemed hardly fair to be damned for not believing in God if it turned out you were, embarrassingly enough, absolutely right.

Martin was told he could leave immediately.

"Where am I going now?" he asked. "Heaven?"

It turned out he was going to Surrey.

The day the dead came back to Earth was one of mixed emotion. Everyone seemed overjoyed to see their loved ones return; there were a lot of tearful reunions and a lot of street parties. The government weren't really sure how to react until they realised that on the whole everyone was very happy about it, so decided in the end they were happy about it too, and acted as if it had been their idea somehow.

But no-one had quite anticipated that the dead weren't going to go back again. Had it just been a flying visit, then fair enough. But by the end of the week most people really felt that they'd outstayed their welcome. The government picked up on the prevailing mood and quickly asserted that they'd *never* been happy about this, that they'd had nothing to do with it whatsoever. And even that new measures would soon be taken against this unwanted invasion of the immigrant dead.

When Moira first saw Martin again, she hugged on to him so hard that he thought she'd never let go. She'd still kept all his clothes and belongings, suitcases full of old knick-knacks that she couldn't bear to part with. She said everyone had told her to give them all to Oxfam, and when she'd refused well-meaning friends had got rather angry with her and worried about her mental health. "So I got rid of them. I've been very lonely. But I knew you'd come back for me." Martin was touched. He didn't want to point out he wasn't back because of her at all but a bureaucratic quirk. "Thank God you came back." And that there was no God to thank, and if there had been there wouldn't have been the bureaucratic quirk in the first place. They made love that first night, and for several nights afterwards, something they hadn't done much even when he'd been alive. And it was surprisingly nice, but not so nice that he minded when they sank back into their usual platonic domesticity. Within a week he was lying in bed next to her, blocking out the snoring with ear plugs. And in the dead of night, when all was still, he could almost believe that he'd never died and been to Hell at all.

At work, however, they weren't so accommodating. For old time's sake, the boss generously gave Martin ten minutes out of his hectic schedule. "And it is hectic at the moment!" he told Martin. "Busy, busy, busy! Well, I needn't tell you. You know what this job's like, you've lived it!" Martin was told that they would *love* to take him back, they *really* would, but they just *couldn't*, not in the present climate. "You can hardly expect to take a leave of absence that long, without any warning, and expect your job waiting when you get back." And besides, the boss admitted when pressed, not everyone felt very comfortable working alongside corpses. Not the boss himself, of course. But even Martin must admit, being one himself, there was something funny about the way they looked. Whereas once he'd been respected for being so reliable, so solid – now, in a very real sense, he wasn't solid any more.

See the dead face on, and you could just about pretend they were normal – that they were living and breathing like all right-minded people. But turn your head to the side and you could see the soul, that all of this skin and bone and individuality was just a façade. It wasn't a thing anyone liked to be reminded of. And it meant that the dead were instantly recognisable. By and large the living would ignore them, some would glare at them with obvious hostility; there were even incidents of target beatings by gangs, but outbreaks of violence became rarer when it was realised you couldn't do anything to kill them. Within weeks the worst that a dead man walking the streets might expect was to be spat at.

Once upon a time, if you'd wanted to separate a race from the rest of society, to make a people stand out and be judged, you'd bring out the yellow badges, you'd start shaving heads. Woofie's masters had done it. But no-one had to isolate the dead; with their souls flapping about for all to see, they'd done it to themselves. And the worst part of it was that they felt ashamed of each other

179

too. A dead man seeing another dead man would turn his eyes in the same way as a living man would; once in a while there might pass a look of sympathy, of understanding, but they'd hurry on, not daring to talk to each other, not daring to reach out and say 'I am one of you'. As if for fear that the vacancy in their eyes, the deadness that had so much more to do with the heart no longer beating and the lungs no longer filling, might be what you looked like too.

Moira didn't like to mention to Martin the fact that he was very nearly two-dimensional. But even her discretion used to irritate him. She'd try to ignore it at first, then to make it go away. She'd make him his favourite meals, fried and fatty, and she'd say it was because she loved him, that she'd missed cooking for him, that she just wanted him to be happy. But he saw the truth.

"You're trying to fatten me up!" he said.

Moira blushed, and admitted that she thought he could do with a little padding out, his body might lose some of its *flatness*, if only if...

"But the food doesn't go anywhere. I eat it, then it vanishes. It doesn't stay in the stomach, I don't have a stomach. For God's sake, I can't even shit."

Moira cried, and said he'd changed, he'd never used to be like this, he didn't love her any more since he'd changed.

And he wanted to say of course he'd bloody *changed*, he'd died, hadn't he? He'd died and gone to Hell, and she *hadn't* died, she'd just stayed cosily alive, what had they got in common any more? He'd gone to Hell and fallen in love with someone else, he'd fallen in love with Hitler's dog. But he couldn't say this, even Martin couldn't be so cruel. It gave him no pleasure to see his widow crying all the time, it just revolted him. "I can't even shit," he repeated numbly. And then, as an afterthought, "I want a dog."

Moira pointed out he didn't like dogs. He was allergic. They made him itch.

"I want a bloody dog," he said, "that's all I bloody want. Get me a bloody dog."

They called the new dog Wuffles. Martin had wanted to call it Woofie, but couldn't quite do it, it was all a bit too raw. Maybe in time he'd rename it, he didn't suppose the dog would mind. Moira had wanted to name him Snoopy, but Martin calmly pointed out that was a bloody stupid name, Snoopy was bloody stupid.

180

Besides, Snoopy was a bloody beagle, wasn't he, and this wasn't a bloody beagle, it was a bloody dachshund, you stupid bitch, it was a bloody sodding buggering dachshund. And then he kissed her gently on the forehead and told her she'd done well, it was a lovely dog. And if she could now bloody well leave him alone to play with it.

The thing was, Wuffles didn't like Martin. He *loved* Moira – he'd wag even at the sound of her voice, wait outside the bedroom door for her, was never happier than when she was petting him or stroking him or touching him. From Martin he'd just recoil. Martin supposed he could see his soul, the same as everyone else. And he quite respected the dog for it – at least it wasn't a hypocrite.

Still, he'd try. He'd take Wuffles out for walks – *drag* Wuffles out for walks, pulling the resistant pet by the leash until it had no choice but to follow. They'd go to the woods. Martin would find a nice fat stick, and throw it.

"Fetch," he'd say.

Wuffles would just stare at him blankly.

"Fetch," Martin would repeat. "Fetch the stick."

Wuffles would look to where he'd thrown it, look back at him, then lie down. He wasn't going to chase after a stick. Not for *him.* For his mistress, anything. But for this flattened dead man, the dog refused to follow orders.

One day Martin dragged the dog to the car instead. They drove far far away. He opened the passenger door. Threw the stick he'd brought with him.

"Fetch," he said.

But Wuffles made it clear that if he wasn't prepared to chase a stick in the woods, he certainly wasn't inclined to do so on the hard shoulder of a motorway. So Martin pushed the dog out of the car anyway, and drove home without him.

Moira was distraught. "It's all right," he reassured her. "He'll be fine. There are lots of rabbits for him to chase out there, probably. And if he *isn't* fine… He was a good dog, he never bit or scratched. He loved his mistress. So at least he can be sure he's going to a happy place."

Martin never saw Wuffles again. But when a few weeks later he opened the door to a dachshund who had rung his doorbell, he thought that his unwanted pet had tracked him down. That he'd have to take him on an even longer journey up the M1.

"No, no," said the dog. "It's Woofie. How are you, Martin?"

"Woofie," repeated Martin. "I didn't recognise you."

"Well, it has been a long time. Can I come in?"

Once inside, Martin asked his old friend whether he wanted anything to eat or drink, wanted to sit down, wanted anything, really. "No, I'm fine," said Woofie. "Nice place you've got here. Very cosy."

"It's not mine, it's hers," said Martin. "It's nothing to do with me. How did you get out of Hell?"

"Oh, they're letting all sorts out now. I wouldn't be surprised if the whole thing hasn't shut down before too long."

"And how did you find me?"

Woofie smiled. "A dog can always find his master. If he wants to hard enough." He let his words sink in. "You do know you're my master, don't you?"

"Yes," said Martin.

"I only think sometimes. That if I'd met you. Right from the start. If I could have given my love to *you*, and not to Hitler... I'd never have gone to Hell in the first place. I could have been great. And I think, too, that with me there beside you, you wouldn't have gone to Hell either."

"No," said Martin.

"We could have been great, you and I. We could have been great."

And Martin kissed him. And he knew that what he was kissing was a dog, and that it was a *dead* dog, but it was all right, it didn't matter, it was all all right.

"Let's get out of here," said Martin. And he got his coat, locked the front door, and put the keys through the letterbox. He considered leaving a note for Moira – but really, what would he have said?

And man and dog went out together. They had no money for food, but that was okay, they had each other. They'd sleep when they got tired, on park benches, in shop doorways, wherever they could cuddle up. And people would avoid their gaze on the street as always, and some would still spit at them. But together man and dog had a strength. They would stare down their persecutors. They showed they weren't ashamed.

182

Early one morning they were shaken awake by an angry farmer. They'd decided to spend the night in an empty barn – the straw was scratchy but warm.

"Get out!" screamed the farmer, with a fury that was mostly fear. "Get off my property!" And he jabbed at them with the handle of his pitchfork.

"There's no need for that," said Martin. "We're going."

"You're filth!" the farmer shouted after them, as Martin and Woofie walked to the door with as much dignity as they could. "You dead bastards. You dead perverted... and on my property! You're filth!"

And quick as a flash, Woofie turned round, leaped up, and tore out his throat.

Martin looked as surprised as the farmer, who, eyes bulged in shock, reached out for a neck that largely wasn't there, before pitching forward onto his face. The blood sprayed across the straw.

"Oh my God," said Martin, bending down. "He's dead."

"Good," said Woofie. "Now he knows what it feels like."

"Oh God, oh shit," said Martin.

"Come on, let's go," said Woofie.

They walked in silence for a while. Martin kept looking at his hands, and every time he did – yes – they were still smeared with blood.

"Oh God," he said at last. "It was an accident. It was an accident."

"It wasn't an accident," said Woofie. "I all but bit his head off."

"Oh God."

Nothing more was said for a few minutes. A man walked towards the pair down the footpath. He gave them the customary glare of hatred and contempt. And then he saw Martin's bloody hands, and the way Woofie openly snarled at him, and there was blood there too, right on the jaws – and he hurried on.

"What's going to happen to us?" Martin moaned.

"What are they going to do? Send us to Hell? Been there, done that."

"Oh God."

"Hitler was like this, you know," said Woofie. "The first time he had a Jew killed. Well, that's it, Woofie, he said. If I'm right, then I have made a blow for justice and the common man. But if I'm wrong... If I'm wrong, I'm damned forever.

"And do you know what I said? What I whispered into his ear. Oh, he couldn't hear me, of course. Dogs can't talk. But I whispered it anyway.

"If you're going to Hell for one Jew, then why not for a hundred? For a hundred thousand. For six million. If you're going to be damned anyway, at least be damned for something impressive. I'd rather be damned for being Hitler's dog than Goering's. Do you understand?"

"Yes," said Martin. "Oh God. I understand. Oh God."

"There isn't a God," said Woofie. "Stop saying that."

"Sorry."

"Do you realise by how much the dead outnumber the living? Do you? Thirty to one. And yet *we're* the outcasts. We're the ones who are spat at. How long do you think that can go on for? How long *should* it go on? Martin?"

"What?" said Martin weakly.

"How long?" demanded Woofie.

"I don't know."

"Then think about it," said Woofie sternly. "For once in your life, just think."

And Martin thought.

"But we mustn't hurt them, Woofie," he said eventually. "We can't do that. We should just put them... I don't know. Out of harm's way."

"For their own good."

"For their own good, exactly. Somewhere safe. Promise me, Woofie. Promise me, whatever happens. That what we'll be doing is good."

Woofie promised, Martin smiled, and on they walked. A man and his dog, making plans.

Machine
by Carole Johnstone

The Bank Holiday was sunny. Sunny and warm. Rain had been forecast, and there were indeed banks of clouds to the west, but these were gradually scudding out to sea and that suited Rick just fine. Rain was no friend to the WW2000+ Experience on any day, much less one as important as this.

He stood just inside a replica of the Dom Tower in Utrecht. Though the bare bones of the tower were stone-built and sturdy enough, the Gothic aesthetic had been achieved through inventive use of MDF and vatloads of casein paint. The high-pointed lantern in which he now stood had been particularly well done. No one looking up from below would ever know that the tower's façade had been built out of fibreboard and glue resin, concealing tiers of scaffolding, ladders and stud props mere feet behind.

He had a good set of guys, most of whom had backgrounds in film and theatre set making, and they rarely failed to come up with the goods, no matter how outlandish his suggestion. As an afterthought, he'd had them dismantle much of the belfry; the real Dom Tower had suffered no such ill-treatment, of course, but its destruction added to the ambience. The crowds loved a blown-up Catholic church.

From his vantage point, he could see out over the majority of the park. *His* park. He still hated referring to it as that; to him the WW2000+ experience was so much more than the twee banality that the word suggested. When it had first opened two years before, one travel show had the nerve to call it a "beach-side amusement facility" – and a mediocre one at that.

Sure, it had its fair share of problems and controversy. He'd had to beef up security around the perimeter fence following the huge protest rallies that first summer, although at least they had got the place some much-needed publicity. Such was the way of the world; there were always going to be different strokes for different folks. His was a tough gig.

The crowds were filtering in nicely now. It was barely ten a.m. and the coach parks were almost full. A cool breeze buffeted him as he leaned over the tower's edge to look down into the streets below. The Dutch quarter was already heaving, its narrow cobbled streets loud and excitable and heavy with the smell of crêpes and savoury *rijsttafel*.

Rick's people mingled with the tourists, handing out flyers and ushering people into the cafés and restaurants, dressed in the vintage 1940s gear that he'd sourced cheap from Islington. Even this many hours before the main event, the whole place was pregnant with an expectation that never failed to set the hairs high on the back of his neck. He loved Bank Holidays, and this was the big one: a centenary celebration of the end of the war.

At all other times, the park's main income came from earnest school and college trips, where circumstance dictated a far less flamboyant approach to proceedings. On public holidays Rick had far more *carte blanche*, and it was just as well. For a moment he was unabashed in likening himself to Vespasian stood atop his mighty Colosseum. *The mob expected it.*

To the north of the low roofs of the Dutch Quarter, the beach and mudflats still loitered in gloom. For a moment Rick frowned. They were not busy yet, but they soon would be. The hundred-yard trench system built into the moorland that abutted onto the flats was always a crowd pleaser. Technically it was harking back to the wrong war of course, but no one cared much about that. They went for the mud and the atmosphere, created courtesy of rabbit warren passages and shrieking, screaming high-def speakers hidden inside spookily lit officer quarters. Rick had wanted to ship in some rats for better authenticity – domesticated of course – but the fun police had refused the application point blank.

The beach, however, was an enduring disappointment and always had been. Though the park had been built on privately-acquired land, and a portion of the beach had come included, it was subject to far more rules and regulations set down by the jobsworths on the local council. Rick had yearned to recreate Dunkirk or the D-Day landings via hourly re-enactments using authentic amphibious vehicles, copious amounts of barbed wire, and perhaps even an outdoor surround sound system for added ambience.

D-Day would have been the far better option of course, and Omaha beach the best template – the real deal. And he'd imagined that having only dead U.S. Rangers and infantry divisions to deal with might satisfy the form filling home front. He'd been wrong.

186

Instead, he'd had to make do with some concrete bunkers hidden unobtrusively under the overhang of Ninian's Bluff, and a replica U-boat tethered to a small pier – the latter a rush job that did well just to float, never mind look the part.

Out towards the edge of Layer-On-Sea proper, the airfield was a flat grey square surrounded by grassland. It was swiftly becoming yet another source of consternation for Rick. The vast hangar now housed only two Junkers, and one of these was held together by little more than glue and goodwill. Fantasies of weekend air displays over the North Sea: an assault of *Blitzkrieg* proportions, accompanied by the roar of propellers and the wailing siren of the *Jericho-Trompete* – gone, just like that. Being so cruelly stymied at every turn would certainly have undone any other man, but Rick was made of sterner stuff. Always had been.

And there was still the consolation of the camp in the west. From his vantage point, it was only a vague collection of low shadows and barbed-wire fences; but in reality it was a vast concreted space more than six hundred yards square, its layout based upon Plaszów near Kraków, which Rick had chosen because it was the one in *Schindler's List*.

For a frankly exorbitant price, people could stay overnight in one of the stark barracks. They could even hire blue and white striped pyjamas bearing triangular badges and ID numbers if they so desired. And much to Rick's initial amazement, plenty had. Plenty continued to do so. Both Buchenwald and Gross-Rosen barracks were booked up solid that night and the next.

When Rick had initially been granted the franchise from Freizeit Industries – an obscure conglomerate of European firms, whose origins were frankly as much a mystery to him as they were to everyone else (despite what the world and his wife thought) – the initial furore had been incredible. A week after its opening, Rick had been invited onto a variety of topical panel shows and investigative TV programmes, the worst being an 'edgy' Channel 6 production hosted by the biggest self-righteous prick he had ever encountered.

When asked about the prudence of opening WW2000+ in the UK (the self-righteous prick had called it a *theme park*, of course he had), Rick had referred the prick to any number of recent action blockbusters, the current climate of political correctness gone mad, people's unquenchable desire for escapism.

Warming to his argument – and not letting the prick get another self-righteous word in edgeways – Rick had waxed lyrical awhile on the theme of circumvention and the innate need to rail against a common but extinct enemy. It was far more acceptable, he had suggested, to hate a bunch of long-dead Nazis than to hate Muslim fanatics with bombs strapped to their bellies. That comment they later took out.

His arguments had been greatly helped by the fact that no one seemed able to decide to what nation or persons the greater affront should be attributed, and thus Rick had initially managed to escape pretty much scot free. He'd eventually come undone on a local news programme, after imbibing a little too much of the free wine on offer in the Green Room. Taking affront at a caller who'd referred to his "chutzpah" in opening such an "abomination", citing the infamous closure of its predecessor in Genoa amid widespread riots and protests, Rick had called the caller something a lot worse than a self-righteous prick. Though *abomination* had still been preferable to *park*.

Rick had also made the mistake of referring to the WW2000+ experience as a "fun family day out". People, of course, had already known that – as evidenced by the huge waiting list for admission tickets, if nothing else. The problem was that some people hadn't wanted to *hear* it. Within the week, protestors had set up camp on the moorlands and in the B&Bs of Layer-On-Sea, and they'd stayed for more than a year.

Despite the welcome publicity, Rick had privately wondered why anyone still cared. If anything, the WW2000+ experience was bloody patriotic. And it wasn't as if he had ever considered building one of the *Vernichtungslager*: an extermination camp complete with gas chambers and crematoria. An iconic pile or two of clothes and shoes and hair. Trèz tacky.

Better than that, he had commissioned a visitor centre next to the Mickey Ds before the main exit. A free-entry concession comprising a museum and an auditorium showing appropriately serious and aged documentaries to the accompaniment of an appropriately dour soundtrack. Overlaid with one of those sombre, preaching to the choir 'lest we ever forget' narratives. What the hell more did people want?

The wind began to pick up, and Rick had to grab hold of a metal strut as he impatiently craned out of the tower. A kid in the street below saw him and screeched in excitement, waving his Dutch flag up at him, a bag of pink candy floss dangling from a ribbon at his wrist. Rick ignored him.

The Benny Goodman tribute band were still setting up in Paris (an hour later than scheduled, Rick scowled, he wouldn't be hiring *them* again), but many of the long tables had already been laid out and and much of the bunting strung up along the wide avenues and neo-classical MDF façades. After the much-hyped invasion of the Dutch Quarter, the VE Day celebrations would kick off in earnest on the Rue de Maris and Rue des États-Unis (a tip of the hat to the growing influx of tourists from over the pond), and Rick was literally banking on the sale of every one of its five hundred tickets.

In a hidden courtyard between France and Holland, the Nazis were a jumbled mass of undone uniforms, flailing limbs and jocular *Sieg Heils*. Rick frowned again, and wondered how many of them had already started drinking.

WW2000+'s real problem was no longer protestors or drunken outbursts on TV shows. It was the growing economic slump. The pound was down against the dollar and the euro again. UK petitions to join the EU Constitution had twice been rejected by every member country. House prices were plummeting as interest rates and energy costs rose. Times were hard, and too reminiscent of the recession that had plagued the early part of the millennium. People were miserable and disillusioned. Fury hung over the country like a growing storm cloud, and the air was thick and static beneath it, as if over sixty million people were holding their collective breath.

As much as Rick liked to deny it, WW2000+ was in immediate danger of going under. He'd had to source every single Nazi from the local job centre: a motley crew hardly comparable with the trained actors that he'd always before employed for public holiday re-enactments. There just wasn't enough money left. Hence the very real need to make this day of all days a success. The 100th anniversary of VE Day – give or take a week – and it had to go off without a hitch. It had to leave people aghast. That was the word that had kept Rick warm at night for many uncertain weeks. *Aghast.*

* * *

At four p.m. the invasion began in earnest. Having returned to his vigil at the top of the Dom Tower, Rick surveyed the streets below in anticipation. His own hundred-year-old war zone, surrounded by the ever-whining twenty-first-century town of Layer-On-Sea. The sight never failed to get his juices going, no matter how dire the circumstances. He lifted his Type 4 rocket mortar – set to deliver sky and bottle rockets with smoke and whistle effects instead of 200mm calibre shells – and balanced its weight on his shoulder.

He watched as the job centre Nazis filed out of their courtyard and into Holland. He watched their flat-footed, jostling advance with a sinking heart. The crowds of tourists gathered within the Dutch Quarter bunched expectantly together. While Holst's 'Mars' blasted out through hidden speakers, explosions of compressed air and propane provoked excited shrieks, and smoke filtered out through narrow pipes secreted inside road drains.

The only real fly in the ointment remained the Nazis. Their advance was still far from ordered or rhythmic. A few of them shook their replica bolt-action rifles and MP40s at the tourists in what Rick suspected was supposed to be a threatening manner; while others shoved through the ill-defined ranks, egging each other on with swinging legs and arms and yells, index fingers pushed hard under their noses. A sniper in one of the rooms above a fish restaurant suddenly fell out. He bounced a few feet along the cobbles, only letting go of his brown-wrapped bottle when another explosion went off close to his head.

A few in the waiting crowd laughed. More of them jeered. Rick put down his rocket launcher. On the Rue de Maris, the bastard Benny Goodman tribute band launched into a celebratory chorus of 'We'll Meet Again', while less than a hundred yards away, the Nazis still invaded Holland five years before. It was all going tits up. The whole shitting thing was going down faster than the Titanic, and he was powerless to stop it.

In the face of growing derision, the job centre Nazis stopped and loitered uncertainly. A few of them shouted at the crowd, but for the most part they hung back, looking to their feet or the courtyard from which they had come. The crowd, perhaps reminded of the price of admission, or perhaps just spoiling for a fight as most crowds were these days, grew ever more vocal.

Kids started throwing stones and running rings around the

closing band of Nazis. No one stopped them, not even Rick's own people, who were either leaving pretty quickly or going back inside the prefab restaurants and cafés. Over on the Rue de Maris, the celebrations were getting louder, and some idiot on the flats out beyond the trenches had begun letting off celebratory fireworks.

Rick closed his eyes. He felt tight with frustration – and something else. Something that tickled the back of his neck with long fingers. A warning not unlike the panicked realisation that he'd gone too far on a topical panel show. Rick twitched his shoulders and tried to ignore it. Given the rising tide of diversions, this was more easily achieved than it should have been.

Shouldering the grey-painted rocket launcher again, he pulled back on the trigger with a curse and the 8oz rocket motor soared out from the belfry, leaving a trail of sparks before erupting into blue stars. For the briefest of moments, the faces below gaped and stared up into the late afternoon sky.

And then it all changed. The gloomy wake of vanished illumination had a terrible quality to it – one that left Rick feeling vaguely unsettled and angrier still. Those faces looked up, but no longer at him. Beyond the enduring flashes of light inside his eyes, Rick perceived a malign, blinking plain of white flesh and cavernous mouths. The air was static, heavy with threat. Rick heard someone laugh: a nervous, flat titter that was quickly stifled. The smell of sulphur and charcoal stung his nose and watered his eyes.

Rick caught only one glimpse of the Nazis before the smoke swelled again, but it was enough to send him scuttling backwards inside the belfry with a cry. He dropped his rocket launcher, and only narrowly avoided plummeting to his death from the tower's opened rear by grabbing hold of a scaffolding joint and ricocheting off plywood.

In the streets below, it had suddenly grown very quiet. That thundercloud hanging over the country might well have finally burst – voiding bile and fury that had too long festered – but if so, it had burst without a further word or shout. Rick tried not to think of those white, gaping faces again; or of him looking down upon their mutinous desertion as if he were Jehovah. Instead, he tried to recall some of that rage for himself.

There were no more explosions, and someone had turned off

the piped music system in the Dutch Quarter. Rick could still hear the Benny Goodman band off to the south, and the odd crack of a rocket out on the flats, but other than that it was almost silent. He could even hear his own erratic heartbeat.

Other sounds began to intrude. A steady snapped staccato that grew swiftly louder and more confident. A whistled wind that suddenly echoed and amplified. An eerie, singular shout that he couldn't hear well enough to understand. As coherence dwindled, his heart began to bite at his bones.

And then the screams – *Christ,* the screams. Never in any picture house or nightmare had Rick heard screams like these. They provoked in him a terror so alien – so *unused* – that he was almost overcome by it. He clutched at the scaffolding pole, gibbering at it like a lunatic before slapping his palms hard against his ears. The screams filtered through like flour poured into a sieve, and Rick began slapping his palms harder and faster so that they might drown the other sounds out. It worked only as long as he could stomach the pain – which fell too obviously short of those suffering in the streets below.

The Machine drove further along Willemstraat, herding the *Untermenschen* towards the vast Dam Square to the southwest. Here there was better accommodation, better facility for their purpose. The *Untermenschen* screeched and screamed like vermin, and their herders grew bolder: rushing stragglers back into their own. Pushing forward, ever forward.

The square was lit by cast iron streetlights with acorn-shaped tops. Two *Kübelsitzwagen* painted Panzer Grey shone headlights onto an empty tent hung with Oranjeboom and Becks Vier banners. The *Untermenschen* still screamed and protested as they were herded deeper into the centre, their wretched mouths always gaping, pleading. Begging.

The massacre was clumsy and exhausting. By necessity, Mausers and MP40s were wielded as clubs and blunt knives, though such inadequacy proved ultimately fortuitous. No hands went unbloodied; no minds escaped the feeble whimper of the inferior; no will went untested or defeated.

Later, while the dead or dying lay in scattered, careless mounds, their killers sat inside the beer tent, toasting and smoking their success, breathing better its meaty copper tang. The distant

192

big band swing suddenly cut off and stained faces looked at one another under the red glow of concave, silhouetted walls. Some frowned; more smiled.

Through the rest of the evening and into the night, the Machine gained pace as efficiently as either purpose or number. Of the hundreds prematurely celebrating in the Rue de Maris or des États-Unis, perhaps as many as two thirds defected quickly and without question upon glimpsing the Machine's collective spectre: turning upon neighbour and friend with little qualm.

Through fabricated street after street, the tattoo of boots and the muttered mantra became absolute: *Nacht und Nebbel. Nacht und Nebbel.* The air was thin and feeble, and a place too far off to matter echoed thinner with muted sirens and alarms. In the streets of Paris, blood was shed for common and justified purpose: for the good of *Das Herrenvolk.* The good of the Machine.

Charlie forced his knees harder against his chin as he crouched at the foot of the basement staircase. There was no house at the staircase's base – only latticed wood and a solitary work-lamp illuminating a dead end – but Charlie hunkered down as low as he could anyway, flinching from the thunder of boots and their owners' clipped and terrible threats. Charlie couldn't translate them, but he understood those threats just fine.

He'd lost sight of his mum and dad long before, and had sprinted for the staircase after seeing an American in beige shorts thrown up against a graffitied wall by two other men. They had been dressed like the baddies in an old Indy Jones film. The baddies that his mum had told him were all dead.

Charlie had recognised the American from earlier on in the Dutch Quarter. He'd bought him the candy floss that his dad had said no to, tying its ribbon around Charlie's wrist and calling it *cotton candy.* Crouching down under the stampeding street, Charlie had watched the American fall back against that graffitied wall, his mouth a black round O as one of those baddies had stabbed a gun into his jiggling belly. Over and over again.

Fingers suddenly grabbed for and scraped against his face, and a woman's bloody eyes screamed at him as she was carried off towards the Rue de Maris. Charlie started crying then: careful hitching sobs that were as silent as he could make them be.

193

* * *

The Machine plucked another *ratte* from its hole. It screamed and cried and pleaded innocence. Children of the *Untermenschen* were already corrupt, and certain to be twisted by perversion. To put them down was a mercy before damnation. The Machine slit the *ratte*'s throat before kicking it back into the basement staircase – though not before plucking the flag from its fist and the Union Jack ribbon from its wrist.

Through established streets and prefabricated silhouettes, the Machine corralled and herded and trapped. In smaller spaces, it forced the fleeing *Untermenschen* into spherical, tightening masses of panic more easily plundered. Within the space of eight hours, the Machine had slaughtered greater than five times its number. Its challenge shrieked wild and long and unanswered.

Rick came to in darkness. He fumbled around, grabbing eagerly at shadows, his efforts rewarded only by ringing metal and its cold fleeting touch. When he tried to stand, he lost his balance too quickly, and the whispered wind atop the belfry reminded him of the precariousness of his position.

He suddenly realised that there were no longer any terrible screams in the streets below, though this development hardly reassured him. Instead, it set the hairs on the back of his neck higher still. His breath hitched deep inside his throat. His heartbeat thrummed.

There were fires out towards the mudflats and the airfield, and more along the beach to the north. Directly below, the Dutch Quarter loitered in silence and in darkness, while Paris sporadically lit up with sprinting lights that scared Rick above all else. All else except the smell that mingled with the salty taste of the sea. The smell of butcher meat.

Rick felt for and caught a scaffolding pole and pulled himself tight against it, resting his forehead at its cold steel hollow. Another sob clawed at his throat, and he drove a free fist into his bladder to stop it letting go. He released the pole only long enough to move his shaking hand towards his head. The skullcap that he only ever wore on days like this – when he was required to give some kind of speech at the climax of festivities – felt horribly wet as he slid it backwards off his head. It made a terrible noise as it

194

slapped against the ground, and he grabbed the pole hard again, closing his eyes and staying that way for many minutes until he was certain that he'd not been discovered.

Eventually reunited with what remained of his courage, Rick started moving himself slowly – and quietly – upwards on the scaffolding pole. A muted scuffle sounded in the street below, though it gave him pause for only a moment. If someone was still alive down there, then good luck to them. There was a jointed plastic rubbish chute that reached from the rear of the belfry to the grassy ground ahead of the beach approach, and Rick intended to ride it.

He'd begun blindly feeling his way backwards, stumbling over tools and sheeted swathes of plastic and cloth, when that scuffle organised itself into a stronger – and louder – rhythm. A sob worked its way up from deep inside his chest. He fought against letting it out, just as he fought against making certain that the skullcap had gone.

He lost his bearings, and in his panic couldn't remember how to reach the rubbish chute. A sudden return to muted light helped to better orientate him, though he was far from grateful. Another hysterical sob escaped him.

They were coming up the stairs. They were coming up the stairs to get him. Any lingering doubt about that was diminished by the dancing orange light that climbed steadily from below, throwing stark shadows against wood and metal and Rick's own skin. And destroyed by the invidious low chant that patiently followed.

"*Nacht und Nebbel, Nacht und Nebbel.*"

Rick knew what the words meant, of course. *Night and Fog.* Warped and stolen words for death, and the leaving behind of no trace. Rick had once considered evolving some kind of playground game out of such code names and their meanings: a bastardisation of *Kiss, Cuddle or Torture.* Kids loved that shit, they ate it up. A queer keening noise sounded in his ears. It grew louder in the instant that he realised it was coming from his own throat.

The Machine stood inside the tower and crowded its narrow mouth. It had no eyes, no face, and one voice.

Rick trembled and begged and pleaded. His heart stalled and overcompensated by thundering too hard and too quick. He dropped to his knees, and watched flickers of orange dance over the orderly lines of boots scuffed and stained dark by their night's labours. Rick screamed and prayed and denied all that he had ever known or pretended to believe in. Everything else he had already forgotten.

The Machine remained unmoved, repeating its mantra in careful, merciless cadences. Moving forward, ever forward. Extinguishing its own light; swallowing its own echo.

Rick scrambled towards it because there was nowhere else left to go. The wind whistled through the blown-out gap behind, and he couldn't bear to give himself up to it. He didn't have the courage. Still sobbing and pleading, he dragged himself forward; and when he was as close as he could bear to be, he dropped himself low to the boards beneath, flattening his arms and palms against them. And he began to lick the first set of boots.

For a moment, the Machine quietened. Rick could sense its grudging favour in a low hum like the purr of a pacified cat. Despite his disgust and sense of shame – and despite the dread that stole all that remained of his will – there was some small part of him that felt exhilaration. Some part of him buried so deep that it had gone untested and unrecognised all of his life. The Machine was his family. The Machine was his right. He needed it; he *yearned* for it. It was belonging.

A retch choked his throat as the Machine rolled over him in disdain. It pulled him apart and tossed him away and filled the space where he had been. It forgot that he had ever existed at all.

For a while the Machine stayed atop the high tower, looking into the night and watching it burn. In the ruins of the Rue de Maris, a gramophone record had caught its needle inside a scratched groove, and the title verse of 'There'll always be an England' played over and over to none. The Machine had few aims and fewer pleasures. It watched and hummed. It had done enough.

The next day, tabloids too jaded or afraid to address the true reality of what had happened inside the microcosm of the WW2000+ Experience buried themselves in its minutiae instead. Many ran with pictures of still-smouldering streets, or of survivors being led out through the broken-down gates: bedraggled tourists and local boys in Nazi uniform, bloody and exhausted faces slack with shock.

196

Many praised the prompt reactions of the emergency services and the citizens of Layer-On-Sea. One of the more argumentative broadsheets went with 'An Accident Waiting to Happen', although no others followed suit. All of them crowed about the end of *Richard Anderson's Nazi Theme Park*, their headlines dominated by exclamation marks and shared scorn.

None spoke of reasons or causes. Of the danger in thunderclouds, or the bile and fury of their forecast storm. The danger in ever forgetting what it was to belong.

After The Ape
by Stephen Volk

It was difficult for her to function with any kind of normality. Not when her lover was lying below, crisscrossed by ropes like Gulliver, people hacking out the insides of his body like whalers from Nantucket.

She'd taken to having her first cigarette while still horizontal, sucking in her already sunken cheeks, drifting into the penumbra of being fully awake. The morning newspaper was always lying outside the door but she didn't read it any more. Always full of stuff she didn't want to hear. Stuff that made her feel angry and sickened. Him. Herself. The lies. The legend. The jungle. What did they know about the jungle? They hadn't been there. None of them had.

In time the salty soreness of her tears compelled her to sit up in the cold of the hotel room, icy shoulders trembling, tiny arms frozen and white.

Doll eyes stared from the mirror. She hadn't set foot outside it for how many days now? How many weeks?

She didn't care: the room was safe. She was untouchable there, alone with her menagerie of thoughts and memories. Sometimes she wondered whether, if she left or was made to leave, those thoughts and memories might remain, like ghosts, her misbegotten soul haunting the building while her physical body was wheeled away on a gurney, nothing left of her but a soft-focus studio publicity shot and an obit in *Variety*. Somehow she knew how the headline would go.

What did they know? *They knew shit.*

That was the Bowery girl talking. That's what she was, after all, down to her raggedy-ass bones. And none of the glamour and pearls and platinum curls of Hollywood could cover that up for her in the end. *Once a bum, always a bum.*

She unscrewed the cap from the Bourbon.

(*Poppa's favourite*)

Prohibition. Joke. There were ways. The tumbler told her it hated to be half full.

The numb, plummeting wash of it brought up an acid reflux that hauled her monstrous hangover with it, dispelling any faint illusion her head was clear. Still, she was grateful for a taste of oblivion. Oblivion was her prime concern, of late. Any other concern – eating, sleeping, dressing – fell poor second. What could you do, when the hangover felt like it would kill you? Keep drinking. Truth is, she barely even tasted it any more.

On her wrist a gift from a producer who had a taste in watching instead of doing said eleven forty-five. Hell. Not that she'd missed anything – just that so much of the goddamn day loomed ahead of her. These days she despised being awake, because being awake meant thinking, and thinking meant remembering.

Twig fingers tweaked at the drapes. She knew sunlight was going to be painful on skeleton skin, but managed to let a gap of a few inches illuminate the scrunched-up sheets, the full ashtrays, the dirty glasses, the scattered shoes, the half-hung clothes, the latest Paris fashion fur coat strewn on the floor – where it would lie forever if she had her way.

Fur.

Those insensitive bastards at the studio.

Fur.

Last time she listened to the radio it was saying they were giving tours of him now. Taking folks on tours *inside* him, now. She pictured his chest cavity lit by strings of lamps like Jewel Cave in Custer, South Dakota she remembered visiting as a frightened, inexpressive, barefoot child. She knew they'd take out *her* insides too, if they could. The birds of prey of the *Herald* and *Times*, the graveyard worms and rats in raincoats with Underwoods where their morals should be.

The Story: it was all about getting the Story.

And the Story was her.

And sometimes in the darkness of night and nicotine with the shakes and spiders (Giant! Huge!) it was oh so appealing sometimes to say, "Here I am you sons of bitches, do with me what you will – here I am, chained, naked, shrieking – and then it'll be over and I'll have peace."

But this wasn't just about her. It was about the special thing that she and her lover had found and lost in a heartbeat, a great heartbeat like a jungle drum, and it was that they wanted to stamp

199

all over with their dirty thoughts and bad jokes and fabrications, and she wouldn't let them. It was too precious. Too rare. Too wonderful. Too strange. Too romantic. Too scary. She wouldn't let them abuse it and she wouldn't let them have it to do with as they pleased. It belonged to *her*. It was all she had left. That and the feeling as she slumbered that once again her lover's giant fingers were closing warmly round her body and she was safe again. It was the one thing, the giant thing they could never, ever destroy. Not with airplanes. Not with anything.

She heard the beeping of taxi cabs from the street far below. The traffic was moving. The traffic always moved.

She wanted to open the window but she daren't. The streets of Manhattan still ran sweet with blood. The oceanic stench of decay – a graveyard up-ended, said the radio – hung heavy in the air, and even as the lumberjacks and slaughtermen changed shifts day in, day out, nothing could be done to diminish it. It was a brave tourist indeed among the throng of sightseers from every state in the Union who wouldn't hold their nose or cover their lower face with a handkerchief when viewing the colossal remains. This Wonder of the World. This hairy Behemoth. This Goliath slain by David.

Goose bumps rose on her arms.

She picked up her dressing-gown embossed with the hotel's elaborate crest and wrapped it round her shoulders. It gave her the warmth of a surrogate embrace. The Bourbon – telling her, don't be shy – gave her another.

It didn't improve on the first. Instead made her feel sour and queasy, mingling with the disquiet she felt in her nerves and far from acting as an anaesthetic as she prayed, made her even more anxious with the hermetic silence of the room.

Not suddenly, but with conviction, she realised the very real possibility that she'd go mad here, and be carted to the nut hatch, or end up howling at the wallpaper, or running out onto Fifth Avenue, half naked like Mrs Partigan, who lost her brain and took to going shopping on icy winter nights wearing nothing but her undies, and would be chauffeured home by Rolly Absolom, the local deputy, with admirably sanguine regularity.

That was in Marshall, Nebraska, where she grew up, cold and unhappy, raised under the jurisdiction of her Aunt Jelly after Ma's last illness. She wished she'd seen her mother before she died –

200

but Brice was on the scene by then and Brice and her didn't get along, which was like saying the Great War in Europe was a difference of opinion. So doll-face, porcelain and pure, skipped off school (never did like it, got beat a lot) and hopped on a cattle train to New York like a hobo, but her Ma was already in the ground and Brice was damned if he'd pay the return fare, so she earned that singing on street corners and in various other manners, with a pair of goodish legs and a singing voice that got her by.

It was a tough climb and mostly she counted herself lucky if she made it to the soup kitchen every day. Hoofer. Chorus girl. Arm candy for a rich guy. Good time Annie for the distracted and misunderstood. Wasn't too choosy. Couldn't afford to be. When you'd slept on a doorstep in the pouring rain, you didn't ask to see a resumé. If the collar was clean, or if there was a collar, the feller was plenty good enough for you. For a night, anyhow: especially if he was paying for a bed. They started saying she should be in movies, and she heard that so many times it turned out to be true. She *was* good at acting. Every day of her goddamn life.

Tired of her own prehistory, she sat on the side of the bed and rang down for room service. The hotel operator's voice was chirpy and infantile, making her wonder if the girl was retarded: nobody could be *that* happy – unless maybe she was on the Bourbon too.

She had a difficult time with the words so she stayed monosyllabic: *ham, bread, eggs.* The girl repeated back her order, making it sound much more coherent and said it would be twenty, twenty-five minutes.

"Is there anything else I can help you with, ma'am?"

The actress spooled through a list of requests in her mind: *a life, happiness...* but said: "No. Just that."

Hung up, thinking, did she know? Of course she *knew*. They all did. Probably snickering up her sleeve right now. Calling her boyfriend, eager with the gossip. *Guess who we've got staying? No! Guess!*

The idea of food made her think of the slabs of meat being shorn off her lover's corpse. The two-man saws at work under the same hefty spotlights the studio wheeled out for the big night at that Broadway theatre when he was shown to the public for the very first time. Before all Hell broke loose. She thought of the massive steaks being packed in ice trucks and sent to the deprived,

201

the poor, the needy. There were placards out there saying it was near as God to cannibalism, but the Hungry didn't care. The Homeless didn't debate. The Jobless didn't grumble. Her lover had died and his flesh was being used to feed the poor. There was something desperately Christian in that, but wholly blasphemous at the same time.

When it came, the knuckle-rap on the door was brisk, snapping her blank stare.

Another glass since the phone call (pointless but effortless), she tucked her breasts inside her robe and tightened the belt with a tug. By the time she opened the door her fringe had drooped over one eye, her belt had loosened and her left tit was about to poke out and say *Howdy* if she hadn't rescued it.

Focusing before her stood a kid with short blond hair, his ears razored islands on the side of his head, standing to attention like a marine. He wore the white jacket with the horizontal epaulettes that was the hotel staff uniform, and first impression was the whole guy seemed as starched as it was. Black slacks straight as ramrods. Black polished shoes at six-thirty. The whole package made her feel even more sluttish and trashy.

"Come in."

The clockwork soldier entered. "Where would you like, please?" The tray.

She waved indiscriminately. "Anywhere."

"Very good, ma'am." Clipped. She tried to pinpoint his accent. European for sure. Hungarian? She should be able to tell. Plenty of those at the studios. Fleeing the old country. Fleeing their wives, too, mostly. Now he was running out of ideas, she could tell.

"Anywhere you can find a space."

He balanced the tray on a foot-stool at the bottom of the bed, uncertainly, and wiped his hands on his behind as he backed away.

She located her purse and spilled out some coins, picked up a few with her thumb and forefinger and dangled them towards him until he held out his palm. He nodded his thanks for the tip and, swear to God, a click of the heels went with it. In the mirror she'd seen his eyes on the bottle of ruin.

As his hand touched the door handle she said: "Can I interest you in an illicit beverage by any chance?"

The kid turned back, painfully polite and not a little nervous. "Thank you, but I do not drink." Eyes anywhere but on her.

"You mean you don't, or you won't?"

His cheeks flushed a little red, which she thought was sweet, and a curse. A display of his unworldliness which must be a burden to carry into adulthood, poor sap. A kind of affliction.

"Come on. Live a little. You're a long time dead. You don't get any prize in the hereafter for being stone cold sober. Not according to the churches I go to."

"I'm sorry. I should explain. The hotel, yes? I will be in a lot of trouble. In USA this is against the law."

"No kidding? What law? The law of the jungle?"

"I'm sorry. These are the rules."

"Oh, get the lead pipe out of your ass and enjoy yourself, kid. What's the worst that can happen? Nobody'll *know*. I won't *tell*. Promise." She put on a Shirley Temple voice: "*Cwoss my heart and hope to die.*" She genuflected and he noticed her fingernails made little white lines in her skin as they brushed it just above the bra-line of her night gown. Her skin seemed soft and still had the sheen of sleep. He looked away.

Turning from him she filled her glass, then turned back to him and drank from it as if demonstrating the procedure.

He looked at the coins in his hand and put them deep in the pocket of his slacks and didn't leave. She thought he was holding his breath, and maybe he was.

She sat on the unmade bed and crossed her legs, positioning the glass on her knee. The hem of her nightdress rode up her bare, shaved calf.

"You're German aren't you?"

He made an apologetic face. "My English is not so good."

"Ditto." She smiled to put him at his ease. "You're doing fine." She wanted him to smile back and he did. "Where you from?"

"Bavaria. Munchen. Munich." He pronounced it moon-itch, like something you'd scratch. "In the south. Close to the mountains."

"Yeah. We got those too. What's your name?"

"Peter."

"Peter," she repeated. "Hi, Peter."

Aged about eighteen, she guessed, he had a good ten, twelve years on her. She liked that. She liked the young. There was something optimistic about them. They didn't know what was to come.

"I – I better go."

"No. Stay," she said. "Talk to me."

He laughed uneasily. "You are a very nice lady, but I don't want to lose my job."

"You won't lose your job. I'm a guest. You're attending to the requirements of a guest. You won't lose your job. Sit down. Relax. Oh please fucking relax, Peter."

Her language shocked him. That wasn't the way women spoke. Not what he was used to. It was another thing that surprised him about America. It made him feel a little sickened and a little excited at the same time.

"OK. I sit."

He could see what was attractive about her. Even now, here, in this state, like some bedraggled bird with a broken wing she had some quality. Downstairs he had wondered if he would be able to tell that by meeting her, and he *could*, in an *instant*. It was true what they said, when they called them stars because they *shone*.

"What do you want to talk about?"

"Oh, surprise me." The arm that propped her up slid down the bed. "I haven't had human contact in seven days. I'm adrift. I'm shipwrecked. Do you know what *shipwrecked* means?"

"Of course. On an island. In stories."

She rested the glass on her forehead. "Not just in stories, baby."

Baby was an American expression. He told himself she didn't mean anything by it. It was a term made by a boyfriend to a girlfriend in this country. It was strange, but it was OK.

"Have you ever been to an island?" she asked.

"America is an island," he said. "A big one, but an island."

"That's not what I mean." She flicked ash onto the carpet. "I mean trees with coconuts on. Big green leaves as big as this carpet. Beaches where no white man has ever trod. You get the idea? Tribes with plumes in their hair and bones through their noses who live in fear of their God. Who sacrifice humans to him with the beating of dinosaur-skin drums." She sipped her poison, her eyes not leaving him the whole time. "That kind of island."

The kid didn't know how to answer. Instead he looked round the room – away from her – as if taking it in for the first time, or pretending to.

"You like this hotel?"

"Oh, it's peachy."

He took a step towards the door. "I can get you something, perhaps?"

"Sit down for Christ sakes, Peter. I want company, that's all. I'm not going to eat you." For some reason she laughed. For some reason this tickled her and she said it again while she was still laughing like a mule: "*I'm not going to eat you!*"

He smiled so that she didn't laugh alone, but he didn't know what was so funny. He looked at her where she lay. Her flat stomach under the silk nightgown shook with mirth until she felt foolish and ceased. He was still looking down at her in silence and she let him.

The room was dark. Sirens broke the air like wild beasts in the distance. It made them both remember where they were, and why.

He coughed and moved to the curtains to open them.

"Don't do that. People can see in. I don't want them to see in. Talk to me." She bent her elbow to prop up her head. Moved the glass to rest on the pinnacle of her hipbone. "Talk to me."

"What do you want me to say?"

She cocked her head to where the light was trying to get in. "Tell me what's happening outside."

"Outside?"

She took a mouthful of liquor and swallowed:

"What's happening to my lover."

She blinked her eyes once, dreamily. He wasn't sure if it was the drink. She looked very sad and alone: he couldn't remember ever seeing someone looking so sad and alone. Her eyes hid back in their sockets like his grandmother's eyes.

"Tell me the truth. I can take it."

Her breasts were tiny, like a girl's, and the space created by the fall of the nightgown was too big for them.

Afraid to go closer – touch her, break her – he leaned back against the wall as if, if he pressed hard enough, he might escape – but did he *want* to escape? A pencil-line of sunlight from behind

205

the drapes cast down his cheekbone, his throat muscle, one bicep, one golden button. The rest was in shadow.

"The traffic is flowing again," he began tentatively. "People are returning to work. President Franklin D. Roosevelt said in a speech yesterday that this great city *might be bloodied* but was *most certainly* unbowed."

He raised a fist but she didn't look at him and he wasn't sure she was listening as he spoke, but he spoke anyway, as he'd been bidden, hiding the fist again self-consciously behind his back.

"They are writing names on the walls of buildings. The relatives. Parents. Husbands. Wives. Writing the names of their loved ones. The ones who died in the slaughter." He saw her flinch a little at the word, and kept his voice low. "There were many, I think. Over seventy on the subway train alone. Many, they say in the bulletins, are missing. Still – what are the words? – *unaccounted for*. The parents and wives and sons sleep on the streets now, asking anybody passing for information. For hope, I guess. Or peace, when the bodies are found. It is a funny word – peace." For a moment he was lost for something to add. He looked at her face as if it might offer him a hint, but it didn't. "The rubble from the destroyed buildings has not all been removed. The trucks come and go through the night but they are hills that do not seem to get smaller. It is a huge job of course. The public services work like crazy round the clock to make stable the buildings they think might collapse and cause more destruction. Oh and dust. Yes. Dust still hangs in the air out there. It doesn't go away. It clings to your clothes. You go outside in a black suit and in five minutes it is white. Even funerals look like they have been sprinkled with icing sugar. Figures from a candy shop. It's not right."

He shook his head. When he looked up his jaw was set.

"Meanwhile the giant... he pays the price. The authorities, they are cutting and peeling off the skin from his arms in long strips, and rolling it up like carpet, taking it away to turn into leather – so the rumour goes – for use as upholstering in government limousines. I don't know if you should believe the rumours."

He wished that a little more light would fall on her but it didn't.

"There is a beggar," he said, filling the silence. "A bearded old Ashkenazer who sells souvenirs outside Macy's. You know

206

the wind-up monkeys who play... *clish! clish!*" Not knowing the word in English, he mimed clapping his hands.

"The toys?"

He nodded. "He has taken the – *clish-clish* off them, so they look like little replicas of the monster opening and closing his arms. But if you look closely you can see the little holes in the middle of their hands. I talked to him about the attack. He just shook his head and said it's Biblical. 'It's *Biblical*', he kept saying."

A memory returned to him and he recounted it quickly and with enthusiasm. "Yesterday when I walked past the scene I saw gang of children bouncing a basketball to each other then tossing it high in the air, trying to get it to land in the dead beast's nostril. Younger kids, on a dare, were plucking out the monster's hair – it took quite a tug, I could see! – and flicking them at each other like bullwhips." He chuckled.

The actress said nothing, and hardly moved. But she wasn't chuckling, he could tell that. His heart tightened in his chest.

"In the kitchen they said it was you. I didn't believe them."

She looked up. "Do I look like the photographs?" Aware of her appearance, she swiftly added: "Don't answer that question."

He laughed, shook his head in disbelief. "I am in the same room as the woman who was held in the hand of a damn monkey."

She lit a cigarette and left the packet sitting between her legs.

"He wasn't a damn monkey. He was a damn gorilla."

He could see the curve of her thighs so clearly it was as if she was naked. He wanted to feel the silk and feel her skin. If it was cold he wanted to warm it for her. If she was cold all over he could hold her to his body. He was not cold.

"Are *you* German? You look German."

She ran a hand through her curls and laughed.

"I've got news for you, kid. I'm not a natural blonde."

He blushed to his bootstraps.

"Greek Scottish on my father's side," she said. "Norwegian English on my mother's. Coat of many colours."

"Bella – she's a Pole who works downstairs washing dishes. She went with her sister and brother-in-law to see it. She was very excited. They all were. Hopping up and down like they were going to a Broadway show. Wrapped up in their scarves. She thought it would be somehow frightening, like a fairyground ride."

"Fairground. *Fairground* ride."

He nodded. "Like Coney Island."

Roll up, roll up.

"Go on."

"She said it wasn't. It wasn't at all." Eyes downcast, he looked unsure whether to continue. "When she came back she was real quiet. Just put her frozen hands in water and got to work. Later I asked her what happened and she said the head of it was as high as two tram cars on top of each other. Huge. As big as a house. You could live in it, she said."

Don't give them ideas, the actress thought, blowing cigarette smoke then waving it gently from her face.

"They looked up and they saw something catching the light. They couldn't work out what it was. Big. Glassy. Round. Then they realised. It was a tear. Frozen. Turned to ice on the creature's cheek. Big as a glitterball in a dance hall, they said. Like I say, they weren't laughing. They came back, like I say, real quiet." He shrugged. "Then the kitchen got busy. A hundred covers. We didn't have time to think about it after that. I don't know."

"What else don't you know?"

He looked up. "Sorry?"

"What else?"

He sighed. "Captain O'Rourke and his men, the pilots of the biplanes, had dinner at the White House." He heard her make a little snort of disdain. "Well, they are heroes, no? They risk their lives for the sake of the Motherland."

"They didn't die. He did."

"The enemy."

"Enemy of what, exactly?"

"I'm sorry... I don't understand."

Shivering, she picked up the fur coat from the carpet and wrapped it round her shoulders.

"Did you see his silhouette against the sunset?"

He shook his head.

"Then you *don't* understand," she said without any note of accusation, hardly louder than a whisper.

Her throat was dry and needy. She struck a match and the lit cigarette dangled from her pale, dry lips, its tip bobbing as she spoke. "Tell me about you. You have a family?"

"In Germany. I will tell them I met you."

"Uhuh. What will you tell them?"

"You are famous."

"I am now."

"You are pretty."

She laughed into a cough. "Once upon a time. This room sure is dark." (She wanted to ask him: *Was I pretty before I was famous?*) "Do you have a girl, Peter?"

"Sisters? Three."

"That's not what I mean. Sit next to me. You're a long way away. I can't see you over there in the gloom."

When he did, she patted the mattress next to her for him to move closer. Then did it again for him to move closer still. She placed her hand on his thigh and saw him shudder.

"Is my hand cold? Am I cold?"

He shook his head. She put it to his cheek.

"Will you take a drink with me? I don't like drinking alone."

He didn't say no, so she held up the bottle of Bourbon and pressed it against his lips. She tilted it up like it was a baby's bottle. Without moving his body he took a mouthful and swallowed; and when the bottle was taken away, with a sucking noise, he gulped air.

"That's it, now. You'll lose your job. They'll smell it on your breath. You've broken the rules, chum."

"I don't *care*," he said, tugging the bottle from her and swigging from it a second time, longer and deeper. She was astonished, and had to take it – *snatch* it – from him before he demolished the whole bottle. *Greedy little –*

Down the hatch.

"What's it for, eh? Booze?" She stared at the label. It swam. "Just a way to get back to the animal: that's all, when you think about it. Look at us. Human fucking beings. We've got hundreds, thousands of years of fucking civilization. We've got intelligence and progress coming out of our ears. We've got motor cars and fashion and society and welfare and adding-up machines and rotivators. And what do we need? When a man and woman get together we need something to evaporate all that. To get us back to the jungle. To wipe out history, to tear up books and wisdom, shed William Shakespeare, Homer, Jesus Christ and Henry Ford, Abraham Lincoln, Greta Garbo, Thomas Edison. To be what we were. Are. *Animals*." She rose to unsteady feet in the middle of the swamp of sheets and pillows. "What's a bed if it's not an island in the room? The island where we return to the past, the scary past, the exciting past, where we live or die on our instinct, on the blood pumping in our veins; not the whim of some bank manager or casting agent. We're at the mercy of the beasts that can eat us or save us or take us or raise us up to the – shit, the heavens!" The bed undulated under her.

He laughed. "Lady, you drink too much."

"And you don't drink *enough*. You better catch up. I'm waaay ahead of you."

"You'll fall."

"I *won't*."

She did. On her back, legs up from under her. Landed flat, breathless, next to him. Her hair dancing as the bedsprings whined like an orchestra tuning up. He leaned over and plucked each strand of hair from her face individually, an archaeologist carefully revealing a piece of precious treasure.

The kid said: "I am not an animal."

She smiled up at him. "I was kinda hoping you were."

Her upside-down eyes glinted.

He placed his hand on her belly and let the warmth spread out from him into her body.

She didn't move, kept staring at the ceiling. She'd had plenty of men touch her before. Boy, and how. Hock Sinnerd who took her to the creek and read to her from the Book of Genesis and told her if she held it a while it would get bigger and guess what? It did. Three guys from Winslow who told her how babies got cooked up, and illustrated, one of them with a hoard of pimples on his neck jumping out at her like frogs. The sweat and beer-breath of a married guy named Ivan Ives: he quoted from the Bible too, as he hitched up his 44-inch pants, as if to convince himself of the fact. Grass stains on your summer dress, carpet burns and hickeys: such a catalogue. The infections and insertions. All kinds, all ways, pleading, threatening, all wanting it then wanting you gone just as fast. Life as a receptacle. That's the way you know it's going to be. Learn pretty fast in this world.

She thought: That wasn't *love*. Not the love *he* gave me. *How could you compare?*

He who owned all he surveyed. Who knew no other of his kind. Who stood alone, Lord of Creation, as far as the eye could see. He saved me from monsters. Took me in his hairy hand and wouldn't let go. Wouldn't let the demons get me, even when they buzzed him and stuck him with their beaks and claws and drew blood. Carried me through the vitriolic swamp like a cannonball – miasma smell making me heady and giddy as a child taking their first sip of champagne. He never let me fall. Held me up to his face, that big dark wall, carnage breath wrapping me like a gift, eyes black tunnels with a freight train coming. Swatted a pterodactyl. Picked my clothes off one by one. Peeled me like a grape. Examined me under the Hollywood chiffon naked and white to see me as I really was. Rolled me to and fro so he could look me over back and front. Blew at my hair. Gazed at me in wonder. Took me to his home in the clouds.

And it wasn't about sex for once because sex was impossible. And that made her so, so safe. And so, so happy then, in a lost world, far away, but found.

She reached down to the kid's hand and held it, to stop it moving.

She said: "I was dreaming of him when his hand came through the window of my apartment. Shards of glass rained down over my bed and he hauled me out into the night sky. I thought I was still dreaming because I was floating. I could hear the wailing traffic a million miles below and the police cars whining and the thunder of his growl getting louder in his chest as he climbed and climbed –" She stopped. "…Do you want to hear this?"

He didn't say anything. He didn't move, epaulettes hunched over her.

She said: "I can still smell his hand, like a big black leather couch, the smell of a hothouse, of the Bronx Zoo, of a Mississippi swamp, of alligator gumbo, of nuts and palm trees and oil and dates and the blood of unsuspecting prey. And if I close my eyes I can see my own reflection right now, frightened and amazed, pinned there in his big brown eyes."

Her own unblinking eyes became baubles of tears. Lost again. From the lost land to lost love: her perilous journey, and now ashore where the rivers were brake lights and the cliffs were Wall Street, and the toucan-calls were *Extra, Extra*.

"He was a wonderful thing. He was a God," she said. "I couldn't escape then and I can't escape now. Because he died for me. I know he did. He placed me down in a place of safety so that

211

I wouldn't get killed when they came on that last figure of eight."
She shuddered and hugged the fur tighter round her. "He knew
what he was doing. He died for love. And nothing can ever be the
same, because that day, when the stream of bullets from the
airplanes tore into his skin, I died inside too."

Her whole body wept.

The kid touched her shoulder. She sat up briskly and
unexpectedly and threw her arms round him and held him tight. At
first he didn't know what to do with his hands, so he wrapped
them round her. He could feel her ribs, her shoulder-bones. He
could feel her heart beating, like a frightened bird's you'd pick up
in your hand, a damaged thing you'd want to save.

The kid didn't want her to die, he wanted her to live.

His fingers sank into her, shocking her. He held her by the
shoulders and pressed his lips onto hers, into hers, forcing her
head back sharply and mouth open and his mouth over it, hard.
Sucking the breath out of her he twisted her and pushed her down
onto her back on the bed. She was weak and frail and it didn't take
a fraction of his strength to overpower her. Was he overpowering
her? No, because she wasn't resisting in the least. She simply lay
there before him, her cage of a chest rising and falling quickly
through the shimmering silk of the nightgown to catch her breath,
eyes flickering like a doe deer brought down by a predator.
Startled, afraid – but the kind of fear, he thought, that meant
excitement and desire and longing and lust and not *Stop*, not *No*. If
she meant *No* she would say *No*.

Sirens and car horns battled in the street a million miles
below.

He knelt across her, Colossus – (or so he thought. Men!) –
taking her hand and putting it on his full erection coiled and
pressing against the cloth of his slacks. She didn't like to take it
away and hurt his feelings. Without a sound he furiously
unbuttoned his jacket from the bottom to the top. In the dark the
golden orbs popped and flew. She watched the vest come up off
over his head and saw that his emaciated chest had hardly any hair
on it. Saw the smoothness, the *pinkness* of him. All she could
think was, he *shone*. Then his pants were down and her nightdress
slid up in almost the same moment, as his weight dropped down
on her. His back made a bridge and he wriggled his hips till the tip
of his thing breached her and went deep so fast she uttered a cry

212

and dug her fingernails into his cold, doughy flesh – not an expression of pleasure, but she'd learned that the male of the species liked this kind of thing. Her knees dropped aside. Memories tumbled on her in a barrage of the past; a wall crumbling on top of her she couldn't stop. He gripped her face and pushed it back into the sheets, smothering her with fingers and thumbs as she struggled to gulp air down her throat. She grunted and sobbed – another requirement, thinking *Why? What? How?* And he was stabbing into her: a noble act, a heroic act, he thought – a Redemption, a Resurrection, yes – *ja, jawohl*. It was time she entered the world of the living again, and he was the man to do it. (Do it! Do it!) She would thank him. She would worship him. He'd be a God. And she'd be renewed and whole again and perfect and pretty and famous and fucked. And just as she was thinking, *Oh God, I wonder if it's possible to enjoy this*, and not the pounding sweat of it, the grunting Bourbon breath of it, the slow, numbing death of it, the disgust of it – it was over.

And he felt the heat of fame washing over him, like reporters' flashbulbs going off, like Valentino's smile, like a tuxedo on fire.

And she only felt the weight of him, the dead weight of him. And not that she didn't want it, but not that she did. And the Grand Canyon like someone had hollowed her out with a big spoon. And the Grand Canyon being full of trash, which was where she belonged, said Poppa, because that was what she was, and that's what she would always be – *you hear me?*

(*But you asked me to, Poppa.*)

(*I believed you, Poppa.*)

He slid his penis out of her, thinking that behind her closed eyes and smiling lips she'd rediscovered love.

(*Poppa?*)

But she was thinking of the ape's tree-trunk finger pressing against her belly atop the Empire State Building, his ebony fingernail a tarnished mirror. His caress so gentle for a big guy.

She rolled onto her side and hugged herself as the chill of the room returned.

They want the Story, she thought. Well you know what the Story is? The Story is: No man has ever come close to how I felt with him. On that mountain-top, on that skyscraper, with him at my side, towering so high, roaring as they came out of the sun.

Stand in front of it, said Poppa.
Look right into the camera, said Poppa.
Look frightened, said Poppa.
Beautiful, said Poppa.
Beautiful!
Beautiful!
Would anyone scare me like Poppa?
Would anyone love me like Poppa?
Then she remembered the blood in her lover's fur, cloying, clammy, clotted. How he swayed from side to side in startled puzzlement. Ageless. A Sequoia hacked down. A century collapsing, a world destroyed, a country eradicated. How she wanted to communicate, but could not. How she wanted to forgive him, but could not. Save him, but could not. How she wanted to be scared but fear was gone. His majesty. His Highness. His – *gone*.

She turned over and saw the German boy's head against the pillow and thought of the giant's head against the pillow of the sidewalk below, at the same angle, eyes non-focused in death.

He rolled his head to her. "It is what you wanted, yes?"

She paused before deciding to nod.

He smiled and lit one of her cigarettes and sat up – you could easily count his vertebrae – and stretched over to pick up his vest and hotel staff jacket, and dressed with his bare back to her as an airplane passed overhead with the monotone murmur of a disappointed voyeur.

Oh, the *pinkness* of him.

Her insides congealed. There was something inside-out about the feeling. The nausea of stepping off a carousel, which was supposed to be an enjoyable experience but wasn't – and yet the relief of *being* off. She didn't want to think about it.

He handed her his cigarette and lit another for himself. She considered the action unbearably familiar and unbearably arrogant. She wanted to cry again.

He stood up, his shadowy cock, now shrunken and unimpressive, dangling under the rim of his white jacket, and peeked behind the drapes at the afternoon sunlight. "Damn monkey." He chuckled as he buttoned up his collar. "We socked him good, huh?"

She pulled the sheets around her in a nest.

214

He got onto the bed on all fours and kissed her with puckered lips, which she endured. His grin was horribly self-congratulatory and she wondered how much of this had been his purpose: to screw the actress in 7205? Perhaps he had announced it to the others as he picked up her tray. Perhaps he'd brag about it tonight in a bar. He had not been violent and hadn't hurt her, even, as others had done – that was exactly it: she felt nothing. Nothing at all. There was a gaping hole inside her where he'd been and it was as if it hadn't happened at all, and she knew with great clarity that was the way it would always be from now on.

She sat up in bed with her breasts and knees covered.

"I hope you don't lose your job."

"Screw my job," he said.

He was a different person now, as they always were. And it was never a surprise to her, but it always hurt.

"You know what they call me in the kitchen? *Sauerkraut.* This was supposed to be the land of the free, the home of the brave, of democracy and opportunity. I came expecting bright, clean Americans like bright clean American automobiles, not sweaty Turks tweaking my ass and blowing me kisses and Italians barking and cursing at me, sticking my hand into boiling water for dropping a plate, a Jew begrudgingly giving me my stinking wages at the end of the week. I expected New York to be like an elevator, going up, always up, like the tall buildings, taller, higher, always higher. A place of money, a place of glamour and power and gasoline. Not foreigners and perverts."

He held his stomach in, puffing his hairless chest as he pulled on his slacks. "My father sent me here to learn the hotel trade. One year, he said: you will learn more than in any university. He owns three of the biggest hotels in Munich, one in Frankfurt, two in Berlin."

He tucked in his genitals. "I always thought the United States would be great, but it is not so great. I expected a strong country, but it is not strong. It is weak. A cripple, like your President. You have no work – no good work. Thirteen million unemployed. Almost every bank is closed. People are losing their farms, homes, businesses. You have no money, no hope…"

"We have movies."

He snorted. "Which is what? Nothing but a sign of decadence." Threading his belt buckle, tugging it to the right hole

215

and poking the pin through. "I have read the history books. This is the way empires fall. Look around you from your high buildings and what do you see? The poor rewarded for doing nothing, immigrants like me given opportunities while patriotic Americans struggle. Your country is sick and your men are standing by watching it happen. They are not fighting for what they value. They are not fighting for the future. They do not have a leader powerful enough to make things change."

The actress held her cigarette vertically with her fingertips and blew on it so that the tip glowed red.

"I'm going back home. Not to Munich. To Potsdam," he said. "I have an uncle there, an industrialist. I know there is always a job there open for me." He waited for a reaction from her but all he saw was a long glowing red puff on her cigarette. The blue smoke hung flatly in the air between them. He crushed his own cigarette out on the plate of cold, untouched food.

"Come with me. A new life. A good life." he said. "America – it is a place for dreams. But for some dreams you have to return to Germany."

She said: "I think there's a Potsdam up in Saint Lawrence County."

The kid laughed through his nose at that – funny girl, crazy girl.

Stupid girl, said Poppa.

"I'm serious. Come. It is beautiful."

Beautiful.

This way. To the camera.

You're frightened. You're amazed. You're terrified.

As the jungle drums began pounding in her heart, she imagined marrying this man. She could, so very easily. After all he thought she was a star. He *knew* she was a star. You could see it in his eyes. He wanted that radiance of fame, of anecdote, of fable, to fall on him. He wanted to be larger than life too. He wanted to have her on his arm, to show her off to bosses and officers and leaders. Own her forever and have her obey his orders. She could see herself making home with him in some little cuckoo-clock house with deer buck heads on the wall, with parties hunting boar or gnawing chicken legs and swilling beer. Or a trophy wife in Los Angeles. She a star – the parts would come knocking ("No jungle pictures!") – him a screenwriter, or producer, or both. Kids,

216

several. Nannies, English. Stern, but not too stern. He'd slap her occasionally, but only when she'd deserve it. He'd have affairs, but then so would she. He'd find some younger, prettier version. So would she. The divorce would be expensive. She'd get the children and dogs. He'd get fat, bitter and twisted, not necessarily in that order.

"You know," she said, "I'm ready for breakfast now."

He gave a broad grin exposing his white, so-perfect teeth. The parenthesis grin of a football player with a chiselled jaw. So American.

"And some good, strong, black American coffee," she said.

He picked up the tray. "You are on the mend, yes?"

"Yes."

"I love you."

Everyone wants to love you, said Poppa, on the boat, during the voyage to the island. And you know what? Let them.

"I know," she said.

When the kid had gone and the door was closed and she was alone again in the room she imagined her lover's gigantic skull, polished and white in the lobby of the Smithsonian, surrounded by a party of eager schoolchildren, any one of them smaller than his pointed teeth. The skeletons of dinosaurs keeping a respectful distance. The stare of aeons in the space where his beautiful eyes used to be.

She got out of bed and took a sheet of hotel notepaper from the drawer. Sitting with her reflection in front of her – who was that woman with ribs in her chest you could count? Pale, gaunt, frightening: why would anyone make love to *that*? – she changed her mind and rummaged in her purse. She spiralled out her lipstick and wrote on the mirror:

Thank you, Peter.

Thanking him for making it clear. Even if he wouldn't understand. Couldn't understand. Could anyone? Then she signed her name. Her autograph. Maybe it would be worth something one day.

(*See, Poppa, I'm worth something after all.*)

She had to hurry now. It would only take so long for the elevator to descend and return.

Light flooded the room like a bomb blast so bright she had to cover her eyes. When she opened them again, blinking, her surroundings took on a different aspect, washed with colour anew. It seemed she was in a different hemisphere now. A different latitude. The world up-ended, transformed, and rare. And she felt no longer weak and fragile and worthless: she felt strong and excited and loved.

The drapes fluttered like flags, horizontal into the room.

She shed the fur from her shoulders. It gathered behind her feet.

She knelt, then stood. Bare feet. Bare legs. Goosebumps. White skin. (The kid with the whitest skin in school – so poor she couldn't afford *shoes*.) Silk dressing-gown (*silk* – how she'd moved up in the world) clinging, a goldy sheen over the dark nipples and black V of her gender – invisible.

Looking down at ants the way he looked down.

Like her lover, she felt no fear.

The unnatural blonde closed her eyes.

Doll eyes.

Drums in her chest.

Took one foot from the window-ledge, then the other.

As it had to be – falling like he fell. Seventy floors, sixty, fifty – then the numbers floated away, irrelevant like everything else. Wind raked through her frizzled hair, an ice-blonde blur as she dropped, pinioned by her plummeting. All her senses peeled away to reveal a peculiar kind of freedom, a strange kind of pleasure that life would not be there to torment her very much longer, and that was fine, that was OK. A euphoric surge enraptured her: *Thank God for that*, and she prepared to enjoy her last few seconds on this earth, unencumbered by the future. And all she could think of was the smallness of it all. And the air rushing past. And that his mighty hand might catch her, even now. And his mighty roar might yet echo in the canyon of the skyscrapers with the mighty beating of his chest. And he would save her. And they would be together on the mountain-top. Because it wasn't like the papers said, oh no. It wasn't "Beauty killed the Beast". It was Romeo and Juliet. Of course it was. And that was how all great love stories ended, didn't they? ...Like this.

* * *

What is the ape to Man? A laughing stock or a painful embarrassment. And Man shall be just that for the Superman: a laughing stock or a painful embarrassment. Once you were apes, and even now, too, Man is more ape than any ape. (...) Behold, I teach you the Superman! The Superman is the meaning of the Earth. Let your will say: the Superman shall be the meaning of the Earth!

– Friedrich Nietzsche, *Thus Spoke Zarathustra*

Zulu's War
by David A. Sutton

"Get a round in, Zulu."

Zulu wasn't black. Nor had he ever been to South Africa. It was just that a distant relative twice removed had been in the Staffordshires at Isandhlwana; some members of his platoon had got wind of the story and the nickname had stuck. Lennie hadn't minded. Zulu was a fucking macho moniker, all right. He secretly saw himself brandishing a great oval shield made of buffalo hide and a spear with a fucking gut-ripping point on the end of it. And while his imagination didn't go as far as having some totally barmy bone through his conk, he did see himself half-naked, with ostrich feathers adorning his privates and cutting up rough with some pompous redcoat-git-officer with a fucking plum in his gob.

The Brasshouse on Broad Street was heaving. On a Saturday night Birmingham's swinging booze belt was red-hot and jam-packed with exposed female flesh. Zulu could smell them, young women eager to ball. He was eager to ball too. He'd not been long back and he didn't feel one hundred per cent, and he was hoping such distractions would help him lay his ghosts.

"Here, don't say I never get you nuffing." Lennie managed to place four pints of lager onto the table without spilling a drop. His companions were sweaty with the heat and the drink they'd already consumed. Their appearance, he noted, was a reflection of him not so long ago... in the desert heat. Sweaty and dirty and eyes lit by an arousal that could be anticipation, or fear. As he sat down his hand automatically fingered the metal souvenir in his pocket. It was much colder than the change from twenty quid he'd been given at the bar. He flexed his biceps and pecs, stretching the tight fabric of his T-shirt. His body advertised its fitness, yet in himself he wasn't right.

Of the four men, Duncan was, like Zulu, in the forces. Phil and Ray were builders, or so they liked to think. But they all had one thing in common: the lack of a stable family upbringing during their formative years and a few juvenile skirmishes in front of the beak; and for Phil, some time in youth custody. They had kept in touch as they grew older, the bonds of burglary and break-ins being stronger ones than the parting of their ways to adult work and careers.

"Seen the news?" Ray asked in his squeaky voice, promptly reducing his pint by half in one open-mouthed gulp.

"What? Somebody nuked the 'ouses of Parliament at last?" Zulu asked. His flippancy hid resentment towards a government that was, he believed, fucking up his life.

"Maybe we should." Ray added dryly.

"Piss off, you Sassenach git." Duncan did a thing with his eyes that made them slant this way and that like he was some Svengali in a silent film. "Who gi's a toss, man. Look at the meat, will ya." The Scotsman sat a head taller than the others, swiveling his neck as if he was a marionette.

They all laughed at the lascivious smile that crossed Duncan's features. Around them in the bar were tons of women, laughing, drinking, and readying themselves for the clubs.

Phil said, "Wasn't there no totty in the casbah, then?" Phil couldn't imagine anywhere where there weren't lap-dancing clubs, massage parlours and scrubbers touring the streets in tight skirts. He was the only of the four who was married, but that didn't seem to hinder his extra-curricular activities.

Duncan's closed fist shot out towards Phil's jaw, converted at the last second into an open palm that gently cuffed him on the neck. "I don't shag Arabs, you English cunt."

"Bet Zulu wasn't fussy about shagging pussy in a burkha," Phil continued, having wrestled Duncan's hand away from his face. "Is that right, mate? Knocking-shop in every village?"

Lennie nodded non-committally, nursed his pint and then took a sip. The booze had started to taste off. Maybe it was. Or maybe it was him. He didn't want to talk about the last few months, but it was expected. You couldn't be a pongo on leave without your mates wanting to hear all about it. Especially the shagging and the shooting.

Duncan answered for Lennie. "If there were any, we didn'a see 'em. And if we did, they were oot o' bounds. I'll take a wank ev'ry night, thank-you-very-much, nay castration by some terrorist Arab pimp! Ay." His laugh was more of a growl.

Lennie took another sip from his glass. Both he and Phil had smoked some skunk on their way to the pub and he was guessing that was what was making the lager taste funny. In fact, *he* was

221

starting to feel quite a bit off, as the skunk messed around with his head, bringing up memories he'd rather stayed dormant.

"Don't tell me you haven't heard?" Ray came back into the conversation. His face glowed with perspiration and gloating. "Couple of your lot been 'ad up. Been a bit rough with the natives apparently."

Zulu's head turned sharply as if he'd suddenly been gripped in an arm lock. "Staffords?" He tried to sound incredulous, as if it was inconceivable that his regiment could ever be involved in... well, what the papers liked to call war crimes.

"Think so," Ray answered, meaning yes.

Duncan gave Lennie a strange look, an expression that tried not to reveal its guilt, and dropped his gaze, nurturing his glass. There was a pause in their conversation and the overcrowded pub's chatter swept over them like white noise.

Lennie hoped that he could hide his demeanor behind that cacophony, but was sure the shame on his face was apparent.

Phil said loudly, "Probably deserved it, ungrateful bastards." No one asked whether he meant the soldiers who had been had up, or their supposed victims.

"You're nay wrong there, Phil," Duncan said. "Things happen none of us like and we see things we don't ever want ta see agin. We shouldn'a be ashamed though – we had a job ta do and we did it. Ay."

All of a sudden, Lennie was back *there*, a flashback triggered by what Duncan had said and the manipulative skunk. His unit was on foot patrol, having been dropped off from the Abu Naji base in Al Amarah, and they were somewhere near Al Uzayr. The Tigris River flowed unseen to their left. The unit was picking its way carefully along the line of reed beds that flanked the river. It was quiet except for the swishing of the reeds, and it was hot. Lennie's fingers were slippery on his assault rifle. He was nervous and almost shivering despite the blistering heat. They were searching for insurgents who had detonated a roadside bomb that half an hour earlier had eviscerated a patrol car and its occupants. He could still see the plume of black smoke rising into the air from the wreckage about half a mile behind him. Duncan was commanding the unit, slightly ahead, and appeared to be as calm and cool as a cucumber. The Scotsman turned and gestured with the palm of one free hand and, as one, the unit dropped silently to a crouching position.

Lennie thought he was going to shit himself. Then his sphincter took control, but the effect was to propel roiling nausea throughout the rest of his guts. He no longer possessed the bravery of a Zulu at Isandhlwana.

The bulrushes swayed in the breeze and rustled. Lennie imagined them concealing a dozen enemy combatants, who might open fire any second. But Duncan was up again and gesturing the men to come forward one at a time, leap-frogging each other round the boundary of marshes and down across a muddy channel where a stagnant finger of the river was half silted up. When it was Lennie's turn to lope forward his gullet wanted to open up and relieve his stomach of that morning's breakfast. He fought the nausea and made his way through the muddy inlet, across and awkwardly up the steep bank on the other side, to take up a firing position with his comrades. Not far ahead of them were the buildings of a small village…

"Still, it's all gone sour, hasn't it," Ray said. "Nobody wanted the fucking war in the fucking first place." Lennie realised that Ray had changed since the last time they'd met. Ray had developed an opinion on the war and was willing to express it.

"I don't want to go back," Lennie said queasily before he could stop himself. He didn't know whether his words had come out as a cowardly plea, or suggested some sort of agreement with Ray's position.

"C'mon, Zulu, you've done your bit," Phil said. "They won't send you back again?" Phil was fond of Lennie, a sort of skunk-induced brotherly camaraderie that he couldn't have analysed even if he'd wanted to.

"Don't be a twat. We've a'ready got oor tickets and tour booked, man!" Duncan spat out the words. It was obvious he was a reluctant soldier boy too, but didn't want to show quite as much spinelessness as Zulu.

"*Fuck.*" Phil couldn't imagine anything worse. All that fighting, plus the regimentation – just like the brawling that went on, and the discipline that was meted out, in Borstal. And the lack of sex.

"It was bad, then, was it, last time?" Ray asked. He sounded contemptuous, as if he would have lapped up a tour of duty in

Maysaan Province and asked to have his leave cancelled besides. But *he* hadn't joined up. *He'd* been sitting on his arse watching the fucking news instead.

"Don't worry," Lennie said harshly, "there's not much chance you'll ever be in the shit like us. The army don't take *weeds*." Ray was short and weedy all right, but Lennie regretted saying so as soon as the words were out, because Ray had been one of those kids who hadn't thrived. He just came down with anything that was going the rounds. It wasn't his fault he was a runt. "Sorry," Lennie mumbled.

Time was standing still as Lennie aimed his SA80. The dwellings a short distance away were ramshackle slums. Litter was strewn around and the walls were pockmarked with the evidence of a firefight that might have taken place last week, or several years ago. He sighted his gun on a glassless window. Beyond the opening there was blackness and silence.

This is going to be it, he thought. The day I peg out. A sitting target with virtually no cover. He was angry and terrified at the same time.

Out of the corner of his eye, fast, several figures moved in the space between buildings. Lennie thought he saw them carrying weapons, but they had moved so swiftly he couldn't be certain.

Duncan was waving for them to hold fire. Hauling himself above the dune, he raised his SA80, the one that was augmented with the under-slung forty-millimetre grenade launcher. Despite its size, the weapon gave almost no recoil as the sergeant fired. A brief second or two passed and Lennie jumped as the ordnance fragmented among the buildings. The thump of it wasn't particularly loud, but the effects were dramatic as a shaft of flame gushed skywards, along with debris and, presumably, some body parts.

As bits of concrete clattered back to earth the firing started…

"Don't be fucking sorry, Zulu, Ray's turned into a fucking pacifist," Phil stated. "Anybody want another drink?" He rose to head for the bar, not waiting for the inevitable reply.

Lennie was tempted to say no to another lager, but thought it would look bad. As in wimpish. In any event, maybe another drink would finally drive away the skunk flashbacks. And make him forget. Except that the thing in his pocket wouldn't let him. The thing in his pocket felt cold and burned like ice. As it had when he'd acquired it...

The walls of the buildings erupted with smoke as forty-five millimetre shells at a rate of seven hundred rounds a minute pocked and ricocheted off the surfaces. The sound of firing and the impacts were deafening. Another grenade punched through a wall and the building it hit almost collapsed as the explosion burst in all directions, throwing up a cloud of dust.

Duncan shouted something that Lennie didn't hear, and all the other men were on their feet, charging towards the village, screaming like banshees. He rose up as well, more in keeping with blind group hysteria than as an individual obeying an order. And they all ran the couple of hundred metres or so between the marshes and the village.

Lennie was amazed that none of the men was hit by returned fire, but they all made it to the shelter of half-demolished walls and their own firing ceased, leaving behind an eerie silence. Smoke was drifting on the air. For a moment Lennie hoped that the village was uninhabited after all, that there were no insurgents lurking, waiting to take him out. Then came the wailing. The pitch of the sound curdled his blood, a rising cry that was choked back as it reached full volume. Then came again. Stopped. *Came again.*

As it started to freak Zulu out, Duncan whispered to the men, sharing out the patrols in different directions, to search the village. "Zulu, you'n me'll find that fuckin' caterwauling and put a stop ta it."

The men moved off warily, while Lennie and Duncan skirted around the ruined building, through a badly-fenced enclosure in which a goat was lying, wild-eyed and stunned by the firefight, and onto the dusty main street. As they did so, the wailing ceased.

"Where'd it come from, d'you think?" Duncan asked.

Across the street there was a dilapidated house with corrugated iron shutters across the windows. The door was shored up similarly, but had been partially bent inwards, leaving enough space for someone to slip through.

Lennie nodded at the house. "Let 'em have it, shall we?" He would rather open fire and blitz the building than attempt to cross the street and risk close combat.

"No, let's check it oot. See the whites of their damned eyes, man!" Duncan was still angry. He wanted revenge for the men

225

killed in the personnel carrier. Lennie did too, but he didn't think he had the guts any more. The war was wearing his resolve.

In seconds they had crossed the dirt road and stood each side of the ruined doorway, weapons ready. Then Duncan used his boot to trash the flimsily-hung corrugated door and it gave way completely. And both men entered the building.

Lennie located the sobbing first, from a room beyond the one they stood in. But it was dark, he couldn't see past the opening in the wall. The crying was pitiful and yet sounded as if its source was trying unsuccessfully to muffle the sobbing.

"Fuckin' civilians." Duncan had ducked under the opening without a thought and was standing, gun pointed downwards. "C'mon, Zulu."

Lennie walked into the room and saw a woman crouched on a bed in a corner, swaying backwards and forwards. She was holding part of her clothing across her mouth, trying to choke back her weeping. Her dark, accusatory eyes were deluged with tears. Her other hand cradled a thickly wrapped bundle to her breast. The cloth of the bundle was red and wet. Shrapnel, a stray bullet? It's the luck of the draw, Lennie dismissively decided. But then something akin to compassion sought to intervene.

"We'll have to help –"

"We'll have to do *nay* such thing." Duncan broke in. "We've nay finished here."

"But..." Then Lennie remembered the insurgents. They might still be hiding in the village. "I'd better check that other room."

"Ay."

As Lennie was about to move, a hand appeared through the open doorway, waving a piece of white cloth. A teenager emerged, eyes wide with fear, holding his flag of surrender high up so that it couldn't be mistaken for anything else. Two other young men followed him into the bedroom; they were no more than boys really. They were jittery with terror.

"What'll we –"

Duncan gestured to the trio to drop to their knees and, using the barrel of his rifle, made them put their hands behind their heads. "If any o' 'em move so much as a fuckin' eye-fuckin'-lid, show 'em that your gun's still loaded."

226

Then he walked, strutted almost, into the vacated room. It went very quiet for a minute, other than for the woman's miserable crying. The three young men crouched, their heads hanging as if in shame. Occasionally one of them would turn to sneak a look at the woman, but Lennie was unable to see what emotions were wrought upon their faces.

In the other room Duncan was turning up things, kicking over furniture. Then his distinctive Scottish lilt came through loudly. "Ay. Knew it, fuckin' *knew* it."

When he came back into the room he was carrying two Russian made sub-machine guns as well as his SA80. The wild madness in Duncan's eyes was unmistakable. Lennie knew that most Iraqis carried weapons, so they probably shouldn't attach too much significance to the find. Duncan, however, was animated. He wanted revenge. Culpability on the part of these teenagers was a minor detail.

The tableau held for a few more seconds and then firing began from somewhere else in the village. A burst from one of their unit's assault rifles that tut-tut-tutted for a few seconds and then stopped.

Duncan did not even flinch.

Lennie's neck returned to its full length again after his head had tried to hunch down within it, and his heart was racing, thumping as if it was a galloping horse's hooves on hard turf. His brain fizzled as if someone was frying bacon in hot fat in his skull. He started to see their captives in a different light, not as civilians but as fighters, which was, after all, what Duncan suspected.

Duncan butted one of the boys in the head with his gun and the woman screamed as he collapsed, squirming in pain at her feet.

"*Shut* up!" One thing Lennie couldn't stand was a screaming woman. He stepped forward, pointing the muzzle of his rifle at her head. "Stitch it, you cunt."

She dropped her bundle and it rolled onto the floor, where it lay soundless and motionless. In her hand, for a fleeting second, Lennie saw a pistol.

His rifle bucked once. At near point blank range half the woman's head disintegrated, flinging bone, blood and brains to splatter up the wall behind her. As the body fell to one side Lennie could see the pistol for what it really was: the woman's own hand, coated in the drying blood from her infant.

The other two teenagers had jumped up and caught Duncan by surprise while Lennie was staring at the woman, and more firing had commenced outside. One of them had grasped Duncan's gun by the barrel and was wrestling with it, the other trying to strangle him. Lennie turned and without thinking his gun popped twice and each boy fell. Duncan stepped over the head-butted third boy and pumped a round into his head.

"Check them over," Duncan ordered. "Leave their guns by them, they'll di as evidence. One more job then it's time ta leave." There was an icy lack of emotion to his voice, as if either the killings had not been sufficient enough for retribution, or having been almost accidental, they did not supply adequate emotional charge to satisfy Duncan's quest to dispatch the killers of the road patrol.

Lennie would rather they left right away, but knew that Duncan would want this neat and tidy, if not forensically unquestionable. "Drag it outside and bury it in the yard." He pointed to the woman's body.

Outside, Zulu turned over the woman's body and watched the half a head that was left attached loll to one side, her dark and staring left eye so motionless and unforgiving above a cheek lacerated by streamers of blood. Something fell from her neck and almost inadvertently he caught up the object. It was a crude metal pendant, rough-shaped, on a short chain. In his palm, it was as cold as ice. He slipped it into a pocket before finding a small spade to dig a shallow grave.

As the rest of the patrol approached down the main street, Duncan took a last look inside the house. "Fuck!" Lennie heard him swear as he hastily scooped the last few shovelsful of sand over the body.

"Nobody here, Sarge," one of the men shouted as they approached. "Except a few villagers!"

"Zulu! Get in here quick."

Lennie waved vaguely, acknowledging the rest of the patrol as he stood up and stepped back inside the house. Duncan was holding the bloody bundle. "Nay time to bury this. Oot back," he ordered, "and chuck it." He held out the infant.

Lennie's innards did a somersault, but the expression on Duncan's face was murderous, so he took it. As he cupped the swathed babe in his arms, he was surprised by its lack of weight. It

228

felt soft beneath its coarse wrappings. The fabric was warm and wet as if the baby needed its nappy changing. He was grateful that he was unable to see its face as he ran back to the stagnant ditch by the river and flung it from him. There was a rustle as if a bird was flapping its wings among the reeds, followed by a watery plop as the little body disappeared from view. Lennie stood numbly for a moment, hardly able to believe what he had just done.

On the way home from the pub, having failed to pull and feeling too wrecked to try the clubs, Phil and Zulu smoked some more skunk. Zulu's flat was close enough to Broad Street to walk the distance. He left Phil at a taxi rank and then headed down deserted side streets. Broad Street had been busy. Traffic streaming along in both directions; exhaust fumes vying with the restaurant smells. The pavements swarming with young men and women, sauntering, hurrying or staggering. Noisy and safe. But now he was alone and he began to feel uneasy. He shouldn't have had that last joint. The streetlamps appeared to be slowly moving towards him and then rushing to pass behind him, but he knew it was the cannabis hit. The discarded sheets of a newspaper flipped up from the pavement and danced, and for a second he saw the dead woman's white clothing and the redness of her blood, but it was just a newspaper and its red-top. Nevertheless, he skirted around the flapping newsprint as if it was intent on attaching itself to him.

Before long, he had reached the low stone wall of the old cemetery, one that he used as a regular shortcut to his home. An old dark church surveyed a small field of dilapidated and skewed tombstones through its dimly-lit windows. He ducked through the lychgate. Litter peeked from behind one of the headstones as the wind cut across the graveyard and he swerved to one side to avoid it. Merely a balled-up fish and chip wrapper, not a mangled face.

Lennie stopped for a minute, his breathing laboured. He was trying to restrain weird fancies that the cannabis was using to terrify him. Gravestones blocked his passage, mocking him with surfaces etched like faces. They marked the passing of beloved relatives; they labelled the dead with names and dates; they stood defending their place against the passage of time. They demonstrated solidity in the face of mortal putrefaction. The dissolution that he had caused, in contrast, went unrecorded. There had been no funeral, no eulogy for that innocent soul so far away.

As his fear-driven abstractions cranked up along with his breathlessness, the textures of the boneyard softened. Rigid stones became dunes of sand. The decaying petals of flowers dissolved into pink blemishes of blood on sand.

The heat of the night was draining. Lennie smelled decay wafting from the dunes. He recalled the stories from many countries, throughout history, of the massacres, the mass graves and the rotting flesh and the wailing. Men embedded in their own history repeating this ritual slaughter.

He was part of it.

His *own* little mass murder.

He lurched on, sand shifting as he walked, where no sand should lie. And then he heard a familiar crying. He sought the church and sanctuary, but there was no longer the old blackened stone or stained-glass windows illuminated from inside by a solitary bulb. Reeds hissed, dry as the pages of musty prayer books opened in unison by pious congregations. Lennie had been forsaken.

When a hummock of sand gave way beneath his feet, Lennie at last expressed his terror; his muffled squeal failed to subdue or drown out the weeping voice.

Something was rising from the sand beneath him. A shape shrouded by a garment creased with dried brown blood. Up it came with a determination, thin bony arms rising between his legs, the hooded face thrusting up, a half skull of dehydrated tissue. The arms grasped his legs, beseeching him for something. Lennie quivered. He thought he knew what it was.

Inside his trouser pocket, the pendant was dry-ice cold. He shook off the rising corpse and removed the pendant as he stepped backwards. Placing it in his palm, he used his other hand to prise open the malleable metal leaves that formed a protection for what was inside. He'd not thought to do this before; after what he had done in Iraq it seemed a final desecration. Lennie stared in astonishment at what was revealed. He was reminded of Sunday school and old illustrated Bibles: small colour plates interspersed between printed pages made of thin, crinkly paper. Paper so insubstantial it seemed only one primitive step from the papyrus from which it had been fabricated. He recalled scenes from the scriptures rendered in muted colours, figures wearing ancient clothing, yet reminiscent of the people back in Iraq... Spreading out the half-crumpled picture, Lennie saw that it depicted a bearded man, God or Jesus, bearing a judgmental sword and with a face darkened by a frown. Haloes of light surrounded the figure, illuminating an idealised idyllic landscape in the background. Did it matter more that he had murdered a Christian, Zulu wondered.

Looking up, the blood-spattered corpse was almost upon him again. As her wrinkled hands touched his ankles, a shiver more ferocious than the most impressive of agues coursed through his body and his thoughts retreated into the fug of the skunk. He managed to take a few steps backwards, stumbling and recovering. He shivered insanely. He turned aside, he could not face making eye contact with the dead woman.

At last, he remembered what she wanted and he cast the religious icon, and its crude metal locket, towards the risen dead. Turning around, he ran.

Within a few minutes he was in his flat and the locked door provided a barrier from the intrusions of the dead. In the darkened room he lit up a joint and inhaled deep enough to stop the shaking. As he became light-headed, Lennie sat and a momentary calm infused him, fogging his brain. But the marshes around the Tigris drifted in and out of his vision, the reeds along the river crackling in the wind, imitating nature's melody and the bullets' random penetration of walls. The village came into view and Zulu saw the house and the shooting; blood smeared his vision as it had smeared walls, flesh and clothing.

When the knock at the door came, Lennie realised that the little Christian image was not the only thing the corpse wanted. There was something infinitely more fundamental he had wanted forgotten. The door banged again, louder, and was followed by an insistent, desperate rapping. The sound clattered around the flat, sending him whimpering into darker shadow next to a drawer unit. A tap was drizzling in the bathroom nearby, imitating a river hissing through bulrushes.

He attempted to clear his thoughts. Nothing came to help, only visions of death and no resurrection. The presence outside his locked door was waiting and would always be waiting for the repatriation of the object he was no longer able to return. Reaching up with his left hand, he awkwardly pulled open a drawer in the unit.

Outside his flat there was silence; outside, the ominous presence had become dutifully patient. There was a resigned endurance to the overwhelming stillness that bided its time beyond the door.

Then came a soft rustling that might have been the palms of anguished hands sliding down the badly painted wood of the door, but which reminded Lennie of the sounds of the rushes bordering the river.

His heart was gyrating frantically. He felt in the drawer as the darkness of the room appeared to intensify. Then his hand clutched the cool metal as if his fingers retained a memory of its shape and position. He lifted the pistol carefully from the drawer and brought it into his lap while he spent a moment in reflection. What was outside waited. He could not give back what he'd taken. Unburied and without ceremony, it lay still amongst the grasses, still and silent, only the wetland whispering its profane fate.

Then came the voice of the water and reeds. And mournful wailing. Lennie lifted the weapon into view. The end of the muzzle was a black and unblinking liquid eye, expressing innocence and surprise, as if shocked by the suggestion that a deadly explosion might be released from its nucleus. Knowing there was only one escape, from his room and everything else, Zulu raised the weapon up and back, and out of his line of sight.

The Death of Dreams
by Thana Niveau

Leann groped sleepily for the ringing phone, knocking over the bedside lamp as she finally caught hold of the handset.

"Hullo?"

"You're not up yet," said a dismayed voice.

"No. Fast asleep. What time is it? Megan, is that you?"

"Then you haven't heard."

"Heard what?"

The silence that followed told her it was bad news. She sat up, instantly awake. "Megan. Tell me."

Her sister took a deep breath before speaking. "It's the newspaper. Well, not the *newspaper*," she qualified with a snarl, "the *Daily Crier*. They've got some pictures. Of you. You and Scotty."

Bewildered, Leann couldn't imagine where this was going. She glanced sharply at the baby monitor as she scrambled out of bed. Her son was just waking up, no doubt sensing Leann's disquiet. "Pictures of what? Me changing his nappy?"

Megan choked back a sob. "No, nothing like that. God, I wish… No, you're – *killing* him. Drowning him in the bath." She began to cry then, loudly and helplessly.

Leann froze, staring at the monitor, watching the baby kick his legs and start to cry. Realisation hit her like a blow in the stomach. She felt cold and weightless, as though every drop of blood had been drained from her. She sank to the floor. "Oh my God."

TV MUM TO MILLIONS WANTS HER BABY DEAD!
Shocking photos of children's TV presenter's
secret fantasies of murder!
Warning – don't turn to page 4 unless
you have a strong stomach!

The monochrome front-page image was grainy and blurred as an ultrasound, but what it showed was unmistakable: Leann Hallier, her well-known face a mask of cruel fury, her hands wrapped around her infant son's throat, holding him down under

233

the water. The article mined the lurid pictures for all they were worth, making a meal of her influential position with children. *Leann's Lullaby*, read the caption beneath one of the photos, juxtaposed with a promo still of Leann surrounded by children on her programme.

Unable to read any further, she shut off the computer and clung to her baby. Scotty was now crying lustily, as though giving vent to Leann's anguish. The pictures were straight out of a nightmare. Leann's own, in fact. That awful recurring nightmare she'd had since the birth of her son two months ago. Night after night she'd woken screaming and drenched in sweat, unable to understand why she was plagued by such hateful dreams. She loved her son desperately. He was her whole world. What demon was planting these terrible visions in her mind?

Dr North had reassured her that such things were completely normal. Simply her mind's way of confronting fear by forcing her to imagine the worst possible scenarios. And while the terrible images were confined to her dreaming brain and her psychiatrist's office, she'd been able to cope. Just. Now the tabloid had turned her private horror into a public freak show.

Reporters were already massing outside and she ignored their assaults on the front door. Now the phone was ringing again. She picked it up and listened until an unfamiliar and breathy voice asked "Is this Leann Hallier?" She hung up and unplugged the phone. Her mobile bleeped with incoming texts from concerned friends but she didn't bother to read them. She rang Dr North's office and the receptionist put her through at once.

"How could you?" Leann demanded. "You promised me confidentiality! You swore no one else would ever see those pictures!"

"Leann, you've got to believe me, I had no idea what was going on until this morning when my colleague showed me the paper." His usually soothing voice sounded shaken.

"I trusted you. You said the Dreamcatcher was safe!"

"It is. And I can't apologise enough for what's happened. Listen to me. You remember my assistant – Shelly? Well, she'd been acting strange all week. Then she didn't turn up for work today and when I saw the paper I realised what must have happened. Your file's gone. She must have stolen it and sold the pictures to the paper. I've already contacted a solicitor."

The words congealed into clarity. Shelly. Yes, his young pretty assistant. The one with the hungry look. Oh God, it all made sense now. Leann had never wanted to see those awful pictures again. The Dreamcatcher was meant to record her nightmares so she could confront her fears and rob them of their power. No one else was ever supposed to see them.

"The paper says they're fantasies, not nightmares," she wept, her defences collapsing, "and they've got some doctor backing it up, saying no one could visualise a thing like that unless there was a real danger they'd do it."

"It's not true, Leann," Dr North said firmly. "It's just tabloid rubbish. Don't lose sight of that. Believe me, we'll sort it out in the courts."

But Leann wasn't listening. She was staring wide-eyed at the two policemen who had suddenly appeared in her living room, their arms outstretched placatingly, as though she were armed and dangerous.

"Just give us the baby, Miss Hallier," said the one young enough to have watched her programme ten years ago, "you don't really want to hurt him, now."

Bleary-eyed and exhausted, Leann asked again when she could see Scotty. It had been several agonising hours since they'd wrenched the child from her arms, though sometimes she was convinced it had been days. She'd resisted all attempts to goad her into an outburst, steadfastly refusing to say a word to either the police or the reporters who'd clustered around her like a cloud of flies.

Now she sat across from an alleged "expert" – on what, she hadn't been told – who identified himself as Dr Mitchell and smiled at her like a politician smugly assured of her vote.

"Look," she said, trying to sound as calm and reasonable as she was able. "I've been having nightmares. Anxiety dreams. That's why I was seeing a psychiatrist. Sometimes I just can't help imagining the worst thing that could happen. It's perfectly normal."

"It's not for people like you to define what's 'normal', Miss Hallier. One doesn't suddenly kill one's baby without first playing it out in the mind."

"But he's not dead! Wherever you took him, he's alive and safe!"

"He's safe *now*," the patronising voice continued, "and once these dangerous fantasies of yours –"

"It was a nightmare!"

"It's no use shouting at me, Miss Hallier. I'm not the one harbouring sadistic desires to harm my baby. Do you really think a woman who can visualise something like that is fit to be a mother?"

"But that's just it, don't you see? I was horrified. That's why I went to Dr North in the first place. He told me it was just my mind's way of lashing out at Scotty's father for leaving when he did. It's nothing I would ever do in reality."

Dr Mitchell's lips twitched into a tight little smile. "So why aren't you fantasising about killing *him*? Why is it the baby you want to kill?"

Fury leapt like flames within her. "I don't want to kill anybody! Why won't you listen to me? It was a nightmare. A terrible, horrible nightmare I never asked to have. You can't help what you dream. And my dreams are nobody else's bloody business."

"Don't you think the public has a right to know what goes on in the mind of someone with so much power and influence over their children?"

She blinked in bewilderment at the question. What did he think she intended to do? Brainwash children through the TV? Was this for real or was it another nightmare? No, she mustn't think like that. He was just trying to provoke her. He wanted to believe she was mad, that she could commit murder. He wanted *her* to believe it. She dug her nails into her palms under the table, drawing strength from the pain.

"No one has the right to gawk at my personal demons. Those images belong to me."

"Ah, but you're mistaken," he said and his triumphant tone suggested that he'd been waiting for her to say that. "You see, this device, this 'Dreamcatcher' your Dr North used, is government property. He had no authorisation to use it in private practice."

"What do you mean? We discussed it. It was part of a clinical trial. All the paperwork was cleared."

Dr Mitchell sighed as though she were the one trying *his* patience. "No, Miss Hallier. We've no doubt he genuinely meant well, but he simply did not have the authority to use his patients as guinea pigs in such a fashion."

"But he *did* help me," she said plaintively. "The nightmares were getting less frequent. And he said there were others it had worked for too."

"That has no relevance here. We're concerned about the security breach."

She laughed bitterly. "Yeah, so am I. Why don't you go after his assistant? She's the one who stole a confidential file and sold it to the papers."

Dr Mitchell pressed his palms together and leaned forward. "That isn't all she stole, Miss Hallier," he said with a sigh. "The Dreamcatcher is gone."

Leann couldn't help finding some satisfaction in that. "Well, well. So your baby's been taken away too."

He eyed her sternly, as though she were a child who'd spoken out of turn. "It's hardly a case of tit for tat. I don't think you fully appreciate the seriousness of the situation. In the wrong hands such a device can be dangerous."

"Oh, really?" When her sarcasm only earned her another admonitory look she grew careless. "You'll have to forgive me if I find it a little difficult to feel sorry for you, *Doctor* Mitchell. Boo-hoo, someone stole your toy. I'm the one whose life has been ruined by your stupid bloody government spyware!"

Dr Mitchell pushed his chair back from the table and stood up, adjusting his tie nonchalantly. "You may feel your life has been ruined," he said loftily, "but your baby's life has been saved by this so-called 'spyware'. The only thing your childish fury will do is reinforce that he's better off where he is now."

Her defiance crumbled under the threat. "No, wait," she whimpered. "Please. You've got to believe me. I'd never hurt Scotty. He's my whole life. Please let me see him. What do I have to do to convince you –"

"In time, Miss Hallier. After a period of rehabilitation you may be allowed to see him without supervision, but for now he'll be placed in care. Where he'll be safe."

Her eyes filled with fresh tears and when she wiped them away she saw her palms were streaked with blood.

It was the ultimate tabloid stealth weapon. And now that it was out in the open, no one was safe. In the months that followed many other celebrities and public figures fell prey to Dreamcatcher scandals. The public howled for blood each time the familiar grainy images appeared on the tabloid front pages, parading the private dreams, fears and fantasies of those they felt should be above reproach.

High-ranking church officials proved easy to dethrone as their subconscious minds sought forbidden imagery like a tongue compulsively probing a sore tooth. A cabinet minister was forced to resign when his recurring dream of sexual humiliation was denounced by government-appointed experts as misogynistic fantasy, despite his insistence that he was himself the willing female victim in the murky photos.

That winter a teenage pop star hanged herself after a taunting exposé of her grandiose dreams of possessing magical powers. The suicide sparked an international outcry, with human rights advocates calling for a ban on Dreamcatchers. But public opinion polls continued to show unwavering support. After all, the UK crime rate was at an all-time low and the general belief was that if one had nothing to hide, then one had nothing to worry about. No one stopped to think what purpose the government could have had in designing the device in the first place, but it hardly mattered now. The prototype had been copied and improved. Its imagery propagated like a virus.

Extreme sickness demands extreme remedies. And as the epidemic of dream exposés spread, so did the desperate need for a counteragent.

Leann looked at the clock. The alarm would be going off in half an hour, so even if she could get back to sleep it wouldn't be worth it. It felt like she'd spent the night tossing and turning on the pavement. With a groan she heaved the covers off and crawled out of bed and into the shower. As she rinsed away the sweat from another restless night she tried to remember the way things used to be.

It had been nearly a year and she was finally on the verge of being granted custody of her son again. He'd grown so much between each weekly visit that she sometimes couldn't help wondering whether it was really Scotty or if he had been replaced by another baby. Or reprogrammed.

"Stop it," she growled, scrubbing herself viciously. "Don't even go there."

The kid she bought Oneirocide from on the street had reassured her that paranoia was a common side-effect of the drug. The human brain needed to dream, he told her. And while the REM suppressant was safe to use occasionally, too much dream deprivation could lead to madness.

In the weeks following the human rights controversy, Oneirocide had risen from the back-alley drug labs like a chemical saviour. It was the only known defence against dream image capture. Naturally, it commanded a hefty price, one its users were more than willing to pay despite the myriad side effects. Headaches, nausea, irritability, paranoia and hallucinations were all typical results of dream deprivation, and prolonged use led to madness. But anything was better than falling prey to the tabloids. In many cases the fear of exposure was enough to generate anxiety dreams where none had existed before. No one could know what lurked in his subconscious mind or how his private thoughts would be interpreted by the witch hunters. Having the power to thwart Dreamcatchers was worth whatever it cost.

Leann refused to trust the short attention span of the public. She'd been raked across the coals once, but she couldn't be sure it was enough for them. It wasn't safe to dream too much when anyone could be watching, especially as now she truly did entertain sadistic fantasies. They weren't directed at her son, however, but at his foster mother, a chirpy young blonde named Kimmy. Leann's heart twisted each time she had to say goodbye to Scotty at the end of their supervised hour together and she wept bitter tears to see how attached he had become to this false mother. In her dreams Leann repeatedly committed unthinkable atrocities on the woman she believed was trying to turn her son against her. It didn't matter how grouchy and unfocused the drug made her; she couldn't afford another dream exposé, so she took Oneirocide each night before she was scheduled to see Scotty.

The sun was out and birdsong filled the morning air, but after a dreamless night her eyes felt gritty and the noise only served to annoy her. She made her way to the bus stop, glowering at the cars that sailed by her on the street. She'd had to sell her Mini to help

239

pay for Scotty's care. "Insult to injury," she grumbled, reluctantly pausing to glance at the papers on display at the kiosk on the corner.

Shock, horror, scandal. Every day the same bloody thing. Here was a schoolyard strewn with bodies, Guyana-style. Some poor primary schoolteacher's nightmare distorted to represent wishful thinking. And here was a celebrity chef feeding body parts into a food processor. A fireman gleefully flinging survivors from the roof of a burning building. Leann's own nightmare felt tame by comparison.

"Enjoying the sideshow?"

Leann turned to see a man in a filthy suit glaring at her. His hand shook as he pointed towards the nearest tabloid.

"Not especially," she said coolly, taking in the man's bloodshot eyes and unkempt appearance, the grim set of his lips.

Every drug had its abusers and Oneirocide was no exception. Dreaming was a basic human need, as essential as food or water. A person couldn't survive without it and stories of bizarre deaths were beginning to compete with scandals for front-page coverage.

The man twitched and then took a jerky step closer to Leann. "Your face doesn't belong to you, you know. They can take it back."

Leann backed away slowly, not taking her eyes off the man. He was pretty far gone. He turned sharply to look behind him, as if in response to a noise he'd heard, and she saw he'd torn out patches of his hair. "Don't touch me!" he shouted, though there was no one there.

"It's OK," she said in a low voice. "I'm going."

"*You're* the freak," he said suddenly, as though she'd accused him. He stared at her until he seemed to forget what he was meant to be angry about. A look of puzzlement crossed his features and he scratched absently at the back of his head. "God damn lizards," he muttered.

A bus shuddered to a halt and Leann shouldered her way on board, exchanging black looks with the woman whose place in the queue she'd just jumped. Most of the seats were taken so she stood like the other shambling commuters, holding onto the overhead rail and trying not to make eye contact with her fellow passengers. Newspaper headlines vied for her attention as though externalising the thoughts of the readers who sheltered behind them.

240

Leann followed the story across the front pages of several broadsheets. The army had been called in to maintain order at a hospital in Edinburgh, where the lunatics had quite literally taken over the asylum. To no one's surprise, the NHS lacked the resources to cope with the number of people being admitted for psychotic disturbances due to sleep or dream deprivation. Oneirocide was already illegal, but new security measures were being proposed to clamp down further on its use. There was talk of more surveillance, more CCTV cameras, as well as new technology that could assess a person's likelihood to commit antisocial behaviour. "You, the public, have a right to know," the Prime Minister was quoted as saying.

Leann looked up to see she'd missed her stop. Tears of frustration pricked her eyes as she pressed the REQUEST STOP button repeatedly, willing the bus to go faster. When they reached the next stop she clambered out with a curse and doubled back on foot. Now she'd be late for the appointment and Kimmy would no doubt use it against her. She was probably cooing to Scotty right now about how Mummy clearly had more important things to do than come visit her son. In his new home.

Bloody cow, Leann thought, remembering the woman's loathsome syrupy voice as she'd smilingly rescheduled the appointment last week. If it had been the usual time, Leann wouldn't have missed the stop. She yawned and scrubbed at her itchy eyes. Three cups of coffee hadn't been enough to wake her up and that was another thing the bitch would probably notice and scribble down in her little file. *Mother would rather be home in bed than make the effort to see her son.*

The pristine Georgian townhouse seemed to mock her with its symmetry and precision. *Look how orderly and well-defined we are,* it seemed to say in Kimmy's voice. She even thought she could hear Scotty giggle in agreement.

"Miss Hallier!" Kimmy exclaimed, as though this were an unexpected surprise. The little bitch even had the temerity to look at her watch, a surreptitious rebuke. "Come in. Scotty's in the living room."

The very thought of being invited into this interloper's house to see her own son was so galling it was all Leann could do to keep from grinding her teeth to powder. "Thank you," she managed.

A bouquet of pungent lilies stood in a huge vase on the coffee table, obscuring her view of Scotty. He was asleep in a carrier on the sofa and Leann suddenly imagined Kimmy drugging him to deprive him of their time together. Leann made her way around the obstacle and the overwhelming stench of the flowers made her sneeze.

"Oh dear," Kimmy said chidingly, "I do hope we won't be giving Baby our cold."

Leann turned with icy calm to face her, noting as she did so the new addition to the wall behind the sofa. A large framed photo of her son hung there. A professional portrait of Scotty with a wide-mouthed grin. In Kimmy's arms.

At least the woman had the decency to look caught out. "Oh, I was going to ask if you'd mind. We've just grown so close and I – "

The heavy vase shattered as Leann brought it down on Kimmy's skull, splashing water and lilies across the immaculate living room. The woman crumpled to the floor, blinking stupidly as blood ran down her face and into her gasping mouth. Behind her Scotty began to cry and Leann felt more deeply wounded than ever as she stood over the howling infant.

"Traitor," she said softly. Then she filled his disloyal mouth with lilies and waited until he was quiet again.

Beyond Each Blue Horizon
by Andrew Hook

Ludio stepped out into the day. As he walked alone through the early morning streets, kicking over yesterday's fast food wrappers with his trainers, he kept his gaze to the hint of the pale mountains in the distance.

Arriving in the city three years ago at night, sleeping with his head resting uncomfortably against the windowpane of the bus, he was ignorant of the landscape that existed beyond the outskirts, beyond the mountains. From street level, because of the density of the surrounding buildings, the mountains appeared further away than they actually were; dwarfed by perspective. Yet from his bedroom window in the shared house, they were visible in their entirety. Standing like sentries, daring you to pass.

The other students in the house kept themselves to themselves and wouldn't have understood his partial obsession. Briony with her head permanently filled with the earpieces from her mini-CD, Gaston shrouding himself with the language-barrier pretence that Ludio knew to be a sham, JJ and his political obsessions, and of course, Khali.

He hadn't spoken to Khali for three days. Not since that night on the sofa, which intimated an inextricable future but which instead had become an inexorable past. It wasn't so much that they had avoided each other, simply that she no longer appeared to exist.

The sun was warming the streets and in the distance the mountains shimmered like a mirage. Suddenly changing tack, Ludio turned off the main street and entered a dusty enclave. One of the small roadside cafés was just opening and he sat down and ordered a coke and some beef broth. Spooning it into his mouth made him realise how hungry he had been. Across the other side of the street, political posters decorated the white wall of the junior school. They only advertised the one party, and Ludio knew that JJ would have something to say about that, but as he wasn't overly interested in politics – especially in a foreign country – he returned to his food and ate greedily; juice slipping off the spoon and trickling down his cheek.

"Here." The wife of the café owner passed him a napkin to dry his face with. He opened his mouth to thank her, but she had already moved into the back of the shop. There was a touch of Khali in the way she walked, and he was reminded of what Khali had said after their initial fumblings on the sofa, accompanied by the sound of the kettle boiling in the background.

"In a world of illusion, you only see what you feel."

Ludio repositioned himself so that his face moved back a little from hers. Their proximity meaning that he couldn't quite see all of her.

"What do you mean?"

Khali smiled, saying nothing. She reached up behind his neck and pulled his face towards her again.

As had happened frequently of late, Ludio found himself returning to the house earlier than intended. After his aborted trip into the mountains he had kicked about the city for a while. His university studies had been temporarily suspended in the build-up to the elections, although he wasn't sure whether the intention was to negate the student population's propensity for subversive behaviour, or simply to allow the buildings to be prepared for their use as polling stations. Whatever, he wasn't concerned about the impact on his studies. The thread of reality had come undone over the previous few days, and he was no longer as interested in anything as much as he should have been.

Inside his house it was quiet, but a restless quiet, as though the inanimate objects in the house had only just settled after sensing his imminent presence. As he moved through the rooms and into the kitchen he had the uneasy feeling that someone was watching him. Switching on the kettle he made some green tea, and then took it upstairs to his room.

His books were scattered across the floor where he'd left them. He placed his tea on the bedside cabinet and walked over to the window. Outside the city seemed vast, barely contained by the mountains that surrounded it, as though it had been crammed into the space rather than growing naturally from within. Children kicked a deflated football in the dusty streets, occasionally making way for a spotless Mercedes or Mitsubishi Pajero, cruising quietly. Ludio didn't want to think on their purpose, but their presence didn't seem incongruous here. It was part of the state of things.

244

Something triggered the hairs at the base of his neck and he went downstairs again. Making sure the house was still empty, he locked the door and returned upstairs. Breathing heavily, he stopped outside Khali's room.

Slowly he turned the door handle and then entered her space.

The curtains were drawn but sunlight shone through the holes that had been torn into the material. Her room was tidier than his, with all her books in author alphabetical order on the shelf above the computer. The air was sweet with the fragrance of freshly-burned incense, and Ludio remembered the smell of it on his skin. There was nothing in the room to indicate she had left, it was as though over the past three days she had slipped into the house through cracks in the walls. On the bed her clothes were splayed as though she had dissolved inside them. Her tights crossed at the knee; her pale blue skirt tucked into her top. There was almost the indentation of her head on the pillow. Ludio bent over to sniff it when he heard the door unlocking downstairs.

JJ was holding discourse on the sofa.

"Of course, once they get in again we'll never get them out. Already I've heard rumours. People are disappearing. No one admits to it of course, but it's happening right before our eyes."

Ludio yawned. JJ hadn't let up for the past half an hour, but he didn't feel like leaving the room and going to bed. Briony sat on the sofa eating beans and flicking through the CD collection that she kept in a custom-made holder clipped onto her leather belt. Gaston was sitting cross-legged on the floor, absorbed in a French novel. Occasionally one of them might nod, or add a comment to JJ's musings, but mostly they were involved in their own worlds. Ludio's only distraction was the constant flickering of his eyes towards the clock that rested against the wall, wondering whether Khali would return home.

"Hey Ludio," JJ shouted across to him, "how does it feel living in a country where you can't vote?"

Ludio grunted. He wasn't sure whether the question was directed at his nationality, or whether it was JJ's attempt to make a political comment about the danger of voting against the government. He knew that the elections were supposed to be free, but JJ's incessant political commentary and the information he'd gathered from some of the other students at the university seemed to prove otherwise.

To break the conversation he said: "Does anyone know where Khali is? I haven't seen her for days."

JJ got up from the sofa and entered the kitchen. Gaston kept his face in his book, and Briony turned up the sound on her mini-disk. Ludio shrugged and stood. "I'm off to bed," he said.

That night he dreamt of her. She had decorated her face with some of the Indian make-up that she liked to use. Her eyebrows were pinprick-sharp black, and beneath them the skin was light pink-powdered, accentuating the smoothness of her face. A red upside-down tear was painted onto her forehead, and her lips were softly rouged. He felt that he could reach out and take her face in one hand, as though she were a tiny being.

"The word *khali* literally means empty," she said – although Ludio wasn't sure if this was part of the dream or of his memory. "However it has special significance in North Indian music. The word implies a wave of the hand which, together with its counterpart, the clap of the hand, forms the basis of timekeeping known as *kriya*."

Ludio wanted to kiss her, but knowing he was within the dream he refrained from doing so. It would break the cycle. But then she dissolved away from him, and his last thought before waking was whether all Khali would ever be to him was a wave of the hand.

He had slept in his shirt and it stuck to his back as he got up. It felt as though he had been lying in a pool of glue. He decided against taking a shower knowing that by the time he dried himself he would be sweating again. The room was filled with the campfire stench of his underpants, and he slipped them off, standing by the window before finding a new pair to wear. Outside, the streets were busy and he wondered how long he had been asleep.

Most of the shops were open and people were already eating and drinking. Motorbikes wove in and out between pedestrians, panniers piled high with green vegetables as the riders made their way to market. The elections were only a few days away, and the number of posters pasted onto the shacks had increased overnight. The slums were reflected back at themselves by the great glass skyscrapers of the prosperous part of the city. The mountains – only truly visible from the upstairs rooms – appeared to hover in the background, a heat haze undermining their foundations, as though they were ready to leave for other worlds.

He felt Khali's hand on his shoulder and his body stiffened. She whispered in his ear. *Beautiful love. Where have you gone?* Ludio hesitated to turn around, knowing that she wouldn't be there. When he did, she wasn't.

He dressed quickly and went downstairs to make some porridge. Briony and Gaston were sitting glumly at the table. They looked up at him and then looked away, disappointed. Ludio whistled as he cooked the porridge, and when the others could stand it no longer they shouted at him.

"How can you be so cheerful on a day like this?"

"Have you no feelings for JJ?"

Ludio stopped stirring. "Why? What's happened?"

"Don't tell me you slept through it," Briony said aghast. "Just like you to be so self-obsessed."

"Slept though what?" Ludio was genuinely concerned now, not least due to a fear that tugged gently at his memories of Khali.

"There was a knock on the door in the early hours of this morning," Gaston elaborated. "Some... people... asked for JJ. Then they took him away."

"He left with them or they took him away?"

"They took him away."

"For what reason?"

"You have to ask."

On the oven, behind him, the porridge rose out of the saucepan and spread across the stove like a lava flow. It seeped onto the concave surface of the hob, and clogged up the gas jets.

Ludio spent the day indoors alone. He had no doubts that JJ would be back; that it was only some aberration of fate that he had left in the first place. But Ludio couldn't help thinking there was a connection between JJ's removal and the disappearance of Khali. Although she had never made her political opinions known – at least not to Ludio – she *was* a free thinker. With the elections looming like the mountains over the city, a streak of independence wasn't the best attribute to cultivate.

He slapped his face in an attempt to clear his head from its sleepiness. The whole thing was nonsense. As if for reassurance, Ludio went up to Khali's room.

As expected, her bed hadn't been slept in. Her clothes and the books on her shelves were still as orderly as they had been the day before. Ludio realised how egocentric his thoughts had been, considering that he hadn't seen her since they had quietly necked. To equate her non-appearance with some reaction to his advances was ludicrous. Perhaps she had, after all, just upped and left.

He traced the outline of her clothes on the bed. The feel of the material tingled his fingertips, sending static shocks into his body. Ludio glanced through the holes in her curtains. Her window faced onto the same view as his, yet something about it was different. He blinked a couple of times, as though clearing sleep from his eyes, and then went to look at the view from his own room.

Something had changed, but he couldn't tell what it was.

"The *khali*," she had said, "is especially important in symmetrical metres, such as *tintal* of 16 beats or *dadra* of 6 beats. It's indispensable for correct orientation of musical rhythm. For example," and here she had placed her fingertips on his lips, shushing the questions from him, "if there was no *khali* then *tintal* would be a confusing string of four-beat measures and it would be very difficult to find the beginning of the cycle."

"Where do you fit into all of this?"

"Nowhere. Khali is simply my name, just as Ludio is yours. What does Ludio mean?"

He thought. "It's Latin. It means *actor*, or so I'm told."

She smiled. "You're the actor then, and I'm the musician."

That was the moment they had kissed.

Ludio realised what the difference was in their window-views. He left his room and tugged on the rope that hung from the attic trapdoor. Climbing the ladder – which had descended when he opened the door – he entered the dark confines of the top of the house and then pushed open the small window that led out onto the rarely-used balcony. A sun-lounger dominated most of the floor space, and beside it was a half-drunk glass of lemonade, the surface speckled with dead flies and greasy film.

Ludio lay back on the sun-lounger, looking up. The sky was mostly clear, but the few clouds dotting his view were grey and promised rain. Immediately above him was the rainbow that he'd been able to see from Khali's room but not from his own. It spread horizontally across the sky, with neither its beginning nor its end disappearing towards the earth. It simply hung there, cut-and-pasted onto the heavens, like a huge multi-coloured grin. Ludio shivered, and as he made to get up he saw the book that was lying on the ground to the right of the sun-lounger. The title read: *Some Is Good, More Is Better, Too Much Is Just Right.*

Ludio went back downstairs.

The house was different. He knew it instantly without knowing why. His own room was untouched, as was Khali's, but as he descended the stairs he noticed a political poster had been fixed to the right side of the stairwell. The message was simple: vote for the current government and stability would be maintained. It was a double-edged sword. Ludio felt his legs shaking as he continued downstairs. Someone must have been in the house whilst he was on the roof.

The living-room looked much as it had done the previous night. He glanced into the kitchen through the open doorway and noticed that the stove was clean. Briony must have cleared up the porridge. He couldn't imagine Gaston having done so. The pair of them had been strangely united at breakfast, instead of being the disparate people that he was used to. For a moment he panicked, hoped that any newfound familiarity would dissipate during the day. He didn't want their potential friendships to be seen as collusion. It was the law that groups of three or more weren't allowed out on the streets, perhaps that might be extended into the home. For the first time that day he felt an urge to get out of the house.

The streets were busy with an explosion of life. Cyclists wove around him, their wheels carving rivulets into the ground that were quickly filled with freshly-fallen rain. Ludio avoided looking into the faces of those he passed. Whilst he wanted to be surrounded by people he also craved invisibility. He needed the anonymity of the crowd, the familiarity of a backdrop.

The mountains foreshadowed the city. They were the walls of the hourglass holding the sands of time.

Khali had been the new arrival in the house. Whilst Ludio was in his last year of studies she was in her first. Yet her life experience had dwarfed his own. He needed her confidence now. That matter-of-factness which was inextricably coupled with her apparent mysticism. Thinking about her, an immediate sexual desire came to him. To his shame he realised he had walked into the section of the city that pandered to less salubrious clients from the business area. He was about to turn back when he caught a flash of pale pink skin.

It wasn't quite Khali, yet it was quite enough.

The prostitute unbuttoned his shirt after he had clumsily negotiated a price. He eased the straps of her dress over her shoulders so it fell to the floor, revealing her nakedness in one take. Her hand reached out and her fingertips unzipped his trousers. He hardened, and she pulled him onto her soft body as she lay back onto the bed. He entered her easily, too easily perhaps, feeling the inside of her rub against him. As he jerked himself out of his fantasy and into a rhythm she mouthed words beneath him. Seemingly nonsensical, one of the local dialects perhaps, his mental processes rearranged them and strove to find meaning, until finally he convinced himself that she was whispering *vote vote vote for them*, over and over again.

He knew he would be alone as soon as he got back to the house. Closing the door on the tumultuous streets he could hear sirens in the distance. The elections were due to take place the following day, and the air was as sharp as it would be before an approaching thunderstorm.

Ludio wondered what his convictions were and whether he would ever stand up for them.

The changes were subtle. In the kitchen the cutlery had been rearranged, and within the cabinets the smaller saucepans had been tidied and placed into the larger pots to conserve space. In the living-room the remote control lay redundant on top of the television that, from now on, would be broadcasting only one channel. Along the stairway the walls had been papered in their entirety with political posters, giving the impression of a long white tunnel. Ludio didn't go into his room, but popped his head first into Briony's and then into Gaston's. Both rooms contained a stripped-down wooden bed and no other furniture. JJ's room was similarly denuded, yet beneath the floorboards lay the thesis he had systematically slotted between the thin slats one page at a time when he had been certain of his pending unofficial arrest. The pages had yet to be discovered by mice.

In Khali's room the books on the shelf had been restacked with their spines to the wall, and the holes in her curtains had been crudely stitched together so they resembled closed eyelashes. Her clothes had gone from the bed.

Ludio lifted up the corner of Khali's bedsheet and slipped beneath the covers, the material imitating her imagined presence, holding him close until he was overcome by sleep.

The *khali*, she had said, forms a convenient method by which vocalists may communicate with the *tabla* player without halting the performance or breaking the musical flow.

Come daybreak Ludio was much refreshed. He rose from Khali's bed and wondered if she had got up early to make breakfast. Dressing quickly he opened the door of her room and tiptoed downstairs, wary of waking the other students and disturbing the tranquillity of the morning.

The curtains were yet to be opened and he relished the new morning feel of the sun filtering its way through the fabric, illuminating the room with a honeyed glow. The smell of fresh coffee came from the kitchen and his appetite was stirred by the thought of newly-baked croissants or bean fritters. His bare feet padded across the linoleum, but stopped moving when he saw the room was empty.

A photograph of Khali was attached to the cork notice-board with a cross drawn over it.

Through the window he saw the mountains.

When he wrenched open the back door the landscape stretched in abject barrenness before him. The ground was flat, a red desert of nothingness that reached from the toes of his feet to the mountains on the horizon. All around him, the vista was the same. Ludio suppressed a gasp as the enormity of what had happened squeezed out of his body and fell to the ground, becoming absorbed by the dry, unforgiving, treacherous soil.

They had stolen everything. Even the city.

Somewhere, he thought, he heard a drum.

The Depths
by Ramsey Campbell

As Miles emerged, a woman and a pink-eyed dog stumped by. She glanced at the house; then, humming tunelessly, she aimed the same contemptuous look at Miles. As if the lead was a remote control, the dog began to growl. They thought Miles was the same as the house.

He almost wished that were true; at least it would have been a kind of contact. He strolled through West Derby village and groped in his mind for ideas. Pastels drained from the evening sky. Wood pigeons paraded in a tree-lined close. A mother was crying "Don't you dare go out of this garden again." A woman was brushing her driveway and singing that she was glad she was Bugs Bunny. Beyond a brace of cars, in a living-room that displayed a bar complete with beer-pumps, a couple listened to *Beethoven's Greatest Hits*.

Miles sat drinking beer at a table behind the Crown, at the edge of the bowling green. Apart from the click of bowls the summer evening seemed as blank as his mind. Yet the idea had promised to be exactly what he and his publisher needed: no more days of drinking tea until his head swam, of glaring at the sheet of paper in the typewriter while it glared an unanswerable challenge back at him. He hadn't realised until now how untrustworthy inspirations were.

Perhaps he ought to have foreseen the problem. The owners had told him that there was nothing wrong with the house – nothing except the aloofness and silent disgust of their neighbours. If they had known what had happened there they would never have bought the house; why should they be treated as though by living there they had taken on the guilt?

Still, that was no more unreasonable than the crime itself. The previous owner had been a bank manager, as relaxed as a man could be in his job; his wife had owned a small boutique. They'd seemed entirely at peace with each other. Nobody who had known them could believe what he had done to her. Everyone Miles approached had refused to discuss it, as though by keeping quiet about it they might prevent it from having taken place at all.

The deserted green was smudged with darkness. "We're closing now," the barmaid said, surprised that anyone was still outside. Miles lifted the faint sketch of a tankard and gulped a throatful of beer, grimacing. The more he researched the book, the weaker it seemed to be.

To make things worse, he'd told the television interviewer that it was near completion. At least the programme wouldn't be broadcast for months, by which time he might be well into a book about the locations of murder – but it wasn't the book he had promised his publisher, and he wasn't sure that it would have the same appeal.

Long dark houses slumbered beyond an archway between cottages, lit windows hovered in the arch. A signboard reserved a weedy patch of ground for a library. A grey figure was caged by the pillars of the village cross. On the roof of a pub extension gargoyles began barking, for they were dogs. A cottage claimed to be a sawmill, but the smell seemed to be of manure. Though his brain was taking notes, it wouldn't stop nagging.

He gazed across Lord Sefton's estate towards the tower blocks of Cantril Farm. Their windows were broken ranks of small bright perforations in the night. For a moment, as his mind wobbled on the edge of exhaustion, the unstable patterns of light seemed a code which he needed to break to solve his problems. But how could they have anything to do with it? Such a murder in Cantril Farm, in the concrete barracks among which Liverpool communities had been scattered, he might have understood; here in West Derby it didn't make sense.

As he entered the deserted close, he heard movements beneath eaves. It must be nesting birds, but it was as though the sedate house had secret thoughts. He was grinning as he pushed open his gate, until his hand recoiled. The white gate was stickily red.

It was paint. Someone had written SADIST in an ungainly dripping scrawl. The neighbours could erase that – he wouldn't be here much longer. He let himself into the house.

For a moment he hesitated, listening to the dark. Nothing fled as he switched on the lights. The hall was just a hall, surmounted by a concertina of stairs; the metal and vinyl of the kitchen gleamed like an Ideal Home display; the corduroy suite sat plump and smug on the dark green pelt of the living-room. He felt as though he was lodging in a show house, without even the company of a shelf of his books.

Yet it was here, from the kitchen to the living-room, that everything had happened – here that the bank manager had systematically rendered his wife unrecognisable as a human being. Miles stood in the empty room and tried to imagine the scene. Had her mind collapsed, or had she been unable to withdraw from what was being done to her? Had her husband known what he was doing, right up to the moment when he'd dug the carving-knife into his throat and run headlong at the wall?

It was no good: here at the scene of the crime, Miles found the whole thing literally unimaginable. For an uneasy moment he suspected that might have been true of the killer and his victim. As Miles went upstairs, he was planning the compromise to offer his publisher: *Murderers' Houses? Dark Places of the World?* Perhaps it mightn't be such a bad book after all.

When he switched off the lights, darkness came upstairs from the hall. He lay in bed and watched the shadows of the curtains furling and unfurling above him. He was touching the gate, which felt like flesh; it split open, and his hand plunged in. Though the image was unpleasant it seemed remote, drawing him down into sleep.

The room appeared to have grown much darker when he woke in the grip of utter panic.

He didn't dare move, not until he knew what was wrong. The shadows were frozen above him, the curtains hung like sheets of lead. His mouth tasted metallic, and made him think of blood. He was sure that he wasn't alone in the dark. The worst of it was that there was something he mustn't do – but he had no idea what it was.

He'd begun to search his mind desperately when he realised that was exactly what he ought not to have done. The thought which welled up was so atrocious that his head began to shudder. He was trying to shake out the thought, to deny that it was his. He grabbed the light-cord, to scare it back into the dark.

Was the light failing? The room looked steeped in dimness, a grimy fluid whose sediment clung to his eyes. If anything the light had made him worse, for another thought came welling up like bile, and another. They were worse than the atrocities which the house had seen. He had to get out of the house.

He slammed his suitcase – thank God he'd lived out of it, rather than use the wardrobe – and dragged it onto the landing. He was halfway down, and the thuds of the case on the stairs were making his scalp crawl, when he realised that he'd left a notebook in the living-room.

He faltered in the hallway. He mustn't be fully awake: the carpet felt moist underfoot. His skull felt soft and porous, no protection at all for his mind. He had to have the notebook. Shouldering the door aside, he strode blindly into the room.

The light which dangled spiderlike from the central plaster flower showed him the notebook on a fat armchair. Had the chairs soaked up all that had been done here? If he touched them, what might well up? But there was worse in his head, which was seething. He grabbed the notebook and ran into the hall, gasping for air.

His car sounded harsh as a saw among the sleeping houses. He felt as though the neat hygienic façades had cast him out. At least he had to concentrate on his driving, and was deaf to the rest of his mind. The road through Liverpool was unnaturally bright as a playing-field. When the Mersey Tunnel closed overhead he felt that an insubstantial but suffocating burden had settled on his scalp. At last he emerged, only to plunge into darkness.

Though his sleep was free of nightmares, they were waiting whenever he jerked awake. It was as if he kept struggling out of a dark pit, having repeatedly forgotten what was at the top. Sunlight blazed through the curtains as though they were tissue paper, but couldn't reach inside his head. Eventually, when he couldn't bear another such awakening, he stumbled to the bathroom.

When he'd washed and shaved he still felt grimy. It must be the lack of sleep. He sat gazing over his desk. The pebble-dashed houses of Neston blazed like the cloudless sky; their outlines were knife-edged. Next door's drain sounded like someone bubbling the last of a drink through a straw. All this was less vivid than his thoughts – but wasn't that as it should be?

An hour later he still hadn't written a word. The nightmares were crowding everything else out of his mind. Even to think required an effort that made his skin feel infested, swarming.

A random insight saved him. Mightn't it solve both his problems if he wrote the nightmares down? Since he'd had them in the house in West Derby – since he felt they had somehow been produced by the house – couldn't he discuss them in his book?

He scribbled them out until his tired eyes closed. When he reread what he'd written he grew feverishly ashamed. How could he imagine such things? If anything was obscene, they were. Nothing could have made him write down the idea which he'd left until last. Though he was tempted to tear up the notebook, he stuffed it out of sight at the back of a drawer and hurried out to forget.

He sat on the edge of the promenade and gazed across the Dee marshes. Heat-haze made the Welsh hills look like piles of smoke. Families strolled as though this were still a watering-place; children played carefully, inhibited by parents. The children seemed wary of Miles; perhaps they sensed his tension, saw how his fingers were digging into his thighs. He must write the book soon, to prove that he could.

Ranks of pebble-dashed houses, street after street of identical Siamese twins, marched him home. They reminded him of cells in a single organism. He wouldn't starve if he didn't write – not for a while, at any rate – but he felt uneasy whenever he had to dip into his savings; their unobtrusive growth was reassuring, a talisman of success. He missed his street and had to walk back. Even then he had to peer twice at the street name before he was sure it was his.

He sat in the living-room, too exhausted to make himself dinner. Van Gogh landscapes, frozen in the instant before they became unbearably intense, throbbed on the walls. Shelves of Miles's novels reminded him of how he'd lost momentum. The last nightmare was still demanding to be written, until he forced it into the depths of his mind. He would rather have no ideas than that.

When he woke, the nightmare had left him. He felt enervated but clean. He lit up his watch and found he'd slept for hours. It was time for the book programme. He'd switched on the television and was turning on the light when he heard his voice at the far end of the room, in the dark.

He was on television, but that was hardly reassuring; his one television interview wasn't due to be broadcast for months. It was as though he'd slept that time away. His face floated up from the grey of the screen as he sat down, cursing. By the time his book was published, nobody would remember this interview.

256

The linkman and the editing had invoked another writer now. Good God, was that all they were using of Miles? He remembered the cameras following him into the West Derby house, the neighbours glaring, shaking their heads. It was as though they'd managed to censor him, after all.

No, here he was again. "Jonathan Miles is a crime novelist who feels he can no longer rely on his imagination. Desperate for new ideas, he lived for several weeks in a house where, last year, a murder was committed." Miles was already losing his temper, but there was worse to come: they'd used none of his observations about the creative process, only the sequence in which he ushered the camera about the house like Hitchcock in the *Psycho* trailer. "Viewers who find this distasteful," the linkman said unctuously, "may be reassured to hear that the murder in question is not so topical or popular as Mr Miles seems to think."

Miles glared at the screen while the programme came to an end, while an announcer explained that "Where Do You Get Your Ideas?" had been broadcast ahead of schedule because of an industrial dispute. And now here was the news, all of it as bad as Miles felt. A child had been murdered, said a headline; a Chief Constable had described it as the worst case of his career. Miles felt guiltily resentful; no doubt it would help distract people from his book.

Then he sat forward, gaping. Surely he must have misheard; perhaps his insomnia was talking. The newsreader looked unreal as a talking bust, but his voice went on, measured, concerned, inexorable. "The baby was found in a microwave oven. Neighbours broke into the house on hearing the cries, but were unable to locate it in time." Even worse than the scene he was describing was the fact that it was the last of Miles's nightmares, the one he had refused to write down.

Couldn't it have been a coincidence? Coincidence, coincidence, the train chattered, and seemed likely to do so all the way to London. If he had somehow been able to predict what was going to happen, he didn't want to know – especially not now, when he could sense new nightmares forming.

He suppressed them before they grew clear. He needed to keep his mind uncluttered for the meeting with his publisher; he gazed out of the window, to relax. Trees turned as they passed, unravelling beneath foliage. On a platform a chorus line of commuters bent to their luggage, one by one. The train drew the sun after it through clouds, like a balloon.

Once out of Euston Station and its random patterns of swarming, he strolled to the publishers. Buildings glared like blocks of salt, which seemed to have drained all moisture from the air. He felt hot and grimy, anxious both to face the worst and to delay. Hugo Burgess had been ominously casual: "If you happen to be in London soon we might have a chat about things…"

A receptionist on a dais that overlooked the foyer kept Miles waiting until he began to sweat. Eventually a lift produced Hugo, smiling apologetically. Was he apologising in advance for what he had to say? "I suppose you saw yourself on television," he said when they reached his office.

"Yes, I'm afraid so."

"I shouldn't give it another thought. The telly people are envious buggers. They begrudge every second they give to discussing books. Sometimes I think they resent the competition and get their own back by being patronising." He was pawing through the heaps of books and papers on his desk, apparently in search of the phone. "It did occur to me that it would be nice to publish fairly soon," he murmured.

Miles hadn't realised that sweat could break out in so many places at once. "I've run into some problems."

Burgess was peering at items he had rediscovered in the heaps. "Yes?" he said without looking up.

Miles summarised his new idea clumsily. Should he have written to Burgess in advance? "I found there simply wasn't enough material in the West Derby case," he pleaded.

"Well, we certainly don't want padding." When Burgess eventually glanced up he looked encouraging. "The more facts we can offer the better. I think the public is outgrowing fantasy, now that we're well and truly in the scientific age. People want to feel informed. Writing needs to be as accurate as any other science, don't you think?" He hauled a glossy pamphlet out of one of the piles. "Yes, here it is. I'd call this the last gasp of fantasy."

It was a painting, lovingly detailed and photographically realistic, of a girl who was being simultaneously mutilated and raped. It proved to be the cover of a new magazine, *Ghastly*. Within the pamphlet the editor promised "a quarterly that will

258

wipe out the old horror pulps – everything they didn't dare to be."

"It won't last," Burgess said. "Most people are embarrassed to admit to reading fantasy now, and that will only make them more so. The book you're planning is more what they want – something they know is true. That way they don't feel they're indulging themselves." He disinterred the phone at last. "Just let me call a car and we'll go into the West End for lunch."

Afterwards they continued drinking in Hugo's club. Miles thought Hugo was trying to midwife the book. Later he dined alone, then lingered for a while in the hotel bar; his spotlessly impersonal room had made him feel isolated. Over the incessant trickle of muzak he kept hearing Burgess: "I wonder how soon you'll be able to let me have sample chapters…"

Next morning he was surprised how refreshed he felt, especially once he'd taken a shower. Over lunch he unburdened himself to his agent. "I just don't know when I'll be able to deliver the book. I don't know how much research may be involved."

"Now look, you mustn't worry about Hugo. I'll speak to him. I know he won't mind waiting if he knows it's for the good of the book." Susie Barker patted his hand; her bangles sounded like silver castanets. "Now here's an idea for you. Why don't you do up a sample chapter or two on the West Derby case? That way we'll keep Hugo happy, and I'll do my best to sell it as an article."

When they'd kissed goodbye Miles strolled along the Charing Cross Road, composing the chapter in his head and looking for himself in bookshop displays. Miles, Miles, books said in a window stacked with crime novels. NIGHT OF ATROCITIES, headlines cried on an adjacent newspaper-stand.

He dodged into Foyle's. That was better: he occupied half a shelf, though his earliest titles looked faded and dusty. When he emerged he was content to drift with the rush-hour crowds – until a news-vendor's placard stopped him. BRITAIN'S NIGHT OF HORROR, it said.

It didn't matter, it had nothing to do with him. In that case, why couldn't he find out what had happened? He didn't need to buy a paper, he could read the report as the news-vendor snatched the top copy to reveal the same beneath. "Last night was Britain's worst night of murders in living memory…"

Before he'd read halfway down the column the noise of the crowd seemed to close in, to grow incomprehensible and menacing. The newsprint was snatched away again and again like a macabre card trick. He sidled away from the news-stand as though from the scene of a crime, but already he'd recognised every detail. If he hadn't repressed them on the way to London he could have written the reports himself. He even knew what the newspaper had omitted to report: that one of the victims had been forced to eat parts of herself.

Weeks later the newspapers were still in an uproar. Though the moderates pointed out that the murders had been unrelated and unmotivated, committed by people with no previous history of violence or of any kind of crime, for most of the papers that only made it worse. They used the most unpleasant photographs of the criminals that they could find, and presented the crimes as evidence of the impotence of the law, of a total collapse of standards. Opinion polls declared that the majority was in favour of an immediate return of the death penalty. "MEN LIKE THESE MUST NOT GO UNPUNISHED," a headline said, pretending it was quoting. Miles grew hot with frustration and guilt – for he felt he could have prevented the crimes.

All too soon after he'd come back from London, the night-mares had returned. His mind had already felt raw from brooding, and he had been unable to resist; he'd known only that he must get rid of them somehow. They were worse than the others: more urgent, more appalling.

He'd scribbled them out as though he was inspired, then he'd glared blindly at the blackened page. It hadn't been enough. The seething in his head, the crawling of his scalp, had not been relieved even slightly. This time he had to develop the ideas, imagine them fully, or they would cling and fester in his mind.

He'd spent the day and half the night writing, drinking tea until he hardly knew what he was doing. He'd invented character after character, building them like Frankenstein out of fragments of people, only to subject them to gloatingly prolonged atrocities, both the victims and the perpetrators.

When he'd finished, his head felt like an empty rusty can. He might have vomited if he had been able to stand. His gaze had fallen on a paragraph he'd written, and he'd swept the pages onto the floor, snarling with disgust. "Next morning he couldn't remember what he'd done – but when he reached in his pocket and touched the soft object his hand came out covered with blood..."

He'd stumbled across the landing to his bedroom, desperate to forget his ravings. When he'd woken next morning he had been astonished to find that he'd fallen asleep as soon as he had gone to bed. As he'd lain there, feeling purged, an insight so powerful it was impossible to doubt had seized him. If he hadn't written out these things they would have happened in reality.

But he had written them out: they were no longer part of him. In fact they had never been so, however they had felt. That made him feel cleaner, absolved him of responsibility. He stuffed the sloganeering newspapers into the wastebasket and arranged his desk for work.

By God, there was nothing so enjoyable as feeling ready to write. While a pot of tea brewed he strolled about the house and revelled in the sunlight, his release from the nightmares, his surge of energy. Next door a man with a beard of shaving foam dodged out of sight, like a timid Santa Claus.

Miles had composed the first paragraph before he sat down to write, a trick that always helped him write more fluently – but a week later he was still struggling to get the chapter into publishable shape. All that he found crucial about his research – the idea that by staying in the West Derby house he had tapped a source of utter madness, which had probably caused the original murder – he'd had to suppress. Why, if he said any of that in print they would think he was mad himself. Indeed, once he'd thought of writing it, it no longer seemed convincing.

When he could no longer bear the sight of the article, he typed a fresh copy and sent it to Susie. She called the following day, which seemed encouragingly quick. Had he been so aware of what he was failing to write that he hadn't noticed what he'd achieved?

"Well, Jonathan, I have to say this," she said as soon as she'd greeted him. "It isn't up to your standard. Frankly, I think you ought to scrap it and start again."

"Oh." After a considerable pause he could think of nothing to say except "All right."

"You sound exhausted. Perhaps that's the trouble." When he didn't answer she said "You listen to your Auntie Susie. Forget the whole thing for a fortnight and go away on holiday. You've been driving yourself too hard – you looked tired the last time I

261

saw you. I'll explain to Hugo, and I'll see if I can't talk up the article you're going to write when you come back."

She chatted reassuringly for a while, then left him staring at the phone. He was realising how much he'd counted on selling the article. Apart from royalties, which never amounted to as much as he expected, when had he last had the reassurance of a cheque? He couldn't go on holiday, for he would feel he hadn't earned it; if he spent the time worrying about the extravagance, that would be no holiday at all.

But wasn't he being unfair to himself? Weren't there stories he could sell?

He turned the idea over gingerly in his mind, as though something might crawl out from beneath – but really, he could see no arguments against it. Writing out the nightmares had drained them of power; they were just stories now. As he dialled Hugo's number, to ask him for the address of the magazine, he was already thinking up a pseudonym for himself.

For a fortnight he walked around Anglesey. Everything was hallucinatorily intense: beyond cracks in the island's grassy coastline, the sea glittered as though crystallising and shattering; across the sea, Welsh hills and mist appeared to be creating each other. Beaches were composed of rocks like brown crusty loaves decorated with shells. Anemones unfurled deep in glassy pools. When night fell he lay on a slab of rock and watched the stars begin to swarm.

As he strolled he was improving the chapters in his mind, now that the first version had clarified his themes. He wrote the article in three days, and was sure it was publishable. Not only was it the fullest description yet of the murder, but he'd managed to explain the way the neighbours had behaved: they'd needed to dramatise their repudiation of all that had been done in the house, they'd used him as a scapegoat to cast out, to proclaim that it had nothing to do with them.

When he'd sent the manuscript to Susie he felt pleasantly tired. The houses of Neston grew silver in the evening, the horizon was turning to ash. Once the room was so dark that he couldn't read, he went to bed. As he drifted towards sleep he heard next door's drain bubbling to itself.

But what was causing bubbles to form in the greyish

substance that resembled fluid less than flesh? They were slower and thicker than tar, and took longer to form. Their source was rushing upwards to confront him face to face. The surface was quivering, ready to erupt, when he awoke.

He felt hot and grimy, and somehow ashamed. The dream had been a distortion of the last thing he'd heard, that was all; surely it wouldn't prevent him from sleeping. A moment later he was clinging to it desperately; its dreaminess was comforting, and it was preferable by far to the ideas that were crowding into his mind. He knew now why he felt grimy.

He couldn't lose himself in sleep; the nightmares were embedded there, minute, precise and appalling. When he switched on the light it seemed to isolate him. Night had bricked up all the windows. He couldn't bear to be alone with the nightmares – but there was only one way to be rid of them.

The following night he woke having fallen asleep at his desk. His last line met his eyes: "Hours later he sat back on his haunches, still chewing doggedly..." When he gulped the lukewarm tea it tasted rusty as blood. His surroundings seemed remote, and he could regain them only by purging his mind. His task wasn't even half finished. His eyes felt like dusty pebbles. The pen jerked in his hand, spattering the page.

Next morning Susie rang, wrenching him awake at his desk. "Your article is tremendous. I'm sure we'll do well with it. Now I wonder if you can let me have a chapter breakdown of the rest of the book to show Hugo?"

Miles was fully awake now, and appalled by what had happened in his mind while he had been sleeping. "No," he muttered.

"Are there any problems you'd like to tell me about?"

If only he could! But he couldn't tell her that while he had been asleep, having nearly discharged his task, a new crowd of nightmares had gathered in his mind and were clamouring to be written. Perhaps now they would never end.

"Come and see me if it would help," Susie said.

How could he, when his mind was screaming to be purged? But if he didn't force himself to leave his desk, perhaps he never would. "All right," he said dully. "I'll come down tomorrow."

When tomorrow came it meant only that he could switch off his desk-lamp; he was nowhere near finishing. He barely managed to find a seat on the train, which was crowded with football fans. Opened beer cans spat; the air grew rusty with the smell of beer. The train emerged roaring from a tunnel, but Miles was still in his own, which was far darker and more oppressive. Around him they were chanting football songs, which sounded distant as a waveband buried in static. He wrote under cover of his briefcase, so that nobody would glimpse what he was writing.

Though he still hadn't finished when he reached London, he no longer cared. The chatter of the wheels, the incessant chanting, the pounding of blood and nightmares in his skull, had numbed him. He sat for a while in Euston. The white tiles glared like ice, a huge voice loomed above him.

As soon as she saw him Susie demanded "Have you seen a doctor?"

Even a psychiatrist couldn't help him. "I'll be all right," he said, hiding behind a bright false smile.

"I've thought of some possibilities for your book," she said over lunch. "What about that house in Edinburgh where almost the same murder was committed twice, fifty years apart? The man who did the second always said he hadn't known about the first..."

She obviously hoped to revive him with ideas – but the nightmare which was replaying itself, endless as a loop of film, would let nothing else into his skull. The victim had managed to tear one hand free and was trying to protect herself.

"And isn't there the lady in Sutton who collected bricks from the scenes of crimes? She was meaning to use them to build a miniature Black Museum. She ought to be worth tracing," Susie said as the man seized the flailing hand by its wrist. "And then if you want to extend the scope of the book there's the mother of the Meathook Murder victims, who still gets letters pretending to be from her children."

The man had captured the wrist now. Slowly and deliberately, with a grin that looked pale as a crack in clay, he – Miles was barely able to swallow; his head, and every sound in the restaurant, was pounding. "They sound like good ideas," he mumbled, to shut Susie up.

Back at her office, a royalty fee had arrived. She wrote him a cheque at once, as though that might cure him. As he slipped it into his briefcase, she caught sight of the notebooks in which he'd written on the train. "Are they something I can look at?" she said.

His surge of guilt was so intense that it was panic. "No, it's nothing, it's just something, no," he stammered.

Hours later he was walking. Men loitered behind boys playing pinball; the machines flashed like fireworks, splashing the men's masks. Addicts were gathering outside the all-night chemist's on Piccadilly; in the subterranean Gents, a starved youth washed blood from a syringe. Off Regent Street, Soho glared like an amusement arcade. On Oxford Street figures in expensive dresses, their bald heads gleaming, gestured broken-wristed in windows.

He had no idea why he was walking. Was he hoping the crowds would distract him? Was that why he peered at their faces, more and more desperately? Nobody looked at all reassuring. Women were perfect as corpses, men seemed to glow with concealed aggression; some were dragons, their mouths full of smoke.

He'd walked past the girl before he reacted. Gasping, he struggled through a knot of people on the corner of Dean Street and dashed across, against the lights. In the moments before she realised that he'd dodged ahead of her and was staring, he saw her bright quick eyes, the delicate web of veins beneath them, the freckles that peppered the bridge of her nose, the pulsing of blood in her neck. She was so intensely present to him that it was appalling.

Then she stepped aside, annoyed by him, whatever he was. He reached out, but couldn't quite seize her arm. He had to stop her somehow. "Don't," he cried.

At that, she fled. He'd started after her when two policemen blocked his path. Perhaps they hadn't noticed him, perhaps they wouldn't grab him – but it was too late; she was lost in the Oxford Street crowd. He turned and ran, fleeing back to his hotel.

As soon as he reached his room he began writing. His head felt stuffed with hot ash. He was scribbling so fast that he hardly knew what he was saying. How much time did he have? His hand was cramped and shaking, his writing was surrounded by a spittle of ink.

He was halfway through a sentence when, quite without warning, his mind went blank. His pen was clawing spasmodically at the page, but the urgency had gone; the nightmare had left him.

He lay in the anonymous bed in the dark, hoping he was wrong.

In the morning he went down to the lobby as late as he could bear. The face of the girl he'd seen in Oxford Street stared up at him from a newspaper. In the photograph her eyes looked dull and reproachful, though perhaps they seemed so only to him. He fled upstairs without reading the report. He already knew more than the newspaper would have been able to tell.

Eventually he went home to Neston. It didn't matter where he went; the nightmares would find him. He was an outcast from surrounding reality. He was focused inwards on his raw wound of a mind, waiting for the next outbreak of horrors to infest him.

Next day he sat at his desk. The sunlit houses opposite glared back like empty pages. Even to think of writing made his skin prickle. He went walking, but it was no good: beyond the marshes, factories coughed into the sky; grass-blades whipped the air like razors; birds swooped, shrieking knives with wings. The sunlight seemed violent and pitiless, vampirising the landscape.

There seemed no reason why the nightmares should ever stop. Either he would be forced to write them out, to involve himself more and more deeply in them, or they would be acted out in reality. In any case he was at their mercy; there was nothing he could do.

But wasn't he avoiding the truth? It hadn't been coincidence that had given him the chance he'd missed in Oxford Street. Perhaps he had been capable of intervention all along, if he had only known. However dismaying the responsibility was, surely it was preferable to helplessness. His glimpse in Oxford Street had made all the victims unbearably human.

He sat waiting. Pale waves snaked across the surface of the grass; in the heat-haze they looked as though water was welling up from the marshes. His scalp felt shrunken, but that was only nervousness and the storm that was clotting overhead. When eventually the clouds moved on, unbroken, they left a sediment of twilight that clung to him as he trudged home.

No, it was more than that. His skin felt grimy, unclean. The nightmares were close. He hurried to let his car out of the garage, then he sat like a private detective in the driver's seat outside his house. His hands clenched on the steering wheel. His head began to crawl, to swarm.

266

He mustn't be trapped into self-disgust. He reminded himself that the nightmares weren't coming from him, and forced his mind to grasp them, to be guided by them. Shame made him feel coated in hot grease. When at last the car coasted forward, was it acting out his urge to flee? Should he follow that street sign, or that one?

Just as the signs grew meaningless because he'd stared too long, he knew which way to go. His instincts had been waiting to take hold, and they were urgent now. He drove through the lampless streets, where lit curtains cut rectangles from the night, and out into the larger dark.

He found he was heading for Chester. Trees beside the road were giant scarecrows, brandishing tattered foliage. Grey clouds crawled grublike across the sky; he could hardly distinguish them from the crawling in his skull. He was desperate to purge his mind.

Roman walls loomed between the timber buildings of Chester, which were black and white as the moon. A few couples were window-shopping along the enclosed rows above the streets. On the bridge that crossed the main street, a clock perched like a moon-faced bird. Miles remembered a day when he'd walked by the river, boats passing slowly as clouds, a brass band on a small bandstand playing "Blow the Wind Southerly". How could the nightmare take place here?

It could, for it was urging him deeper into the city. He was driving so fast through the spotless streets that he almost missed the police station. Its blue sign drew him aside. That was where he must go. Somehow he had to persuade them that he knew where a crime was taking place.

He was still yards away from the police station when his foot faltered on the accelerator. The car shuddered and tried to jerk forward, but that was no use. The nearer he came to the police station, the weaker his instinct became. Was it being suppressed by his nervousness? Whatever the reason, he could guide nobody except himself.

As soon as he turned the car the urgency seized him. It was agonising now. It rushed him out of the centre of Chester, into streets of small houses and shops that looked dusty as furniture shoved out of sight in an attic. They were deserted except for a man in an ankle-length overcoat, who limped by like a sack with a head.

Miles stamped on the brake as the car passed the mouth of an alley. Snatching the keys, he slammed the door and ran into the alley, between two shops whose posters looked ancient and faded as Victorian photographs. The walls of the alley were chunks of spiky darkness above which cramped windows peered, but he didn't need to see to know where he was going.

He was shocked to find how slowly he had to run, how out of condition he was. His lungs seemed to be filling with lumps of rust, his throat was scraped raw. He was less running than staggering forward. Amid the uproar of his senses, it took him a while to feel that he was too late.

He halted as best he could. His feet slithered on the uneven flagstones, his hands clawed at the walls. As soon as he began to listen he wished he had not. Ahead in the dark, there was a faint incessant shriek that seemed to be trying to emerge from more than one mouth. He knew there was only one victim.

Before long he made out a dark object further down the alley. In fact it was two objects, one of which lay on the flagstones while the other rose to its feet, a dull gleam in its hand. A moment later the figure with the gleam was fleeing, its footsteps flapping like wings between the close walls.

The shrieking had stopped. The dark object lay still. Miles forced himself forward, to see what he'd failed to prevent. As soon as he'd glimpsed it he staggered away, choking back a scream.

He'd achieved nothing except to delay writing out the rest of the horrors. They were breeding faster in his skull, which felt as though it was cracking. He drove home blindly. The hedgerows and the night had merged into a dark mass that spilled towards the road, smudging its edges. Perhaps he might crash – but he wasn't allowed that relief, for the nightmares were herding him back to his desk.

The scratching of his pen, and a low half-articulate moaning which he recognised sometimes as his voice, kept him company. Next day the snap of the letter-box made him drop his pen, otherwise he might not have been able to force himself away from the desk.

The package contained the first issue of *Ghastly*. "Hope you like it," the editor gushed. "It's already been banned in some areas, which has helped sales no end. You'll see we announce your stories as coming attractions, and we look forward to publishing them." On the cover the girl was still writhing, but the contents were far worse. Miles had read only a paragraph when he tore the glossy pages into shreds.

How could anyone enjoy reading that? The pebble-dashed houses of Neston gleamed innocently back at him. Who knew what his neighbours read behind their locked doors? Perhaps in time some of them would gloat over his pornographic horrors, reassuring themselves that this was only horror fiction, not pornography at all; just as he'd reassured himself that they were only stories now, nothing to do with reality – certainly nothing to do with him, the pseudonym said so –

The Neston houses gazed back at him, self-confident and bland: they looked as convinced of their innocence as he was trying to feel – and all at once he knew where the nightmares were coming from.

He couldn't see how that would help him. Before he'd begun to suffer from his writer's block, there had been occasions when a story had surged up from his unconscious and demanded to be written. Those stories had been products of his own mind, yet he couldn't shake them off except by writing – but now he was suffering nightmares on behalf of the world.

No wonder they were so terrible, or that they were growing worse. If material repressed into the unconscious was bound to erupt in some less manageable form, how much more powerful that must be when the unconscious was collective! Precisely because people were unable to come to terms with the crimes, repudiated them as utterly inhuman or simply unimaginable, the horrors would reappear in a worse form and possess whomever they pleased. He remembered thinking that the patterns of life in the tower blocks had something to do with the West Derby murder. They had, of course. Everything had.

And now the repressions were focused in him. There was no reason why they should ever leave him; on the contrary, they seemed likely to grow more numerous and more peremptory. Was he releasing them by writing them out, or was the writing another form of repudiation?

One was still left in his brain. It felt like a boil in his skull. Suddenly he knew that he wasn't equal to writing it out, whatever else might happen. Had his imagination burned out at last? He

269

would be content never to write another word. It occurred to him that the book he'd discussed with Hugo was just another form of rejection: knowing you were reading about real people reassured you they were other than yourself.

He slumped at his desk. He was a burden of flesh that felt encrusted with grit. Nothing moved except the festering nightmare in his head. Unless he got rid of it somehow, it felt as though it would never go away. He'd failed twice to intervene in reality, but need he fail again? If he succeeded, was it possible that might change things for good?

He was at the front door when the phone rang. Was it Susie? If she knew what was filling his head, she would never want to speak to him again. He left the phone ringing in the dark house and fled to his car.

The pain in his skull urged him through the dimming fields and villages to Birkenhead, where it seemed to abandon him. Not that it had faded – his mind felt like an abscessed tooth – but it was no longer able to guide him. Was something anxious to prevent him from reaching his goal?

The bare streets of warehouses and factories and terraces went on for miles, brick-red slabs pierced far too seldom by windows. At the peak hour the town centre grew black with swarms of people, the Mersey Tunnel drew in endless sluggish segments of cars. He drove jerkily, staring at faces.

Eventually he left the car in Hamilton Square, overlooked by insurance offices caged by railings, and trudged towards the docks. Except for his footsteps, the streets were deserted. Perhaps the agony would be cured before he arrived wherever he was going. He was beyond caring what that implied.

It was dark now. At the end of rows of houses whose doors opened onto cracked pavements he saw docked ships, glaring metal mansions. Beneath the iron mesh of swing bridges, a scum of neon light floated on the oily water. Sunken rails snagged his feet. In pubs on street corners he heard tribes of dockers, a sullen wordless roar that sounded like a warning. Out here the moan of a ship on the Irish Sea was the only voice he heard.

When at last he halted, he had no idea where he was. The pavement on which he was walking was eaten away by rubbly ground; he could smell collapsed buildings. A roofless house stood like a rotten tooth, lit by a single streetlamp harsh as lightning. Streets still led from the opposite pavement, and despite the ache – which had aborted nearly all his thoughts – he knew that the street directly opposite was where he must go.

There was silence. Everything was yet to happen. The lull seemed to give him a brief chance to think. Suppose he managed to prevent it? Repressing the ideas of the crimes only made them erupt in a worse form – how much worse might it be to repress the crimes themselves?

Nevertheless he stepped forward. Something had to cure him of his agony. He stayed on the treacherous pavement of the side street, for the roadway was skinless, a mass of bricks and mud. Houses pressed close to him, almost forcing him into the road. Where their doors and windows ought to be were patches of new brick. The far end of the street was impenetrably dark.

When he reached it, he saw why. A wall at least ten feet high was built flush against the last houses. Peering upwards, he made out the glint of broken glass. He was closed in by the wall and the plugged houses, in the midst of desolation.

Without warning – quite irrelevantly, it seemed – he remembered something he'd read about years ago while researching a novel: the Mosaic ritual of the Day of Atonement. They'd driven out the scapegoat, burdened with all the sins of the people, into the wilderness. Another goat had been sacrificed. The images chafed together in his head; he couldn't grasp their meaning – and then he realised why there was so much room for them in his mind. The aching nightmare was fading.

At once he was unable to turn away from the wall, for he was atrociously afraid. He knew why this nightmare could not have been acted out without him. Along the bricked-up street he heard footsteps approaching.

When he risked a glance over his shoulder, he saw that there were two figures. Their faces were blacked out by the darkness, but the glints in their hands were sharp. He was trying to claw his way up the wall, though already his lungs were labouring. Everything was over – the sleepless nights, the poison in his brain, the nightmare of responsibility – but he knew that while he would soon not be able to scream, it would take him much longer to die.

Malachi
by Simon Bestwick

"I won't be five minutes."

She was worried; no, she was frightened. Who could blame her? "Mark..."

"It'll be alright. I have to go out." He reached out and touched the swell of her belly. "Try to stay calm."

"I know, I know. There's three of us now."

"That's right."

He went to the door of the narrow, squalid little flat. The walls were patchy with damp; a roach scuttled across the carpet and from the kitchen came the trickle of the tap that he couldn't, despite their best efforts, shut off. "Don't open the door for anyone."

"Except you."

"Except me."

She lowered herself onto the threadbare sofa, bone-weary. "You going to look in on Mr Rosen?"

"May as well."

"What's he going to do?" She shook her head. Pregnant, the world going to hell in a handbasket all around her, living in a small corner of the hot place itself, and afraid – afraid for herself, afraid for her husband, for their unborn child, afraid for and of almost everything – but she could still care for the old man. Such moments reminded him of why he loved her. Of late, with all the pressure and the fear and the angry helplessness of being trapped where they were, he'd needed every one of them. But, with luck, not any more. After tonight, they could breathe easier, at least for a while. For however long it took the killing tide to well over the Dover Cliffs and into the Channel, and spread out to lap onto another, freer shore.

He crossed the room again to kiss her, stroking her long, crinkly hair, relishing the feel of it. How long since he'd been relaxed enough to enjoy so simple a caress? "I don't know, Susie. I offered to try and get him out too, but he wouldn't. Said he'd run one time too many."

"He's got one of those tattoos on his arm, you know."

"Yes. I've seen it."

Susan took a deep breath and tried to keep herself composed, but her shoulders hitched. "People don't seem to learn anything, do they?"

"Shh." He stroked her face. He'd always been pale; the contrast of his skin against hers was so stark, like cream and chocolate. "You're beautiful," he whispered.

She snorted a laugh. "Yeah, with my swollen ankles and bags under my eyes and –"

"You are." He kissed her eyelids gently. "You're so beautiful."

"You're so biased."

He laughed and kissed her lips. How could anybody hate her? But there were those who did – not for who she was, but what – and him too for bedding her, and the knowledge of their existence made his thoughts redden with a hatred all their own.

"I love you."

"You too, Mark. Please, be careful."

"I will. You know I will."

Then he quickly got up and went out.

Mr Rosen's flat was on the floor below. Mark knocked gently on the door and listened to the shuffling footsteps approaching. A beat of silence. The click and rattle of locks and chains. And the door opened.

"Hello, Mark. Do come in." The English was impeccable, but the German accent lingered still.

"Hi, Mr Rosen. Look, I can't stop long. I have to go out and see Spider."

"Spider...? Oh, yes. Him."

"I wanted to ask you..."

"No. Thank you, Mark, but I'll stay here. I'm too old to run any more. But when they come for me, they won't take me alive. You can be sure of that."

It was unnerving to hear him talk like that. Frightening. But Mark knew that the things he talked of would come to pass. That was why he was going.

"You've been a good friend to me, Mark. You and Susan both. I wish you luck."

Mark looked at him. A sagging, wrinkled prune of a face, thinning white hair, the last wisps of a beard clinging to his wattled chin, or maybe he just couldn't be bothered to shave any more and this was all that would grow.

There wasn't much in the flat. It was barer even than Mark and Susan's own. There were no pictures, no books. Only, on the mantelpiece above a gas fire that didn't work (who cared about the people who lived on the Blackheath Estate?) a small clock, its ticktock relentless and slow as though measuring out each of the old man's dwindling seconds of life, and a menorah. Odd, as Mr Rosen wasn't even a practising Jew. A British citizen since the forties, he was an atheist. But faith they didn't care about. Only blood.

Mr Rosen had once told him the menorah came from his home in Germany. His father had hidden it before the SS came to take them away to Auschwitz, or was it Dachau? To his shame, Mark couldn't remember. Mr Rosen had been back home once, to retrieve it. It had still been there, where it was hidden. Somehow, Mr Rosen had said, he had known it would be.

They talked for a little while, but there was nothing much to say. Mark and Susan were leaving, hopefully tonight; Mr Rosen was staying and waiting to die.

"I just wish I could take a few of the bastards with me when I go," he said with sudden fire. They were dying down in him to embers, all his flames, but now and again they would flare up, and Mark would wish he'd known the old man in his youth.

"Ah, well." He sighed. "I wish that I believed, Mark. That I would see Rosa and the boy again. Samuel, he was called. My family. They never came out. I did. They didn't. Not even a grave. Only ashes, mixed with those of a million others..." He blinked rapidly, clearing his eyes. "Rosa Rosen. Hell of a name, eh?"

"Yeah," said Mark softly. What else could he say? Once you had anger, once you had fire. And now? Only regret. And ashes. And the sorrow of lessons never learned.

"No, Mark, it's the right thing that you are doing. Get out now. Raise your family somewhere better than this. But one day... when things have changed – as you must believe they will – come back home. I should have gone back to Germany, claimed my homeland back off them, but... there were too many memories, you know? But not for you, perhaps. If you get out now."

274

The clock ticked on. Mark glanced at it. "Mr Rosen, I'm going to have to go."

The old man nodded gravely, and shook his hand. "Shalom."

Mark nodded, not trusting himself to speak. Sometimes parting was a sorrow without any sweetness to it. He closed the door on his way out.

Half the lights on the Blackheath were out, smashed. Darkness made their work easier.

The coppers patrolled the estate very lightly, mostly confining their presence to its outskirts. The job was to make sure that all the scum stayed there, where they belonged. Who cared whether or not they ripped each other's throats out? Not the law.

The danger was the Jackshirts, the young bloods with their shaved heads and red, white and blue T-shirts in all weathers, even the bitter heart of late November, like now. Looking for a chance to impress, to prove themselves – it stood you in good stead, these days, if you went for a job with the police, or the elite special patrols. The Jackshirts roamed the estate by dark, looking for someone, anyone. Everybody here was a legitimate target.

He wore his hair long. That was to mark him out as one of the oppressed. Some of the Asian lads on the estate banded together in vigilante groups. If you were one of the white people here, by the time you convinced them you weren't the enemy, you could be dead, or maimed at the very least.

He still had an old flyer – or had until this morning – handed out by one of the far-right groups they'd had around in the old days, when there were still elections, before the stupid sods had elected the BPA. British Patriotic Alliance. Bastards. He'd found the flyer sorting through some old things, sorting out the stuff to pack into his case. One case each, Spider had said. No more. Christ knew how it had got there.

Our aims, the leaflet had declared. He only remembered one of them, right now.

To execute all white race mixers.

Mark walked on down the street. The only sound was the squelch of his leaky trainers on the tarmac. He couldn't afford another pair. *What are they so afraid of?*

He sighed. He could chase his tail all night trying to work that one out.

* * *

Spider had been some sort of socialist or anarchist before the BPA
came in. He was thin and pale with ginger hair down to his
shoulders in dreadlocks. He'd been in a council flat. Easy meat.
They'd just relocated him. He'd been lucky to escape arrest. The
'subversives' had been the first ones to be rounded up. Most likely
to organise something.

But here, he had connections. On the estate, as everywhere
else, there was a black market. People who could see a profit to be
made and would risk the grief running the checkpoints could bring
in exchange for it. Cigarettes, coffee, dope, little luxuries like that.
That was how Mark had raised this money, buying their dope and
then selling it on. And always the risk of treading on some other,
bigger dealer's toes.

They ran stuff into the Blackheath, and all the other places
like it, all the dumping grounds, all the ghettoes while the
unwanted and the impure waited for their turn on the chopping
block. And sometimes, if you had enough money, they could run
people out again.

Mark gave Spider the money. Spider counted it, then went to
the phone and made a call.

"It's done," he said. He scribbled a note on a piece of paper
and passed it to Mark. "Be there in one hour. Dead on the dot. If
you're late, it's blown."

Mark read, memorised and shredded it, then nodded. "OK.
Thanks, mate."

Spider shook his hand. "Just wish I could do more around
here."

Spider would never leave, Mark knew. Because in a perverse
way he was in his element. Before the BPA came, he would never
have hoped to make so concrete a difference. He would stay here
until they came to take him away in one of those unmarked vans,
the ones you never came out of alive.

Face flushed with relief, heart banging like a victory drum, he
stepped out onto the pavement and started walking. Rounding the
corner, he could see the apartment block. His home no more, after
tonight. Who was he kidding? It had never been.

276

A foot scraped on the pavement behind him. Mark walked on. A little faster than before.

More footsteps. *Clump, clump, clump.* More than one set.

Oh, God... he didn't believe, but he started to pray.

Clump, clump, clump. Faster, and faster. The sounds changed. They weren't just directly behind him now. They were spreading out.

Walk. Walk. Don't run. Don't look back.

"Oi!"

Walk don't run, don't look back, don't answer. It wasn't far now. Only a couple of hundred yards, surely? Not that far.

Far enough, he knew. Far enough to die before you were home.

"Oi! Longhair!"

"Girlboy!"

"We're talking to you! Yeah, you!"

And then he did it. Big mistake, but he knew they'd have come for him anyway. But he still shouldn't have done it; like Lot's wife at Sodom, he turned and he looked back.

The Jackshirts started running.

There were five of them. All young, all fast. Mark wasn't exactly old bones himself, but he knew he couldn't outrun them. Still, he tried.

But they were on him, outpacing him, spreading to outflank him. One, then two swerved onto the pavement in front of him. He slowed, backed up, but the others were behind him and to his left. On his right there was only a high, flat brick wall, too high and too flat to climb.

They closed in on him. One held a length of chain, another a knife. The others, knuckle-dusters, a club.

"Well, look who's out after curfew," one of them said, one of the boys with the knuckle-dusters. His shaven head gleamed as the moon peeped out from behind a bank of thick cloud. Mark put him at about twenty-two, twenty-three. The eldest, he guessed. The ringleader.

Oh Christ, why now, tonight of all nights?

"Thought it was a bird at first," said the one with the chains. Mark looked around for a gap in the ranks, one he could dart through, and run for the apartment, have a chance of making out. God knew how they'd get out again, but –

The leader punched him in the solar plexus, with the knuckle-duster. Mark doubled up, the air whooshing out of his lungs. The pain. The pain was terrible. Just that blow could have killed him.

The chains crashed down, across his back. He hit the pavement. A kick caught him in the side.

With a strange sense of detachment, he thought: *They're going to beat me to death.*

But no, they'd stopped. For now. Please God, let them have stopped for good. He couldn't take much more and they'd barely started. One of them was going through his pockets. They had his wallet. Was that all they wanted? If he just lay still they might leave him alone. They were welcome to it anyway. There was no money left, Spider had it all. There was nothing in his wallet except –

"Ooh, look at this, lads."

Oh no. Oh please. Oh no.

The photo. The photo of him and Susan. Oh, no. Stupid. Stupid. Stupid.

"Looks like we've got ourselves a race mixer."

The leader pulled his head up by the hair, hawked and spat glutinously in his face. It rolled down his cheek. He wanted to wipe it away but didn't dare. "Knock me sick, your sort. How can you do it? God knows what you catch. So come then, where is it you live? Think me an' the lads'd like to come and see your bit of black. Pay our respects, like."

They did this sometimes. Came into the flats, busted down the doors, and had their fun. And the neighbours would hear the screaming, but who'd intervene?

"Fuck... off," Mark croaked.

They yanked him up and the leader kicked him in the groin. *Christ!* He doubled over. Didn't they wear steel-capped boots? Oh God, the pain, the pain...

"Come on, wog-lover. Tell us where she is."

I won't. Won't. Won't.

Wouldn't he? Just say no. Like those stupid drugs adverts when you were little, remember them? Just say no. All you have to do is keep saying it.

But they'd barely started hurting him, and how long can anyone hold out? For all the heroes who keep their jaws shut and

278

save their last breath to spit in the torturer's face, there's a dozen at least, or more, who crack and spill their guts and welcome the bullet when it comes and finishes them off, ends the torment of knowing that last capitulation, the enemy's final victory.

They caught him by the hair and pulled him up again.

Glass crunched underfoot.

"What?"

They were turning. A tall man was crossing the street towards them, from the mouth of a dark alley. He wore a dark suit, shirt and waistcoat – waistcoat? who wore them any more? – a long, light-coloured coat. Bareheaded. Dark hair. A pale angular face. Something familiar about the face. Something. What?

The chief Jackshirt let Mark go, stepped forward. "What you looking at?"

The man just looked at him.

"You want some too, that it?" The Jackshirt leaned forward and poked the tall man in the chest. "Listen –"

The tall man reached up, grabbed the two poking fingers, and bent them back. A sound like dry twigs breaking on a clear winter morning. The Jackshirt screamed. The tall man let go of his hand and hit him in the neck. There was another, louder crack, and the Jackshirt was flung aside like a used rag. The tall man came forward.

The one with the knife lunged at him. Did he get him? Mark couldn't tell; the tall man grabbed the shaven head with both hands and twisted. *Crack.*

The tall man sprang forward. The other three Jackshirts might have run, but he didn't give them time. The club and the chains swung; the knuckle-duster punched out and all met empty air. The tall man punched the man with the knuckle-duster and the man with the club, ferocious lunging blows like a woodsman chopping trees. Two more loud cracks of breaking bone; two more Jackshirts fell and were still.

One left, the one with the chains. He swung wildly at the tall man once more, then turned to run. But the tall man caught him. Picked him up as if he weighed nothing. And then flung him at the brick wall. The *crunch* of impact was loud and unpleasant, and very final.

The tall man was on the pavement now, offering a hand. "Can you stand up?"

Mark was doubled over in agony, but he could, just about. "Thanks."

"Are you alright?"

"I think so. You –?"

But the tall man swayed now, and put out a hand to steady himself against the wall. There was a glistening darkness on his waistcoat. *The knife*, thought Mark. "Ah..." the tall man sighed. He didn't seem frightened, or even surprised. He looked up at Mark and smiled.

"Malachi."

The tall man looked around. Mark followed his gaze. A woman was standing in the mouth of the alley from which he'd emerged. She was holding a child in the crook of one arm; with the other, she reached out towards him.

"Malachi, come home now."

The tall man – Malachi – stepped away from Mark and started across the road. He stumbled as he went, swayed, but kept going. Halfway across, he turned and looked back. "You'd better get back home now, Mark," he said. "Susan will be worrying. Get yourselves out. The three of you." He smiled tightly. Then he turned to stumble the rest of the way across, onto the pavement, before his legs gave way and buckled underneath him. He collapsed at the mouth of the alley. He managed to half rise. The woman reached down towards him. He clutched at her hand, and she pulled him up.

And then they were gone, as if the shadows filling the alley had welled up and overflowed to engulf them.

Mark sagged for a moment against the alley wall. It didn't seem real. None of it did. Well, that wasn't quite true. Whatever the origins of the tall man, the five bodies strewn around him weren't in his imagination.

He turned and started staggering back towards his flat.

"Mark! Shit! What...?"

"Jackshirts. Susan, it's alright. I'll explain later. But we haven't time now. Come on."

They staggered down the stairs with the cases. On the floor below, Mark stopped.

"Mark?"

"Wait a second."

"I thought you said we didn't have time?"

"I'll be a minute."

"You said that last time." It wasn't much of a joke, but it was all they had.

The door of Mr Rosen's flat was ajar. Mark pushed it open and went inside.

Mr Rosen sat in his armchair, eyes closed, mouth open as if in mid-snore. But he wasn't snoring.

Mark knelt, wearily, his bruises throbbing.

"Mark." Susan whispering from the doorway.

A dark stain had dried from red to brown on the old man's shirt.

"He's dead."

"Oh god. Mark…?"

There was something in Rosen's cooling hands.

Mark stared at it for a long time, then prised it loose. "Hang on." He stood, still holding it. A black and white photograph of a family of three. A man, woman and child.

"Poor old guy," he heard Susan whisper. "We never even knew his first name."

The man was tall, with black hair, clad in a suit, waistcoat and a long, light-coloured coat. "Didn't we?"

"Mark, I'm sorry about him. But we can't do anything. We have to go."

"Yeah." He slipped the photograph into his own pocket. A reminder. But she was right. There was no more time.

Get out now. Raise your family somewhere better than this. But one day... when things have changed – as you must believe they will – come back home.

"Shalom," he said softly.

He closed the door behind him.

Author biographies

Nina Allan's fiction has appeared in the magazines *Interzone, Black Static, Midnight Street*, and in the anthologies *Subtle Edens, Catastrophia, Strange Tales* from Tartarus and *Best Horror of the Year Volume 2*. Nina won the Aeon Award in 2007, and has twice been nominated for the British Fantasy Award for best short fiction. Her first story collection, *A Thread of Truth*, is published by Eibonvale Press. She lives and works in London.

rj krijnen-kemp does not exist. Living in the deep, raw, dark dungeon of himself, where he chooses to remain, afloat upon oceans of absinthe and black ink, he carefully scribes the cartography of his inner nightmare. Life, he has concluded, is nasty, brutish and thankfully short, while art is long and the atrocities to which art must bear witness are endless.

Lisa Tuttle was born in the United States, but has been resident in Britain for almost thirty years. She began writing while still at school, sold her first stories at university, and won the John W. Campbell Award for Best New Science Fiction Writer of the year in 1974. She is the author of eight novels (most recently the contemporary fantasy *The Silver Bough*) and many short stories, in addition to several books for children, and editor of *Skin of the Soul*, an anthology of horror stories by women. Her story 'Closet Dreams' won the International Horror Guild Award in 2007. Ash-Tree Press is to publish a multi-volume collection of her short fiction, beginning with *Stranger in the House: Collected Ghost and Horror Stories, Volume 1* scheduled for September 2010.

John Howard was born in London in 1961. He is the author of *The Silver Voices* (2010) and *The Defeat of Grief* (2010). With Mark Valentine he is the author of the collections *The Rite of Trebizond and Other Tales* and *The Collected Connoisseur*. John's short fiction, solo and in collaboration, has also appeared in the anthologies *Beneath the Ground* and *Strange Tales*. John has published many articles on various aspects of the science fiction and horror fields, especially on the work of classic authors such as

Fritz Leiber, Arthur Machen, August Derleth, M.R. James, and the writers of the pulp era. He contributed essays to the Fritz Leiber special issue of *Fantasy Commentator*, as well as to *Fritz Leiber: Critical Essays* and *The Man Who Collected Psychos: Critical Essays on Robert Bloch*. John has reviewed genre books for a wide range of magazines and journals for nearly thirty years.

Tony Richards sold his first short story at the age of twenty-one, and hasn't stopped selling fiction since. He has written SF, mystery, and mainstream tales, as well as dark fantasy, and has appeared in most major magazines and anthologies in the genre. His work has been praised by the likes of Ed Gorman, Ramsey Campbell, Graham Joyce, and the late Ronald Chetwynd-Hayes, and he has been nominated for both the Bram Stoker and British Fantasy Awards. When not writing, he likes to travel, and has based a good deal of his fiction on his journeys to far-flung corners of the world.

His debut novel with Eos/HarperCollins, *Dark Rain*, was the first in a series of tales set in the fictional town of Raine's Landing, Massachusetts, the premise being that there were real witches in Salem back in 1692; they simply got wind of the forthcoming trials and decamped to this other town instead. It was mostly inspired by Tony's visits to Massachusetts and to small towns in New York state. The second book, *Night of Demons*, is now available. The third Raine's Landing novel – *Midnight's Angels* – is due out shortly. Tony Richards lives with his wife in his native town of London, England.

Alison J. Littlewood lives in West Yorkshire, England, where she hoards books, dreams and writes short fiction—mainly in the dark fantasy and horror genres. She is currently working on a novel. Alison has contributed to *Black Static, Murky Depths, Dark Horizons, Not One Of Us* and *Read By Dawn 3*, among others. Visit her at www.alisonlittlewood.co.uk

R.B. Russell is the author of two collections of short stories, *Putting the Pieces in Place* (Ex Occidente) and *Literary Remains* (PS Publishing), and a novella, *Bloody Baudelaire* (Ex Occidente). Born in Sussex in 1966 and now living in the Yorkshire Dales, he runs Tartarus Press with his wife, Rosalie Parker.

284

Mat Joiner is a member of Birmingham Writers Group. This is his first published story; another (a collaboration with Joel Lane) is forthcoming in *Postscripts*. He's currently working on a novella-length sequel to that, and a series of interconnected fantasy short stories. Interests and influences include walking the Grand Union Canal or Birmingham backstreets, real ale pubs, 1890s art and fiction, folk music and electronica, and playing the Omnichord.

Rosanne Rabinowitz lives in South London and earns a crust as a freelance sub-editor. Other forms of toil have included stints as a life model, oral history researcher, part-time mental health worker and full-time dole claimer. She has a story in NewCon Press's *Conficts* anthology, and her novella 'In the Pines' appears in the award-winning anthology *Extended Play: the Elastic Book of Music*. Other published fiction includes stories in T*he Slow Mirror: New Fiction by Jewish Writers, Postscripts* and *Midnight Street*. 'Survivor's Guilt' first appeared in *Black Static 14* and is part of a recently completed novel, *Noise Leads Me*. Rosanne is now putting the finishing touches on a novella and working on a novel about a woman leader of the Adamites, the radical and free-loving faction of the Hussite revolution in 15th-century Bohemia.

Rhys Hughes was born in Cardiff in 1966. His first published story appeared in 1992 and his first book in 1995. Since then, he has embarked on a mammoth project of writing exactly 1000 tales that will form a single connected story-cycle. The overall title of the project is 'Pandora's Bluff'. His most recent books are *Twisthorn Bellow*, a novel; and the collection *Tallest Stories*, which is a sort of microcosm of his big story-cycle. He enjoys music, astronomy, hiking, cycling, travel and the outdoors life, and his website can be found at: http://rhyshughes.blogspot.com

Simon Kurt Unsworth was born on Valentine's Day in 1972 somewhere in the northwest of England. He spent the years between then and now growing, the result initially of hormone surges and biology and more latterly as a result of a weakness for pizza. He lives in Lancaster (just below the Lake District) with his wife and child, which is a good place to live if you like that sort of thing – it has all the things that a town needs: a river, some pubs, shops, roads of varying quality, pizza restaurants and only one or two places that mortal man should fear to venture. He writes when he's not working as a trainer for a national charity, spending time with his family, cooking, walking the dogs, watching suspect movies or lazing about. He would like to believe that equality and fairness are within our grasp, if only we could think about other people rather than ourselves for a change: in this belief, he is happy to be accused of naivety. His first collection, *Lost Places*, was released by Ash-Tree Press in March 2010. His second, *Strange Gateways*, is out from PS Publishing in 2012.

Joe R. Lansdale is the author of over thirty novels and two hundred short stories/articles. He has received two New York Times notable books, an Edgar, seven Bram Stokers, a British Fantasy Award, and many other recognitions for his work. One of his novellas, *Bubba Ho-Tep*, was filmed under the same name and is a popular cult film. His most recent novel is the Vintage edition of *Vanilla Ride* which appeared last year from Knopf.

Kaaron Warren's short story collection *The Grinding House*, CSFG Publishing (published as The Glass Woman by Prime Books in the US) won the ACT Writers' and Publishers' Fiction Award and was nominated for three Ditmar Awards, winning two. She has three novels with Angry Robot Books. The critically acclaimed *Slights* was nominated for a number of awards and won the Australian Shadows Award. Her short story collection from Ticonderoga Press, *Dead Sea Fruit*, was published in 2010. Kaaron lives in Canberra, Australia, with her husband and two children. Her website is http://kaaronwarren.wordpress.com

Steve Duffy's stories have appeared in numerous magazines and anthologies in Europe and North America. His third collection of short supernatural fiction, *Tragic Life Stories* from Ash-Tree Press, was launched in Brighton, England, at the World Horror Convention 2010; his fourth, *The Moment Of Panic* will be published by PS Publishing in 2011, and will include the International Horror Guild award-winning short story, 'The Rag-and-Bone Men.' Steve lives in North Wales.

286

Gary McMahon's short fiction has appeared in numerous acclaimed magazines and anthologies in the UK and US and has been reprinted in yearly 'Best of' collections. He is a multiple-award-nominated author/editor. His work includes the novellas *Rough Cut* and *All Your Gods Are Dead*, the collections *Dirty Prayers, How to Make Monsters* and *Pieces of Midnight*. His novels to date are *Rain Dogs* and *Hungry Hearts*. Angry Robot Books is publishing *Pretty Little Dead Things* in November 2010 and Dead Bad Things in September 2011. He has signed a three-book deal with Solaris – the first of which, *The Concrete Grove*, will be published in 2011. Gary's website can be found at www.GaryMcMahon.com

'Damned if You Don't' is taken from **Robert Shearman**'s first collection of short stories, *Tiny Deaths*, published by Comma Press in 2007. It won the World Fantasy Award for best collection, and was also shortlisted for the Edge Hill Short Story Prize and nominated for the Frank O'Connor International Short Story Prize. One of the stories from it was selected by the National Library Board of Singapore as part of the annual Read! Singapore campaign. His second collection, *Love Songs for the Shy and Cynical*, was released late last year to great acclaim, and has won the Shirley Jackson Award and the Edge Hill Short Story Reader's Prize; it is currently nominated for three British Fantasy Awards. His third collection, *Everyone's Just So Special*, comes out early 2011.

He's probably best known as the writer who brought back the Daleks for the BAFTA award winning first series of the revived *Doctor Who* series starring Christopher Eccleston. His episode was runner-up for a Hugo Award, and his award winning contributions to the audio range of *Doctor Who* released by Big Finish have been broadcast on BBC Radio. He has written many plays for Radio Four, mostly produced by Martin Jarvis; he has won two Sony awards for two series of his interactive short story project for BBC7, 'The Chain Gang'. As resident dramatist at the Northcott Theatre in Exeter, Robert was the youngest playwright in Britain ever to be honoured by the Arts Council in this way, and he subsequently became a regular writer for Alan Ayckbourn at the Stephen Joseph Theatre in Scarborough. His theatre awards include the World Drama Trust Award, the Sunday Times

Playwriting Award, the Sophie Winter Memorial Trust Award, and the Guinness Award for Ingenuity in association with the Royal National Theatre. He has recently been commissioned for a new play for the London West End, to be produced in 2011. A collection of seven of his plays, called *Caustic Comedies*, is to be published in autumn 2010. 'Damned If You Don't' was nominated as best short story at the World Fantasy Awards.

Carole Johnstone's first published story appeared in *Black Static #3* in early 2008. Since then she has contributed short stories to numerous magazines and anthologies including *Grants Pass, Dead Souls, Close Encounters of the Urban Kind* and PS Publishing's forthcoming post-apocalyptic anthology, *Catastrophia*. 'Dead Loss' (*Black Static #13*) was recently reprinted in Ellen Datlow's *Best Horror of the Year, Vol. 2*. Her first novella, *Frenzy*, was published by Eternal Press/Damnation Books in August 2009. Her website can be found at www.carolejohnstone.com

Stephen Volk was the creator and lead writer of ITV's award-winning paranormal drama series *Afterlife* starring Lesley Sharp and Andrew Lincoln, and the notorious, some say legendary, BBC TV 'Halloween hoax' *Ghostwatch*, which spooked the nation, hit the headlines, and even caused questions to be raised in Parliament.

His latest feature film, *The Awakening*, now in production, stars Rebecca Hall, Dominic West and Imelda Staunton. Other credits include Ken Russell's *Gothic*, a trippy retelling of the Mary Shelley/Frankenstein story starring Gabriel Byrne and Natasha Richardson; *The Guardian*, directed by William Friedkin; *Superstition*; and *Octane*. For television, he has written stand-alone scripts for Channel 4's *Shockers* and BBC1's *Ghosts*. He also won a BAFTA for his short film script *The Deadness of Dad* starring Rhys Ifans.

His first collection of short stories, *Dark Corners*, was published by Gray Friar Press in 2006, from which his story '31/10' (a sequel to *Ghostwatch*) was nominated for both a British Fantasy Award and a HWA Bram Stoker Award. More recently his novella *Vardøger* has earned him a nomination for both a Shirley Jackson and a British Fantasy Award. He has also appeared in *The Year's Best Fantasy and Horror, Best British Mysteries* and has been selected for *The Mammoth Book of Best New Horror*. He writes a regular comment piece 'Electric Darkness' for the magazine *Black Static*.

David A. Sutton lives in Birmingham, England. The recipient of the World Fantasy Award, The International Horror Guild Award and twelve British Fantasy Awards for editing magazines and anthologies (*Fantasy Tales, Dark Terrors*). His first professional anthologies were *New Writings in Horror & the Supernatural* (two volumes) and *The Satyr's Head & Other Tales of Terror*. More recently he has edited *Phantoms of Venice*, which was reprinted in paperback by Screaming Dreams in 2007, and *Houses on the Borderland*, a selection of novellas from The British Fantasy Society in 2008. He has also been a genre fiction writer since the 1960s. Recent appearances have been in *When Graveyards Yawn* (Crowswing Books), *The Black Book of Horror 1 and 2* (Mortbury Press), *Dark Reign* (eBook from Screaming Dreams), *Dead Ends* (Screaming Dreams), Su*btle Edens: The Elastic Book of Slipstream* (Elastic Press) and in *The Black Book of Horror 4. The Fisherman*, published in 2007 as a chapbook from Gary William Crawford's Gothic Press, was selected by Stephen Jones for *The Mammoth Book of Best New Horror 19*. His debut short story collection is *Clinically Dead & Other Tales of the Supernatural* (Screaming Dreams). David's non-genre interests are Rambling which, for the Birmingham group, he edits their quarterly newsletter and is secretary, and genealogy, where he finds that his Chimney Sweep ancestors hold a bizarre attraction.

Thana Niveau lives in a crumbling gothic tower somewhere near a place called Wales. She writes horror and shares her re-animated life with the mad surgeon who stitched her together from pieces of fallen women.

Andrew Hook was born in 1967 and lives and works in Norwich, UK. His short fiction has appeared in over 70 magazines and anthologies since 1994. Some of these stories have been collected in three books: *The Virtual Menagerie* (Elastic Press, 2002), *Beyond Each Blue Horizon* (Crowswing Books, 2005), and *Residue* (Half-Cut Publications, 2006). Whilst primarily a short

289

story writer, Andrew has also written novels, with the comic satire *Moon Beaver* appearing from ENC Press in 2004, and a shorter work, *And God Created Zombies*, published through NewCon Press in 2009. Forthcoming books include *Ponthe Oldenguine* (Atomic Fez, late 2010), and *Shipping Tomorrow Backwards* (under negotiation). Andrew's website can be found at www.andrew-hook.com

The *Oxford Companion to English Literature* describes **Ramsey Campbell** as 'Britain's most respected living horror writer.' He has been given more awards than any other writer in the field, including the Grand Master Award of the World Horror Convention, the Lifetime Achievement Award of the Horror Writers Association and the Living Legend Award of the International Horror Guild. Among his novels are *The Face That Must Die, Incarnate, Midnight Sun, The Count of Eleven, Silent Children, The Darkest Part of the Woods, The Overnight, Secret Story, The Grin of the Dark, Thieving Fear, Creatures of the Pool* and *The Seven Days of Cain*. Forthcoming is *Ghosts Know*. His collections include *Waking Nightmares, Alone with the Horrors, Ghosts and Grisly Things, Told by the Dead* and *Just Behind You*, and his non-fiction is collected as *Ramsey Campbell, Probably*. His novels *The Nameless* and *Pact of the Fathers* have been filmed in Spain. His regular columns appear in *Prism, All Hallows, Dead Reckonings* and *Video Watchdog*. He is the President of the British Fantasy Society and of the Society of Fantastic Films.

Ramsey Campbell lives on Merseyside with his wife Jenny. His pleasures include classical music, good food and wine, and whatever's in that pipe. His website is at www.ramseycampbell.com

Simon Bestwick lives in mournfully resigned bachelorhood (or more precisely, Lancashire) and is the author of two short story collections, *A Hazy Shade Of Winter* and *Pictures Of The Dark*, and a novel, Tide Of Souls. His novella 'The Narrows' was shortlisted for the 2009 British Fantasy Award and reprinted in Ellen Datlow's *Best Horror Of The Year*. Another novella, 'Angels of the Silences', was published by Pendragon Press in 2010, and his short story 'Sons of the City' will appear in the forthcoming Solaris Books anthology *End Of The Line*. He's also written numerous radio scripts. He likes folk, blues, rock and jazz music, films (unless directed by Michael 'the Antichrist' Bay), books, hill-walking, the sea and single malt whisky. He still enjoys admiring beautiful women from afar but has now progressed to going over and talking to them as well. This has actually happened a couple of times recently without any restraining orders being issued. Which is nice.

Daniele Serra is a professional illustrator. His work has been published in Europe, Australia and the United States, and displayed at various exhibits in U.S. and Europe. He has provided illustrations for authors such as Brian Stableford, Rain Graves, Steven Savile and Allyson Bird. He has also worked for DC Comics, Image Comics, *Cemetery Dance*, *Weird Tales*, *Black Static* and other publications.

Allyson Bird's debut collection, *Bull Running For Girls*, won best collection in the British Fantasy Awards, 2009. Her collection, *Wine and Rank Poison*, introduced by Joe R. Lansdale is to be published in September 2010 by Dark Regions Press. Allyson's debut novel *Isis Unbound*, will be published by the same publisher in 2011. She has had stories in *The British Fantasy Society Yearbook 2009* amongst other publications and her almost most recent story 'The Black Swan of Odessa' is in *The Master in Café Morphine: A Homage to Mikhail Bulgakov* published in September by Ex Occidente. She lives on the edge of the South Yorkshire moors in England, with her husband and daughter.

Joel Lane lives in Birmingham. He is the author of three collections of supernatural horror stories, *The Earth Wire*, *The Lost District* and *The Terrible Changes*; two novels, *From Blue To Black* and *The Blue Mask*; a novella, 'The Witnesses are Gone'; a chapbook, *Black Country*; and two collections of poems, *The Edge of the Screen* and *Trouble in the Heartland*. A third collection of poems, *The Autumn Myth*, is forthcoming. Joel has edited an anthology of subterranean horror stories, *Beneath the Ground*, and co-edited (with Steve Bishop) the crime fiction anthology *Birmingham Noir*.

Organisations and publications

Some anti-fascist and anti-racist organisations (UK):

HOPE Not Hate and *Searchlight* magazine
PO Box 1576
Ilford IG5 0NG
020 7681 8660
www.hopenothate.org.uk

Stop Racism and Fascism Network
http://srfnetwork.org

Unite Against Fascism
PO Box 36871
London WC1X 9XT
020 7801 2782
www.uaf.org.uk

Youth Against Racism in Europe
PO Box 858
London E11 1YG
020 8558 7947
www.yre.org.uk

Some human rights organisations (UK):

Amnesty International UK
The Human Rights Action Centre
17-25 New Inn Yard
London EC2 3EA
020 7033 1777
www.amnesty.org.uk

English PEN
Free Word Centre
60 Farringdon Road
London EC1R 3GA
020 7324 2535
www.englishpen.org

Equality and Human Rights Commission
www.equalityhumanrights.com
Helplines: England 0845 604 6610, Scotland 0845 604 5510,
Wales 0845 604 8810

Arndale House, The Arndale Centre, Manchester M4 3AQ
0161 829 8100 (non-helpline calls)
info@equalityhumanrights.com

3 More London, Riverside Tooley Street, London SE1 2RG
020 3117 0235 (non-helpline calls)
info@equalityhumanrights.com

3rd floor, 3 Callaghan Square, Cardiff CF10 5BT
02920 447710 (non-helpline calls)
wales@equalityhumanrights.com

The Optima Building, 58 Robertson Street, Glasgow G2 8DU
0141 228 5910 (non-helpline calls)
scotland@equalityhumanrights.com

Index on Censorship **magazine**
SAGE Publications Ltd
1 Oliver's Yard
55 City Road
London EC1Y 1SP
020 7 324 8500
www.indexoncensorship.org

The Sophie Lancaster Foundation
12 Bury Road
Haslingden
Lancashire BB4 5PL
www.sophielancasterfoundation.com

Lightning Source UK Ltd.
Milton Keynes UK
11 February 2011

167363UK00001B/12/P